S0-AAZ-729

I love you, David. I'll always love you. I won't let the children forget you. Nor will I.

Slowly she made her way to where the children waited. Tad handed her the reins to Nancy, her docile buttermilk mare. Livi swallowed hard. "Mount up," she said.

Livi looked down the road toward Lynchburg nearly six days away. Back there were friends, a town she knew, a life she had come to enjoy. All that was safe and familiar pulled at her. It was a tether she did not want to break.

She turned to look to the road ahead. The trees crowded close, hemming it in, shrouding it in shadows. David had told her often enough what lay ahead: steep, rocky trails; fast-flowing rivers and streams that must be forded; rugged mountains to bar their way. Wilderness, wild animals, Indians.

Kentucky.

Livi shivered and looked long and hard at David's grave. Then she kicked her mount forward, west on the Wilderness Road.

Avon Books are available at special quantity discounts for bulk purchases for sales promotions, premiums, fund raising or educational use. Special books, or book excerpts, can also be created to fit specific needs.

For details write or telephone the office of the Director of Special Markets, Avon Books, Dept. FP, 1350 Avenue of the Americas, New York, New York 10019, 1-800-238-0658.

A Place Called Home

Elizabeth Grayson

AVON BOOKS ◆ NEW YORK

If you purchased this book without a cover, you should be aware that this book is stolen property. It was reported as "unsold and destroyed" to the publisher, and neither the author nor the publisher has received any payment for this "stripped book."

A PLACE CALLED HOME is an original publication of Avon Books. This work has never before appeared in book form. This work is a novel. Any similarity to actual persons or events is purely coincidental.

AVON BOOKS
A division of
The Hearst Corporation
1350 Avenue of the Americas
New York, New York 10019

Copyright © 1995 by Karen Witmer-Gow
Front cover art by David Gatti
Excerpt from Elizabeth Grayson's next novel copyright © 1995 by Karen Witmer-Gow
Published by arrangement with the author
Library of Congress Catalog Card Number: 95-94483
ISBN: 0-380-77845-9

All rights reserved, which includes the right to reproduce this book or portions thereof in any form whatsoever except as provided by the U.S. Copyright Law. For information address Jane Rotrosen Agency, 318 East 51st Street, New York, New York 10022.

First Avon Books Printing: December 1995

AVON TRADEMARK REG. U.S. PAT. OFF. AND IN OTHER COUNTRIES, MARCA REGISTRADA, HECHO EN U.S.A.

Printed in the U.S.A.

RA   10   9   8   7   6   5   4   3   2   1

To Eileen Dreyer
and the conquest of Everest

❧Acknowledgments❧

So many people come to the aid of an author during the writing process that I find myself wanting to thank everyone—including the Pizza Hut delivery boy. Certain individuals, however, do stand out.

In the area of research, I would like to both thank and bless Eleanor Alexander, who served as my research assistant and sounding board for the sections of the manuscript concerning Native American culture. In sharing her time, her books, her enthusiasm, and her expertise, she gave me a wonderful basis for the sections of the manuscript that deal with the Creek way of life.

Once again Charles Brown, at the Mercantile Library Association of St. Louis, has proved himself wonderfully able in providing me with a wealth of information on Kentucky and the Wilderness Road from Mercantile's seemingly inexhaustible American history collection.

I would also like to acknowledge John Villeneuve, who has long been my source on period weaponry and hunting. His ability to tell me more than I ask and his willingness to play "what if" make him a resource I truly value.

My friend and lecturer extraordinaire Joyce Schiller, of the St. Louis Art Museum, has once again come through with several delicious tidbits to give veracity to the world my characters inhabit. Her enthusiastic support for what I do is a gift I appreciate from the bottom of my heart.

I would also like to give a big hug to my husband, Tom,

for his ongoing help in researching my books. In this case, that took the form of negotiating the still fairly rustic highways along the route of the Wilderness Road. That he did this from period maps and in a driving rainstorm, with a companion who was busy seeing pack trains and pioneers, attests to his qualifications as both a pathfinder and my hero.

On the professional level, I would like to thank both Meg Ruley and Ellen Edwards for encouraging me to spread my wings and write this book, even when it meant trying things I'd never done before.

No set of acknowledgments would be complete without a mention of my writer friends who have read, critiqued, and gone out of their way to say the right things at the right moments. My wonderful colleagues are: Eileen Dreyer, Linda Madl, Kim Cates, and Elizabeth Stuart. And I would like to say a special thank you to Karen Harper for recommending and sharing.

And last but not least, I want to express my appreciation to my "Mom Consultants"—the ladies who shared their expertise in word and deed with one of the uninitiated: Kim Bush and Eileen Dreyer, Linda Madl and Libby Beach, Debbie Dirckx-Norris and Johann Stallings. And especially my sister-in-law Renée Witmer, who went above and beyond the call of duty by getting pregnant so I could take notes.

Thank you all!

A Place Called Home

✎↶ Prologue ↷✎

On the Wilderness Road
March 1782

David Talbot awoke to a living nightmare. To a feral,
dusky scent drifting in the dank night air. To the chill
of a sinister presence tickling along his skin. To a knot of
anticipation snarled beneath his ribs. The stealthy pad of footsteps passing close outside the tent brought both dread and
confirmation. There was someone in their camp.

Clearly, his wife had sensed it, too. "Someone's out there,"
she breathed, reaching across to manacle icy fingers around
David's wrist.

"It'll be all right, Livi," he whispered back.

Coiling out of his bedroll, David nudged open the tent flap
with the barrel of his pistol and peered outside. By the light
of the waning moon, he could make out two figures rifling
through their packs on the far side of the campfire. Talbot
could see the sway of the men's breechclouts as they moved,
the feathers in their hair. Indians bent on thievery, David
thought. Not something to fear on this side of the mountains.

He turned to the woman beside him. Even in the darkness
he fancied he could see the terror blazing in her eyes, turning
them green and bright as bottle glass. They'd been on the trail
less than a week, and already Livi was being forced to con-
front her fear of the wilds, her fear of the Indians. David

1

longed to take her in his arms, longed to soothe her with the stroke of his hands.

"It's going to be all right," he whispered again. "It's only a couple Indian braves bent on mischief."

Knowing full well that his actions belied the comforting words, David cocked his pistol and pushed the butt of it into Livi's palm.

"Just don't shoot me by mistake," he murmured, checking the prime on his long rifle. "Stay here in the tent. Don't come out unless I shout for you."

He glanced back at the two children still nestled in their bedrolls. "And don't let Tad out of the tent, either. Now that he's twelve, he's got some damn peculiar notions about being grown up."

He could sense Livi's panic spiraling, smell the fear on her skin. He would have sold his soul to spare her this.

"It's going to be all right." He leaned across and kissed her hard. "Just leave this to me." Turning, David bolted from the tent.

"You there!" he bellowed. "What are you doing with those packs?"

The two Indians stiffened and jerked around. Shawnee, Talbot realized. What the hell were Shawnee doing this far east?

He'd barely finished the thought when one of the pack-horses snorted off to his left. A glance in that direction revealed two Indians clinging to the packhorses' leads and two more beyond them at the edge of the woods. In the faint light of the moon, he could see their faces were painted black and vermillion, the colors of war.

Chills prickled up Talbot's back. No raiding party had ventured this far east in a decade.

One of the men came out of the trees. "Where is it?" he demanded in Shawnee.

"Where is what?" David answered in the same language.

"What have you done with it?"

David stepped back a pace and raised his gun. "We don't have whatever it is you want. Get out of here."

As he spoke, one of the men who had gone back to poking through the packs gave a grunt of acknowledgment. "Here," he exclaimed. "It's here."

The brave came to his feet holding a deerskin medicine bag.

David saw the spiraling bead designs, the trailing rawhide fringe. His gut tightened.

Grim-faced, he leveled his gun. "Put that down," he ordered in Shawnee. "You can't have that."

The brave clutching the medicine bag glared defiance.

David edged away from the tent, skirting the campfire. When he was close enough, he reached for the bag. "I'll take that," he said. "Give it to me!"

With his left hand the brave extended the medicine bag toward David. With his right he jerked a knife from the sheath at his waist. The blade flashed in the half-light as he lunged.

Pain burned through the flesh of David's upper arm. He dodged away and fired.

The ball caught the brave full in the chest. He looked down, his eyes glazing, widening. He staggered backward and fell.

The doeskin bag spun from the Indian's grasp, skittering across the ground in a swirl of fringe.

As the shot boomed deep into the hills, David heard Livi and the children stirring inside the tent. He could sense their confusion and alarm. He shifted to his left, preparing to defend them.

Then a whoop of fury split the night, shattering the momentary stillness. The warrior at the edge of the woods pelted down the rise, his hair flying. As he ran, he raised the war club in his left hand.

Recognition sizzled along Talbot's nerves, the certainty of what was about to happen.

"I'm sorry, Livi," David mumbled under his breath as the man raced toward him. "I'm so sorry. Oh, God, I'm sorry."

With ferocity scored in every movement, the warrior swung his war club. It scribed a long, wide arc, a slash of fury whistling through the night.

Talbot raised his empty gun to ward off the blow. The force of the clash jarred up David's arms. It bashed his rifle aside.

The man set his feet. He swung again.

Talbot fumbled to raise his gun a second time.

This blow came swifter, harder. It battered the rifle from David's hands. It smashed into the side of David's skull.

The world flared hot and bright before his eyes. Pain ripped apart sight and sense and consciousness. The last thing David Talbot heard was the shattering terror of Livi's scream.

1

*I*t was raining in the mountains, a chill, persistent drizzle that wrapped the world in a haze of gray. Clouds shrouded the towering peaks and blurred the jagged lines of ridges that faded into the distance on the east and west. Rain slicked the rocky outcroppings that pushed toward the sky, darkening the striations of gray and gold to shades of charcoal and ocher. It was raining in the forested hills that huddled at the knees of the mountains, wafting into the bristle of barren trees that grew on their slopes, spattering into the mat of last year's leaves strewn on the forest floor, drizzling down to feed the streams that gathered and flowed the length of the valley at the mountains' heart.

Through that broad, lush valley a road funneled down from the north. It was a road that began in the wild green hills of western Pennsylvania, a track that charted the turns and hummocks on the valley floor and mounted the rising hills at its lower end. It pushed relentlessly south and west, fighting through miles of rough terrain, challenging the heights at the Cumberland Gap, spilling into the promised land on the opposite side.

During these last unsettled years when a nation was struggling to be born, the road had been worn deep into the rich Virginia earth. Now, with the coming of peace, it would be worn deeper still, trod by untold thousands seeking a better life. Many who passed this way would fulfill their dreams; many others would bury them.

Today, on a rise at the side of the road, a woman and two children stood over a raw, fresh grave. Their story was not a new one to the high, encircling hills. Those seeking a home beyond the mountains were damned to play out the tale of hope and loss and fortitude again and again. Only the faces of the mourners changed.

This woman stood tall and spare, a damp red braid drooping down her back. A shabby dark green cloak swaddled her from head to toe, but beneath the brim of the chipped-straw hat she had affected to keep off the rain, her face shone with a rare, deep beauty that not even her sorrow could weather away.

A girl-child nestled close against her mother's side, a soft and dreamy child, a fair and tender girl. The kind so easily lost on a trek as dangerous as this. A boy edging toward manhood held himself a little way apart. Lacking the confidence to comfort or the maturity to share his grief, he shuttered his feelings close inside.

In a voice thick and grainy from crying, the woman finished reading from the Bible she cradled in trembling, mud-stained hands: ''. . . that whosoever believeth in Him shall not perish from the earth, but have everlasting life.''

Soft, murky silence had long since closed around her words when she finally lifted her eyes from the mound of red Virginia dirt, from the two peeled sticks lashed inexpertly together to form a cross.

You deserve better than this, David. Better than a shallow grave at the side of the road. Better than we three mourners to mark your passing. Better than I have been able to give you.

She shivered in the cold, dank wind that swept out of the hills; breathed the earthy musk of woodlands awash with rain; watched this strange and hostile world through tear-wet eyes. And wondered where she should go from here.

After a time, Tad Talbot lay a hand on his mother's arm. ''Shall I strike the tent, Ma?'' he asked. ''Shall I saddle the horses?''

His questions rolled over Livi with all the force of a breaking wave, battering her with new responsibilities, drowning her in confusion. Her chest tightened as if she were battling for breath; her ears rang with the roar of mounting panic. She clung to her Bible as if to an anchor, to keep from being swept away.

Using a soft, frayed ribbon to mark the page, she closed the Bible and steeled herself to face her son. He stood before her with the wide, fresh face of a twelve-year-old and the eyes of an infinitely older man.

"We should be getting packed up, shouldn't we?" Tad prodded her. "Pa would want us to go on to Kentucky."

"Kentucky." Livi spit out the word as if it were ashes in her mouth. That Tad should speak it standing over his father's grave smacked of the vilest blasphemy.

Still, she knew her son was right. David would expect her to carry on. He would expect her to pack up their belongings—in spite of his death, in spite of the Indians—and claim the acres beyond the mountains. He would expect her to make a home for the three of them on his land. But how in God's name could she do that when she loathed the very thought of Kentucky, when every mile between here and there teemed with all-too-imaginable terrors?

"Mama?" Her daughter's voice was barely louder than the patter of rain through the trees. "Mama?"

Livi looked down to where her four-year-old snuggled close, down at her rumpled rose-gold curls, down into her whiskey-brown eyes. They were eyes that would ever mark the girl as David's child.

"What is it, sugar?" she asked, seizing the diversion, eager to put off the decision she did not know how to make.

"When we go on to Kentucky, is Papa coming with us?"

Cissy's question dropped the weight of an anvil on Livi's chest.

In the horrid, garbled hours between midnight and dawn, when David had lain breathing but beyond her help, Livi had done her best to explain to her children what dying meant. Tad was older; he'd understood. But Cissy . . .

"Don't be a goose, Cissy," Tad snapped. "Of course Pa isn't—"

Abruptly Livi turned on her son. "Let me answer her," she admonished, having no idea if she could.

Livi went down on her knees beside her daughter, took her small, soft face between her palms. The hope and confusion in Cissy's eyes swelled the ache around Livi's heart. How could she explain David's death to Cissy when she didn't understand it herself? What could she possibly say that would make losing the father she adored easier for his little girl?

"We talked about this last night," Livi began in a voice thick with suppressed tears. "Don't you remember? I told you Papa died, that he went away."

The girl's eyebrows skewed together. "But Papa hasn't gone away. He's right under there. We wrapped him in the daisy quilt to keep the dirt off his face. We put him to sleep in the ground just like you said."

At Cissy's words, the reserves of patience and compassion Livi had been clinging to crumbled away beneath her fingertips like tinderbox char. She didn't have any soft, sweet words to soothe her daughter. She didn't know how to fill the void David's death was leaving in all their lives. If it weren't for the trust in Cissy's dark eyes, Livi would have succumbed to the hopelessness and walked away.

Instead she drew a shaky breath and tried to explain death to her daughter another way. "Do you remember when Tad's dog, Rusty, got so old he could hardly get around? How he lay down by the fire one night and never woke up? Well, something like that happened to your father."

"Papa's not old like Rusty was."

"No, but sometimes younger people die. There's nothing we can do. When someone's dead we bury them."

"Like we buried Rusty."

The roar of fear and impatience inside Livi dropped to a hum. She was breathing a little easier. "Yes, that's right. We buried your papa's body, and his spirit has gone away to heaven. He'll stay there with God forever."

The child's face stiffened; she jerked away. "No, he's my papa. He loves me. He'll come back."

Livi wanted to believe that herself; knew that, in spite of his silence, Tad wanted to believe it, too.

"Cissy, no," she insisted gently. "Heaven's so glorious and wonderful that people never come back."

"Papa came back from Kentucky and he liked it there."

Livi narrowed her lips and fought down the burn of frustration. Death wasn't something open to debate. It was final, irreversible.

"I wish it were different, sugar," Livi finally managed to

say, "really I do. But going away forever is what dying means."

"No!" Cissy shook her head. "No! Papa will come back! He will. He will!"

Livi absorbed the sounds of her daughter's distress. They swelled the tide of helplessness, unworthiness, and desolation rising within her. She didn't know what else to do. She'd used up all the strength it took to think, or act, or comfort, digging David's grave, wrestling his broken body into the ground, lifting shovel after shovel of dirt to cover it. There were no reserves left for her to draw on, no wise, brave things left for her to say. Why, for the love of God, couldn't Cissy just accept that she would never see her papa again?

With a moan of effort, Livi wrapped her arms around her daughter and lifted the child on her hip. Cissy was too old to be held like this, with her bare, skinny legs sticking out and her skirt hitched up. Livi hugged her anyway, swaying in the age-old rhythm all mothers know.

"I'm sorry," Livi crooned. "I'm so sorry. I wish with all my heart I could make things different. But your papa isn't coming back."

The girl wriggled in her mother's arms, pushing hard against her chest. Livi held on as Cissy struggled to break free. She held on as David's daughter fought the words, the truth, her mother's compelling embrace.

"I'm sorry," Livi murmured, swaying again. "I'm sorry, but it isn't right to lie to you, especially about this."

Cissy fought on, fought with one fist jammed in her mouth and tears streaking down her face.

Then all at once, Livi couldn't bear to be pushed away. Not when she'd lost David. Not when Tad and Cissy were all she had. With a final burst of strength, Livi crushed her daughter in her arms, buried her face in her tumbled hair, breathed the balm of Cissy's childish hope and innocence.

The girl capitulated, melting into her mother's body, limp, defeated; sobbing as if her heart would break. Livi's heart was breaking, too—for her children, for herself.

Slowly she became aware that the tempo of the rain had picked up around them. It came rippling through the trees, plopping onto Livi's hat, sopping into the heavy cloak that wreathed her back and shoulders. The crumbled clods of earth at the edges of the grave threatened to turn slippery and treacherous underfoot.

With a long, deep sigh, Livi cupped her hand to the back of Cissy's head and carried her daughter down the rise. Tad trailed them back to camp, catching his mother's arm before she could seek refuge in the tent.

"We *are* going on to Kentucky, aren't we, Ma?"

The question hung heavy between them.

"Shouldn't we move out today?"

Livi took a breath and let it go. She refused to look at her son.

"What if the Indians come back?" he demanded when she did not reply. "What will we do then?"

Livi lifted her gaze to the hills rising on every side, to the ridges mounded up behind them, to the road that probed the wild unknown. This vast, imposing place was David's world. Going west was David's dream. It was not hers. *It had never been hers.*

As she held her daughter against her heart and considered the question in her son's dark eyes, Livi groped for words to reassure both her children. It was a long and futile search.

Deciding lies offered only transient comfort, Livi chose to tell the truth. "I don't know if we'll be going on to Kentucky," she said, fighting to steady the tremor in her voice. "I don't know what we'll do if the Indians come. I don't know anything, Tad. Not anything at all."

We can't stay here, Livi Talbot thought, raising her eyes to the ring of hills, visible now through the pink of dawn. After what had happened to David, it was only by the grace of God that they had survived a second night in this miserable place. Though the Indians had slunk away, taking their dead, it was possible they could have returned.

But leaving the tiny campsite and her husband's grave would have forced Livi to decide where they would go and what they would do. She couldn't have done that yesterday. Not when her thoughts were warily circling the reality of David's death. Not when turmoil skimmed the surface of her world with black. The pain of losing David was every bit as sharp today, but the darkness was receding. In its place came the imperative: it was time to move ahead or back.

There was no question what David would expect of her. Kentucky had enthralled him from the moment he heard the name. He'd been mesmerized by the promise of this vast new world, obsessed with owning a piece of it. When they set out from Lynchburg, David had waved extravagant good-byes to everyone they passed, burst into song as they rode into the open countryside. The sound of his voice rang in Livi's ears, a memory as strong and vivid as David had been. But instead of the three hundred acres in Kentucky that he'd fought for and sacrificed for and cherished beyond all else, David had ended up with only a grave-sized plot of coarse Virginia dirt.

David's land still lay waiting on the far side of the mountains—waiting now for her. Just knowing that, Livi went weak and weightless inside. Every instinct clamored that she was incapable of braving the wilderness. With her upbringing, her terrors, and her doubts, how could she be? After seeing their father killed by savages, what mother could drag her youngsters through country rife with Indians? And how in God's name could a woman with a babe in her belly survive a trip over such rough terrain?

If by some stray miracle she and the children got as far as David's claim, could they plant the fields and harvest enough corn and beans and squash to see them through the winter? A cabin and its outbuildings would have to be constructed. They'd need fences and furniture, barrels and basins, a hundred other essentials Livi did not know how to provide. The enormity of the task set panicky desperation fluttering in her chest.

Livi had to consider the baby, too—David Talbot's final mark upon this earth. As her pregnancy advanced, how able would she be to plow and lift and hoe and weed? Would she have the stamina to work from dawn until dark? Would she die in childbirth, leaving Tad and Cissy to fend for themselves? Could she care for an infant along with all the rest?

Could a lone woman and two children do what needed to be done to build the homestead her husband had envisioned? The fact was, they couldn't. No matter how much she'd loved David. No matter how much she owed him, Livi couldn't live up to David's legacy.

I'm sorry, David. I know this is all you ever wanted, all you ever dreamed about. I know this is what you expect of me. But

I can't reach Kentucky on my own. With you to guide me, I might have managed the trip, might have learned to live on the frontier. But there's no one to teach me now, no one to protect me while I learn.

And if I fail—oh, David, if I fail, our children will pay the forfeit. If I'm not strong enough, or brave enough, or wise enough, they will die. Our children, our babies, are all I have left. How can you expect me to gamble their lives for the sake of a dream?

Shattered, hollow, raw, Livi huddled before the fire with her face in her hands, tears drizzling hot between her fingers. Giving up David's dream was like losing him all over again; giving up David's dream brought comfort and relief.

Returning to Lynchburg made far more sense. She could draw strength from familiar surroundings, from people she knew. She could give birth to David's child attended by women she counted as friends. The people of Lynchburg had looked after her when David was off fighting with Colonel Clark; surely they would be willing to help her and the children now. Still, the house and blacksmith shop were gone, sold off to buy packhorses and supplies, and Livi had no idea how much money was left. What would she do for more when that money ran out? No Chesterton had ever accepted charity, and after eloping with David, she could hardly go to her family for help.

Wrapping her icy fingers around the mug, Livi took a sip of tea to quell the churn of nausea. She couldn't decide the rest of her life in a single moment. She couldn't make this kind of decision when other lives were at stake.

Livi had barely completed the thought when Tad stumbled out of the tent, snarling like a bobcat. "The sun's been up for an hour or more. Why didn't you wake me?" he demanded, his fair, tousled hair standing up around his head. "Why haven't you started packing?"

"I'm not certain where we're going yet."

"Not certain?" Tad stopped dead in his tracks and stared at her. "We're going on to Kentucky, aren't we, Ma?"

"I told you yesterday I wasn't sure, and now that I think on it, I don't see how we can. How are we going to plant the fields, Tad? Who's going to build a cabin? What are we going to do for food until the crops come in? Besides, there's the whole of the Wilderness Road between here and there.''

Fire kindled up, replacing the confusion in his eyes. ''We can do it, Ma. I know we can! We can meet up with some folks at the Block House just like Pa planned. We can travel with them over the mountains as far as the Crab Orchard or Hazel Patch. Pa's land isn't more than a few miles beyond them. I'm sure I can read his maps and journal well enough to find it.''

Livi only wished the trek to Kentucky were as easy as Tad made it sound.

''And when we get there,'' he went on, his voice rising in excitement, ''I'll plant the fields. I'll build the cabin. I'll work day and night if I have to—''

''Tad,'' his mother offered gently, ''you're only a boy. I can't ask you to do a man's work; you can't expect that of yourself. It would make far more sense for us to go back to Lynchburg—''

''Lynchburg?'' the boy spit. ''That piss-poor excuse for a town? How can you think about going back to Lynchburg when you know the land in Kentucky meant everything to Pa?''

She could see the essence of his father in the set of Tad's jaw, in his fierce and boundless optimism. The guilt of a double betrayal bit deep.

''Tad, your father's dead,'' Livi said, working to steady her voice. ''We can't base our decisions on what he wanted. We have to make them on what's best for the three of us.''

''This isn't best,'' Tad insisted.

''I think it is.''

Cissy emerged from the tent, rumpled and sloe-eyed, the knuckle she hadn't sucked in two full years jammed deep in her mouth. ''What are you two yelling about?''

Neither Tad nor Livi answered her.

''Fine, then! Fine!'' Tad shouted at his mother. ''You do what's best for you and Cissy. You go back to Lynchburg if you want. I'm going on to Kentucky. I'm going to claim Pa's land. It's what he would have wanted me to do.''

''Don't talk foolishness, Tad!'' Livi snapped. ''You can't go on a journey like that alone! You're only twelve years old!''

Tad bent and began cramming his belongings into a battered

pair of saddlebags. "I *can* make the trip on my own! I won't take much with me—just my clothes, a little food, Pa's gun and horse and maps. You don't give a damn where those acres are anyway."

Tad really meant to go, to brave the wilderness by himself. The thought shocked Livi, swelled the barely controlled panic lodged beneath her ribs. What madness possessed her son to make him think he could make the trek to Kentucky alone, could pick up the broken standard of David's dream?

"For God's sake, Tad," she argued, fear for her firstborn gripping hard. "You have no idea what you're getting into. You have no idea what dangers you'll be facing. Please don't do this."

"I am going to Kentucky! I can chop trees and dig dirt as well as any man. I can handle Pa's gun if I have to, and I'm good with animals," Tad proclaimed. "And once I make Kentucky, I'll look up Reid Campbell. He's Pa's best friend. He'll help me plant Pa's fields. He'll help me raise a cabin."

"Reid Campbell!" Livi jerked up like a toy on a string. "I won't have you seeking out that blackguard's help."

"But I like Reid," Cissy piped up.

"It's Reid Campbell who put these crazy notions about Kentucky in your father's head," Livi raved. "It's Reid Campbell who came around with his wild stories and his promises of free land. He'd talk until your father's eyes began to shine, and off they'd go into the hills. And when they came back your father would be restless, all stirred up. He'd be ready to change our perfectly settled life for some dangerous dream."

Tad continued as if he had not heard. "Once Reid learns what's happened, he'll help me start the farm. He might even want to live there permanent-like."

"Oh, I wouldn't count on that if I were you," his mother advised. "Reid Campbell's no farmer, and he'll never settle down. He's not good at anything but hying off to explore the woods. He's unreliable as summer rain, never around when you've need of him."

Tad's shoulders stiffened at her words. "Well, I warrant if Reid had been in camp night before last, my father would be alive today. Reid would have done something to save Pa's life."

The accusation that she'd failed to save David hung thick and poisonous in the air. A tingle of faintness danced along Livi's skin. Wetness gathered under her tongue, and she thought she might be sick.

Questions she'd smothered with her grief and drowned in her tears slithered to the surface. If she had come out of the tent a moment sooner, could she have saved her husband's life? If she had raised and fired the pistol, would David be alive today? Livi would never know. The moment was irretrievably gone, the answers lost forever.

Even through the haze of pain, Livi realized Tad had no idea what he'd said, what he'd implied, how deeply he'd hurt her. Tad had been trailing Reid Campbell around from the time he could toddle, staring up at the big half-breed as if he were some mystical forest spirit come to life. Tad had only been protecting his hero from her wrath, and Cissy was far too young to understand concepts like guilt and culpability. Livi was the one who would carry the question for the rest of her days, the one who would read condemnation or absolution in David's eyes when her life on earth was done.

The thought of facing her husband's disapproval once she reached the world beyond, and the realization that if she didn't follow the road to Kentucky she would lose her son, made Livi's decision inevitable.

"Strike the tent, Tad," Livi finally said, "and douse the fire. Cissy and I will begin loading and saddling the horses."

They broke camp as silently and as efficiently as they could without David's help. Livi suddenly wished she were strong enough to heft the packs onto the saddles by herself; wished she'd learned the neat, tight knots that David had used to secure the ropes that linked the animals together; wished the small of her back didn't seem ready to snap when she bent or lifted. It took far more time and effort than Livi would ever have imagined to prepare her little band for the trail.

Once they were ready, she walked alone to the top of the rise. This was where the bones of David Talbot would lie for all eternity: here on this barren knoll, in the heart of the rolling Virginia hills. Here, more than two hundred miles from where his heart and his soul would ever be.

Bending beside her husband's grave, she laid a small bouquet of pussy willows on the mound of earth. It was too early in the year for flowers to be blooming in the woods, but the soft gray buds had burst through their winter coats. The graceful branches seemed the right offering for David somehow; they suited his optimism, his tenderness. Tears blurred Livi's vision again.

I love you, David. I'll always love you. I won't let the children forget you. Nor will I.

There was so much more she wished she could say, so many questions she needed to ask. She wanted to pour out her frustration and fear, to demand assurances, to assuage her guilt. But David was no longer there with her.

Slowly she made her way to where the children waited. Tad handed her the reins to Nancy, her docile buttermilk mare. He helped her mount and arrange herself as comfortably as possible on the slippery leather sidesaddle. He slung Cissy up behind her.

These were duties that David had performed for Livi every time they'd ridden together, every time for thirteen years. And David had always patted her knee when he was done. Tad didn't know to do that.

Livi swallowed hard. "Mount up," she said.

As she waited, she looked toward the three packhorses and the cow that were strung out behind her. Tad had four more packhorses and David's mount tied to the back of his saddle. It would be difficult for the two of them to manage so many animals.

Livi looked down the road toward Lynchburg, nearly six days away. Back there were friends, a town she knew, a life she had come to enjoy. All that was safe and familiar pulled at her. It was a tether she did not want to break.

She turned to look to the road ahead. The trees crowded close, hemming it in, shrouding it in shadows. David had told her often enough what lay ahead: steep, rocky trails; fast-flowing rivers and streams that must be forded; rugged mountains to bar their way. Wilderness, wild animals, Indians.

Kentucky.

Livi shivered and looked long and hard at David's grave. Then she kicked her mount forward, west on the Wilderness Road.

2

Bedraggled, sodden, and chilled to the bone, Livi Talbot peered down the long, dim arch between the trees. The road ahead was swallowed in gloom, hazy and indistinct with misty rain, lost in a filigree of shifting branches. Before it got too dark to see, they needed to find a place to spend the night.

Unfortunately, Livi had no idea what criteria David had used in selecting a campsite. A clearing set well back from the road, she supposed, high ground, running water. Remembering the smugness that had hitched up one corner of his mouth as they'd turned down the road to the west, she dismissed the notion of asking Tad for help.

Somehow he must have sensed her concerns, because a few minutes later, Tad pulled up beside her at a wide spot in the trail. "Do you suppose we should look for somewhere to camp?" he asked, sounding at once deferential and contrite.

Livi nodded, her brow furrowing a little in spite of herself. "We've never had to make camp without your father's help."

"We'll manage," Tad offered, angling a grin in her direction.

Livi glanced back at her son. Had David taught Tad about living in the wilds, or was the boy whistling in the dark?

"Well," she murmured, accepting to his assurances, "if you see a likely place . . ."

Tad kicked his roan forward, taking the lead, the pack animals trailing after him. Half an hour later, he gestured off to

16

the right. "There's a clearing just ahead. I'll poke around and make sure it has everything we need."

Livi reined in beside him and dismounted, still uneasy about leaving such an important decision to her son. Cissy trailed along as they explored.

The clearing was located slightly uphill from the road, sheltered on one side by a rocky overhang and ringed with pines. The deep black pockmark of old fires gave evidence that many travelers had rested here.

"Is there a stream nearby?" Livi asked fretfully.

Tad gave her one of David's smiles, said what might well have been David's words. "In this rain—*Livi*—set out a pot and you'll have all the water you could possibly want."

They found that a spring trickled down to form a clear, deep pool on the far side of the rocks, and Tad set about bringing the horses up to the clearing, one by one. No boy had ever loved horses more, and Livi happily delegated care of the animals to him.

Once Tad removed them, Livi wrestled the packs and saddles into a pile beneath the lip of the overhang and threw a tarpaulin over the lot to keep out the worst of the wet. While Tad watered and fed the horses, Cissy tended the shoats and chickens that had been strapped in cages on the horses' backs.

With the last of the goods stowed away, Livi addressed what remained, a jumble of canvas, sticks, and curved wrought-iron stakes that went together somehow to form a tent. She'd always been too busy making supper to notice how David had pounded and pinned and strung the thing together. She wished now she'd paid closer attention. Knowing there was no profit in regrets, she began struggling with what seemed like an armload of sticks and acres of canvas. Soon Tad joined her at the task.

The first time they tried to erect the tent frame, they set the uprights so far apart that the notched cross-member wouldn't bridge the gap.

"You should have measured," Tad admonished her.

"I did measure—then you moved your end back!"

The next time, they pounded one of the uprights in too deep. The lintel pitched steeply toward the back.

At last they managed to coordinate the uprights and the top of the frame, sliding the notched pieces together with only a modicum of difficulty. It was a minor victory, but mother and son grinned at each other in triumph.

After unrolling the main body of the tent, Livi and Tad dragged the stiff, linseed-oil-treated canvas over the pegs at the top of the frame. Neither of them was tall enough to fit the corners from above, so they worked from beneath the yards of draping cloth. It was like wrestling with a phantom. Both of them were disheveled and panting by the time they were done.

Carefully they spread the wide white wings of canvas and pegged the edges into the earth. Though their finished tent listed sharply to the left and the roof ruffled freely in the breeze, Livi and her son were bursting with pride at their accomplishment.

Tad had just barely begun to lay and light the fire, and Livi was searching out a bucket to milk the cow, when a gust of wind swept up the rise. It caught the underside of the tent and set it to billowing. The roof swelled like dough put out to rise, popping each of the tent pegs out of the earth. The whole structure lifted for a moment like a huge white bird. It fluttered, dipped sideways, then dropped with a loud and graceless thud.

Tad and Livi stared at the ruin of their handiwork.

"Must be your side wasn't pegged properly," Livi grumbled to her son.

"Could be you didn't pull the canvas tight enough."

"This wasn't a tug of war."

"And if it was a tug of war, do you really think you could best me, Ma?"

"I *might* not be able to best you in a tug of war, Thadius, but there are other things I can certainly best you at—like checkers and arithmetic and making biscuits."

"How about riding bareback, Ma? Or cleaning fish?"

Livi made a face at her son.

Whether at her expression, the banter, or the jumbled wreckage of the tent, Tad and Livi began to giggle. Why a twisted ridgepole and pulled-up pegs or even a few good-natured boasts, should set them off, neither Tad nor Livi could explain. Staggering a little with mirth, they drew Cissy into the circle, too. Arms linked, hands joined, faces turned to the darkening sky, they held one another fast and howled with laughter.

The bout of hilarity ran its course. "Oh, Lord, but we're a sorry pair," Livi finally muttered, wiping tears from her eyes.

Tad nodded in agreement. "Did Pa ever tell you about the time the tent collapsed on him and Reid? They woke the whole of Colonel Clark's encampment with their shouting before they figured out it was the wind that knocked it over—not a British attack."

David hadn't told her, not a story with Reid Campbell in it. Not considering the way she'd always felt about Reid. "I guess we didn't do so badly, then," she conceded.

"At least this didn't happen in the middle of the night."

It was full dark when they finished erecting the tent a second time. Tad quickly turned his attention to the fire, building it higher than was necessary to push back the dark.

After tending the cow, Livi began to prepare the simple fare for supper. She mixed milk with salt and cornmeal into a thick yellow batter she would pat into loaves and fry in bear grease. But as she crumbled dried herbs and jerked deer meat into the mixture, a now-familiar nausea twisted her insides.

Hastily handing the bowl to her daughter, Livi staggered into the trees and lost what little food she had managed to gag down when they'd stopped at noontime. She'd been sick first thing this morning, first thing the day before, and the day before that. She'd never had a pregnancy like this, not with Tad or Cissy, not with any of her miscarriages, not with the two babies she'd left behind in the churchyard at Lynchburg. Hollows shadowed her cheekbones and ringed her eyes; her ribs and collarbone stuck out. She'd been sick so often this past month that Livi wondered if the babe was getting nourishment at all. Closing her eyes, she steadied herself against a tree and waited for the light-headedness to pass.

David had been so excited when she announced she was expecting. He'd been happy, filled with plans. Inured to loss and dreading the journey ahead, Livi had vowed not to think of the baby at all. But now she had to think about it, had to accept that the child she carried was the last act of love and creation she and David would ever share. It was a gift more precious than any David had ever given her, but it was also a horrendous complication to all that lay ahead. Was she mad to press on to Kentucky with this babe growing inside her?

"Ma, are you all right? The fire's really going good."

Livi took a shaky breath and turned back to where Tad and Cissy were waiting.

"You feeling better, Ma?" She read concern in her son's face.

"I'm fine," she reassured him. "It's just the baby that makes me ill. Sometimes it takes a while for one to settle in."

Tad nodded warily. Like most men, he didn't want to know about the mysteries of pregnancy and childbirth. Men cared only about the pleasure that gave a babe its start. They left their women alone when it came time to pay the price for sharing their passion and their seed.

Returning to the fire, Livi chided herself for lamenting something God Himself had decreed. As her mother always said, a woman mustn't think too much. And good advice that was, she conceded—at least if a female was to be content with her lot.

Bending over the footed frying pan that had been heating in the fire, Livi set the cornmeal loaves to sizzling. Soon they were trailing steam into the air. She divided all but one between Tad and Cissy and ate that smallest portion herself. Washed down with a cup of her precious tea, the simple fare warmed her after the cold, wet day and settled about as well as anything had in weeks.

The rain sputtered to a stop shortly after they made camp, but the air hung dank and chill. Livi sent Tad and Cissy to their beds as soon as supper was over and joined them there when she'd put the last of the wood on the blaze. There would be no fire at breakfast tomorrow, but it seemed more important to beat back the shadows as long as she could.

Exhaustion dragged Livi down into the pile of blankets. Her head was fuzzy and her bones weighed heavily with weariness. She couldn't remember when she'd slept. Last night Cissy had needed to be held, and the night before—

Livi shuddered. She didn't want to think about the night David died.

"Mama?" Livi could tell by the sound that Cissy had a knuckle jammed in her mouth. "There won't be Indians around tonight, will there? No bears will come?"

"You'll be fine, Cissy. Go to sleep," her big brother answered her. "Ma and I are keeping watch."

"Mama?"

Tad gave a disgruntled snort.

Responsibility hung over Livi in a way it never had before, grave, constricting, overwhelming. How had David borne it all so effortlessly?

"Tad's right," she answered, scuttling across the blankets to where her daughter lay. "We won't let anything happen to you."

When she bent to hug Cissy, Livi could feel the tension across the girl's shoulders and down her back. She settled in at the edge of the bed, holding her daughter's hand, stroking her brow, and crooning lullabies until she slept.

Without disturbing either of her children, Livi crept back to her own pile of blankets. David's long rifle lay on one side, propped up on a stick to keep the powder dry. As she nestled in, she cradled David's loaded pistol between her breasts. The guns were less than ideal bedfellows, but necessary. The welfare of her family rested with her.

Instead of dulling as she stared into the dark, Livi's senses seemed to sharpen. She watched the pale pink tint on the side of the tent fade as the last flickering light of the fire died away. She smelled the embers and the damp, the biting musk of a skunk passing in the woods, and the sharp, clear scent of pine. The wind picked up, humming a little in the trees, making the roof of the tent flutter. Something creaked a short way off. She raised her head to listen, breathing softly, her mouth gone dry. Gradually her tension ebbed away in the stark black silence.

She curled deeper into the chilly blankets and tried to rest. Cissy whimpered in her sleep. Livi soothed her and lay down again. Her ears rang. Her eyes burned. Her thoughts drifted and swirled.

A crackling of brush jerked her out of a doze.

Livi rolled onto her knees and peered outside. The crackling moved, coming closer. A footfall sounded, the rustle of slippery leaves. Was it a bear, a deer, an Indian? Her heartbeat thundered, reverberating against the wall of her chest. Livi waited, straining, quivering.

An owl hooted. Another answered. It was Indians! Hadn't David told her they signaled just this way?

She crept toward the back of the tent and reached for Tad. He started awake. "There's someone out there," she breathed.

"Who?"

Livi shook her head. "Indians, maybe."

Tad nodded, took up his father's rifle, and crept toward the opening at the head of the tent. The crackling came closer. Tad coiled beside her, his muscles strung tight, his breathing repressed.

"What do you think we ought to do?" she whispered.

"Wait it out, I suppose. See what they want."

Livi cocked the pistol anyway.

The crush of leaves, the snap of branches, came from just beyond the fire. The bushes pitched and sawed. Tad and Livi both stopped breathing.

With ears laid back and noses twitching, three of the biggest raccoons Livi had ever seen gamboled into the clearing.

"Raccoons," Tad breathed, wilting with relief.

The creatures sniffed their way around the campsite, looking for food.

Livi gave a fluttery laugh. "I never thought it might be—"

Something thudded onto the tent, right above their heads. Both of them jumped. The pistol in Livi's hand went off, blowing a hole in the roof.

The raccoons hightailed it into the trees.

Tad rolled sideways, covering his head.

Cissy woke up screaming.

"It's all right, sugar." Livi handed Tad the smoking pistol and caught her daughter in her arms. "My gun went off accidentally. There isn't anything to be afraid of. Tad, tell her it's all right."

But Tad was poking around outside. She could hear the crush of his feet on the pine needles as he circled the tent. When he got back he was grinning from ear to ear.

"Looks like you blew the hell out of a pine cone, Ma."

Heat flared in Livi's cheeks. A pine cone? Was that all?

"Don't swear, Tad," Livi admonished her son. "Tell your sister that's all it was."

He did as he was told, but Cissy clung to her mother like moss to a tree. She sobbed against Livi's neck, craving contact, reassurance, comfort. "I want Papa," she whimpered. "I want to go home."

Livi soothed her as best she could, sitting cross-legged in

the nest of blankets, holding Cissy close. It didn't help that at this moment Livi shared her daughter's sentiments. She hated the world of darkness outside the tent, the noises in the night. She hated all that lay ahead, hated that she must face the dangers alone. Was it too late to change her mind about pushing on to Kentucky?

After reloading the pistol, Tad stretched out on his blankets. She could hear the smile in his voice as he said good night.

David would think this was funny, too, Livi thought with a huff of impatience. He would have chuckled under his breath and teased her about the pine cone for weeks.

But Livi didn't share her menfolk's sense of humor. Like Cissy, she was scared to death—and it was hours yet till dawn.

"We stopping at noontime, Mama?" Cissy asked and shifted slightly in the saddle behind her mother.

"You hungry, sugar?" Livi dug into the deep canvas pouch she'd taken to slinging across one shoulder and passed her daughter a strip of jerky.

"Tad said maybe I could ride Papa's horse for a while this afternoon," Cissy wrangled. "Do you think I can?"

She'd scrapped with Cissy about riding David's horse just this morning, and Livi's opinion hadn't changed. Only her willingness to argue about it had.

"Your brother had no right to tell you that."

"But Papa would let me . . ."

David probably would have let her ride the gelding, Livi thought. Fathers allowed their children to do all sorts of things mothers never did. Perhaps that was why God gave children two such disparate beings for their parents, one to encourage a child to challenge the world and one to offer comfort if things went wrong. In any case, Livi had no intention of letting her four-year-old ride David's skittish gelding, especially on a road that was little more than a quagmire.

The track they'd been following since dawn churned thick with mud, the earth beneath their mounts' hooves slick and treacherous. As the land rose before them, the horses puffed and blew, slipping and sliding in the muck, fighting their riders and their leads.

"Please, Mama, can I ride Papa's horse?"

"Absolutely not," Livi answered her daughter with what she hoped was a note of finality.

Slowing her pace even more, Livi looked back to check the packhorses tied to the back of her saddle. Both Tad's string and her own bobbed along in the same syncopated time. The milk cow mooed discontentedly at the end of her rope, the piglets in their crate snorted a constant lament, and the chickens cackled softly as if grumbling among themselves. The animals weren't any more sanguine about this trip than she was.

Pulling her horse to the side of the road, Livi slung her daughter down and dismounted into ankle-deep mud.

"Are you going to let me ride Papa's horse?" Cissy piped up.

Livi ignored her and made her way back to where Tad was waiting. She produced more jerky from inside her pouch, added a hoecake and a handful of parched corn for each of them. "I figure, with the shape this road is in, we won't make the Block House until day after tomorrow," Livi said around tiny bites of corn cake.

The Block House was where David had intended to meet up with other settlers bound for Kentucky. The dangers and hardships of the trail that scaled the Cumberland Gap were legendary and made travel in large groups mandatory. Though he'd made the trek before, even David hadn't been willing to travel Boone's Trace alone.

"Pa said we had to be at the Block House by noon tomorrow if we were going to get over the mountains by the first of April," Tad offered, reciting the timetable his father had set. "I think we can still do that if we try."

Livi compressed her lips. "Your father hadn't taken the weather into consideration, for one thing. And besides, we just can't travel as quickly without him." Or as safely. Or with as much food, Livi amended, sorely missing her husband's hunting skills. What she wouldn't give just now for a few bites of rabbit stew!

"And, Tad, I want you to let Cissy ride with you this afternoon."

"Aw, Ma! I don't want her riding with me. Let her take Pa's horse."

Livi ignored both her son's comment and the eagerness that shone in Cissy's face. "I'll take two of your pack animals and the cow behind me if you let her,'' Livi bargained.

Without waiting to hear a counteroffer, she headed off to water her horses at the roadside stream. Muttering under his breath, Tad did the same. A short time later, they moved on.

Livi let Tad and Cissy take the lead. The land had leveled out, and it was an easy enough trail to follow—the only two-rut road in this part of the country. Closing her eyes, she swayed in time to her mare's plodding footsteps and let her thoughts spin away. Once again she hadn't slept. Cradling Cissy in her arms most of the night, she'd sat tense and listening, wondering if the creaks and scratches and rattles heralded the approach of a bear or bobcat, of dangerous white men or hostile Indians. She'd kept the guns well within reach, though after the pine cone incident, how effective she'd have been with either weapon was anyone's guess.

This morning she'd let Tad take his father's long rifle across his saddle. The boy had proved his coolheadedness the night before, and David had been taking Tad hunting for over a year. In truth, Tad probably knew a good deal more about loading and firing a gun than Livi did. Still, she'd kept the pistol for herself—just in case.

As the afternoon advanced, the way turned steeper. Hills crested to the north and west, forcing the road to twist and narrow as they climbed. The talus surface had washed out in the recent rains, turning the way crumbly and uneven underfoot. As they approached the top of the rise, the land dropped off sharply to the left. A ravine fell away far below, and beyond it was a vista stark with scattered boulders and barren trees.

Slowed by the drag of the additional pack animals and the ache in her bones, Livi realized suddenly how far she'd fallen behind. Up ahead she could see the children riding together and picking their way through the mud.

Though nothing seemed amiss, a sulfurous singe of disaster burned up Livi's nostrils. "Don't ride so close to the edge, Tad," she called out, giving in to the surge of uneasiness.

Livi saw him raise one hand in a wave of acknowledgment, fancied that he moved to obey her. As he did, Tad's rear pack-horse suddenly shied, skittering toward the edge of the cliff. The overhanging bank crumbled beneath the little mare's weight. A shower of stones rattled down the steep wall of the ravine. Larger clods of dirt followed them, rumbling and smashing as they fell.

"Oh, God!" Livi gasped, her chest gone tight. Slapping the reins against Nancy's haunches, she urged her buttermilk up the rise. The trailing pack animals anchored Livi where she was, too far away to aid her children.

"Cissy! Tad! Hang on!" Livi yelled and jerked her knife from the sheath at her waist.

Up ahead, the little bay was floundering, fighting to keep her feet. Hampered by the weight of the packs, the mare stumbled, fell. More of the road gave way. Screaming, the horse teetered at the edge.

Goods tumbled from the baskets on her back. A kettle broke loose and clattered down the slope. A bolt of calico unfurled as it fell. A sack of precious wheat flour detonated at the bottom of the cliff, leaving a powdery stain on the rusty earth.

"Hang on!" Livi screamed and hacked at the line that bound her to her pack animals. "I'm coming!" Savagely she kicked her mare up the slope.

The bay's struggles were hauling the other animals in the string toward the lip of the embankment. Clinging to her brother, Cissy shrieked shrilly and long.

Tad dug in, fighting to overcome the drag. He shouted and kicked. He flailed his horse with the reins. Pebbles scrambled and rolled. His roan just wasn't strong enough to pull away. They skidded backward toward the edge.

Livi drove her mare harder, plowing into the melee of thrashing animals. The contact nearly jolted her out of her seat. Locking one knee around the saddle horn, she strained toward the flailing horse's lead. The blade in her hand snagged and bit. The taut rawhide snapped back with the force of a whip.

Deprived of its tether, the little bay pitched backward down the cliff. Freed of its weight, Tad's roan lurched up the slope.

Livi jerked her own mount away from the edge. Clods flew from beneath the horses' hooves. The air hung thick with the smells of mud and sweat and fear.

Ahead of her, Tad reined in his roan. It quivered with exertion. Foam speckled its heaving sides. Pulling up behind it, Livi leaped from her mare and snatched her daughter from where she clung to her brother's back.

"Mama! Mama!" Cissy sobbed.

Livi crushed the girl to her chest, knotting her fists in her daughter's clothes. Tad hurled himself into his mother's embrace the moment he was out of the saddle. Livi held tight to the solid breadth of him and pressed her face into his thick, unruly hair. The three of them hugged one another, breathing hard.

How close she had come to losing her babies! How precious they were in her arms. Livi thanked God that they were safe. Without her children, she'd have nothing left.

Tears scored trails down Cissy's muddy face. Livi couldn't stop panting. Tad closed his eyes and simply held on.

Minutes passed before they took note of the bay mare's screams. The pain and panic in the sound sent shivers up Livi's back. Loosening her hold on her children with great reluctance, she moved toward the edge of the cliff and peered over the embankment.

The drop was sheer, all gray-white rock and crumbled earth. Livi jerked back reflexively. After a moment, she edged up to take a second look.

Thirty feet below, the packhorse had come to rest on its side at the base of a tree. She could see its ribs rising and falling as if pumped by a bellows. From the angle of its legs, she judged at least one to be broken. Still, the beast flailed and twisted as if determined to rise.

"What are we going to do?" Cissy wanted to know.

What would David have done? Livi took a shaky breath. "I'm going down," she said at last. "Tad, bring your papa's pistol from my saddlebag."

Using Cissy to steady her, Livi eased herself over the edge. The undercut bank had given way, and loose dirt rolled beneath her boots. With roots and branches for handholds, she worked her way across and down the slope. It was a slow, dirty business, but at last she reached the little bay.

Up close, she saw the blood on the ground where the mare's stark white ribs protruded through its hide like shattered barrel staves. One rear hock was broken and the right foreleg lay limp and useless. Exhausted by its struggles, the horse rolled its eyes, frantic and filled with pain. Livi fancied that there was trust in the bay's expression, as if it expected her to make things better somehow.

At that moment Tad came skidding down to join her. "How is she?" he asked.

Livi shook her head. "There's nothing we can do for her. You'll have to put her down."

She heard Tad suck in his breath and turned to look at her son. His eyes had gone wide in his chalky face, blank with horror, blurry with tears.

Until that moment Livi had simply assumed Tad would be the one to take care of this unpleasantness. Men did these things; women weren't expected to.

But Tad was not yet a man. He was big and brave for twelve years old. He was conscientious and determined. Since David's death, he had hidden his grief, shouldered responsibilities far beyond his years. In asking him to shoot a horse he had fed and curried and cared for, she had demanded too much.

Her son's courage had a brittle delicacy about it, an untried purity. He wasn't ready to face such cruel realities as this. And suddenly Livi did not want him to be.

That she might have to shoot the horse instead appalled her, unnerved her. "Did you bring the pistol?" she asked at last.

Tad extended the gun for her to see.

"Are you sure it's loaded?"

He nodded.

"Thank you for seeing to that."

Livi closed her fingers around the gun. Though she'd held and fired it the night before, the weight of the pistol surprised her. Or perhaps it was holding death in her hand that weighed so heavily.

Before them, the horse struggled, strained to rise.

"Now, if I just put the barrel to her head . . ."

This was a living thing she was about to destroy. How could she bring herself to do that?

Gorge filled her throat, but she forced it down. She refused to be sick in front of her son. Not over this, not when Tad would pay for her weakness with his guilt.

"I can . . ." There was shame in the boy's face. "I'll try . . ."

"It's all right, Tad," she assured him. "I'll do it. It was wrong of me to ask you."

Beside them, the beast shifted again.

Livi's palms were slick. Her breath came harsh and quivery.

"It would help if you could hold her head. The last thing I want to do is miss."

Tad moved to grasp the bridle.

Livi cocked the pistol and nestled the barrel above the mare's left eye. Was this the right place? Would this kill her?

The bay puffed and blew. Livi tightened her finger around the trigger. Tad closed his eyes.

With a blast and a flash, the gun went off. The concussion jarred up Livi's arm.

Tad cried out.

The horse went still.

Livi sank back on her haunches against the hillside. There was a whining in her ears. Her hands tingled and went numb. She had never killed a living thing before, never deliberately taken a life. She'd even made David wring the chickens' necks. Around her the whining intensified.

As if from a distance, she felt Tad slip the pistol from her grasp, felt him close his hand around her shoulder, gripping hard.

From the road high above, Cissy was shouting. "Did you kill the horse? Why did you kill the horse?"

"Because we had no other choice, goddammit!"

She should warn Tad not to swear at his sister, Livi thought as a wave of dizziness took her. She'd do it just as soon as she dredged up the energy. Instead she closed her eyes and waited for her heart to stop pounding in her throat, for her legs to stop quivering. That took a good long while.

As her head cleared, she began to notice their belongings scattered here and there. There was a single leather book between her feet. A pitcher lay shattered nearby. Her best lace fichu fluttered in the breeze, snagged like a web in a bramble bush. Slowly she raised her gaze, seeing the contents of the horse's packs spilled across the face of the hill.

Livi climbed unsteadily to her feet and surveyed the wreckage. Tad and Cissy squatted nearby, waiting for direction. Rubbing her forehead with the back of her wrist, Livi tried to think what should happen next.

"We'll have to see to the horses on the trail," she finally said.

"Cissy and I did that already," Tad answered. "They're all

kind of wild-eyed, as if they understand what's happened. We tied them to the trees so they wouldn't wander off.''

"Thank you." Livi managed to smile at her son. "If I remember correctly, there's a clearing back a mile or so. Let's make camp there and gather up what's left."

It took some time to prepare the campsite, to get a fire going, to ferry back what goods could be salvaged. They had lost not only a horse, but one of the precious packsaddles. David had made each one of them by hand, selecting branches that grew at exactly the right angle to span a horse's back, using hickory withe to weave the baskets on either side. Deep and commodious, each of the creels, or panniers, held more than a hundred pounds of goods, things essential for establishing a farm in Kentucky.

Some of the goods the little bay had been carrying were irretrievably lost. Livi's best straw bonnet was smashed flat. Two tin candle molds were twisted and useless. They could find only one of Cissy's extra pair of shoes. Some of the bedding was so mud-stained Livi wondered if it would ever come clean. Still, they were lucky they hadn't lost more. But with one less horse to carry the load, Livi faced the inevitable decision of what to leave behind.

Some things were essential: gunpowder and shot, seeds and farming implements, quilts and blankets, iron kitchen ware, axes, knives for cooking and skinning, clothing for the children and herself. It was madness to consider leaving food behind. They would run out of sugar and flour soon enough. She only prayed that the cornmeal would last until harvest.

Livi fed several wooden bowls, a bucket, and her disassembled loom into the campfire, figuring that she might as well make use of them. She drank a last cup of tea from one of the four china teacups painted with a bright Forget-Me-Not pattern. The cups and a matching teapot were the only indulgences, the only "fancy bits," as David had called them, that Livi had allowed herself. But where they were going, such things were superfluous—and they took up space.

She asked the children if they could think of things they wouldn't need. Tad sacrificed a crudely painted checkerboard, a box of checkers, and a boat Reid Campbell had carved for him. He also did his best to discard a slate and two of his schoolbooks. He didn't have Cissy's quick mind for letters and such, and he would have been delighted to leave them behind. Livi prevented that. After much knuckle-chewing, Cissy picked three rocks from the collection she had been lugging around for as long as Livi could remember. With the rest, she erected a monument at the edge of the trail and held a private funeral for the little mare.

Once Livi herself had tucked away David's most valuable things, his journal with instructions for crossing the mountains and finding their land, his watch and pocket telescope, she went through the rest of his things. She found a brass key she decided to keep, a pair of boots she knew would fit Tad eventually, and a waistcoat she'd made for David's birthday only three weeks before.

With no small difficulty, they unloaded the heaviest of his blacksmithing tools and half the iron bars he'd brought. They set aside his brass-buckled dress shoes, which were all but worn through, his embroidered frock coat and nankeen breeches. It was doubtful that he would have had use for such finery in the Kentucky wilderness anyway.

This is what makes it so difficult when someone dies, Livi thought. It's not just that they're gone, that you'll never see them, or hold them, or hear their laughter. For those who are left behind, dying doesn't just happen once. It's a series of losses that go on and on.

Last night she had missed David's presence, David's strength, David's reassurance in the dark. Today she was being forced to leave more parts of her husband behind. What would she give up tomorrow, and the day after that? How long would it take for even her dearest and most precious memories to fade?

As if to stave off the inevitable, Livi wrapped David's linsey-woolsey hunting shirt over her own mud-spattered gown. The garment was huge, hanging on her slender frame, drooping well down her thighs. But the moment the shirt settled around her shoulders, David's essence enveloped her. His warmth fell across her back; his scent drifted around her like a balm. Reassurance emanated from the sturdy cloth as if some last scrap of the man who had been her husband still resided there. Livi felt loved, protected, soothed, and she refused to deny herself the comfort she'd unwittingly discovered in the yards of cloth. Doubling the hunting shirt across her breasts, she belted it tight at the waist and turned back both sleeves. With its tough fabric and its broad, caped collar, the hunting shirt made an odd but completely serviceable garment for Livi to wear as they traveled. With a new sense of serenity, she continued with her chores.

Between her and the children, they repacked the creels and set aside the goods they would tie to David's saddle in the morning. The night passed without incident, though Livi slept very little. She lost her breakfast almost as soon as she'd eaten it and wept over the things they were leaving behind. But when she turned onto the road shortly after sunup, they headed west once more.

3

The Block House lived up to its name. Livi and the children had seen it standing foursquare and resolute on a rise at the mouth of a wooded valley long before they reached the security of its walls. They clattered through the open gate just short of midday: a train of straggling pack animals; a slender woman worn weary by the miles; and two fair-haired children riding together, clearly out of patience with traveling and each other.

A tall man with graying hair and a military bearing strode out of the main building as they rode into the yard. "Welcome to the Block House," he greeted Livi. "I'm Captain John Anderson."

Livi nodded in acknowledgment. "I'm Olivia Talbot and these are my children, Tad and Cissy."

"Have you come far?" the captain asked.

"From Lynchburg," Livi replied.

"Come all that way by yourselves? How long did it take?"

"A bit more than a week."

Livi could feel Anderson's assessing gaze slide over her. "More than a week," he echoed.

"We had some trouble," Livi felt compelled to answer.

John Anderson perked up like a hunter on point. "Trouble? What kind of trouble?"

The memory of David sprawled shattered and bleeding at her feet roared through Livi's head, drowning out any coherent response.

Tad spoke up in his mother's stead. "Well, the roads haven't been the best," he began. "And we lost one of our packhorses day before yesterday. She got spooked and went over an embankment. Broke two legs."

"Mama had to shoot the horse," Cissy added from where she was sitting behind her brother. "I made a funeral for her, too. Just like—"

Under the drape of his sister's skirt, Tad reached around and pinched her into silence. Cissy sucked in her breath and punched him back.

Her children's behavior jerked Livi free of the memories. As she drew breath to admonish them both, Tad abruptly raised his head.

"Is that stew I smell cooking?" he asked. "I swear I'm hungry enough to eat a bucketful."

"As it happens, son," Anderson said, grinning at the two scrappy youngsters, "you've arrived just in time for our noon meal. You're more than welcome to join us. I can have someone see to your animals, if you like."

"A hot meal sounds wonderful," Livi conceded, "but I'd just as soon see to the animals myself, Captain Anderson, if you think there's time."

The big man seemed to approve of her concern. "Then go on around this building to the right. You'll see a paddock and the stable. Why don't you stow your goods in there for the time being?"

Livi did as Anderson suggested, and she was pleased with the facilities.

They had barely dismounted at the stable door when Cissy turned furiously on her brother. "Why'd you pinch me, Tad?" she demanded. "I didn't do anything to you!"

Tad glared down at his little sister. "Because I didn't want you blurting out how Papa died."

Livi turned to her son, saddlebags in hand. "Why shouldn't we tell these folks what happened? We can't very well keep your father's death a secret."

Tad met his mother's gaze. "I know we can't. No one would believe a mother and two children setting out on this trip alone. But I think we should be careful what we say."

Livi came a step nearer. "Just what do you mean?"

"I think what happened will go against us when we try to

find folks to travel with. Pa said people band together to cross the mountains because they're afraid of the Indians. If they hear we've already had Indian trouble, how willing are folks going to be to let us join them? You said yourself, Ma, we're likely to be hard pressed to find a group to take us on.''

''Yes, that's true,'' Livi admitted. ''But, Tad, don't you think we need to warn these people about the Indians who attacked our camp?''

''Don't you think if that raiding party was still around, Captain Anderson would know about it by now?'' Tad reasoned aloud. ''Pa was killed five days ago.''

Five days? Livi found herself thinking. Was that all it had been? Those five days seemed like an eternity.

''Reaching the land in Kentucky depends on being able to travel with a group, doesn't it, Ma?'' Tad pressed her.

''Yes.''

''Can we afford to scare them off? Should we give them one more reason to refuse us passage?''

''I suppose not.''

''Then we can't tell anyone how Pa died.''

Livi nodded in agreement, amazed by the complexity of her twelve-year-old's logic, his instinctive understanding of the settlers headed west.

While Livi pondered, Tad addressed his sister, nestled at Livi's side. ''You want to go on to Kentucky, don't you, Cissy?''

Chewing on her knuckle, the little girl stared up at him.

''You want to see the place Pa picked for us to live, the one Reid told us stories about. You want to live by the creek with the pretty stones and all the fish, don't you?''

Slowly, without removing her fist from her mouth, Cissy nodded.

''Then you have to swear not to tell anyone what happened to Pa.''

Cissy looked to her mother for confirmation.

Livi shifted the weight of her ambivalence and nodded. ''That's right. We can't let these folks know your father was killed by Indians.''

''But what if they ask me?'' the girl wheedled.

''I'm sure they won't,'' Livi assured her.

''But what if they do?''

Livi exchanged a long look with her son. "If anyone asks how your papa died, tell them he was sick."

"Very sick," Tad put in.

"But that would be a lie," Cissy insisted primly. "Papa told me never to lie to anyone."

"Pa will forgive you for lying this once," Tad assured her.

When had her son become so sanguine about lying? Livi wondered. When had he learned that sometimes lies were necessary?

Could two children keep such a volatile secret? Could Livi herself go on without confiding her fears and grief to anyone? Yet what choice did they have? If they were going to reach Kentucky and settle David's land, they had to find passage with other travelers going west.

"If things were different, I wouldn't ask you to do this," Livi murmured, looking down into her daughter's dark eyes.

The child answered with a nod. "All right, Mama. I'll do what you say, if you're sure Papa wouldn't mind."

"You need to swear not to tell," Tad insisted.

"Tad!" Livi snapped. Bending the truth to reach Kentucky was one thing. Swearing a four-year-old to secrecy was another thing entirely.

"No, Ma, she has to swear."

The little girl nodded, obviously caught up in some childish ritual Livi had long ago forgotten. "What do I have to do to swear, Tad?"

"Repeat after me: I promise—"

" 'I promise—' "

"Not to tell anyone how my pa died—"

" 'Not to tell anyone how my pa died—' "

"Until we get to Kentucky."

" 'Until we get to Kentucky.' "

"Then cross your heart and spit in your hand," Tad instructed.

"Tad!" Livi admonished him a second time.

Cissy performed the appropriate ritual and Tad did the same. He took her hand in his and pressed their palms together.

Livi grimaced.

"Now you've given me your sacred word," he told her solemnly. "You can never break it as long as you live."

Cissy stared wide-eyed at her brother as if she had been part of something mysterious and infinitely important. "Oh, I never will!"

"Now," Livi muttered when they were done, "do you suppose I could have some help unsaddling these horses?"

She and the children went about their task with newfound proficiency, making short work of getting the animals fed, watered, and settled in. After a quick wash at a basin in the yard and a few swipes of a comb, they joined Captain Anderson and a dozen or so others at the long plank table in the Block House's main room.

Since its construction in the opening days of America's War of Independence, the formidable log structure and the meadow around it had become a gathering place for travelers headed to Kentucky. Built at the junction of the trail from the Holston River settlements and the road that ran the length of the Shenandoah Valley, the Block House was the final bastion of civilization on the fringe of the frontier. Designed for defense with a second story that overhung the first, the Block House and its palisaded yard now seemed to serve more as an inn and trading post than as a refuge from marauding Indians. Still, Livi welcomed the foot-thick walls; the high, barred gate; the sense of invulnerability about the place. It was the first time she'd felt truly secure since they'd left Lynchburg.

All manner of people were gathered around the dining table on the Block House's commodious first floor. They stared at Livi and the children as they sat down, sizing them up as potential traveling companions. Livi stared back with the same intent.

John Anderson made introductions, but the spicy tang of the rabbit stew Mrs. Anderson began ladling into bowls made Livi incapable of concentrating on anything else. It was as if the woman had somehow discerned all of Livi's fancies and fulfilled them with a stir of her spoon. The taste of the stew lived up to its aroma, the meat succulent and tender, the vegetables cooked to perfection, the gravy savory with a hint of rosemary and dill. There was a knob of dark bread in the center of the table, and Livi used her third piece to swipe up the last of the stew in the bottom of her bowl.

Finally sated, she returned her attention to her companions. There were a round-faced man and woman and their round-faced sons; a shy young couple with a baby asleep in its mother's arms; an old man and three strapping boys. There were several single men at the table, too: one with a patch over his eye and a red mustache, another great bear of a man missing most of his teeth, and a sallow-complected fellow who kept to himself.

At a glance David would have known which of these people would be the most dependable and congenial on the trail. He would have known how to approach them, how to form an alliance that would weather the miles. Livi had no idea at all how to do that.

"Ma, can I be excused?" Tad asked when talk around the table turned from tales of Kentucky to a debate about the merits of certain varieties of seed corn.

"If you take your sister with you," Livi replied.

"Aw, Ma!"

"It's safe for them to wander as far as the edge of the woods," Mrs. Anderson put in helpfully as she cleared the meal away.

"You heard her," Livi warned as the children headed toward the door.

"There's a bed and a trundle still available upstairs, Mrs. Talbot," Jane Anderson continued, "should you and the children want it."

Livi asked the price, then gave the older woman a nod. "A bed sounds like heaven after sleeping on the ground even these few nights."

"As soon as I've seen to the dishes, I'll show you the way."

The room at the end of the hall was dark and airless but scrupulously clean. There were fresh linens on the bed and a washstand in the corner. Livi could not have been more delighted if the pitcher and bowl were English porcelain and the bed a tester hung with silk.

The loopholes plugged with big wooden pegs and the trapdoor in the floor that enabled defenders to fire down at an enemy storming the walls reminded Livi that she and the children had ventured far beyond everything that was safe and familiar and comfortable. They also made her feel as if she might dare to sleep tonight.

"Your husband joining you soon?" Mrs. Anderson inquired, breaking into Livi's thoughts.

"No, he's not." Livi could feel her throat close up. She

fought to weigh her words. "He—" Livi swallowed hard. "David . . ."

"Your man die recently, then?"

Livi refused to meet the other woman's gaze. "On the trail."

Jane Anderson offered an indelicate snort rather than the questions or the words of sympathy Livi had been expecting.

"And you're going over the mountains anyway? Alone with those two children? All the way to Kentucky?"

Livi's chin came up. "David claimed his three hundred acres for serving with Colonel Clark during the war. We were supposed to start a new life out there."

She knew it wasn't a new story. Half the people who passed through the Block House must be headed for land they'd garnered fighting for Virginia or North Carolina in these past years.

Jane Anderson gave Livi a long, assessing look. "And you're going ahead with his plans."

Livi nodded.

"You know what you're getting into, girl?"

"No."

"Kentucky's not the best place for a woman alone."

"I haven't anywhere else to go."

The other woman mulled that over. "You have someone to fell the trees and build a cabin? To clear the fields?"

"David cleared several fields when he was in Kentucky last fall. We'll be able to put in corn as soon as we arrive. I figured I might find someone going west who would trade his services for some of my land."

"It'd have to be the right man," Mrs. Anderson mused, leaning thoughtfully against the doorjamb.

As long as Jane Anderson was in an expansive mood, Livi decided to take advantage of it. "What about the men at the table today?"

"Well, you don't want Red Swazey—the man with the patch. He's a scrapper and a boozer. And Billy-boy Bryant is hardly better. Les Winslow ain't half bad, but he sets to wheezing sometimes. He'll never make old bones; you mark me well."

"Perhaps I'll find someone once I get there."

Jane Anderson's eyebrows conveyed her disbelief. "Well, perhaps."

"When are these people moving out?"

"Tomorrow morning. But by the look of you, I'd say you need a few days' rest. You ain't slept much since your husband passed on, have you? And unless I miss my guess, you're breeding, too."

Livi's mouth dropped open. "How did you know?"

"I saw the way you ate at dinner. A woman built like you don't pack away that much food unless she's carrying. You going to be able to keep it down?"

"I'm not sure." Livi had never spoken so frankly to anyone, let alone a stranger. "But no matter how I feel, there isn't time for me to rest up if these people are leaving in the morning."

"There'll be other folks through here soon enough," the older woman said. "We had lots of them pass by while there was snow on the ground, and there will be more in the next few weeks. We just got to find the right ones for you and your young'uns to travel with."

"You mean you'll help me?"

"Lord, girl!" Jane Anderson laughed. "Half of what me and John do is set folks up together for the trek over the mountains."

"I can't afford to wait too long. I need to get the corn in by the middle of April."

"Just where is your husband's land?"

"South and west of Logan's Station."

The older woman nodded. "Then you've got a week or two yet. Lots of time to find some suitable traveling companions. Though the good Lord knows there won't be many willing to tote a lone woman and her children all that way."

"I can take care of myself and my children!" Livi insisted.

Jane Anderson gave another derisive snort. It was unnerving the way this woman saw through Livi's every pretense.

"You just lie back on that bed and have a good sleep," Jane advised sagely. "You got circles under your eyes as dark as lantern soot. I'll keep watch over your young'uns for you this afternoon, and we'll talk later about the rest."

Mrs. Anderson swung away and disappeared down the hall before Livi had a chance to so much as thank her.

*   *   *

Jane Anderson was right. Lots of people stopped at the Block House on their way to Kentucky, more each day as the weather improved. Not one of them was willing to add a widow and two children to his party.

"Now, just why would a pretty lady like you want to settle in a wild place like Kentucky?" the men would ask when Livi approached them about passage west.

"I have land near Logan's Station."

"Do you indeed? And just what do you intend to do with that land once you reach it?"

"I intend to do the same as you, build a cabin and start a farm."

"Alone?" they would demand, their voices rife with laughter and incredulity. "A woman like you won't last a week in the wilds. Hell, a lady like you'll never make it beyond the Cumberland Gap."

Each refusal turned Livi harder, grimmer, more desperate. Each day she and the children spent at the Block House called into question the decision she had made, weathered away a few more grains of her confidence and determination, made Tad more itchy to be on his way. A boy his age might well be hired on by a party going west to help with the chores. Concern for his mother and sister kept Tad at the Block House—but for how much longer?

When a group of travelers from a church near Petersburg pulled in late one afternoon, Jane Anderson quickly alerted Livi.

"Surely they'll take pity on a widow woman," Jane murmured encouragingly as they watched the group make camp in the meadow beyond the Block House's open gate.

Livi stiffened. She didn't want the settlers' pity; what she wanted was passage over the mountains. But she had to admit that this group offered what might be her last and very best chance.

An hour after the churchmen rode in, Livi found herself preparing to meet their leader, the good Reverend Amos Lindenwood. Securing her heavy coppery hair in a knot at the nape of her neck and placing a crisp, bleached-muslin cap atop her head, Livi peered into the scrap of mirror suspended on the wall above the washstand.

Haunted moss-green eyes stared back at her. New hollows sharpened the sloping line of her cheekbones and highlighted the angle of her jaw. With her wide-set eyes and broad-boned face, her mouth seemed pale and small and vulnerable. She looked more frightened than determined. More like eighteen and inexperienced than self-possessed and twenty-nine.

She pinched color into her cheeks and bit her lips. Tawdry tricks, but necessary. She tied a fresh apron around her still-slim waist, infinitely grateful that her pregnancy hadn't yet begun to show. It was the one liability no one could see, and Livi had no compunctions about keeping it secret.

She glanced in the mirror one last time. Did she look calm and strong and capable enough to brave the trip? Could she convince Reverend Lindenwood to grant them passage? She swallowed hard and reminded herself she had no choice.

Tad was pacing circles in the yard when she came down. She could see he'd washed up good and slicked back his hair.

"Do you want me to come with you?" he asked when he saw her standing in the doorway.

Tad knew as well as she that time was running out for them. If they didn't start up Boone's Trace by the first of April, they might as well give up on David's dream.

"I thought it might go better if I went, too."

"I think I have to go alone," Livi answered him. "It's me they'll be having doubts about."

Tad turned the brim of his hat in his hands. "It's just that it's getting so close to planting time . . ."

Livi's breath fluttered, trapped beneath her ribs as much by ambivalence as by nervousness. "I know, Tad. I intend to do everything I can to convince this Reverend Lindenwood that we'll be an asset to his party—not a liability. I just don't have any way of knowing how charitable this group of Christians is prepared to be."

"I know you'll do your best, Ma."

The weight of those words settled over Livi like a yoke.

Before she could think of how to answer her son, John Anderson came out of the Block House.

"You 'bout ready, Olivia?"

Livi dredged up what she hoped was a cocky grin. "Got the horses already saddled."

Anderson laughed and headed for the gate.

"Good luck, Ma," Tad called after them.

It helped to have John Anderson beside her as they crossed the field where the settlers were pitching their camp. By making the introductions, he added the weight of his recommendation to her request for passage. Surely his willingness to do that meant that John had faith in her, that he believed her capable of making the trek to Kentucky, of working David's land.

Around them, the churchmen were putting up tents while their women shook out bedding and unpacked food. Older children hauled water from the stream, and younger ones carried logs from the two huge stockpiles Anderson provided for the travelers' use.

They found the Anglican pastor splitting wood. With his shirtsleeves rolled up and a sheen of perspiration on his brow, Amos Lindenwood looked a good deal less intimidating than he might have, done up in clerical robes and standing by the sanctuary door. He was a big, bluff man in his middle years, and Livi liked the looks of him immediately.

"I'm pleased to meet you, Mrs. Talbot," Lindenwood said, setting his ax aside and wiping his face with a bright bandanna handkerchief. "The captain says you want to travel with us to Kentucky."

"That's right, Reverend Lindenwood. My husband's land lies near Logan's Station. My children and I need to reach it as soon as we can."

"And why isn't your husband escorting you, dear lady?" the pastor inquired with real concern.

"My husband is dead, sir. He died on the trail some miles east of here."

Lindenwood reached across to take her hand. It was the practiced gesture of a man who had comforted scores of widows in his time. "Then may the Lord grant you strength and solace in your time of loss."

The reverend's sonorous tone reverberated in Livi's chest, brought an unexpected need for comfort to the fore. Resolutely she ignored it. "Thank you," she answered, lowering her eyes.

"With your husband so recently taken from you, dear lady, wouldn't it be wiser for you to go back where you came from? Surely you have family who can see you through this crisis."

Not once in all the years since she'd turned her back on the

Tidewater plantation where she'd grown up had Livi considered going to her family for help—not when she realized how hard life with David was going to be, not when her husband marched off to war, not when she lost her babies. She would not turn to the Chestertons now. Still, the reverend's suggestion brought a clutch of unexpected desolation.

"There's no one to go back to," she answered quietly. "We must press on."

"You aren't going to live on the land in Kentucky all by yourself, are you, dear?" Lindenwood asked.

After Livi had been refused passage so many times, she and Jane Anderson had concocted a story to assuage any fear the men might have of being held responsible for Livi and the children once they crossed the mountains.

"No! Oh, no," she assured the reverend with what she hoped was sufficient conviction. "We won't be living there alone. My husband's brother is at the cabin now. But— George—has no way of knowing what happened to David, no way of knowing we're stranded here. We have no way to join him unless, of course, you're kind enough to let us accompany you."

Deceit never sat well on Livi. In the face of Lindenwood's obvious sincerity and genuine concern, it rankled even more. And surely it was doubly wrong to dupe a man of the cloth. That Anderson had heard the recitation and said nothing was either a tribute to Jane Anderson's persuasiveness or even more evidence of his confidence in recommending her.

"Well, I'll have to discuss this with the others in my party before I can give you an answer," Lindenwood told her. "It's highly irregular, a woman traveling alone. Still, I can see the need of it . . ."

"Then I leave the decision to you," Livi said with what she hoped was just the right amount of approbation. Experience had already taught her that these men might demand a strong and capable woman for life on the trail, but she must be soft-spoken and infinitely biddable when she wasn't saddling horses or loading rifles for the camp's defense.

Lindenwood asked her a few more questions before he let her go and promised he would give her his answer after supper. Livi felt more hopeful than she had in days, and when she returned to their room at the Block House, she found Tad and Cissy packing.

The dawn's first rays slanted through the trees, tinting the mist that veiled the meadow a diaphanous amber rose. Even at that hour of the day, the area around the Block House was astir with travelers striking tents, rolling bedding, and saddling horses. Children laughed and chased one another through the drifting banks of fog. As they finished their chores, women gathered around the few remaining campfires, drinking coffee and talking, their voices low and vibrant in the cool, still air.

The dew-damp grass whispered against Livi's skirt as she and her children led their animals toward where the party of churchmen was preparing to get under way. A ring of men stood conferring in the midst of the confusion, leaning on their long rifles as they made their plans.

As Livi approached, their circle subtly shifted, minutely closed. At first she thought it might have been some vague, unconscious movement, but as she came nearer she could see the squaring of the men's shoulders, the tightening of their stance. Though Reverend Lindenwood had given her permission, these men clearly opposed adding a widow and two children to their party for the journey west.

Feeling both intimidated and strangely belligerent, Livi paused a yard or two from where the men were standing. "Good morning, gentlemen," she said softly but distinctly.

They ignored her to a man.

"Good morning!" She tried again, forcing the words past the knot in her throat.

Amos Lindenwood turned at the sound of her voice, genuinely surprised to see Livi standing behind him. The preacher was the only man in the circle who hadn't noticed her.

"Mrs. Talbot, good morning. Come meet some of the others of our little band."

Begrudgingly the men shuffled aside, looking Livi up and down as she took her place among them. She was dressed for the trail with David's altered hunting shirt belted over her bodice and skirt. The canvas sack filled with necessities— parched corn and jerky, salve and bandages, a needle, thread, and tinderbox—was slung across one shoulder. Jane Anderson had given her an old, indestructible, wide-brimmed hat that shaded her face and gave her what Jane called "substance." Livi wasn't sure what "substance" was, but she figured it wouldn't hurt to have some in the days ahead. She also clung to David's long rifle as if it had been grafted to her hand.

What the men thought of her was anyone's guess, but Livi stood her ground in spite of their flaying scrutiny.

After everyone had looked his fill, Reverend Lindenwood went on with introductions. "This is my church deacon and friend, George Willoughby, George's brother, Sam, and Sam's oldest boy, Jacob."

The three men were stocky and not very tall, with shocks of bristly dark hair that seemed to have successfully resisted all attempts to tame them. Livi nodded in greeting.

"Next is Lem Stewart. Lem and his sister are going to their aunt and uncle's place just west of Hazel Patch." Lem looked washed out, weary, odd in a man of such tender years.

"And this is Hyram Boggs. He and his missus seem to have taken God at His word and been 'fruitful and multiplied.' Your youngsters will certainly find companions among his brood."

"Mr. Stewart." Livi acknowledged them. "Mr. Boggs."

"I'm Joss Smiley," said the next man, a handsome, sandy-haired fellow.

"And I'm Turnip Carter."

Looking at the stringy little man with his round, flushed face and scraggly beard made it clear to Livi that Turnip lived up to his name.

"I'm pleased to meet you, gentlemen. I'm Olivia Talbot. These are my children, Tad and Cissy. We want to thank you for letting us join up with you."

There was a moment of silence, a moment of lowered eyes and shifting from foot to foot.

Apprehension twisted beneath Livi's breastbone. Surely they weren't going to deny her passage at this late date. Not when her horses were already saddled and her creels already packed. Not when her children were so eager to get under way. Not when she had finally managed to gather her courage for the trek ahead.

"About that, Mrs. Talbot." Hyram Boggs broached the subject hanging thick in the air. "Just why is it you are traveling to Kentucky alone?"

Livi drew an unsteady breath. Sensing that these men were

going to be far more stringent in their questioning than Reverend Lindenwood had been, Livi tried to shoo her children away. Cissy went gladly, having already discovered playmates among the churchmen's children. Tad stoically sat his horse, guarding his mother's back.

"My husband died a little more than a fortnight ago, shortly after we left Lynchburg," Livi began. "He filed his claim for land just west of Logan's Station and cleared a section of it last fall. His brother's there now, getting ready for planting. I need to reach the farm with the seed corn as soon as I can."

Livi told the lie far more convincingly than she had the previous evening and raised her chin a notch when she was done.

The men nodded, still frowning, still eyeing her. "Let me be frank with you, Mrs. Talbot," Boggs went on. "We have some reservations about taking you and your family with us. We're going to be passing through some rough and dangerous country, and we're concerned about you keeping up."

"I assume we can keep any pace your own wives and children can," Livi offered levelly.

"What about food?" Lem Stewart wanted to know. "You've got no man to hunt for you."

"Tad will do a bit of hunting when he can, and Captain Anderson was kind enough to sell me some smoked and salted meat. If we run out on the trail, perhaps I can buy what we need from one of you."

As much as she'd hated to sell David's horse, John Anderson had given her a good price for it. Now the additional coin might help to smooth their way.

The men murmured among themselves and finally Boggs asked the question Livi had been dreading. "But can you and your boy defend yourselves on the trail, Mrs. Talbot, if it comes to that?"

She straightened as if a ramrod had been inserted up her spine. "Do I look like the kind of ninny who has never fired a gun?" she demanded.

To them, she probably did. Surely she had earned that distinction, coming from a long line of women who spent their days doing petit point and drinking tea—ninnies by these men's definition. Doubtless she bore the stamp of it.

Livi focused her fiercest scowl on the men and shifted the

long rifle across her arm as if the stance were second nature to her. Any doubts she had about defending her family she kept to herself. John Anderson had schooled her in the basics of handling firearms, in loading and cleaning and shooting them. But if truth be told, her accuracy left much to be desired. Nor was she certain she would be able to shoot a man if it came to that. To her eternal shame, Livi hadn't been able to pull the trigger on the gun the night her husband died.

Around her, the men rolled their shoulders and shifted their feet. They beetled their brows and grumbled under their breath, but in the end, they took Livi at her word. Even Hyram Boggs backed down. In the days to come, these men would watch her and test her and do their best to bully her, but for the moment they had accepted Olivia Talbot as one of them.

After a brief discussion, the group broke up. Livi hooked one foot in the stirrup and vaulted into the sidesaddle without so much as a helping hand. At Tad's whistle, Cissy came running across the wind-washed field.

As they waited, Tad reached across and patted his mother's arm. "You did good, Ma."

"Did I?" Livi asked almost breathlessly.

"Yes, Ma, you did."

Tad's words warmed her, fanned the spark of pride and determination that had begun to smolder inside her chest. Somehow she had managed to get this far, secure passage for the journey west. It brought them one day closer to Kentucky, one day closer to fulfilling her husband's dream. And for the very first time since David's death, Livi Talbot began to think she might somehow face what lay ahead.

4

"*Y*ou managing to keep up, little lady?"

Livi had watched Hyram Boggs canter the length of the pack train. She'd seen him smile and nod benevolently at others as he rode, but his patronizing tone as he asked after her and the children stirred the rich roux of uncertainty bubbling in her chest. "We're doing as well as anyone could expect, Mr. Boggs," she answered with as much gumption as she could muster.

"We should be making camp in an hour or so," he went on. "Dark comes early once you get into the hills."

They had indeed gotten "into the hills." In the course of today's march they'd splashed through the ford on the North Fork of the Holston River, traversed the Clinch Mountains at Moccasin Gap, and were following Little Moccasin Creek to the west and north.

"I suppose we'll be climbing Troublesome Creek Gorge tomorrow," Livi offered. While stranded at the Block House, Livi had made it her business to familiarize herself with the landmarks described in David's journal. "From what I understand, it lives up to its name."

"That's true enough, little lady," he answered, lifting heavy, wedge-shaped brows. "Tomorrow we'll find out just how game the members of this pack train really are."

Boggs's challenge lingered even after he'd spurred his horse to where the Carter family was bringing up the rear. Though he had other reasons for riding the length of the pack train, it

49

was obvious Boggs expected to find her and the children lagging. He had been looking for a chance to bedevil her, to point out just how ill-suited she was for the wilds. Just as Reid Campbell always had.

If she were more certain about their ability to keep up, if she weren't quivering with exhaustion, Livi might have thought fast enough to answer Boggs. But she wasn't sure how she and the children would fare in the rough terrain, couldn't imagine what words could put a man like Hyram Boggs in his place, and didn't dare risk his wrath.

In the saddle behind her, Cissy broke off singing a nonsense song about apples, beans, and turnip greens. "When will we be stopping for supper, Mama?"

"Mr. Boggs said in an hour or so."

"But I'm hungry now."

As Livi fumbled in the canvas bag for a piece of jerky, a new blaze of nausea surged up her throat. With an effort she quelled the queasiness, just as she had been swallowing it down all day. Living and eating and sleeping in close proximity with so many others, Livi knew she couldn't keep her pregnancy secret for long. She just hoped that when her companions discovered that she'd deliberately misled them, they'd be too far from the Block House to send her and the children back.

The sun was setting behind the hills when the party of churchmen and their families turned into a U-shaped meadow to the right of the trail. Already cloaked in shadow, the field was swiftly being divided into campsites. Since Livi and the children were second to last in line, the choicest places had all been taken when they arrived.

Tad immediately saw the way of things and circled around to the left, motioning toward a hollow beneath an arc of pines.

"This campsite lies lower than I would like," he grumbled, sounding very much like David, "but unless we get rain tonight, it should do us well enough."

Cissy pointed to the roseate glow tinting the sky beyond the hills. "Red sky at night," she piped in singsong, "sailors delight. Red sky at morning, sailors take warning."

"That's very good, Cissy," Tad said. "But we're not exactly on the ocean here."

"Doesn't that rhyme count on land, Mama?"

"I suppose it does," Livi answered with a grunt, lifting a creel off one of the horses. "At any rate, the stars are coming out, so it seems unlikely it will rain."

"Oh, they *are* coming out, Mama. And the sky is just like apple fritters."

Livi paused, the packsaddle in her arms. "Like apple fritters?"

"Like the sugar on the top," her daughter enlightened her, one corner of her mouth hitched up in exasperation.

After wrestling the saddle to the relative protection of the pine's shaggy branches, Livi stepped back to look. High above, the heavens shaded in a few quick strokes from scarlet through orchid, mauve, and violet to a clear, almost iridescent blue. Stars were popping out across the hazy expanse, sparks of faceted white shimmering through the merge of colors.

Livi gave her daughter a secret smile. The stars did look like granules of sugar sprinkled on a batch of apple fritters.

"I think the campsite will be fine for tonight, Tad," she said, turning to reassure her son. "But tomorrow—"

"I'll take care of tomorrow," he promised her.

With unprecedented ease and alacrity, Livi and the children set up the campsite. Tad and his mother erected the tent; Cissy gathered wood. While Tad made the fire, Livi stirred together batter for the hoecakes that were a staple of life on the trail. A few slices from a slab of bacon sizzled beside them in the frying pan, sending up tendrils of sweet, salty smoke that turned Livi's stomach inside out.

For a time, the other families were similarly employed. But as soon as the meal was eaten, the dishes washed and put away, others in the pack train began to filter past the Talbots' campsite. Some stared long and hard as they made their way toward the stream. A few nodded in greeting. Some of the children Tad and Cissy played with at the Block House stopped by to say hello.

In the course of the evening, three of the women in the party wandered over to introduce themselves. The first, Ada Lindenwood, the reverend's wife, made her "duty call" to welcome Livi and the children. The moment she opened her mouth, Livi knew how much Ada disapproved of them.

"Why, my dear, this is such a brave and *unorthodox* thing for a woman to do," Ada trilled, "to continue on to Kentucky when you've no man to protect you. How very—*resourceful* you must have become since your husband was *called home*. Darling Amos so *admires* your determination. He saw it as his *Christian Duty* to allow you and your *precious* children to accompany us to Kentucky. Just as I see it as my *Christian Duty* to make you welcome."

Livi ground her teeth to keep from telling Ada Lindenwood where she could take her welcome and her "Christian Duty."

Tacy Boggs came by some minutes later, one baby on her hip and another growing beneath the pleats of her apron. She didn't even bother to veil her hostility. "Hyram says you got no business being on the train. Hyram says you're putting us all in danger being here without a man. Hyram says—"

"If Hyram has anything to say," Livi cut in, her cheeks burning, "you tell him to come and see me himself. I don't fancy hearing his words chewed twice."

Tacy Boggs went off in a huff.

Aching with disappointment, Livi watched her go. She'd counted on finding some common ground with the women on the pack train, on forming bonds with others braving the same dangers and hardships as she.

There was no doubt that her situation was different from theirs. Widowhood granted her certain rights the other women did not have: to consult with the men on issues pertaining to the journey west, to express her opinions, to vote for or against a course of action that would affect them all. They were rights that gave her unprecedented freedom, rights that weighed with unaccustomed responsibility.

But Livi was a woman and a mother first. She'd hoped for someone with whom she could commiserate when her back ached and exhaustion dragged her down. She'd wanted friends who would join her around the campfire, who would make her forget she was frightened and alone. *She'd wanted someone she could turn to if things went wrong.*

"Mama?"

Cissy's soft voice scattered Livi's thoughts. Turning, she faced two dark-haired, dark-eyed girls whose ages must bracket Cissy's own, and the woman who was certainly their mother.

"These are my new friends, Ann and Verity," Cissy told her.

"And I'm Ann and Verity's mother, Molly Baker. I thought I'd stop by and see how you were settling in."

Gratitude swelled in Livi's chest. "I'm pleased you did."

"You met my pa this morning," Molly went on. "Turnip Carter?"

Livi nodded and watched as the three girls sat down in front of the tent to play with their dolls. Ann's and Verity's were dressed in chintz and calico. Cissy's wore a tattered tabby gown.

"Are you traveling with your husband, too?" Livi asked, turning her attention to the woman beside her. She was every bit as done up as the dolls, in a fashionably cut bodice, bustled-up overskirt, and bright red shoes.

Molly Baker shook her head. "Pa and Ma took the girls and me in when Ben was killed at Yorktown," she volunteered. "I've been sewing dresses for ladies in Petersburg to earn our keep."

"There won't be much call for dressmaking in Kentucky," Livi observed. "Nor money for fripperies."

"I'll work on Ma and Pa's place till towns sprout up. It won't be long at the rate folks are crossing the mountains. And how is it that you and your young'uns are traveling alone?"

Livi sacrificed a bit of her precious tea to make a new friend and told Molly as much of the story as she dared.

"Aren't you purely terrified of where we're going?" Molly asked, wide-eyed. "After your David up and died, how can you bear to brave the hills alone?"

"What choice do I have?" Livi answered, the simplicity of the words startling her. Making the decision to go on to Kentucky hadn't been simple at all.

"Besides," Livi went on, "it's better traveling with a group. I was terrified to be in the woods by myself."

"I agree." Molly nodded emphatically.

As she settled on her pallet a good while later, Livi's own words came back to her. There was comfort here in the camp, companionship, security. She could hear the crush of the sentry's footsteps as he made his rounds, the hum of voices, the piping of weary children drifting toward sleep. Faint golden

light warmed the canvas walls of her tent. In spite of the lack
of acceptance, there were people here to call on, to count on.
With that knowledge clutched close, Livi drifted into dream-
less sleep.

During her years in Lynchburg, Livi had grown accustomed
to the smoky ridge of mountains on the horizon. She'd learned
to like the way they framed the stores and houses and barns
of the small James River settlement. She'd found them protective, calming, benign. But neither those hills nor the ones
she'd passed through since had prepared her for the pinch and
press of the mountains they encountered three days out on
Boone's Trace.

Just beyond the Clinch River ford, hulking gray rocks shouldered close to the road. Boulders jutted out of the broken earth.
Trees stood sentry wherever they could, clinging to the edge
of the trail, risking impossible slopes, teetering on ledges, their
roots trailing down like raveled rope. High above, the mountains compressed the wide expanse of sky to a narrow vein of
dusky blue. Even the stream the pack train followed and
forded, and forded again, had to fight and twist to make its
way along the jagged scrap of valley floor.

The mountains weighed on Livi—like responsibilities she'd
accepted, decisions she'd made. Her lungs labored and her
skin crawled. Like the sliver of chasm rising around her, the
life she'd chosen seemed harsh, unforgiving, inescapable.
With David here, the way mightn't have seemed so torturous
or so terrifying. David would have helped her, shielded her,
borne the weight. But David was gone; he'd left her to face
this wild, exacting world alone.

As the day progressed, the trail moved laboriously upward,
the track narrow, the pace slow. The horses picked their way
over the uneven ground, their haunches working, their forelegs
braced for steep descents. There were no long vistas here, just
ranks and ranks of mountains, brows of distant hills.

They drew off the road at Little Flat Lick in the early afternoon. As one, the travelers let out their breath. For all its
relative brevity, it had been a grueling day. While the women
busied themselves setting up camp, the men gathered rifles and
powder horns, muskets and shot. They hied off into the woods

to hunt. Before she could gainsay him, Tad slipped away, too, taking David's rifle with him.

From time immemorial, the saline spring that bubbled to earth in this wooded glade had been a gathering place. Animals came here to lick the salt, women to dip and evaporate the water over smoldering fires, and men to hunt. Game was plentiful at such a place, and soon rifles were cracking and booming deep in the woods.

Livi was just boiling up a pot of gruel when she heard the tramp of footsteps crossing the compound, the rumble of masculine voices. Glancing up, she saw her son stalking toward her, bare-chested and streaked with blood.

Her breath snagged in her throat. Tad was hurt—shot or stabbed. Gore smeared his bony chest. His hands were gloved red to the elbow. She started toward him at a run.

Only as she closed the distance between them did she notice that Tad was leading a swaggering procession in the direction of their campsite. Men with guns on their shoulders and grins on their faces. The two walking directly behind her son were carrying a white-tailed deer strung up on poles.

Livi let out her breath in a little hiss as the band of hunters shambled to a halt before her. She could smell the excitement on them, the sweat, the tang of blood. Her stomach lurched.

"Boy got his first big kill," Sam Willoughby crowed in explanation. "Shot this buck here slick as you please."

Tad flushed, his eyes wide and flickering with golden sparks. "That buck came right down to the lick, Ma. Right down to the lick! Stood there pretty as you please. Still like. Listening, I guess. Almost as if he was waiting for me to raise my gun."

All Livi could think about was running her hands over her son, making sure none of that blood was his.

"And when the boy did raise his rifle"—Joss Smiley took up telling the tale—"he dropped that deer as if he had been hunting for fifty years."

"Handles that gun well," Lem Stewart added with a hint of awe. "Damn well."

These men were as proud of her boy as he was of himself.

Livi nodded, beginning to understand, a husky prickle starting at the back of her throat. David should be here, she realized. David or Reid Campbell, at the very least. Some man who could fully appreciate Tad's triumph. Someone who'd watched her son grow up.

She sucked in a ragged breath and quelled the flood of regrets. To show anything but pride would negate Tad's first act of manhood, betray all he was struggling to prove. And for all her reservations, Livi Talbot was desperately proud of her son.

Swallowing the lump of feelings lodged in her throat, she reached out to ruffle Tad's fair hair. "Good shooting, boy," she pronounced. "By the size of that stag, we'll be eating off it for a week."

Tad grinned, flushed with his mother's acknowledgment. "Guess I did all right."

Livi fought to muster an answering smile.

"You be needing help with butchering, boy?" Sam Willoughby asked as the others drifted away.

"I'd be happy for the help," Tad answered, assuring a share to the other man's family. "We'll cut some for Joss and the Stewarts, too."

"Be back with my apron and my knives," Willoughby offered as he turned to go. "Your pap sure taught you well, boy."

Livi saw Tad's jaw stiffen. She saw the wash of color recede from his face. She shared the raw, parching pain of his sudden desolation.

"Tad," she began, instinctively reaching toward her son.

With a jerk, he shrugged away.

"Tad, please." She wanted to tell him it was all right to miss his pa, that there were times when a boy needed a man beside him. Tad's straight back and squared chin denied her any rights where comforting was concerned.

"I'm a man, Ma," he said, the words hollow, bleak. "I killed my very first buck today."

The fragility of the declaration tore at Livi's heart. Tad was too young to call himself a man, for all that he had earned that right. He hurt too much to deny his grief for his father, yet he stubbornly refused to turn to her.

There was only one thing to say. "Your father would be proud."

"Yes, Ma." There was a harsh, wretched twist to Tad's lips. "You know, I think he would."

* * *

In dry weather, fording the Powell River would have been easy. After two days of persistent rain, it was anything but.

Sitting her horse well back in line, Livi watched with mingled impatience and apprehension as a continuous string of riders skittered down the muddy embankment and plunged into the dun-green water. The current ruffled against their horses' fetlocks and knees, swirled under their bellies and up their chests. In the best of circumstances it took skill to stay a ford's predetermined course. Without being able to see bottom or watch for the ripple of water passing over a bar, it was nearly impossible. With the river running high, the current threatened to push both horses and riders off the hairpin shoal and drag them into the churn of rapids thirty yards beyond it. That the river was awash with debris made passage even more treacherous.

When they'd reached the bank of the Powell, the heads of the families met to decide what to do. "My husband's journal says the ford runs chest-deep and twenty feet wide," Livi offered. "Today it must be twice that. I think we should wait for the water to drop."

"Not all of us can afford to do that, Mrs. Talbot," George Willoughby put in. "We need to clear land before we can plant our crops. Every day we delay is a day we'll be short at harvest time."

A general murmur of assent ran through the group, though Lem Stewart came down on Livi's side. "Seems like we're taking an awful risk crossing the river while it's so swollen with rain."

"There's been Indian sign on this side," Sam Willoughby argued.

"As if a little high water could keep the Indians on this bank if they've a mind to cross," sniffed Turnip Carter.

Hyram Boggs cast his vote. "I say we forge ahead. You, Reverend?"

Lindenwood's words would decide the matter. "We need to believe that the Lord will provide," he intoned.

Livi thought that what He had provided was a good deal more river than was good for them.

The men did make concessions to the uneven footing and the current. Four stationed themselves along the width of the shoal to assist the party as they crossed. Still, it was slow going, traversing the river a single rider at a time, ferrying pack horses over in twos or threes.

Livi shifted in her saddle, trying to ease the knotted muscles in her back. She hated the inactivity, the waiting, and she blessed Molly Baker for keeping Cissy occupied. Tad sat his horse beside Livi, bearing the wait no better than she.

The Lindenwoods, the Willoughbys, the Stewarts, and about half of the Boggs family had successfully crossed the ford when Joss Smiley, who was next in line, took out and lit his pipe. Ripe, pungent, and sickly-sweet, the tobacco smoke trailed in Livi's direction. It brought a flush of sickness up the back of her throat. Her ears rang and her mouth went wet. She was certainly about to disgrace herself.

There was no time to dismount, no time to seek the privacy of the distant woods. Tossing the pack animals' lead line in Tad's direction and urging her horse down the slope, Livi dodged around a rocky overhang. Once she was out of sight, the nausea took her in earnest. Clinging to the saddle horn, Livi bent double and lost what little she'd eaten at noontime. A whirring filled her head; the trees danced circles around her. She closed her eyes and hung on until the spinning stopped. When she finally managed to raise her head, she'd gone hollow inside. With an effort, she lifted the water bag and rinsed her mouth.

Now they'd all know, she thought wearily. They'd all know about her pregnancy, that she'd deliberately held back the truth to gain passage for her family. Tonight the men would gather, pack their pipes, and debate what should be done with her. The women would shake their heads in sympathy and hold their peace. In the end, Livi knew what the judgment must be: she and the children would be sent back to the Block House for her deceit.

But she just couldn't trek those trails again. She couldn't fight the high, constricting mountains; couldn't brave the forest and the Indians on her own. Livi's breathing shuddered and her eyes burned. Then outrage fought its way through the tears. What right did these men have to send her back after she'd come so far and survived so much?

Resentment was coursing hot through her veins when Livi

heard a clamor off to her right. What she saw when she turned to look made her blood run cold.

Somewhere upstream, a century-old tree had been ripped from the bank and was bearing down on the ford—and the pack train—like a vengeful Medusa. Its huge trunk rolled and churned in the current. Its branches clawed the water. A snarl of roots trailed out behind.

The people at either edge of the ford were out of harm's way, but caught halfway across was Hyram Boggs's oldest girl, Jemima. While she kicked at her mare for greater speed, her little brother Marcus clung to the saddle behind her, his bony arms locked around Jemima's waist.

The children foundered in the boil of the current, helpless against its strength, dwarfed by the size of the tree bearing down on them. So young and small and frightened. Over the roar of the river, Livi could hear them shrieking.

Livi watched with her heart in her throat as the branches loomed above them. Then, just as the tree was about to run them down, the trunk rammed into a boulder rising out of the water a few feet above the ford. The tree caught there, lodged. Wood ground against rock. Splinters flew.

The children plunged toward the western bank.

Then the huge tree began to swing, scribing a long, slow arc across the surface of the river. Gnarled limbs reached toward where the children were fighting to get out of the way. The long, tapering branches stretched and curled. They snagged Marcus's suspenders and snatched him off the horse's back. Both children screamed.

Lem Stuart charged toward Marcus from the near end of the ford. Hyram Boggs bolted down the opposite bank. Neither man was close enough to grab the boy as the tree dipped over the shoal and lurched downstream.

"Papa!" Marcus shrieked as the river swirled up his chest. "Papa!"

The boy's cry swooped to silence as the tree bucked and rolled, plunging Marcus beneath the surface. Everyone on the bank went silent as they watched, waited. As they feared for Marcus's life.

Livi sat with her hands clamped around Nancy's reins. Marcus was drowning, and there was nothing they could do for him.

The branches abruptly rose again. Marcus still dangled among the twisted limbs, battered and streaming, choking and pawing. He was a speck of boy caught in the bobbing mass of tree. A fragile child battling forces he could not hope to overcome.

Livi suddenly realized she might be just far enough downstream to make a grab at the boy as he washed by. "Damn stupid thing to do," she muttered as a vision of her children spun through her head. She kicked her horse forward anyway.

Livi's buttermilk mare took off like the spirited hunter she'd been a decade before. With grace born of generations of good breeding, Nancy cleared a fallen log. Two more strides took her to the edge of the bank. She gathered herself and leaped as if the swollen river offered no more challenge than a water jump.

Livi closed her eyes and hung on. There was no telling how deep the river was, no telling what the bottom was like, no time to make plans. The jar of landing slammed her teeth together. Spray flared high. Stunning cold battered her chest and belly.

Hunching forward, Livi pulled Nancy's reins to the left. The mare lurched sharply downstream.

Glancing over her shoulder, Livi located Marcus as much by sound as by sight. The boy wailed piteously as the current by turns doused him in the river and jerked him out. It was a thin sound, choked and warbly. She homed to it anyway, maneuvering her horse.

If she moved fast enough, if the timing was right, she just might intercept the tree and Marcus a few yards above the first white foxtails of the Powell River rapids.

She could sense the tree looming behind her. Dark and malevolent. Overwhelming and powerful. Livi deliberately held back. She mustn't misjudge her timing and waste the single chance she'd have to snatch the child.

The web of branches whooshed past. She made her grab. Her fingers snagged Marcus's shirt. His fragile rib cage flexed beneath her hands. Her thumbs dug in at his waist. Tad had never seemed this wiry and thin.

She strained to wrench Marcus free.

The jolt of resistance all but unseated her. Marcus's braces were snarled in the branches of the tree like a ruined skein of darning thread. She tightened her grip and pulled again.

Marcus flailed. He turned his head. His mouth opened in a cry she could not hear.

White water frothed around them. The tree bobbed and trembled. Livi's grip shifted as the branches took a slow, inexorable dip, dragging Marcus down. Water closed over his head. She could feel him squirming. It took everything she had to hold on to the struggling child.

Locking her knee around the saddle horn, Livi yanked. Branches jabbed her ribs. Twigs raked her face. Mass and water dragged at her arms as if they were taffy. The rapids seethed around them. With the crackle of breaking branches, Livi jerked Marcus free.

She dragged the child against her chest and tightened her forearm to anchor him there. She felt his ribs expand and heard him coughing. She gave the mare her head.

The tree abruptly wheeled. Though Livi fought to get out of its reach, one limb swung around to smack her between the shoulder blades. It knocked her forward, nearly out of the saddle. Another blow glanced off her temple, sending comets bursting before her eyes.

The white water sucked them downstream. Still, Livi clung—to Marcus, to the reins, to the graying film of consciousness.

Livi felt the mare surging toward the bank, churning through the shallows, stumbling up the slope. She heard the river's rush recede. But she was most aware of Marcus in her arms, the way he shivered and sobbed against her. Alive. He was alive and safe.

As they came to a stop, people engulfed them. A blur of faces. A circle of noise. Hyram Boggs appeared at her side. He reached for Marcus, and Livi placed the child in his father's hands. She saw Hyram stroke the boy's face and hair, run one trembling palm along the length of his back. Marcus twined his arms around his father's neck. There were tears on Hyram's cheeks.

There were tears on Livi's, too.

With tremendous difficulty, she untangled herself from the sidesaddle and slid to the ground. Her knees wobbled and the sky wheeled.

Beyond the press of bodies, the murmurs of appreciation,

the pat of hands, she could see the river churning, wide and fast and dangerous. She could see the tree, powerful and vicious, tearing apart in the rocky shallows. For the first time, she realized what she'd done, what she'd risked to accomplish it. She might have been crippled. She might have been killed. *She might have left her own two babies alone in the wilderness.*

The buzz of praise receded. Livi's vision dimmed. Hands that had stroked her were supporting her, easing her down. Consciousness narrowed and stole away.

When Livi came to herself again, her head lay pillowed in Molly's lap.

"Are you all right?" Molly was asking. "Are you truly all right?"

Livi cautiously raised her head. Though she was wet and cold, battered and weary, she was all right. The baby she'd carried in secret, David's last and most precious child, still seemed nestled safe inside her.

Before she could answer, Tad was elbowing through the crowd with Cissy at his heels.

"You all right, Ma?" her son demanded, dropping to his knees beside her. Cissy settled, weeping, on her opposite side. "Are you all right?"

"I'm fine," she answered to reassure her children. But she wasn't fine. Not if Molly knew about the baby. Not if Molly had told the others.

With an effort, Livi worked her way to her elbows. She needed Molly to hold her peace. But before she could think of how to ask for Molly's pledge, Hyram Boggs was looming over them.

Livi scoured every cell for the fortitude to face the man who'd picked at her and plagued her ever since they'd left the Block House. There wasn't a gram of gumption left for her to find.

"Why did you do it?" Boggs demanded, standing above her, looking grim. "I never wanted you on this pack train. I told everyone you'd be trouble, that you'd never keep up. I've done my best to show you that you and your children aren't welcome here. So why did you rescue my Marcus after all of that?"

Livi stared up at him, at where Tacy Boggs stood at her

husband's shoulder, at Marcus's sallow, tear-streaked face.

"How could I do anything else?" Livi answered softly, ducking her head. "I expect anyone in the pack train would have done the same."

Boggs hesitated just long enough to indicate he wasn't sure what she claimed was true. "Be that as it may, Mrs. Talbot, you've done me and my family a great service. One my wife and I can never repay. Both of us want to thank you. And let me say how wrong I was about you and the children, and that I'm sorry."

Livi nodded and lay back. With Boggs in their debt, no one would ask them to leave the pack train now. She heaved a heavy sigh. As far as Kentucky, they were safe.

5

Martin's Station was the single knot of civilization on the long, ragged string of the Wilderness Road. Slightly more than fifty miles beyond the Block House and nearly a hundred and twenty miles to English Station in Kentucky, Joseph Martin's settlement was no more than a trading post, a smithy, and a good, sweet spring. Still, nearly every pack train stopped there, bound west or east. It was a chance to buy—at exorbitant prices—whatever items had run out, worn out, or been lost on the trail. It was a place to mend the harness, the saddles, and have the horses shod. It was a respite where travelers could catch their breath either before or after their assault on the Cumberland Gap.

Three days beyond the Powell River, Reverend Lindenwood's pack train of churchmen arrived and set to mending and shoeing and preparing. Livi, worn by the strain of the journey and the first months of pregnancy, declared it Sunday and lay down for a nap. While Molly looked after Cissy, Livi slept, finally wandering over to the Carters' campsite in the early afternoon. It wasn't until she had returned and found Tad's message chalked on his slate and propped up against the tent post that she learned what her son had been about.

GON TO SHOOT US SUM DINNER

The words sent Livi Talbot blundering forward, dragging aside the tent flap for confirmation. David's rifle was gone.

"Damn that boy!" she muttered. "Who does he think he

64

is, going off without asking me?'' This wasn't the woods around Lynchburg where Tad knew every path and stream. This was back-country Virginia. The forests here grew thick and wild. Indians lurked among the trees. Hadn't Joseph Martin warned all of them that his scouts had spotted a party of savages just this morning?

Angrily Livi prowled the campsite, a knob of concern in her chest. Turnip Carter, who was ambling back from the trading post, sensed her agitation.

''It's Tad, Mr. Carter,'' she told him when he asked her what was wrong. ''He's gone off hunting somewhere.''

''He go alone?'' the little man wanted to know.

''To be honest, I'm not sure.''

''Well, Joss Smiley and Sam Willoughby are out hunting, too. No doubt Tad went with them.''

Livi did her best to rein in her concern. It was daylight. Tad was hunting with men who would look after him. It was going to be all right.

''But what if Tad *is* out there alone?'' she asked in spite of herself.

Turnip Carter took her hands, his round, ruddy face turned up to hers. ''Now see here, missy. That's one fine boy you got there. Has more gumption than some folks twice his age. Got his pappy's rifle with him, hasn't he?''

Livi nodded, tears welling.

''Then hush, girl,'' Carter admonished her. ''One way or t'other, he'll be all right. You don't want to embarrass the boy by making a fuss. Shooting his first buck cut him loose of his mama's apron strings. You want to tie him up again?''

''Maybe I do,'' Livi answered. Still, she knew what Turnip said was right.

''Now don't you fret,'' he went on. ''Tad will be back by suppertime—probably toting something good to eat.''

Livi settled herself by the fire and tried to concentrate on her mending: hems torn out from her squatting by the fire, sleeves snagged on branches, precious bone buttons lost in the woods. While her needle danced of its own accord, she watched the encampment, searching for a shock of wheat-gold hair, listening for a young voice raised in triumph.

''Tad not back yet?'' Molly asked when she returned Cissy

to the Talbot campsite. It was late afternoon; the hunters should soon be coming back to camp.

"I don't know what gets into that boy," Livi grumbled, rubbing at the knot in her chest. "Killing that buck seems to make Tad think he doesn't have me to answer to, that he can go off whenever he pleases. He acts as if he's a full-grown man."

"Haven't you been treating him like one?" Molly asked, her voice gentle. "You been leaning on him, Livi, expecting him to shoulder most of David's load. Tad's only doing what he thinks you expect."

Livi's mouth narrowed. She didn't want to examine what she'd asked of Tad since David died.

"He'll be along any time now." Molly soothed her friend.

Livi could only nod, hoping he would.

The sun was melting over the drifts of hills when Joss Smiley and Sam Willoughby entered the compound. On legs that quaked, Livi went out to meet them.

"Isn't Tad with you?" she asked, her voice rising in entreaty.

"We haven't seen the boy all day," Sam explained.

"Did you see his tracks? Did you hear his shots?"

The men glanced at each other, then shook their heads.

"If he'd asked, Tad would have been welcome to come along."

"I know he would, Joss. I know you and Sam would look out for him."

"He'll turn up, Olivia," Willoughby offered. "Been lost in the woods a few times myself, and don't think I'm any the worse for it."

Lost. In the woods. In the dark. With wild animals and Indians. Her son, her *child*. The lump in her chest swelled, making it impossible to answer, to breathe.

Under the cover of her silence, the men slunk away.

With dread whining through flesh and bone, Livi set out to search for Tad herself. She circled the frontier settlement, moving through the woods in an ever-widening pattern. She pushed through the underbrush, stumbled up hummocks and down ravines, peered into the heavy growth of trees, probed the forest as deeply as she dared. She shouted Tad's name until her voice rasped raw.

Pressing into the deepening dark, Livi wished, just this once, that Reid Campbell were here. David claimed that since he'd spent those years with the Indians, Reid could track a snowflake over solid rock. That was the kind of skill she needed tonight—something certain and infallible. Her baby was out there somewhere, frightened, hungry, and alone. And there wasn't one damn thing his mother could do to find or comfort him.

When her voice gave out, when it was too dark to see, Livi dragged herself back to her campsite to hope and wait.

Reverend Lindenwood stopped by after supper. Holding her hand in both of his, he bowed his head and entreated God to keep Tad safe. But more than the reverend's prayers, it was his promise that searchers would go out at first light that comforted Livi.

She fussed over her daughter as they prepared for bed, washing her face and hands with lilac-scented soap, lingering as she brushed out Cissy's silken hair. She sought comfort in the sound of the little girl's voice piping familiar songs. It was Cissy's questions that were more difficult and disconcerting.

"So where is Tad sleeping tonight?" Cissy asked, looking up at Livi with a four-year-old's certainty that mothers had answers to everything.

Livi wished she knew. "I expect he's sleeping in the woods."

"Out there with all the animals?"

With the animals and the Indians.

"Tad won't get eaten by a bear, will he, Mama?"

"No, of course not. He has your father's rifle with him. He'll be fine."

"When will he be back?"

"Tomorrow." Livi spoke the words with a conviction she wished she felt. Tad would be back tomorrow, wouldn't he?

Livi rocked her girl-child in her arms until she slept, taking comfort in the warmth of that small, solid body curled against her own.

But outside the tent, the darkness beckoned. Where the world seemed even more hostile and vast than it did during the day. Where even the brightest campfires illuminated no more of the night than a handful of fireflies. The darkness invited the imaginings that the sunshine and her daughter had kept at bay: of Indians dodging through the trees, chasing her son; of braves catching him, dragging him down; of them drawing knives from rawhide sheaths . . .

Livi knotted her fists in the folds of her cloak, blinking to rid herself of the grainy afterimage that lingered at the backs of her eyes. It was a picture so strong that only seeing Tad and holding him—and shaking him until his teeth rattled—could possibly wipe away.

Around her, silence reigned—the sound of safety and heavy sleep. These families had gathered their children, banked their fires, and said their good-nights. These families were strong and whole. Livi seethed with envy. What had she done to deserve losing so much?

She prowled the campsite and stared into the close, thick darkness, her eyes burning with the drift of smoke and unshed tears. Was Tad out there somewhere—huddled cold and frightened? Was he sprawled still and lifeless, his eyes open to the endless sky?

Was Tad gone forever because she'd expected him to take his father's place, because she had demanded too much? A sob worked its way around the burr in her throat. How could she live with herself if this was her fault?

Oh, David, please watch over Tad tonight. Watch over him and keep him safe. After losing you, I couldn't bear—I couldn't bear to lose him, too. Take care of him for me, David. Bring him home safe.

There was no sense that David had heard, no sense that he was here with her. Sometimes Livi felt as if she would turn and find her husband beside her; sometimes she heard his laughter in the wind. But not tonight. Tonight she was alone with her fears and recriminations.

The searchers went out at dawn, every man from the pack train and half a dozen from the station itself. Not one of them complained about the traveling and planting time they were losing by looking for her son. Still, Livi understood their sacrifice. Grim and determined, they nodded to her as they passed by. Their demeanor told her what no one had the courage to say: that they thought Tad was dead, that the child she'd loved and nurtured was lost forever.

Livi watched them go, clinging to the frail, wavering conviction that the men were wrong.

The day went on around her. Newly cut wood replenished the dwindling pile beside her fire. Gruel and tea appeared where she could reach them. Women came to sit with her. Livi kept Cissy close at hand.

Hours passed, each one shriveling the precious kernel of optimism she hoarded deep inside. By midafternoon the worry and the waiting had baked it brittle and dry.

Then from the woods to the south came the sound of voices whooping, echoing, chorusing through the forest. The women stopped to listen. The yelling came again.

Slowly Livi rose. She scooped Cissy up in her arms and moved toward the sound. As she walked, a soft careful flutter of hope unfurled inside her chest. The knob of fear began to melt.

The shouts grew louder, shouts of joy, shouts of victory. Livi picked up her pace.

The men burst from the trees, nearly a dozen strong, their faces animated, flushed. And in their midst was a boy, a tall boy, dirty, tattered, fair-haired. Carrying his father's gun.

Livi began to run, closing the distance between herself and Tad.

His weight and solidity battered into her chest and ribs and hips as they came together. The contact took her breath. His long, sinewy arms closed around her.

She knotted her fists in his clothes, buried her tear-wet face in his shaggy hair. *Thank you, David*, she thought. *You heard me after all.*

Around them, their fellow travelers laughed and shouted and slapped one another on the back.

Livi hung on as long as Tad would let her, crushing Cissy between them, demanding her mother's due. But finally, with a flutter of pats, he squirmed out of Livi's embrace.

"Did you sleep in a tree like the man Papa told us about?" Cissy wanted to know. "Did you see any Indians? Were there bears in the woods?"

Watching her son with possessive eyes, reassuring herself with a hand tucked tight around his elbow, Livi let out her breath. It really was all right. Tad was safe and here with her.

Unexpected, bright crimson anger crowded close on the heels of that relief. *Did Tad have any idea what he'd put them through?*

"Thadius Chesterton Talbot," Livi demanded, setting Cissy on her feet, "just where have you been?"

Tad shrugged and looked away. "Lost, I guess."

"Lost!?" Livi breathed the word as if it were a curse. "Just how did you get lost? Didn't you mark your trail like your father taught you?" Even in her own ears her voice seemed shrill, dancing at the edge of hysteria.

"I guess I forgot."

"God Almighty, Mrs. Talbot." George Willoughby spoke up in the boy's defense. "Even Dan'l Boone misplaced himself in these hills once. For three whole days, as I recall. I've heard him laugh about it myself."

"This is hardly a laughing matter, Mr. Willoughby," Livi fumed, her gaze never leaving her son. "You made these people lose a whole day's travel."

"We figured the horses could do with another day's rest," Joss Smiley put in.

"And don't you realize the worry you caused?"

A flush crept up Tad's jaw.

"We're just glad the boy is safe," Reverend Lindenwood offered.

Livi stood her ground. "I think you owe these folks an apology, Tad, for holding them up. You owe them your thanks for all their help."

Tad ducked his head. "I'm sorry you all lost a day's travel because of me." There was sincerity in his demeanor and tone. "And it was good of you to look for me."

"You're welcome, lad," Lem Stewart said, patting Tad on the shoulder as he turned to go.

"You're a game one—just like I told your ma." Turnip Carter grinned. "You'd have found your way back here soon enough."

With another flurry of backslapping and waves of mumbled good wishes, the families filtered back toward their campsites. The drama of the reunion was over.

Taking Cissy's hand, Livi turned in the direction of their own tent, their own fire. There was no question that Tad would follow.

"I ought to cut a hickory switch," Livi threatened as they burned a path across the compound. "I ought to make you cut it!"

That had been her own father's brand of torture when she'd done something sufficient to draw his notice.

"I ought to tan your hide," she went on. "It's what your father would have done."

But as she closed in on their own campsite, Livi became suddenly afraid she was going to cry, that she wasn't strong enough or wise enough to raise this boy herself. She was suddenly afraid Tad would sense her weakness.

To prevent that she caught the fabric of Tad's shirtsleeve and gave it a furious shake. "Heading off into the woods alone, you risked your life—and the lives of everyone who looked for you! What could you have been thinking of?"

Tad lowered his head. "I'm sorry, Ma," he said. He sounded exhausted, chastened, contrite.

She allowed herself to glance across at her son. He seemed unbearably young, unbearably vulnerable. He seemed disillusioned with his own prowess for the first time in weeks.

Livi studied him, seeing more this time than the dirt and scrapes and bravado. She saw that his lips were bitten raw, that the skin was bruised and dark-looking beneath his eyes. Clearly he hadn't slept. And he wasn't walking with that cocky, hitched-up stride.

"I really *ought* to tan your hide, Tad," Livi repeated, the words caught in a sigh. "But I think it's something that will wait—at least until you've had a rest and something to eat."

"You coming, Cissy?" Livi called out, savoring a long, last swallow of her tea. It was unusual for her daughter to lie abed any morning. It was particularly unusual on the day they would brave the Cumberland Gap.

Livi washed and packed her cup away before shifting her gaze to the white limestone wall towering above them. Glowing with all the rich translucence of alabaster, the rock seemed to possess a magic, a fire, a promise that even Livi couldn't deny. It stirred excitement inside her and something else—something tentative and fragile, something ever so slightly like hope. Far above, hidden in the majesty and mysticism of those rugged hills, lay the gateway to the promised land—the gateway to Kentucky.

"Hurry up, Cissy!" Livi called a second time. "We need to strike the tent."

For all her dreaminess, for all her made-up songs and imaginary companions, Cissy was an eager child, and Livi couldn't understand her dawdling today. But just as Livi was losing patience, the girl burst from between the tent flaps, hairbrush in hand.

"Mama, braid my hair," she demanded.

Livi wrapped the leftover hoecakes and stuffed them into her canvas bag before taking up the brush and ribbon. Gently she worked her way through the fall of rosy curls, amazed that some trick of heredity had given Cissy those ringlets when her own hair hung straight as a mason's plumb.

"Haven't you and Cissy got that tent down yet?" Tad admonished, leading three of the horses to the edge of the campsite. "If this whole pack train has to wait for us, don't you dare blame me!"

Livi gave a final tug on the ribbon that fastened the end of Cissy's braid and turned to help Tad with the packsaddles. They'd all been lagging a little this morning, she reflected, and began loading the last of their gear.

The trail to the Cumberland Gap took them up the side of a deep ravine to Poor Valley Ridge. That ridge skirted Pinnacle Mountain, the last obstacle to their final assent. As one, the churchmen and their families stopped to stare as they rounded the final bend at the mountain's base and the Cumberland Gap came into view. The opening in the hills gaped broad and snaggle-toothed, the rugged white peak to the north towering above the rounded contours of the cliff to the south.

Mindful of the danger of an Indian ambush in the narrow pass, Sam and George Willoughby went ahead, while the rest of the party stopped to gobble down a noon meal and water the horses. The brothers returned, their faces flushed, exhilaration humming around them like a swarm of bees. Caught up in their excitement, the pack train set out again, laboring up the final slope.

One by one, Livi's companions paused in the palm of the Cumberland Gap as if taking a moment to mark the true beginning of their lives in Kentucky. As the pack train snaked forward, Livi tensed with anticipation, craving the feeling of awe the others seemed to be experiencing, needing the reassurance that she'd made the right choice for her family and herself.

Though she'd read her husband's journal and heard him describe this journey a hundred times, nothing had prepared her for the vista that lay before her when she reached the fabled swath of level ground. Mountains rose on every side, hulking, magisterial. The peaks crowded close, fighting to reach the scrap of tattered blue-gray sky. It was a wilderness of such ruggedness and scope that their party of churchmen seemed a mere trickle of humanity in its midst.

Livi paused in the hollow between the hills, waiting for some wondrous revelation, for a sense of belonging that called her home. But as far as she could see, this was no utopia of lush fields and forests thick with game. It was not a land of plenty and of ease. What she saw from the heights of the Cumberland Gap was more of the harsh, broken country they'd been toiling through for days.

Livi stared, desperate for reassurance, desperate to find some indication of the new, sweet life David had promised her. Instead she felt betrayed.

Even through the blaze of her own disillusionment, she recognized that David would have drawn strength from this endless sweep of earth and sky. Beside her, Tad's eyes blazed; her daughter's face was flushed with excitement. Around her, the churchmen seemed enervated and renewed. This wild new world seemed to hold some wondrous secret she could not comprehend. That others could sense the magic isolated her, pointed up some flaw she had no way to rectify, convinced her she was less than whole.

Reid Campbell had seen the deficiency years ago, Livi suddenly remembered. He dared to tell her the truth, and she had loathed him for it.

"Kentucky isn't the place for a woman like you," Reid had assured her. "It's miles of wilderness, of hills and hollows, of forests and wild animals. It's years of danger and backbreaking work, of hardship and loneliness."

She'd always hated Reid for looking into her heart and finding her wanting, hated him for believing that David could never reconcile the land and life he coveted with his love for her. Now she saw that Reid had known her—and this land—far better than her husband had.

All Livi was able to see in this landscape was the grinding hours of toil, the obstacles to overcome. She wasn't able to see the promise. She had never been able to envision it. This hadn't been her dream.

Then her moment was gone. As others of the party crowded up behind, Livi urged her horse through the fabled gateway and down the slope on the westward side. She rode in silence most of the afternoon, keeping pace with the other riders yet somehow set apart. Cissy seemed to mirror her mother's mood, nodding in the circle of Livi's arms.

They made camp in the valley near Yellow Creek. Her thoughts a-tangle, Livi went through the motions of pitching the tent and cooking dinner. Molly Baker and her girls came by just as Livi was packing the dishes away. But instead of going off to play with Ann and Verity, Cissy curled up in Livi's lap while the women talked.

"Not feeling poorly, is she?" Molly asked.

Livi felt her daughter's forehead with a practiced hand. Cissy was warmer than she would have liked.

"You feeling all right, sugar?" she asked, stroking the girl's flushed face. As she did, Livi encountered a cluster of small red bumps beneath the drape of Cissy's hair and bent to examine them more closely.

"What is it?" Molly asked.

Livi turned to her friend with fear in her eyes.

"What is it?" Molly demanded, drawing aside the child's hair to see for herself.

Livi heard Molly's indrawn breath. "Smallpox."

"No!" But the denial wedged in Livi's throat.

"It's smallpox." Molly came to her feet with a jerk.

"It must be something else. How could Cissy have contracted smallpox?"

"It is smallpox, I tell you! My brother died of smallpox. I'd know those blisters anywhere."

"It's not!" Livi insisted desperately.

But Molly was already gathering up her girls, already sweeping them out of the campsite. Out of harm's way.

Livi watched Molly go, a tight, dry knot of fear coiling just beneath her ribs.

Breathing denials, Livi lifted her younger child in her arms and carried her into the tent. As she removed Cissy's clothes, she could see that clusters of the splotches marred the skin of her chest and back. More were rising under her arms and between her legs. Cissy whimpered as Livi swathed her in a nightdress and bundled her into bed.

"This isn't smallpox." She whispered the ragged litany in words too low for her daughter to hear. "This can't be smallpox."

"Ma?" Tad pushed aside the tent flaps and peered inside. "Is Cissy sick?"

Livi rose and came out of the tent to speak to her son. "It's not anything," she assured him, icy fingers clenching around his arm. "It's not what they think."

"Smallpox." Even a boy of twelve knew the danger, knew enough to be afraid. She could see her own fear mirrored in his eyes.

"It's not smallpox," she insisted.

"But, Ma, if it is—"

"Mrs. Talbot?"

It hadn't taken long for word of Cissy's illness to spread through the camp. Turning, Livi clamped her hands together to still their trembling. Reverend Lindenwood had brought a contingent of churchmen and their wives to her campsite. It was a contingent that stopped short at what they must consider a "safe" distance.

"We heard that your daughter has been taken ill," Lindenwood said, "and, of course, we're concerned for her welfare. Is she—is she suffering from any complaint that might be contagious?"

Livi swallowed. She didn't know how to answer him.

"What the reverend wants to know"—leave it to Hyram Boggs to come straight to the point—"is whether your daughter has smallpox."

Livi fought the urge to weep. Not smallpox. *Oh, please, not smallpox.*

"Go sit with your sister," she instructed Tad, fighting for time to frame an answer. Tad nodded, his face gone grim.

"I don't know what complaint Cissy is suffering from," Livi finally said. "She's running a fever and there's a rash . . ."

A flare of voices smothered the rest of her words.

"Is it smallpox?" someone demanded.

"It could be any one of several things . . ." Tears thickened her reply, undermined her credibility.

Reverend Lindenwood raised his hand for silence. "Is there anyone who can examine the child to be sure?"

A murmur passed through the crowd. No one wanted to expose himself to the dread disease.

"I know smallpox when I see it," Turnip Carter's wife, Lila, finally said. "Lost my boy to it two years back."

Livi watched Lila Carter approach. She carried herself with gravity, as if in making this determination she bore some horrendous weight. Livi saw the loss of her child in the older woman's eyes, the hurt, the hollowness. It was something Livi recognized; she'd lost children, too.

Livi took Lila inside the tent and came to her knees beside her daughter's pallet. Murmuring reassurances, she saw to the blankets and lifted Cissy's nightdress. There seemed to be more of the puckered blotches than before. Panic shot through her, stole her breath.

"She been sick for long?" Lila asked.

"I only noticed she was running a fever a short while ago."

"Has she been listless, tired?"

Livi nodded.

"For how long?"

Livi couldn't say. She'd been too wrapped up in her own concerns to take proper note of her daughter's well-being.

She read the diagnosis in the older woman's face.

"I'm sorry," Lila said, clasping Livi's hand. Condolences passed from one mother to another.

The horror sank in, viscous and black. Courting desperation, feeding fear. "What shall I do?" she demanded. "How can I help her?"

Lila Carter paused and tightened her grasp. "Let her go peaceful-like when it's her time."

The words battered Livi's chest, set her heartbeat staggering. "I can't," she whispered. "I can't!"

Lila Carter shrugged and took back her hand.

Back outside, the crowd was waiting. "It is," Lila told them as she passed by, heading toward her own campsite.

The voices of the churchmen rose all around her, but Livi was barely aware of them. It was only a few spots, a touch of fever. How could Cissy have smallpox? How could she be so desperately ill? God wouldn't take her baby girl when she'd already lost so much.

It was Reverend Lindenwood's approach that penetrated the fog of denial and grief. "Mrs. Talbot? Olivia?"

Livi looked up, dazed.

"I'm sorry about your daughter's illness."

"Thank you," she answered. But there seemed to be more he wanted to say. She could see it in his face.

"This is difficult, Mrs. Talbot, but you must try to understand our position . . ."

"Your position?"

Lindenwood lifted his hands in a gesture of futility. "That when we head out tomorrow, we're going to have to leave you and your family behind."

"You're what?"

"We can't let you continue to travel with us and expose everyone on the pack train to smallpox," he reasoned. "We have no choice but to leave you here while we go on."

Fear migrated north from her belly, setting her chest ablaze.

"It's not smallpox," Livi said, the words quiet and desperate.

"Lila Carter says it is."

Livi looked away, battered, wavering on her feet. Her daughter might be dying, and these people meant to abandon her.

"But it's seventy miles to the nearest settlement," Livi whispered.

"We've got to save ourselves," Lindenwood explained. "Surely you can see that."

Seventy miles to the nearest settlement, with one child who might never survive the trip and another who could just as well fall ill.

"Please don't do this," she breathed, looking up into Lindenwood's furrowed face. "Please, I beg you."

She gazed beyond Reverend Lindenwood to where the others waited. "You can't do this! If you leave us, we won't have a chance. If you leave us, we'll die!"

Lem Stewart hung his head. George Willoughby looked away. She could see the anguish in Molly Baker's face. That Turnip Carter should be the one to answer decimated the last of Livi's hope. "We're sorry, girl, but we've got to see to our own kin first."

"We'll leave you all the food we can spare." Lindenwood's

The people on the pack train were doing what they thought was best, doing it reluctantly, but doing it with a resignation that was impregnable. They were leaving her and her family to fend for themselves.

What would she have been willing to do to ensure her children's well-being against such a scourge?

Not this, she hoped. Not this.

Bitterness burned against her breastbone, and she fanned the flame. She let her outrage fuel the enormous effort it would take to survive.

Cissy's fever had risen during the night as the rash gained purchase. Livi sat up, bathing her brow and swaddling her in blankets. It was the accepted remedy for fevers of every kind, but against an illness as fierce and deadly as smallpox, such measures seemed hopelessly inadequate.

Livi's tear-wet gaze swept the mountains towering on every side. Here, miles from a settlement, miles from help, she must find a way to keep her family warm and fed and dry. In spite of her doubts, her inadequacies, her pregnancy, she had managed to hold her family together after David died. She had managed to secure them passage over the mountains. But this was too much, far more than a woman like her could manage. She wasn't brave or strong enough, didn't know enough about surviving out here in the wilderness. How could she expect—

"Are they gone, Ma?" her son demanded, coming out of the tent tousled and half dressed.

"They pulled out a few minutes ago."

"I didn't think they'd really leave us, that they'd really go. Not Joss and George. I thought they cared about us. I thought they were our friends." Livi could hear the disillusionment in her son's voice, see the confusion in his eyes. "How could they do that, Ma? How could they turn their backs on us?"

"Smallpox is a dangerous disease."

It was the truth; both of them knew that.

"But could you do what they did? Could you leave a family behind like they've left us?"

Livi had wrestled with the question herself. "I'd like to think I wouldn't," she conceded.

Tad took his time considering the shades of uncertainty in her answer. Then he threw back his head and gave his judgment. "Cowards!" he shouted, his voice echoing back from the encircling hills. "Goddamned cowards!"

Livi didn't argue with his assessment. She didn't admonish her son for swearing. With what she was about to ask, with what she had asked of him already, Tad had earned certain rights.

She took a long, slow breath before she began. "I've been thinking that we're too visible here, too vulnerable camped in the valley. We need somewhere to hole up until Cissy's better, somewhere off the road, with water and grazing for the horses. And it can't be too far."

Tad turned his gaze from where dust was rising above the distant trees.

"Don't want much, do you, Ma?" A wry smile hitched up one corner of his mouth.

"Do you think you can find us a place like that?" she asked. "Do you think you can find it without getting lost?"

A spark flared in his whiskey-gold eyes. "I suppose I could unwind a ball of yarn as I go."

Livi caught his arm as he spun away. She understood his anger; she must make him understand her concern.

"It's not that I doubt your abilities, Tad," she told him. "It's just that I couldn't bear to lose you, too."

After a moment she felt the rigidity seep out of him, heard him heave a heavy sigh. "You won't, Ma. I promise, you won't."

Livi waited out the day, alternately bathing Cissy's brow and soothing her whimpers of pain and confusion. Not for so much as a moment was her son out of her mind. Was Tad having trouble finding a safer place to camp? Where was he, and what would she do if he didn't return by nightfall?

They were questions Livi had no need to answer. Tad returned in the late afternoon, and together they struck the camp. The cave he'd found in the limestone bluff to the north of Boone's Trace was more than Livi had dared to hope for. The entrance, half hidden by a cleft in the rock, opened into a dome-shaped chamber that rose to a height of five or six feet. A fire-ring set well back from the entrance made it clear that others had taken refuge there, though there was no evidence of recent occupation. The sloping walls were rough and blackened with smoke, but with blankets laid out on the sandy floor and a fire crackling, the place seemed almost hospitable.

While Tad saw to the horses, hobbling them to graze in the woods at the base of the slope, Livi bent over her daughter. Cissy's fever was up and the small red sores had blossomed everywhere, in her hair, between her fingers, on the soles of her feet. Livi had no idea what to do for her, what symptoms might develop next.

By midnight Cissy was tossing and muttering in her sleep. Livi, listening to her daughter's labored breathing, smelled the dry, sour scent of fever. The smallpox threatened her baby's life, her sight, her rare and fragile beauty. All Livi could do as she stared into Cissy's swollen face was take the child in her arms and hold her close. And as she did, Livi tried to accept that not even a mother's love could keep her children safe.

As she held her daughter, Livi looked across at her son, curled up in his nest of blankets, his body slack, his lashes dark against wind-burned cheeks, his hair tumbled in its usual disarray. Would Tad catch smallpox, too? Would she have to stand by helplessly and watch him succumb? And who would care for her if she fell ill?

The terrible fear came again—stronger because the world was dark; because she had never felt so hollow, so inadequate; because no living soul knew their plight or cared enough to aid them. They could all die here in this cave, and the world would never mark their passing. Their bones could turn to dust without anyone to scratch out a shallow grave or whisper a prayer for their salvation.

Tears of fury and fear and hopelessness stung her cheeks as she rocked her daughter against her chest, as she watched her son sleep. The need to hold and defend her family weighed on her, dragged her down. It was a load David had always carried, one she had been hefting and shifting and balancing since the night he died. The illness, the isolation, and the stark, blank terror of what lay around them made her yearn to shake the burden off. But there was nobody else.

"David," she whispered, tears running down her face, seeping hot and salty into her mouth, dampening her daughter's matted hair.

"David," she sobbed, her chest raw and heaving with suppressed emotion. *How could you leave me when I need you so?*

Worn beyond weariness, crushed by responsibility, Livi closed her eyes and willed her thoughts to other days.

6

S *tep right. Step left. Turn and curtsy. One. Two . . .*
Livi Chesterton paused in her counting to cast what she
hoped was a scintillating glance at her dancing partner, a whey-
faced young lawyer from Williamsburg. Now that she had met
him, seen his uneven teeth, and heard his priggish lisp, she
couldn't imagine why her mother had been so pleased when
Samuel Carson responded to the invitation to Livi's sixteenth-
birthday fete. But perhaps capturing the affections of such a
man was the best she could hope to do.

"It's not as if Olivia has much to offer," her father had harrumphed the day Jessica Chesterton pointed out that their
youngest daughter had reached marriageable age. "She's plain,
solemn, and far too tall. All she cares about are books and
horses. And she grows that hideous-colored hair."

"Red," her mother had acknowledged with a sniff.

"How can we hope to make a suitable match for such a
girl?" he'd gone on, heedless that Livi stood listening. "How
can we hope to ally ourselves with one of the better families
when she's neither pretty nor accomplished?"

That was where her father's ambitions lay, with snaring a
Fairfax, a Merriweather, or a Lee. Richard Chesterton coveted
ties to Virginia's best families so that Livi's younger brother,
Randolph, her father's only heir, could gain entrée to the high-

83

est echelons of colonial business and society. Both her sisters, Arabella and Felicity, had made the kind of marriages their father craved. Livi had so hoped that if she managed to look her best for the party tonight, could remember her manners, her dance steps, and everybody's name, she might make one of those eligible gentlemen look at her twice.

Yet despite being the guest of honor, Livi had danced no more than a handful of times. Not one man had offered to bring her punch, sat with her after his "duty" dance, or suggested a stroll in the gardens behind the house. Instead Livi had plastered a smile on her face and watched while other girls flirted and teased and fluttered their fans, snaring beaux Livi knew were meant for her.

"Well, it's not as if Olivia has either Felicity's wit or Arabella's beauty," she heard her mother say to one of the other matrons as Samuel Carson returned Livi to her side.

"It's been a pleasure," he mumbled before shambling away.

Having offered his felicitations, Carson was off to devote himself to the punch bowl, the gaming tables, or the cigars and the port in the billiard room. Or perhaps he was bound for more romantic pursuits with one of the girls he'd been eyeing while he danced with her.

As Livi steeled herself for her mother's subtle but inevitable rebuke, the parlor fell still. Glancing around, Livi's gaze came to rest on the man poised in the doorway.

Though she had never once set eyes on him, Livi recognized Reid Campbell instantly. He was the estranged son of the wealthy trader whose plantation abutted their own. That the younger Campbell had returned to visit his father's plantation after years in the wilds, that he bore a very evident disdain for his father's land and money, had stirred speculation the length of the James. Why such a man had deemed it expedient to put in an appearance—late though it was—at Livi's birthday fete was something she could not fathom.

Livi did know that all over the room heads were swiveling in the newcomer's direction, that fans were stilling in mid-flutter. She heard a ruffle of whispers rise and fall.

No doubt this man's looks would have caused a stir at any gathering. Few men were as tall or as imposing. Nor could any who frequented the parlors of Virginia's finest homes claim a Creek princess as a grandmother, or sport her legacy with such audacity.

That Indian woman had gifted Reid Campbell with heavy blue-black hair, a countenance that was all bones and hollows, and—if the gossips were to be believed—a clan deep in the wilderness that had taken him in when his father and stepmother had all but disavowed him a decade before.

Still, there was no question that Campbell's Scots-Irish fore-bears had marked him, too. Ruddy skin, startling sky-blue eyes, and a square jaw bespoke generations of virile Campbell men. But whatever his ancestry, in this man was a serendipitous mingling of traits fully capable of stealing a maiden's breath.

Certainly Livi was having trouble catching hers.

In utter silence Campbell stalked the length of the room. As he closed the distance between them, Livi could not think, could not breathe. His vitality surged over her like a river in flood, setting every cell to tingling. She fought an urge to turn and run.

"Are you Olivia Chesterton?" he asked, his deep voice reverberating inside her. "Is it your birthday we've come to celebrate?"

Though Campbell's questions were couched in the most genteel manner, orthodoxy decreed that someone else should have made the introduction. Not one of the etiquette books her mother had forced her to read had mentioned handling such a gaffe, and Livi was sure she'd muck this up in front of everyone.

"Yes, I am Olivia," she finally answered, her voice quavering.

As if she were a princess and he a courtier, as if he had never been reputed to brandish a tomahawk or wear feathers in his hair, Campbell caught up her hand and brought it to his lips. "Then let me offer you my good wishes on such an auspicious day."

Flustered beyond coherent thought, Livi flushed. "Thank you," was all she managed.

Then, as Campbell loosened his hold, his fingers trailed along the tips of hers. A frisson of energy danced up her arm. It was hot and tingly, all at once. It sent her heart tripping, brought a wash of color to her cheeks. Livi looked down at their two linked hands, wondering what he'd done to her.

It was then she saw the wide, blue comma-shape that marked him. Inscribed with swirls of subtle patterning, the design curved across the back of his hand from thumb to wrist and disappeared up his sleeve.

A tattoo! Livi thought, shocked and scandalized. *He has an Indian tattoo!*

"Miss Chesterton?" Reid Campbell still stood over her. A stiff, parched smile had appeared on his face.

He knew exactly what she'd been thinking! Livi blushed again.

"I'd beg your leave," he continued, "to present my friend David Talbot."

Livi struggled to regain her composure, to prompt a tremulous smile to her lips. "Certainly, sir, I would be pleased to meet your friend."

At that a second man stepped from behind Campbell, a man nearly as tall, with his own undeniable magnetism and the gold of a thousand candle flames glinting in his hair. For Livi, it was as if the sun had come out from behind a cloud.

"David Talbot," she said, needing to speak the name, to try the shape of it in her mouth.

"Yes." He took her hand in both of his, a gentle gesture of extreme respect.

The simple pressure of his skin on hers kindled a warmth in Livi's chest. It roused a sweet, confusing ache that tightened down the midline of her body. She stared, mesmerized by the glow in his amber-brown eyes.

His voice came to her from far away. "Will you allow me the favor of this dance, Miss Chesterton?"

She knew the dance was promised to someone else. Yet Livi could no more have denied David Talbot's request than she could have denied herself another breath.

With her fingers cradled in his, David led her away from Reid Campbell and onto the dance floor. His hand curled possessively against her waist as he guided her into their places for a country dance.

"You're so lovely," he whispered as the musicians struck up the tune. "I never thought I would find anyone as sweet and beautiful—"

Livi hung on his fading words as the figures of the dance took them apart. Her heart beat wildly as she watched him cross the room with a big man's grace. It beat wilder still as the music brought them together again. When they clasped hands and looked into each other's eyes, some deeper melody seemed to swell in each of them.

Livi couldn't tear her gaze from David Talbot, from the waves of his tawny hair, from the broad planes of a face that seemed to mingle all the tenderness and strength and humor a woman could want. As they bowed and turned, the breadth of his shoulders and the solidity of his body dwarfed her, enticed her, awakened yearnings Livi had never felt. Yearnings she had never imagined she could feel.

His smile lit wonder inside her, a feeling so marvelously strong, deliciously new, that she could scarcely take it in. More miraculous still was that Livi saw the same wonder in David Talbot's face, sensed the same yearnings in the clasp of his fingers on her own. When the dance ended, he seemed as reluctant to let her go as she was to break the contact between them.

"May I show you the garden behind the house?" he finally asked. "They say it's one of the most beautiful in all of Virginia." Then color rose in his face. "But you already know that, I suppose, since Chesterton Oaks is your home."

Livi knew with certainty that her mother would disapprove of her leaving the parlor with a man she barely knew. Since it was her father's plan to make a brilliant match for his youngest daughter, he would abhor any breach in decorum. But for the first time in her life, Livi didn't care what her parents thought.

"Then perhaps *I* should show *you* Chesterton Oaks' garden, Mr. Talbot," she suggested.

The night was alive with the last full flush of Indian summer, the air heady with the dusky scent of fallen leaves and the poignant sweetness of the flowers that remained. Though the gardens were not all they had been in July, there was remarkable beauty to the pathways that wove through the drifts of careful plantings. Boxwood hedges hemmed the perimeters of many flower beds. Roses clung in clusters to the banks of bushes. Asters nodded, their colors muted by the cool, crisp light of the moon. As Livi and David wandered farther from the house, the sounds of music and voices faded away.

They came to an arbor swathed in wisteria vines and found a bench amid the flickering leaves. David spread his handkerchief on the seat and settled Livi as if she were something rare and fragile. She motioned for him to sit beside her. Silence fell; the awareness of their solitude and each other became a barrier neither knew how to surmount.

Every nerve in Livi tingled. She wanted to touch this man, taste him, breathe him in.

"You feel it, too, don't you?" David Talbot said at last. "As if the two of us were meant to meet."

Livi nodded, barely able to answer for the wonder and the uncertainty constricting her throat.

"As if we were meant to be together," David went on.

"Yes."

"I didn't know this could happen. That you could fall in love in an instant. That you could know that what you feel is strong enough to last a lifetime."

"I feel part of you already," Livi whispered in awe, "as if this was destined to happen."

"And I feel a part of you."

As he spoke he cupped her face with his callused hands, splayed his fingers along her jaw. With the brush of his thumbs, he charted the curve and contours of her cheeks. He drew her closer, as gentle and tender as a man could be. Yet when he covered her mouth with his, the contact was fierce, bright, exquisite.

Livi caught her breath, sinking, shivering, aching with delight.

He fit her lips to his, teaching her the multitude of pleasures to be found in a kiss. He showed her that the brush of his lips might be fluttery and light, the next fiery and long. He taught her that others could be deep or sweet or as sultry as a summer day.

Livi did her best to return his kisses, arching into his embrace, opening her mouth to the probe of his tongue. She gasped at the shocking, salacious glide as his came to mate with hers. She moaned with deepening pleasure as he tantalized her with feathery strokes, making the heat wash through her in a soft, dark tide. Livi couldn't breathe, couldn't think, couldn't do anything but want what this man seemed more than willing to give.

His arms curled around her shoulders, cradling her, holding her as if she were delicate and infinitely precious, as if she were revered and cared for. And adored.

At length David Talbot raised his head. She could hear his ragged breathing, see the tender curve of his mouth. "I love you, Olivia Chesterton. I wouldn't have believed it could happen like this, but I want you with me for the rest of my days."

"Oh, David," Livi answered, wondering if one could fall in love with just one dance, with a single kiss. While her mind refused to accept that, her heart knew something else. "Oh, David, I love you, too."

She drank tenderness from the depths of his eyes, pressed a kiss into his palm when he touched her cheek, raised her face to his for another kiss.

Instead of accepting her invitation, he turned away.

Livi tried to swallow her disappointment. Why, if he loved her, hadn't he taken the opportunity to kiss her again?

David drew toward the opposite end of the bench, a furrow between his brows, a narrowing at the corners of his mouth. "Listen, Olivia, we need to go back. People will notice that we're gone, and I don't want anyone to think . . ."

"Think what?"

"That I—that we—"

David took a moment to compose himself. "If you love me, if you're sure you want to be with me, we need to do this right. I'll have to ask your father's permission to court you."

To court her? Elation flooded through her veins in a fierce, sweet rush. David Talbot wanted her as his wife. After the confidences and kisses they'd exchanged tonight, the idea that he must ask her father's permission to bring her flowers and hold her hand seemed archaic, ridiculous.

"And then what?" she asked.

Until tonight, marriage had been an abstract idea, something her mother and father discussed. Something that had nothing to do with her. Now, with unbelievable intensity and speed, Livi had discovered the man with whom she wanted to share all of herself. A big man, whose hair shone like sunshine and whose eyes were warm and kind. A tender man, who made her feel protected and revered.

A man she had known no more than an hour.

"After we've courted for a time, I'll ask in earnest for your hand."

"And then?" Livi's face flushed, her skin atingle.

"I'll take you as my bride." His eyes brightened as if the thought filled him with the same delight it had begun to spark in her. His mouth swooped down for a kiss that brimmed with promise.

"Talbot?" Reid Campbell's voice interrupted them from the direction of the garden path. It made Livi and David leap apart. "Is that you, David, off there in the bushes?"

"Damn," David muttered. "But it's better that Reid should find us together than others I could name." Pulling Livi to her feet, David smoothed her hair and gown and led her out of the arbor.

Livi only barely withstood the scorch of Campbell's disapproving gaze, but when he spoke, it was as if she were invisible. "For God's sake, David, she may be a pretty little thing, but stealing away the guest of honor at a party is chancy, don't you think?"

"We were just headed back inside," Talbot answered. "It was a lovely night for a walk."

"A walk indeed." The inexplicable acid in Campbell's words made Livi want to shrink against David's side. In silence the three of them made their way to the house.

Livi could feel the weight of Richard Chesterton's scowl down the length of the parlor, and she had no choice but to obey when he summoned her with a nod of his head. She could only whisper a good-bye before she left David in the doorway.

The rest of the evening passed in a blur. Livi knew David dared not approach her again, but no matter where she was or with whom she danced, Livi followed Talbot's presence like the tide follows the moon. She felt breathless when she chanced to look up to see that David was watching her. He was her beacon in the murk of humanity. And for those few moments when their gazes held, they might as well have been alone. Livi felt bound by whispered words, by emotions too deep to deny. She seemed touched but untouched, joined but not yet promised.

When the last of the guests had clambered into their carriages and waved their farewells, Livi returned to the room of her childhood irrevocably changed. She stood silent as her maid stripped away the butter-yellow gown and dancing shoes, and she stood staring into the pier glass clad only in her chemise. Once the woman was gone, Livi plucked the pearl-tipped pins from her hair and watched those shimmering russet locks flare in the candlelight as they tumbled down her back. Studying the girl in the looking glass with great deliberation, Livi noted the glow that warmed the curve of her cheek and the graceful line of her throat. With trembling hands, she molded the soft muslin of her shift to the rise of her breasts, traced down her ribs to the nip of her waist and over the swell of her hips.

What did David Talbot see when he looked at her? A tall girl with coppery hair and wide green eyes. A voluptuous child-woman with a vulnerable mouth. Would David touch her one day as she touched herself?

Her skin flushed as she imagined his fingers tracing the curve of her throat, riding the ridge of her collarbone, contouring to the swell of her breasts. Her mouth went dry, the images she'd conjured making her unbearably conscious of her body, arousing a restlessness that was mysterious and compelling.

With wonder she lifted one hand to stroke her burning cheek. She seemed never to have lived inside this skin until today. Never to have dwelled in this flesh and bone and sinew. Never to have known the physical extent of Livi Chesterton until David helped her define it. And there was more he could teach her, more she must learn, more to discover about herself. More to explore at David's hands. She could not wait through the courting and the betrothal to a wedding a year or more away. She so yearned for the chance to feel and experience and know.

This is me, Livi thought, focusing on the girl in the mirror, pleased with the image for the first time in her life. This is Olivia Elizabeth Chesterton. And David Talbot loves me.

Livi rushed up the wide hall stairs, invigorated by the crisp November air, the flame-blue sky, and her morning ride. She could never remember feeling so wonderful. She'd wanted to skip all the way from the stable, dance through the gardens, throw back her head and laugh at the sun. She'd managed to meet David Talbot every day for a week. She'd touched his face, held his hand. She'd learned to kiss him in a dozen wanton ways that were undeniably naughty and utterly delicious. For the first time in her life, Livi overflowed with energy and confidence and hope.

The first sign of trouble was the half-full trunk in the middle of the upstairs hall. The second was the housemaid's wariness when Livi demanded to know why her things were being packed. The third was a summons to her father's study.

She loathed the small, cramped room at the back of the house that served as Richard Chesterton's retreat. No good had ever befallen her behind that door. It was where her father meted out punishment, a switching for taking his stallion out for a run, for stumbling through the piece she'd been asked to play for her mother's company, for teaching the slave children their ABC's. The mere thought of her father's study made Livi's stomach churn.

Richard Chesterton was seated behind his desk when she arrived. With an imperious nod of his head, he motioned her to a chair.

"Is something the matter, Father?" she asked when he finally looked up from the accounts he had been totaling.

"Olivia," he began, "David Talbot came by this morning—"

Livi could feel the warmth rise in her cheeks, feel the leap in her pulse at the mention of David's name.

"—to ask permission to pay you court."

Livi was relieved that David hadn't waited to approach her father. It had been difficult stealing away to meet in secret, difficult lying to cover her lengthening absences.

"And I want you to understand," her father went on, "why I sent young Talbot away."

It took a moment for the meaning of his words to reach her, to penetrate the haze of happy anticipation.

"You sent him away?" she gasped.

"Obviously your mother and I never expected you to attract the kind of wealthy, influential men your sisters did, but it never occurred to us that someone like this David Talbot fellow would make the first offer."

"But I love David!"

Her father gave a derisive snort. "Posh, girl! What could a sixteen-year-old possibly know about love?"

"I know that David makes me feel as if I am the most beautiful woman in the world," Livi explained. "The smartest, the kindest, the most . . ."

Richard Chesterton's frown brought her words to a stumbling halt. "Surely you can see how unsuitable Talbot is for you. He's the son of James Campbell's indentured servants, for God's sake! Riffraff. How could you possibly expect me to agree to his suit?"

The truth was, Livi hadn't known. When she and David were together, there were far more pleasant things to do than talk about their families.

"And have you any idea how he makes his living?" Livi recognized the shift in her father's tone from bullying to battering. "Your David's a sharecropper. He works for a blacksmith three days a week. It's honest work, I grant you, but he barely keeps body and soul together. Surely he can't afford to take a wife."

"If you give us your permission, we'll be fine," Livi pleaded, her voice unraveling as she spoke. "Loving David is all that matters."

"Perhaps to you, but I wonder if it's really you he loves."

"Of course he loves me." It was the only thing of which Livi was utterly sure.

"I suppose he clasped his hands across his heart and said he was 'stricken with love for you.' I suppose he vowed he'd 'never felt this way before.' " Her father came around the desk and loomed above her chair. "And just why did all this happen so suddenly, Olivia? Is it because you're fair of face? Because you're witty and accomplished? Because you're exactly the kind of wife a sharecropper needs?"

"I don't know why David loves me. He just does."

"Well, I can hazard a very good guess about his motives. Your David Talbot took one look at this house, at this land, at the horses and the slaves, and he thought, 'I could learn to love this man's daughter. I could marry her and have a better life.' "

"No!" Livi breathed in protest.

"He realized that with a little flattery and a few stolen kisses he could win your heart. And he has, hasn't he?"

been drawn by the Chesterton riches and not by love for her. The realization tore deep into the already threadbare fabric of her self-respect, but she hid her hurt and disappointment behind uncharacteristic truculence. She refused to kiss her mother or tell her father good-bye.

The role of outcast suited her. She was being unjustly punished. She was being banished for loving the wrong man. Betrayed by both her family and David Talbot, Livi allowed herself the luxury of tears only after the coach had rolled away.

As the carriage bucked and swayed along the river road, a gauzy mist boiled up, shrouding the familiar landscape, laying thick as batting in the hollows. The dank, heavy fog matched Livi's mood. Her future was murky and dark. Without David she had no chance of happiness.

But not five miles beyond the gates to Chesterton Oaks, the coach abruptly slowed. Livi leaned out the window to ascertain the cause and found a masked horseman at the edge of the woods brandishing his pistol at the driver.

Highwaymen? In Virginia? She jerked back in surprise and alarm.

"Ho up, there," the man called out. "We won't harm you. All we want is a word with one of your passengers."

Livi recognized Reid Campbell's voice, and a moment later a second masked man with sunshine-bright hair appeared at the window on the opposite side of the carriage.

"David! You came!" she cried out.

"Of course I came," he said, removing the scrap of black silk covering his face and crushing it into his pocket. Though a slow smile curled the corners of his mouth, his eyes held hers with smoldering intensity. "How could I do anything else? We have to settle things between us."

"Now just a moment, Mr. Talbot!" Arabella jumped to intervene. "There is nothing for you to settle with my sister. Father has forbidden her to speak to you."

"But Father isn't here now, is he, Bella?" Livi asked as David dismounted and came around to help her from the coach.

He led her well out of earshot before turning to her. "Your father told me he would rather see you in hell than married to

me," David declared, his face set with determination. "I've
come to ask you how you feel."

At the expression in his eyes, all Livi's doubts fell away.

"I think my father is right," she answered. "It *would* be
hell loving you and being married to someone else."

At her words, some terrible tension inside him seemed to
ease. "You will marry me, then?" David asked. "Without
your father's permission or his blessing?"

"Will you have me as your wife without the Chesterton
holdings as inducement?"

She saw his eyes widen, heard his gasp of surprise. "Oh,
Livi, no. Is that what he said? How could you let him make
you think that your family's fortune is more important to me
than you are?"

It was all the reassurance Livi needed

"If you choose to be my wife," David pressed on, "you
must realize all you'll be giving up: your home, your family,
more money than I'll see in a lifetime. I'm a blacksmith, Livi,
and a sharecropper. I can't provide you with the ease and
comfort you're used to, with the life you'll be leaving behind."

Her fingers closed reassuringly around his arm. "While you
see what I'll be giving up, I see all I have to gain: a man who
loves me, a man who believes I'm someone very special, a
man who wants me as much as I want him."

A smile returned to David's face. "You'll come with me,
then? You'll come with me today?"

"I will."

"And we'll be married?"

"Yes."

"This evening?"

"If you like."

He kissed her hard, then spun her back toward the coach.
"Then we need to get your things."

While David unstrapped her trunk and Reid Campbell un-
hitched the coach horses, Arabella did her best to dissuade her
sister.

"Olivia, darling, think this through! You'll have no life at
all with a man like him. You'll live in a one-room shack, work
like a darky from dawn to dusk, ruin your figure with a baby
every year." Livi gathered her belongings from inside the

coach, heedless of Arabella's words. "You'll never have tea or oranges or peppermints. You'll never own another silk dress or feathered bonnet!"

David came up behind Livi, took her jumbled things, and stuffed them into a saddlebag. "What your sister says is true, Livi. It isn't too late to change your mind."

Instead of acknowledging David's words, Livi spoke to her sister. "It doesn't matter what the future holds as long I'm at David's side. I love him, Bella; I really do."

"But we'll never see you again if you marry him!" Arabella wailed, her distress as real as the threat.

Livi might try to convince herself that her father would forgive her, but both sisters were aware that Richard Chesterton did not tolerate defiance. He would disown his daughter rather than accept a marriage he so stringently opposed. Livi and Bella knew their father was a cold man, capable of gross and subtle cruelties. Yet in spite of that, Livi's family was the only forfeit she was reluctant to make.

Behind her, David drew his mount up close beside the coach and swung into the saddle. It was time for them to go, and there was nothing else to say.

Arabella wept into her handkerchief as Livi threw her arms around her and held her tight. "Tell Mama and Papa that I'm sorry they forced me to make this choice. Tell them that I love them and that I'll write."

"Oh, Livi, please don't do this," her sister sobbed. "We'll all miss you terribly. And what will Papa do to me when he hears I've let you slip away?"

"Tell him it wasn't your fault. Tell him I'm only willing to marry a man I truly love."

Before Bella could respond, Livi turned, slid one foot in the stirrup, and let David hoist her behind him into the saddle. He wheeled his horse away, leaving Reid Campbell to tug and curse at Livi's heavy trunk and follow reluctantly in their wake.

They rode for some time, though Livi was barely aware of the passing countryside. She wept against David's back, drifted into a hazy resignation, then roused to weep again.

Around midday Livi began to take note of her surroundings. The road was more heavily traveled here, and farmsteads speckled the landscape. At a crossroads, David pulled up before a prosperous-looking inn. The innkeeper ushered them upstairs to a simple, well-scrubbed room. From David's conversation, Livi learned that this was to be the site of their wedding, their marriage celebration, and their first night as man and wife.

She flushed at the thought, only vaguely aware of what that first night entailed. Before she could ask for any kind of clarification, David hustled out and Reid Campbell arrived, her humpbacked trunk balanced on one broad shoulder. He heaved it to the floor with a resounding crash.

"Thank you for bringing up the trunk and for your help with all the rest," Livi offered shyly. They were the first words she had spoken directly to Campbell since the night of her birthday fete.

"There's no need to thank me. I'm doing this for him." The statement reeked of Campbell's disapproval.

"I'll do my best to be a good wife," she promised.

"Yes, I suppose you will," he conceded, his blue eyes piercing and stark in a savage's face. "But surely even you can see it will never be enough. David needs a helpmate who'll work as hard as he does, who'll encourage him to pursue his dreams."

"I will work hard; I'll learn to help," she offered, desperate to win him to her cause. "And just what are these dreams that marrying me will undermine?"

Even Campbell seemed taken aback. "If David hasn't told you what they are, it's certainly not my place to do it."

"And just how is it your place to condemn me, Mr. Campbell?" Livi heard herself say, nearly as surprised by the words as Campbell was.

He glared at her long and hard. "I dare to condemn you, Olivia Chesterton, because I know what's best for him. Because I know David better than he knows himself. And because any fool can see you're too pampered, too fragile, too damn weak to be the wife he needs."

"But I love him, Mr. Campbell," she insisted softly.

"Yes." Reid shook his head with regret as he turned to go. "I'm afraid you do."

Her mother would have pointed out that *all* brides were beautiful on their wedding day. Dressed in a blue-and-ivory gown of ribboned silk, with a fichu of Belgian lace and a matching cap, Livi did indeed feel beautiful. Not only did she feel beautiful, but she felt special, very, very special. And it was David who made her feel that way. It was David and the knowledge that he loved her, that within a matter of minutes their lives would be joined forever.

The wedding party consisted of a minister, Reid Campbell and the innkeeper as witnesses, David and her. How David had arranged the ceremony, complete with a parson to hear their vows, Livi would never know. But once they were married in the eyes of the church, nothing short of an annulment could separate them.

"Well, my children," Reverend Schofield intoned, opening his prayer book, "shall we begin?"

Clutching the small bouquet of wild asters and Michaelmas daisies David had somehow found time to pick for her, Livi stepped up beside the man she had chosen as a husband. At the brush of his hand, yearning seeped through her. It was a yearning that went deeper than desire, a longing for tenderness and tolerance and acceptance, a craving for reassurance and constancy.

"Dearly beloved," the reverend began, "we are gathered here today to join the lives and spirits of David and Olivia . . ."

Yet she and David were already joined. Any vows they spoke would only reaffirm what each of them had sensed the moment they met: that they were meant to be together. From that first clasp of hands, they had accepted that they would rise together each morning and lie down together each night, that they would share life's joys and sorrows all their days. Still, they repeated the reverend's words, declaring that they loved each other, that they wanted to be together always.

Then all at once the ceremony was over. David was smiling down into her eyes, clasping her fingers as if he would never let them go, brushing a kiss across her lips. Livi kissed him back and blinked away happy tears.

The wedding supper passed in a blur. Reverend Schofield ate sparingly and took his leave. Reid Campbell watched David and Livi with smoldering eyes and drank deep. The innkeeper bustled to and fro, clearing dishes and replenishing

"I should leave you now," he murmured, his callused thumb scoring circles against her bare shoulder. "I should allow you time—"

"Time for what?"

"To undress. To prepare yourself."

"Prepare myself how?" Livi's stomach fluttered with uncertainty, the first she'd felt since David had taken her from her father's coach.

"Hasn't your mother explained what happens—" David shook his head. "No, of course she wouldn't. Certainly not before you were betrothed. Probably not until just before the wedding . . ."

"Explained what?"

He raised one hand to cup her chin. Tenderness curled the corners of his lips and warmed the amber gold of his eyes. "Explained the greatest pleasure of married life. But then, perhaps it is just as well that I show you all of it myself."

"Does that mean you're going to stay?"

Nodding, David reached around and plucked the pins from Livi's hair. Tendrils drifted down, drooping lengths of vibrant red, bright and shimmering against her shoulders.

"Lovely," he whispered, veiling her breasts with the silky strands. "You have hair like polished copper, the color of dawn."

"You like it?" Livi dared to ask. No one in her family had one kind thing to say about her hair.

"Love it," he corrected, curling his fingers into the slippery mass, "nearly as much as I love you."

Bending his head and plying her with sultry kisses, he reached for the tapes at the back of the tight, closely boned underbodice.

Livi felt the bows slip, felt the constriction ease as he loosened the ribbon laces. Once he'd teased the garment free, he worked the cluster of ties at her waist, letting the skirts and panniers and petticoats ripple to the floor.

Standing in the center of the mound of bright fabric, clad only in her chemise, Livi flushed. She'd imagined this moment more than once, but she had never anticipated how exposed she would feel, how overcome she would be by the flare of heat in David's eyes. An answering heat blossomed in her chest and radiated through her.

The fierce wonder in his face drew her beyond the circle of skirts, into his embrace, into his kiss. The pleasure of his lips moving against her own, the tantalizing stroke of his tongue, deepened the bond between them. David coaxed her further still until her mouth burned hungry and hot, and her limbs seemed weighted with some mysterious lassitude.

"David?" she whispered, raising her gaze to his. "I feel so breathless and quivery . . ."

Smiling, he lifted one hand to cup her breast, found the knot of her nipple with his thumb. Livi gasped and tried to pull away as he began slow, circling motions that sent fresh waves of heat and confusion washing through her.

"David?" she breathed.

"Hush, love," he murmured. "This is the way you're supposed to feel. This is desire, Livi. This is how a man shows a woman he cares for her."

"It is?"

"Oh, yes. And there is so much more."

Giddy, mesmerized by the swell of new sensations, Livi arched against her husband. "How can there be more?"

Accepting the access she granted him, David showed her. He drizzled kisses along the line of her collarbone, down the swell of her breast. Through the veil of her chemise, he sought the nipple just barely visible through the drape of cloth. Livi moaned in protest and pleasure as he took the puckered bud into his mouth.

Bright streamers of delight drew taut, trailing down her breasts and belly toward the apex of her thighs. She was melting inside, her most secret place gone liquid with this thickening, seeking sensation David called desire.

Crooning her name as if it were a melody, he lifted her in his arms and carried her to the curtained bed. The draws and the covers had been thrust back so that the sheets rippled with golden highlights from the fire. Settling Livi at the edge, David untucked his shirt. He had discarded his coat and waistcoat earlier in the evening, so that when he pulled the billowy fabric free, he stood bared to the waist before her.

Livi had never seen a man without his clothes. Though she always appreciated how much bigger and stronger they were than women, she had never seen such graphic proof of it. David's shoulders bowed broad as an ox yoke. The muscles of his chest flexed firm, well defined, and hazed by a growth of downy-gold hair. Mesmerized by the pliant flow of his flesh, Livi watched as David bent to remove his boots and stockings. But she blushed and turned away when his hands dropped to the waist of his breeches.

After a few moments, he came to stand before her. When she refused to look, he turned her face to his. "I am as God made me, Livi, for your admiration and your pleasure," he told her. "You may look at me and touch me as you please."

With blood burning her cheeks, she allowed her gaze to drift, back to the breadth of his shoulders, down his massive chest, across the muscles that bound his ribs and hips. Coming upon the rampant jut of his manhood brought another blush to Livi's cheeks. She looked away.

David chuckled at her reticence, but let her have her way. Instead he leaned over her, bearing her back onto the bed and sprawling beside her. Knotting his fingers in her hair, he stared down at her hard and long, as if she were a mirage that might shimmer and fade before his eyes.

"I can't believe you're here," he whispered at last. "I can't believe you're mine. I don't know what miracle made you love me, Livi, but I swear, as long as I live, I will do my best to make you happy."

The pucker between his brows, the serious line of his mouth, the intensity of his eyes, brought a constriction to Livi's throat. She wanted to reassure him, but what could she say?

Instead of answering, she twined one hand in his golden hair and drew him to her. The kiss swelled and pooled between them, exquisite in its intensity, a promise of passion, of spirit, and of flesh. It turned thick and sweet, viscous, wildly intoxicating. It renewed the wanting in their blood.

Losing patience with the billow of her chemise, David pushed beneath the hem, his rough palm abrading the satiny texture of her thigh and hip. He pushed higher, to the hollow beneath her ribs and up the rise, cupping the swell of her breast.

Uneasy with this new intimacy, Livi twisted against him. Still David's hands skimmed over her, gentling her to his touch. Then all at once the delicate scrape of his work-roughened fingers against the tightening nubs of her nipples set her quivering. The vibrations swelled and grew, quivers of sensation deep within the core of her.

In a world that had become a shimmer of shadow and firelight, David was her only reality. The harsh, uncompromising lines of his body; the pleasure in his touch; the secrets of life and love he seemed so eager to share.

"David," she whispered, her emotions a tumult of eagerness and fear and confusion. "David?"

"Stay with me, love," he answered as he inched one hand along the midline of her body. Her breath caught harsh and fluttery in her throat. Inside she thrummed, heat and tension pulsing deep. His palm closed over the nest of coppery curls, stirring helpless, breathless wildness in her. His fingers probed deeper, pressing, seeking, taking up a slow, sweet rhythm Livi seemed instinctively to recognize.

With the escalating intensity of those first strokes, Livi came apart. Sensation swamped her, ripples of delight wafting outward, washing up her spine and down her legs. Shivers curled and peaked and drew her down. She went liquid, formless, soft, melting into David, lost in him, in the pleasure he offered unstintingly. Gradually the tempest inside her stilled. She curled into the bastion of David's embrace.

"That was 'more,' wasn't it?" she breathed after a long, unfettered time. "That was what you meant to show me."

"A part of it." She heard the smile in his voice.

With the tip of one finger he had begun to draw distracting, feather-light patterns on the surface of her skin. He traced from the slope of her shoulder to the rise of her breast, from the dip of her waist to the flare of her hip. Something about those repetitious, barely discernible strokes turned her restless and trembly again. In time he trailed lower, skimming the curve of her belly and the line of her thigh. Livi's breathing fluttered; her head went light. She felt the warmth and fullness gathering.

Then David bent to claim her mouth, to caress her breasts. Sensation flared, a tumult of desperation and desire. Livi rose against him, her back arching, her hips lifting.

David accepted what she seemed ready to give. He rolled above her, eased her legs apart, and sought his haven between her thighs. The union took her breath, not for the intrusion of manhood into virgin flesh, but for a sense of completion. It came so strong, so filled with elation, that tears clogged Livi's throat and trickled from the corners of her eyes.

For a space she and David hung suspended, on a plane apart. Their gazes fused, their bodies joined, their souls forever one.

"I love you, David," Livi whispered, the words fragile, pure.

"And I love you."

This, then, was the quintessence of their vows: a communion so intense that nothing else existed, a perfection that nothing in the universe could change. Then the clarity of that realization began to blur, the edges fraying with the sharp, insistent pulse of physical yearnings. Their gazes held as the intensity swelled between them, becoming more than they could bear. David's mouth captured hers in a kiss that arced sweet illusion and reality.

Chests heaving, hearts thundering, they began to move together. Each of his thrusts sank deeper as Livi welcomed her husband home. Life and hope and love hummed in their veins as they twisted together, as the world shimmered and shattered around them. They gloried in the frenzy and the fury, the ecstasy and the emotion, the surrender and the sweetness. They clung each to the other as wonder and exaltation swept them away.

They lay together for a long and hazy time, claimed and claiming, sated and sating, loved and loving.

Finally Livi raised her head. "Am I truly your wife now?"

"In every way."

"And you'll never leave me?"

She felt David stir and gather her closer still. He brushed his lips across her brow. "Man and wife," he whispered, as if the reality evaded him even now. "From this moment on, we'll be together. I give you my oath, my solemn vow. Always, Livi. Always."

7

Livi awoke with David's words ringing in her ears and the taste of ashes in her mouth. *You should never have promised me always,* she thought, caught in the dregs of the dream. Life was too fragile, too uncertain. But they'd been young. They hadn't believed that trouble or grief or death could intrude on their safe little world. David had promised her always, and she had believed.

Groaning, Livi coiled out of the tangled bedclothes and took stock of her surroundings. Pale gray light was just beginning to delineate the mouth of the cave—a half-moon of hope in a dense black world of uncertainty. Beside her, Cissy lay lost in feverish sleep. Livi could see that more of the angry red splotches had emerged on Cissy's face during the night. The realization gave a quick, hard tug on the panic already snarled in Livi's chest. Cissy had to get well; Livi couldn't bear it if her daughter died.

Across what was left of the campfire, Tad sprawled in his blankets, deeply asleep and apparently well. She thanked God for that and for His help in these past days. Beyond Tad lay the jumbled hulks of their packsaddles and creels.

Easing away from her daughter, Livi rose, added wood to the fire, and prodded the coals to life. She knew how critical it was to keep Cissy warm; she should never have let the fire get so low. She should never have closed her eyes last night.

Ignoring the faint churn of morning nausea, Livi crept to the head of the cave. Fog dense as day-old porridge filled their little hollow to the rim. The boulders that guarded the opening shone with wet, and trees farther down the slope blurred to shadows.

As she stood there, Livi noticed that the water bucket by the entrance stood empty. Though she was loath to leave her children alone, she knew she must fill it before she could bathe her daughter's brow or fix their breakfast. With the weight of the primed pistol she'd taken to carrying bumping against her thigh, Livi hefted the pail and stepped out into the half-light.

Fog roiled thick and frigid in her lungs as she picked her way along the path. Fingers of damp probed her clothes and scattered pearls of condensation in her hair. Livi could just make out the hazy shapes of the pines and hawthorns through the blur. From somewhere near at hand came the lowing of their cow and the gurgle of a mountain stream.

Ahead, a clear vein of silver pooled in the lee of a wooded bank, the only solid shape in a ragged, shifting world. Livi knelt beside the water and filled her bucket to the brim. After carefully scanning her surroundings, she dipped her hands into the icy stream and bent to wash her face. The water was like a slap, startling her, clearing her head. She splashed her face again, bathed her arms to the elbows, then drank deep.

Fortified, clearheaded for what seemed like the first time in days, Livi sat back on her heels. If Cissy recovered, if neither she nor Tad fell ill, if they could keep body and soul together and the Indians didn't find them, they might eventually resume their journey.

And then what? she wondered.

Livi could never remember being so tired, so down-to-the-bone weary as she'd been in these past weeks. Every step took effort. Every decision loomed formidable and unwieldy. Her emotions ruled her common sense.

She knew carrying the baby sapped her strength and turned her moods. The hours she'd spent waiting for word when Tad was lost and sitting vigil over Cissy had worn her down. Pressing ever onward through rough terrain pushed her to the brink of physical exhaustion. Was she strong enough to see her children safely to David's land? Had she been a fool to go ahead instead of back when she'd had the chance?

She'd indulged herself the night before by turning to thoughts of David for comfort, but David could not help her now. Livi had decided their fate. She had taken this responsibility on her own shoulders three weeks ago, and she must find a way . . .

"Ma!" Tad's voice sliced through the fog and her recriminations. "Ma!"

"Here, Tad," she called back, staggering to her feet. Hefting the bucket, she rushed toward their camp. "Is something wrong?" she panted.

"It's Cissy!"

Livi scrambled upward, her knees trembling as she made the climb. "What is it?" she demanded when she reached the mouth of the cave. "What's wrong?"

Tad's brows were drawn together over dark-ringed eyes. "Cissy's mumbling in her sleep. She's wet with sweat. I can't make her keep the covers on."

Livi thrust the bucket at Tad and ran to her daughter's bedside. The boy was right. Cissy's face was beaded with perspiration and her hair lay dark and damp against her temples.

This is good news, not bad, Livi told herself as she tested the heat of her daughter's forehead with the back of her hand. *This was good news.*

The fever had broken. Cissy was better. Livi closed her eyes against the slow, sweet seep of relief.

Beside her, the boy stood quivering. "Is she—Did I—"

"It's all right, Tad," Livi assured her son. "Cissy's better. Sweating is good when someone's had a fever. Now, if you could get me a basin of water . . ."

The boy jumped to do her bidding.

Cissy awoke at midday. "The spots itch, Mama!" she whimpered. "And I'm hungry."

Livi smiled through a haze of sudden tears. "I'll see what I can do," she promised and pulled her little girl close.

Miles of rugged trail stretched before them. A wilderness rife with dangers lay in wait. But with her daughter gathered in her arms, Livi was content. Cissy was going to get well, and Livi had to believe that somehow they would find their way through all the rest.

The world changed almost overnight. The wind's sharp bite lost its teeth. The earth sprawled soft and fecund beneath an azure sky. A pale pink flush swept the uppermost branches of the barren trees. It was spring. It was planting time. *It was time to press on to David's land.*

The imperative nagged Livi like a crone.

To everyone's overwhelming relief, Cissy recovered with remarkable speed. Her fever dropped; her energy returned. Only the spots remained, scabbed over and as Cissy proclaimed, "itchy as a thousand mosquito bites." Less than a week after they'd been abandoned by Lindenwood and the company of churchmen, Livi and the children, the horses, the piglets, the chickens, and the cow set off down the Wilderness Road again.

Fortified with an herb-and-bear-grease mixture to ease Cissy's scratching, with two rabbits Tad had snared, with the directions in David Talbot's journal, they traced the course of the Yellow Creek to the west and north. They penetrated cane breaks where winter-dry stalks clattered in the wind and the air hung fetid with the roux of decay. They climbed into the hills again, where the delicate yellow-green furls of leaves fought for precedence over shadowy groves of cedars and pines. The forest floor was astir with life, scatterings of violets, clumps of star-bright trillium. Carpets of bluets were flung in profusion over the broken ground.

Livi and the children made good progress that first day, pitching their camp just south of Pine Mountain Gap. They should be able to traverse the gap tomorrow and ford the Cumberland River by early afternoon. A sense of well-being settled over Livi as she prepared their meal. Firelight filled the campsite with an amber glow. Doves cooed in the trees overhead. The children were sitting by the fire, Cissy writing words on her slate and Tad struggling to read aloud from a battered copy of *Pilgrim's Progress.* Livi allowed herself a tiny, satisfied smile.

Her contentment held until she looked up and saw the tall, fierce figure looming on the far side of the fire. His face was striped with red and black. Garish feathers bloomed from his vermillion-tipped scalp lock. He bore a war club in one massive hand.

Warmth drained from Livi's face. Her hands went numb. Images of David and what the Indians had done to him blared in her head.

Around the first man, other braves appeared. Suddenly. Silently. As if the trunks of the trees encircling the camp had been transformed from bark to flesh.

A hot, heavy dollop of rabbit stew spattered from the spoon Livi had been holding into her lap. It startled her to action. With a cry, she tossed the spoon aside and dove for David's rifle an arm's length away.

The first brave hurdled the campfire and caught the muzzle of the gun just as Livi tightened her grip around the stock. He jerked it toward him. Livi jerked it back. She fumbled to cock the hammer. He did his best to twist the weapon out of her hands. She tightened her finger around the trigger and fought to aim. The rifle exploded with a flare and concussion that pounded over all of them.

Cissy howled and covered her head.

The brave thrust the smoking barrel aside and loomed over Livi. Tad leaped to his mother's defense.

"No, Tad," Livi cried, but the brave was wheeling to face this new threat.

Livi grabbed for the pistol tucked in the pocket beneath her skirt. The hammer snagged in the opening of the seam.

The brave battered Tad aside as Livi fought to jerk the pistol free. Staggering, the boy turned and charged again. The warrior met his attack with a slashing, backhand blow. The sound of the impact resounded through the clearing. Tad dropped like a stone.

Livi scuttled toward her son. The brave glared a threat that froze her in her tracks. Instead she drew Cissy close, comforting the child as best she could.

Sobbing and shuddering, the girl burrowed into her mother's lap.

The other Indians came out of the trees.

Cautiously Livi reached across to where Tad was beginning to stir. "Are you hurt?" she whispered.

Blood trickled from a gash at the corner of his eye. It gleamed dark in the firelight, like the track of a single savage tear. The boy took a moment to assess before shaking his head.

The trip-hammer thud of Livi's pulse slowed a little. Even Cissy cast a teary glance in her brother's direction.

"It's going to be all right, sugar," Livi reassured her daughter.

"I w-want Papa," the girl whimpered and hid her face again.

Livi registered the words: acknowledgment that she could never provide for and protect her family as David had, acknowledgment that Tad might feel compelled to do something foolish to try to keep them safe.

"I don't want you taking any more chances," Livi told him in an undertone as a tall, impenetrable circle of Indian braves closed around them. As it did, Livi saw the tangled hanks of hair—fair and dark, curly and straight, thick and long—hanging from several of the men's belts. Recognition jolted her to her fingertips.

Scalps. These men had taken scalps!

Panic swarmed over her, itchy and hot. Her muscles bunched in the effort to keep still when she wanted to run.

With tears of frustration backing up in her throat, Livi eased her hand through the opening in the seam of her skirt and began to work the pistol free. She had a single shot to save her children. A single shot. It was such an inadequate defense for something so precious.

Livi didn't think she could be more terrified until one of the men jerked Tad to his feet.

"*HoΘaawa? Takawe.*" said the brave, one hand pulling at her son's shaggy hair. "*NiΘakaskitepeena.*"

The Indians laughed.

Tad tried to jerk away.

The smooth wooden stock of the pistol weighed reassuringly in Livi's palm. Under the cover of her skirt, she raked the hammer back.

The warrior who'd wrenched the rifle away came to squat beside her and ran his fingers the length of Livi's braid. "*Mskwiskitepe.*"

Her muscles quivered. Her nerves hummed.

Cissy sobbed and raised her head.

Livi looked into her daughter's face for what might be the very last time. A soft, sweet oval. Eyes dark and huge with fear. Skin peppered with spots that might never have a chance to heal. Smallpox, they'd thought.

Smallpox!

The thought echoed in Livi's head, suddenly louder than her thundering heart.

Not taking time to consider what she was giving up, Livi loosed her hold on the gun. She slid her hands beneath her daughter's arms and hefted the child to her feet.

Cissy sobbed and clung when Livi tried to make her stand.

"Look up at them, sugar," Livi breathed. "Be brave for me, Cissy."

How could she ask this when her baby was so afraid? How could any mother demand such courage of her child?

"No," the girl whimpered.

But this was far too important to be Cissy's choice.

"Please, baby girl, just look at them once," she pleaded, knowing it was for all their lives.

Cissy seemed to gather her courage. She raised her head. She stared at the man kneeling beside her, the man with the feathered scalp lock and painted face.

For an instant he simply stared back.

"*Noomekiloke*," he shouted and scrambled away. "*Noomekiloke!*"

The word echoed around the clearing, rising in alarm from a dozen throats. The men recognized the scourge that had wiped out scores of their villages. They well knew the white man's disease that was devastating Indian nations. Smallpox.

The braves withdrew stealthily and swiftly—from the fire, from the family, from the child whose illness might prove more deadly than rifle or knife. Without a sound they melted back into the woods.

Relief sang in Livi's veins as she watched them go. She sucked in great, shivery draughts of air and hugged her daughter tight.

"Where did they go, Mama?" Cissy asked.

"Back into the woods, sugar. You scared them away." Livi was laughing and crying all at once.

"I did?"

"They were afraid of your spots," Tad explained.

"They didn't want the itches, either?"

It seemed so simple; it had been so difficult. How could any mother live with herself after demanding what she had of this fragile four-year-old? How could she have forced her baby girl to meet her nightmares head-on? But Cissy had done it. She'd conquered her fears. She'd saved their lives.

"No one ever wants the itches," Livi confided, reaching

out to grab Tad's hand. She needed to acknowledge her son's own act of courage. She needed the feel of her children's flesh to reassure herself of their safety.

"You were brave to face that Indian," Tad told his little sister. "I know you must have been really scared."

"It wasn't so very bad," Cissy assured him in a very small voice. "I might—I prob'ly—could do it again. If the Indians come back."

If the Indians came back. The laughter died to silence on Livi's lips. What would the wilderness demand of her babies next? She closed her eyes and prayed that the worst of this journey was over. She just couldn't believe it was.

A new sense of foreboding arrived with the dawn. An ache across her shoulders. Pressure at the base of her throat. Livi tried to shrug it off. After the Indian incursion the previous evening and the hours she'd lain awake, she had reason to be jumpy as a June bug. She'd stared into the dark, living those moments of horror and helplessness again and again. Last night she and her babies had escaped the savages unharmed, but next time . . .

Dear God, what would happen next time?

In a haze of restless exhaustion, Livi rose before dawn and threw herself into preparing for the trail. She cooked a hearty breakfast and repacked the creels. She helped Cissy feed the cow, the chickens, and the piglets, and worked with Tad to hitch the horses. In spite of her best efforts to drive it away, the eerie feeling clung like a sodden cloak. It was not the clutch of imminent peril, not the squirm of being watched, yet it stirred a restiveness in her, a dread she could not name.

Livi did her best to blame it on the mountains that lay ahead: slabs of harsh gray stone jutting skyward, slopes so ragged and steep that only a sprinkling of trees dared to brave the barren face, peaks that prodded the lowering sky. It was land that might overwhelm the most courageous scouts, swallow the largest pack trains without a trace. And she and her children would face it alone.

Responsibility lay even more heavily than the dread. She must have been mad to consider this course. But had she ever been given another choice?

With dogged perseverance, Livi and the children put the

Pine Mountain Gap behind them. They reached the Cumberland River ford just ahead of the rain. In a fine, drifting mist they traversed the gravel bar, coming out unscathed on the opposite bank.

The trail beyond the ford skirted the mountains by tracing a narrow path at the base of the gorge. On that ledge a wonderland revealed itself. Rocks shimmered iridescent in the wet. Raindrops glittered like crystals scattered on a bed of velvet moss. The leaves of the waving ferns were limned with silver.

But even such rare and fragile beauty could not dispel Livi's foreboding. She ached with it, fought for breath beneath its weight, trembled with its growing power. As she led her little party forward, she wrapped her daughter closer than before and wondered if the damp had compromised the prime of her pistol.

Several miles beyond the ford, the valley opened up to reveal a world awash with rain. The forest swayed in the waves of wetness. The clouds hung low. The mist boiled out of the trees like lost souls escaping to heaven.

An unearthly chill crawled the length of Livi's back. The rime of fear came sharp and bitter on her tongue. Whatever she had sensed lay just ahead.

The horses felt it, too. They snorted and blew and fought their leads.

Livi tried to focus, to prepare.

"What *is* that?" she heard Tad ask. "That smell—"

And suddenly Livi knew—knew what horror lay in wait for them. Certainty swamped her. Sick, hot dread filled her to the brim, driving the air from her lungs, coherent thoughts from her brain. She had just sense enough to crush Cissy against her chest and draw the protective wing of her cloak around her daughter before they topped the rise.

Livi's fear was given form at the brow of that hill. Vile, violent impressions assaulted her. Images she would carry for the rest of her days. Revulsion that scarred her soul. Carrion birds rose from where they'd been about their grizzly work. The beat of their wings was the only sound in the hollow, hissing silence.

Then from somewhere behind her, she heard Tad retching.

What lay in this little valley was too vivid, too abhorrent, too vile for even an adult to assimilate—let alone her twelve-year-old son. What lay in the little valley was the desecrated remnants of Reverend Lindenwood's pack train, the broken bodies of the people with whom she and her family had briefly shared their lives.

Crushing Cissy against her chest, Livi turned to where her whey-faced son was wiping his mouth with the back of his hand.

She wanted to draw Tad to her and hold him, too. She wanted to beg his forgiveness for not warning him away. But the time was past for all of that.

"Indians?" he finally asked and looked as if he might be sick again.

"I suppose," Livi answered, knowing that the marauders were gone, that they'd been gone for several days.

"Do you think anyone escaped?"

She doubted it, but let her gaze skim the little valley, trying not to look too closely. She saw a few piles of wood, a few half-constructed tents. The Indians must have swept down on the churchmen in the bustle and confusion of making camp.

"If anyone did, they're long gone by now."

She heard Tad draw a shaky breath. "What are we going to do?"

The inevitable question.

"We're going to move on. Around the encampment if we can. Through it if we must."

"We're not—" Tad swallowed and composed himself. "We're not going to stop and bury them?"

"The two of us alone, Tad? How could we do that?"

His voice dropped, going raspy and small. "But Sam and Joss might be here . . ."

She narrowed her eyes against the sting of tears. She couldn't bear to put a human face on what lay before them. "I'm sorry, Tad. They were my friends, too, but we really have no choice."

He nodded his head and looked away.

With the river to the left and the rock wall rising just beyond the trees, there was no way around what had been the churchmen's camp.

"Don't look, Tad," she admonished him as she tugged her balky animals into the shallow valley at Four Mile Creek.

"It's too late, Ma," he said and rode in after her.

Holding Cissy under the drape of the cloak despite her squirming, Livi rode tall, her eyes focused ahead. Still, at the periphery of her vision, images intruded. Broken bodies sprawled where they had fallen. Faces stained dark with blood. Women with their skirts rucked up. She saw a pair of bright red shoes and knew they belonged to Molly Baker, saw Ellen Stewart's fine embroidery ground into the mud. A carved Noah's ark lay at the edge of the trail; Amos Lindenwood's youngest, Aaron, had been so proud of it.

Not the children, she thought, new revulsion rising inside her. *Oh, please, God, not the children.* She knew they would fare no better than the adults, though some might well have been taken captive.

Every glimpse Livi caught of the carnage drained away a bit of her strength, annihilated a bit of her courage. It would be horrific to come upon a massacre if the people had been strangers. That she had laughed with these people and argued with them and cursed them when they'd abandoned her and her family, deepened her despair. The scope of the loss, the cruelty with which their lives had been taken, devastated her. So many gone, she thought. So many savaged.

It could have been us. The realization burst somewhere behind her eyes. If Cissy hadn't taken ill . . . If they had stayed with the pack train . . .

A wave of cold swept through her. Livi bound her daughter tighter than before. *It could have been us!*

"Dear God." The entreaty was on her lips before she realized she was speaking the words aloud. "Please receive the souls of these departed friends. They were good people in their way and lived their lives as well as any of us mortals can. Welcome them home to heaven and give them comfort there."

"Amen," she heard Tad murmur.

And thank you for watching over me and my family, she added silently. *Thank you for keeping us safe.*

They put Four Mile Creek behind them, pushing themselves and their animals as hard as they dared. They rode so far and fast that they outdistanced the rain. They rode until the sky was streaked silver and peach and peacock blue. They rode until Livi found the campsite that suited specifications she hadn't even thought about the night before: a scrap of high, open ground with rocks at her back; a place where she could see or hear her enemies coming.

Sleep eluded them all that night. Tad tossed and turned. Cissy whimpered softly. And for a very long time Livi lay taut and trembling with the pistol clutched against her chest. It could have been us, she kept thinking. *It could have been us.*

8

$\mathcal{L}$ ivi's hand closed reflexively around the stock of the pistol as she jerked awake. For one cold, clammy moment she was sure she was dreaming, dreaming of the night that David died. There was the same pad of footsteps from outside the tent, the same hot wash of danger spreading down her back. But this was not the dregs of some bitter dream. This was reality. Someone was in their camp.

Raw terror ripped through her chest. *No!* she raged. I can't face this. I can't do this. Not again.

She burrowed deep into the bedclothes, tears of fear and exhaustion scoring down her face. "I can't," Livi whispered into the dark. "I can't." Except that she had no choice.

A thud from somewhere near where she and Tad had stacked the creels made her start nearly out of her skin. There was someone out there. She had to find out who.

Livi gathered up the threadbare strands of her courage and crept toward the opening of the tent. Looking outside took an act of will. She nudged open the flap with the mouth of the pistol. She swiped at her eyes and peered through the dark.

By the faint red-orange glow of the campfire, she could see two crouched figures going through the packs. One was large, a good-sized man, judging by the set of his shoulders. The second was huddled in the first man's shadow, impossible to see. Though she looked long and hard, Livi could make out neither the sway of breechclouts nor the gleam of beads. No feathers blossomed in the robbers' hair. Then again, who but

Indians would be plundering campsites in the dead of night?

Livi spared a look for any raiders who might be lurking at the edge of the woods, then crawled back to where Tad was sleeping. Her son came awake with a jerk, Barlow knife in hand.

"There are men outside going through our packs," she whispered. "Bring the rifle."

Tad nodded, tense and wild-eyed. After being terrorized by the Indians the night before, after riding through the massacre this afternoon, Livi wondered how much more Tad could assimilate. She knew just how close she was to shattering. How much worse must this be for her son?

Still, Livi wasn't about to repeat David's mistake and face the marauders alone. Together she and the boy crept to the front of the tent. Their breathing was harsh and muffled as they assessed the situation.

"You go to the right," Tad instructed, his understanding of tactics instinctive and better than hers. "Keep the fire between us and them."

With an uneasy nod of acknowledgment, Livi burst from the tent with Tad right behind her. "Stop!" she shouted, training her pistol on the smaller of the two intruders. "Put that down."

"Raise your hands above your heads," Tad instructed.

The big man took one step forward and pulled up sharp, unwilling to argue with the muzzle of Tad's rifle. He lifted his hands. His companion followed suit.

The man was a Negro, Livi realized as he stepped in the firelight, not an Indian. Tall and rawboned, of middling years, he exuded strength and stoicism the way some men did the smell of sweat. His companion came nearer, too: a wisp of a woman in a tattered gown.

"Mama? Mama!" Cissy's frightened cry echoed around the campfire.

"I'm out here, sugar," Livi called. "We have visitors."

The child came out of the tent, trailing her blanket. Though Livi bent and lifted Cissy on her hip, the barrel of her pistol never wavered.

"But who *are* these people, Mama?" the girl demanded.

"Just what I was about to ask."

The man bobbed his head, the creases in his brow deepening. "I'm Eustace Hadley, ma'am, and this here's my woman, Violet Mae."

"And just what are you doing in our campsite in the middle of the night?"

"I confess, ma'am, we was stealin' food."

"And why is that?" Tad demanded.

" 'Cause we's hungry. 'Cause we ain't et in three days." The woman's voice was like drifting smoke.

Livi nodded and set her pistol aside long enough to offer up the hoecakes she'd been saving for breakfast. "I suppose we could remedy that before we go on."

While her son glared, Eustace and Violet tucked into the corn sticks with a relish that seemed to confirm their claims.

"And just why are you here, a hundred miles from any-where," Livi asked, "with nothing to eat?"

"We ain't runaways, if that's what you think," the woman answered around a mouthful of food.

"Truth is," Eustace elaborated, accepting another hoecake, "we was with Mr. Titus Wagner and his family, bound for Kentucky when our party got set upon by Indians. Killed everyone while Violet and me was gettin' water down at the creek. We was a-scared to stay near the camp after that and headed off into the woods."

"And how long ago was that?"

"Nigh a fortnight, seems to me."

"And do you know anything about the massacre near Four Mile Creek?" Tad demanded. "A big party of churchmen?"

Eustace shook his head. "We been hidin' in caves mostly. Though there been war parties through here regular, like."

Livi considered the man's story, watching the way he ate, liking that he didn't grab for more until she offered it. She took note of the work-roughened hands, the bulk of his fore-arms and wrists. She watched the woman, too. There wasn't much to her but bones, defiance, and big dark eyes. Violet must have had to fight for what she got; it was an ability Livi was beginning to respect.

"Well, you and Violet are welcome to sleep by our fire," Livi offered, "and travel with us tomorrow if you like."

"Ma!" Tad admonished sharply.

"But should you choose to come with us, I'll put up with no thievery," she went on before either Eustace or Violet could answer. "If I'm missing so much as a pinch of salt, I'll put a hole in both of you."

"Ma!"

"My family and I are willing to share what we have in return for work, but I need to know right now if you're going to stay and abide by my rules or if you're going off again."

"*Ma!*" There was no more denying Tad.

"Make your decision," Livi said, "while I speak with my son."

Toting the pistol in one hand and balancing Cissy on her hip, she led Tad to the shadows in the lee of the tent.

"What the hell can you be thinking of?" he demanded in a furious whisper. "Two escaped slaves wander out of the woods to steal our food—"

"Violet said they weren't escaped slaves," Cissy corrected.

"—and you ask them to join up with us! God Almighty, Ma! You don't have any idea if they're telling the truth about what happened to the rest of their party. You don't know if you can trust them."

"You're right. I don't," Livi answered calmly.

"For God's sake, Ma, they could be anything!" Tad warned. "They could kill us in our sleep."

"Seems to me they'd have done that if they intended to."

"What possessed you to ask them to travel with us?"

I did it because I'm tired and afraid. Because I can't face the wilderness and the danger by myself anymore. Because it could have been us lying dead at Four Mile Creek.

"What are you suggesting, Tad?" she asked instead. "That we leave Eustace and Violet here to starve? That we abandon them without a chance of reaching a settlement? It makes sense for them to join us. Sense for them and sense for us."

"We've been managing," Tad mumbled defensively.

"Well, I like them!" Cissy piped up. "Violet's little like me, and she has lots of spunk."

"You've got spunk, too, sugar," Livi acknowledged before turning back to her son. "We can use help with the chores and the animals. Things will be easier—and maybe even safer—if there are five of us instead of three."

"I don't know . . ."

"Ma'am." Eustace was standing by the head of the tent. "Ma'am?"

Livi turned. "What have you and Violet decided?"

"We'd sure 'nough like to take you up on your offer. We'd like to stay on if your husband says it's all right."

"Wonderful!" Tad muttered under his breath.

"My husband's dead, Eustace," Livi said, ignoring her son. "If you're going to stay, you'll be dealing with me."

Eustace nodded. "I promise you, ma'am, you won't be sorry you took us in. We's both hard workers. Violet cooks a fine meal when she got proper fixin's. I'm a fair hand with horses, and do all kinds of farmin' . . ."

"This isn't a fancy rig, as you can see," Livi responded, "But we'll be glad to have your help. I'm Olivia Talbot, and these are my children, Tad and Cissy."

"We's pleased to be travelin' with you, Miz Talbot."

On the far side of the fire, Violet sketched a curtsy. It was a token of respect that must not have sat easily on a woman like her. That Violet should offer it up now—and to a pioneer woman who certainly worked every bit as hard as she—said much about the couple's gratitude. Livi responded with an inclination of her head.

Taking a blanket from one of the creels, she offered it to Eustace. "I think we'd all better get some sleep," she suggested. "Dawn will come far too soon and we've many miles to go."

Curled up in her blankets once more, Livi lay listening. Cissy's breathing had already gone soft and deep. Tad shifted at the rear of the tent, angry and restless. Out by the fire she could hear the grainy murmur of voices and the rustle of people settling in. Livi eased down the hammer of the pistol and nestled the weapon against her chest. It was a comfortable enough pose, one she'd grown used to in these past weeks. Still, it was almost dawn when she closed her eyes.

Livi reviewed the passage in David's journal that dealt with crossing the Rockcastle River, then looked out from her perch on one of the boulders along the bank to make sure she knew just where the shallows were. For a mostly unlettered man, David had left remarkably complete directions for everything from picking their way through the canebrakes to ferreting out mountain passes. But Livi cherished the book for far more than its accuracy. David's scrawled, uneven hand and unconventional spelling underlined the labor it must have taken for her husband to complete the journal. It was an act of love, simple and pure. Having the journal made Livi feel as if David were with them still, watching over them, guiding them to Kentucky by way of the grimy, much-thumbed pages.

Livi curled her fingers around the tiny volume and blinked away unwelcome tears. She missed her husband with a deep, persistent ache that seemed to intensify the nearer they got to his land. It was a constant struggle to keep her emotions in check, but Livi refused to give way. Not when she barely had the privacy to heed the call of nature. Not with Violet and Eustace looking on. And certainly not in front of her children. She'd mourn David at her own time, in her own way.

From behind her, she heard Eustace call her name. "Here's some tea and hoecakes, Miz Talbot, ma'am."

"I told Violet not to light a fire," Livi grumbled, taking the offering.

"She thought you might be needin' a bite to settle you," he said.

It hadn't taken Violet Mae Hadley five minutes to surmise that Livi was pregnant, and the woman had hounded her unmercifully ever since. She all but poured milk down Livi's throat, gave her the largest portion at dinner, and made sure she got her rest. Building a fire in the middle of the day so Livi could have tea was just another example of Violet's infuriating disobedience.

Livi sipped and nodded begrudging thanks. The tea was exactly what she needed. How had Violet known?

Turning her face to the sun, Livi reflected that they'd made good time these past three days. They'd come from just this side of Big Flat Lick through swamp and canebrakes, past Raccoon Spring and Hazel Patch. These were landmarks David had talked about, written about. Landmarks that brought her that much closer to David's claim.

Livi surprised herself by being both eager and reluctant to arrive. There were so many dreams and so much resentment tied up in that single plot of ground that she couldn't imagine how it would feel to climb the rise where David said he'd build their house or walk those wide, cleared fields all by herself. Could the land possibly be worth all the grief and discord it had caused?

Livi was just finishing her tea when she heard the clatter of approaching riders. They'd encountered so few people on the trail that Livi wasn't sure if she should wave in welcome or meet them with her pistol drawn.

Two men came into view at the opposite end of the ford. Livi's uneasiness grew as they navigated the crossing. They were unshaven, roughly dressed, and looked like they were moving fast.

She scrambled down from the boulder and headed for where her children and the Hadleys were clustered on the bank above the ford. She had one hand wrapped around the stock of her gun when the men splashed out of the river.

"I think you'll fin' it a easy crossin'," the heavier man greeted her, drawing his horse up a few feet from where Livi stood. "Your man about?"

It didn't seem wise to offer the information that they had no man to protect them. "He's off hunting just now," she told the stranger. "If you've something to say, sir, you can say it to me."

The two men exchanged glances before the first one went on. "I'm Slay Grover and this here's John Bean. We're slave catchers from Virginie, checkin' the ownership of all the niggers we fin' on the Kentucky Road."

"It's amazin'," Bean put in, "how many runaways are headin' west. An' how many folks is willin' to help 'em."

"Really?" Livi answered coolly, though her pulse had begun to dance. "Well, you needn't worry about my people. Violet and Eustace have been with me for years."

At the periphery of her vision, she saw Tad curl his fingers around his sister's arm.

"An' just how long is that, Mistress . . ."

"Talbot, Olivia Talbot. Since just after I was married thirteen years ago. David bought Eustace and Violet for me as a wedding gift."

David hadn't had two pennies to rub together then, but it didn't matter. What mattered was that Livi knew slave catchers to be hard and vicious men. What mattered was that even if the story about their owners being killed by the Indians was true, the Hadleys had no way to prove it. And if they'd lied . . .

"Violet helped deliver Tad," Livi went on. "She was the

first person to hold Cissy after she was born. Even before her papa did.''

"Such fine, strong young'uns," Violet added with quiet pride.

"I don't know what I'd have done without her." The longer they played this game, the more likely it was that one of them would reveal too much. Nor did Grover or Bean seem overly impressed with the theatrics.

"I suppose their papers are in with our things," Livi offered. It was a bluff, one she hoped would forestall any further questions.

"It just so happens, Mistress Talbot," Grover drawled, "that we'd purely like to see them papers."

Livi tried not to blanch. "I don't know where they are exactly, so it might take a while to find them." She'd claimed Violet and Eustace as her slaves, and now she had to find some way to make these men believe her—papers or not.

"We can wait," Grover assured her and swung down from his horse.

"Well, then," she offered brightly, "perhaps Violet can make a pot of coffee while I look through our things."

John Bean's voice followed her as she turned away. "You do know, don't you, Mistress Talbot, that harborin' 'scaped slaves is agin the law?"

Livi suppressed the shiver that slid the length of her back. She'd known a couple in Lynchburg who'd run afoul of the law for helping slaves escape. There was no way of knowing how such matters were settled here. It was certain, though, that no matter what they did to her, far worse things would befall Eustace and Violet. They would be beaten, chained, and force-marched back to Virginia at the very least.

While the men waited, everyone played his or her part. Cissy helped Violet make the coffee. Tad and Eustace lowered the creels to the ground. Livi pawed through the baskets.

By the time Bean and Grover had finished their coffee and every last one of the hoecakes, Livi was quivering inside. There were no ownership papers for her to find. What she had come across in one of the creels was the oilcloth packet that contained all of David's important papers. His militia discharge and their land grant were inside, along with their marriage compact, the children's baptismal certificates, and several other things. She thumbed through the documents, wondering what papers that attested to a Negro's ownership looked like. Had she ever seen copies in her father's house?

If only she could steal off by herself, she might be able to fabricate—

"You find them papers yet, Mistress Talbot?" Slay Grover inquired, one eyebrow tilted speculatively. "I'm beginnin' to think you was funnin' us when you said these folks belonged to you."

Livi's time was running out. She shuffled through the packet one more time and withdrew two sheets from inside. "Eustace's and Violet's papers are right here," she said, trying to still the tremor in her voice.

Grover set aside his empty mug and took the papers in hand.

"I had some trouble learning my letters," Livi admitted. lowering her eyes. "That's why it took so long to figure out which ones they were."

He answered with a grunt and scanned first one document, then the other. Each had "Bill of Sale" across the top and bore an official-looking seal in the lower corner.

"You want to take a look at these, Bean?" he asked, impaling Livi with a narrow-eyed stare. It took every ounce of her gumption not to flinch.

Bean sauntered over and took a look. "Never saw slave papers with all them gewgaws on 'em before."

Livi's pulse fluttered in her throat. Her ears rang like a church bell calling the faithful to Sunday services. "Well, Mr. Grover," she declared in spite of it, "those are the only papers the broker gave my husband."

The two men conferred again.

If they made her wait much longer, Livi was going to faint.

Finally Grover raised his head. "Well, Mistress Talbot, these here bills of sale do seem to be all you claim."

"Of course they are." Livi took back the papers with a little huff, as if she'd never had any question about their authenticity.

All of them watched the slave catchers fetch their horses.

"You take care on that ford, Mistress Talbot," Grover warned, swinging into his saddle. "And keep them papers handy. There's others who'll want a look at 'em."

"Oh, I will, Mr. Grover," Livi answered. "Have care on the trail."

Bean and Grover were hardly out of sight when Eustace doused the fire and Violet began repacking the creels. No one spoke as they readied themselves for the trail. No one asked about the papers, but when Livi withdrew the oilcloth packet from her shirt to tuck them away, Tad silently held out his hand.

He took several minutes looking them over, laboring with the complicated legal phrases. Finally he glanced up, giving his mother a grin that stretched from ear to ear. "Is this really what you gave them?"

Livi nodded. "The bill of sale for the house and the one for your father's blacksmith shop."

Tad shook his head and grinned again. "By damn," he said as he mounted up, "it sure is handy knowing how to read!"

"We need to take precautions so that nothing like this happens again," Livi insisted as she huddled over the campfire with Eustace and Violet Mae. The children had long since been sent to bed, though she would bet Tad was lying awake listening.

"But what you told the slave catchers worked," Eustace argued. "They believed the papers you showed them."

"They wouldn't have believed them if either of those men had been able to read," Livi insisted. "What I need to do is write up something that says you and Violet belong to me."

Eustace's face hardened in resistance. "Papers that say you own us."

"Well, yes," Livi answered. "But I'd only write them up to protect—"

"I don' want no papers like that made!" Eustace jerked to his feet. "I don' *ever* want to be owned again!"

Livi stared up at him, sensing the depth of his resistance, his agitation, his fear. Raised in Williamsburg and then at Chesterton Oaks, she had grown up with Negro servants in the house and in the fields. They were part of the background of her life, silent, efficient, obedient. She'd never considered how they might feel about their servitude.

It made her wonder what it was like to be bought and sold, to labor and have nothing to show for it. To live and die by

another's will. Intolerable, she thought. Unbearable for anyone
with intelligence, ability, or pride.

In spite of her newfound sympathy for Eustace's concerns,
Livi knew it was essential to have papers drawn in case they
were questioned again. "Eustace," she offered gently, "the
papers wouldn't be real."

"What would keep them from bein' real?"

"Well, they won't be stamped the way bills of sale really
are, and all the signatures will be forged . . ."

"But we free now, Miz Talbot!" he exclaimed. "We been
free since the day Marse Wagner died, and I don't want no
papers sayin' we slaves again!"

Livi recognized the fire in Eustace's eyes, the passion in his
voice. They were the fierce, unfettered expressions of a man
who, for the first time in his life, belonged only to himself.

Or so he thought.

"Well, no," Livi answered, thinking back to what had transpired when one of their neighbors in Lynchburg died.
"You're not exactly free. What you are is part of Mr. Wagner's estate."

Violet, who had been watching the exchange through slitted
eyes, removed the stem of the clay pipe from between her
teeth. "What's estate?"

"In this case," Livi explained, "it means the things that
belonged to someone who's dead. Things that are passed on
to his kin or sold to pay his debts."

Eustace dropped down beside Violet like a quail shot in
mid-flight.

"You mean we ain't free?" The natural huskiness of
Violet's voice deepened. "Marse Wagner owns us even beyond the grave?"

"In a way. I suppose the thing to do," Livi went on, thinking aloud, "is to make out papers saying I bought you from
Mr. Wagner several weeks ago . . ."

"Then we don't belong to him; we belong to you," Eustace
pointed out miserably.

"Well, not if I write manumission papers, too." When she
saw their puzzled expressions, she went on. "I could write
papers saying that you were my slaves, and that I am granting
you freedom."

"I heard tales of that," Eustace allowed. "Manumission, you call it?"

"Or emancipation."

"Emancipation." Violet tried out the word in her mouth. "I like the sound of that."

"Well, then," Livi began, "I'll make you a proposition. I need help clearing and planting and building a cabin when we reach my husband's land. If you agree to let me write ownership papers now, if you stay until the cabin's built and the crops are in, I'll write manumission papers for both of you."

Eustace fixed her with a narrowed gaze. "You mean, if we help you get set up on your husband's place, you'll give us papers sayin' we free."

"That's right."

"And how long will settin' up take?"

"The fields are cleared. We'll need a house, and a barn for the animals." She hoped there wouldn't be more to do than that. "It should take two months. Maybe three."

Livi gave Eustace and Violet a moment to mull that over.

"Or," she continued, "you can stay for a year and work for free. If you do that, I'll give you the emancipation papers and twenty acres of land to do with as you please."

Livi had been considering the proposition for several days, ever since Eustace and Violet had wandered into camp and she'd realized how much they could help.

Across the fire, she watched the Hadleys' faces. They were marked with confusion and suspicion, though she sensed that each of them wanted to believe in what she was offering.

"Why you doin' this?" Eustace finally asked.

Livi shrugged. "Because I'm a woman without resources. Because I'm trying to make a life for my children. The land in Kentucky is all I have. I can't build a home on it or tend the fields or clear more ground all by myself. I'm offering you a share of what I have in exchange for your help."

There was nothing so potent as the truth.

The slaves looked at each other, and Livi could see the effect it had on both of them. Violet's mouth softened. Eustace's shoulders dropped.

"Do I get to pick the land?" he bargained, still looking out for tricks.

"From any land I don't already have cleared and cultivated

at the end of a year. From any that doesn't block my access to water.''

"And can we have a place of our own in the meantime?"

"As soon as we can get it built."

Without so much as a word or a glance passing between Violet and him, Eustace nodded.

"In order for any of this to work," Livi said, hating the restriction and knowing it was necessary, "I need to forge a bill of sale for you and Violet. And I need to do it tonight."

Eustace stirred, restless and reticent again.

"She needs that paper to protect her babies," Violet put in. "What woulda happened to her and her young'uns if those slave catchers hadn't gone away?"

The black man's mouth narrowed. A furrow came and went between his eyes.

"If those men had know'd their letters, Miz 'Livia woulda been as deep in trouble as us. Is that what you want?"

The two women waited in silence for his reply. Eustace finally gave in. "Make up the papers," he said.

Go three mils past Crab Orchard. Look for a streem on left under high stone banc. Follow the streem south a mile and a haf to wher I cleard the fields.

L ivi knew the passage by heart. The last one in David's journal. The passage that would lead her and her children to David's land. She searched the road ahead for landmarks, her hands damp on her horse's reins, her heart thudding thick and loud beneath her ribs. She'd traveled two hundred miles to reach this place. She'd fought terrible hardship, unendurable loss. Before this day was out, Livi would walk the open fields her husband had loved, feather the fertile soil between her fingertips. And when she did, she would finally understand. She would finally claim her share of David's dream.

They had descended the mountains the previous afternoon. As the road wound its way out of the hills, long vistas opened up. They traversed sweeps of forested plateau where drifts of spring-green trees rustled in the wind. They rode by rocky rills that trickled at the sides of the trail; stopped in flower-studded meadows that lay lush and green in the sun. Kentucky was a beautiful land, a bountiful land. But was it, Livi found herself wondering, a land she would have been willing to trade for David's life?

Today they'd passed through countryside knobby with humpbacked hills and creased with shallow side valleys.

They'd ridden through the area David called the Crab Orchard, and as they passed, the petals from the blossoming apple trees fluttered in the wind like gentle snow. From the Crab Orchard they'd continued to the west and the north, anticipation growing with every footfall.

Then Livi spotted the first of the landmarks David had described. Her heart soared at the sight of the trailside stream, the promise of their journey's end after all these weeks of traveling.

"There," she cried, turning to where Tad was guiding his pack horses, back to where Violet walked with Cissy, and Eustace led the cow. "That's the stream David wrote about."

Gurgling around a towering limestone overhang, the water pooled in the curve of a rocky creek then swept downstream. As Livi urged her horse along the natural path that traced the bank, the forest deepened around them. The trees grew taller, broader here. The canopy of new leaves thickened overhead. The verdant majesty of the woods closed in, breathtaking in its magnificence. Silence descended, the loamy earth muffling every sound. Even their voices, raised in cries of wonder and excitement, seemed lost and small.

The stream bed narrowed, passing around a ruffled curve. Still in the lead, Livi pushed her horse for greater speed as they climbed the trail above the water. The ground rose steadily, and from the crest of the hill Livi could see the whole of David's dream spread out before her.

"Our land lies in a basin between the hills," he'd told her more times than she could count. "It's a small green valley with a creek winding through and a good, sweet spring."

This little hollow was everything David had promised, serene and lush and beautiful. Livi expected her spirits to soar like a kite in the wind, waited for the sense of belonging to envelop her.

And felt nothing at all.

"Are we home?" Cissy demanded breathlessly, topping the rise. "We're home now, aren't we, Mama?"

Livi let out her breath on a ragged sigh. She didn't know how to answer.

Not waiting for her mother's reply, the little girl darted down the hillside. Tad swung out of the saddle and followed his sister.

Livi stared after them, abandoned and lost.

"You goin' on ahead?" Eustace asked her, coming to gather up the reins to Tad's horse.

She nodded and urged her mare toward the four cleared fields that lay below. More than an acre of ground had been hacked out of woods grown thick with black walnut, sugar maples, and honey locust; with sumac, wild grape, and may-apples. How hard her husband must have worked, she thought, to open this patch of earth to the sky. How wounded he would be by her indifference to all of it.

Then Livi saw something David had never seen fit to mention, something that softened the first terrible moments of alienation. Tears blurred her sight. Her chest contracted with almost unendurable grief. She bypassed the fields where her children were whooping and chasing each other around. She clopped across the bridge that spanned the creek and eased her horse up the rise.

Standing on the knoll overlooking those four cleared fields and that rippling stream was a fine, strong cabin. Set on a solid limestone foundation and facing south, the cabin was comprised of two separate buildings roofed in tandem. The cabin on the left was by far the larger, its wide oak door padlocked with one of the brass-and-iron locks David had crafted himself. It explained the mysterious key she'd found among his things.

Sliding down from her horse, Livi rummaged at the bottom of her canvas bag and pulled out the key. She mounted the wide stone steps that ran across the front and fit it into the lock.

The dank mustiness of a closed-up house rose to meet her as the door swung wide. By the slash of sunlight that fell across the rough, planked floor, Livi could see that the inside of the cabin was commodious, slightly longer than it was wide. A head-high limestone fireplace dominated the west end of the room, with andirons and a lug pole already in place. Above the room was a half-open loft, its access ladder set into the wall.

The children swept past where Livi stood frozen in the doorway.

"Is this our house, Mama?" Cissy demanded, her small

voice echoing from the shadowy corners. "Is this where we're going to live?"

"Of course," Tad answered. "There's even a bed."

Indeed there was, not just a bedstead propped up and wedged into the corner, either. It was a tall, freestanding bed frame lovingly crafted of peeled logs and already laced with rope. Nor was the fine bed the only furniture. An oak-slab table with puncheon benches stood just to the right of the fireplace.

Livi moved inside on a tide of overwhelming gratitude and devastating loss. David must have worked so hard to prepare this place for them. He must have been so sure about the future. Her throat tightened and her eyes burned.

"Miz 'Livia, ma'am," Eustace interrupted. "They's a woodpile 'round back. You want me to get a fire goin' to chase off the chill?"

Livi could only nod. She made her way to one of the benches and sat down hard. They were here in Kentucky. Finally. On David's land. And all she felt was tired. It took an effort to move, to breathe.

The children ran out to continue their exploration.

"Don't you go too far, now," Livi heard Violet admonish them in her stead. "We can't have you gettin' lost first thing."

Violet came in with a broom and began to sweep. Eustace bustled past with a load of logs in his arms.

She should stir herself, Livi thought. See to the horses. Unload the packsaddles one last time. She could set her house to rights at last. This beautiful house. This strangely empty house.

She was still sitting on the bench when Eustace approached. The fire was lit and casting warm yellow light on what she suddenly realized was whitewashed walls.

"Oh, David," she breathed. "How hard you tried to make this place like home!"

"Miz 'Livia, ma'am," Eustace offered deferentially. "Miz 'Livia? This paper was on the mantel shelf."

Livi's hands trembled as she opened the folds. A note, she thought. From David.

But instead of her husband's scrawl, this writing was broad and graceful. She recognized it as Reid Campbell's hand.

David—

I have gone off to trade for furs as we discussed. Hope your journey from Virginia was swift and uneventful. Will be back this way once I have run out of things to barter.

Reid

Reid, she thought. Oh, God, Reid! Even here in the house David had built for her, the house that sang of her husband's devotion more clearly than any love song, Reid Campbell had found a way to intrude.

Resentment rose in her. She could not bear to think of him here, within the walls of the cabin David had built. She could not bear to think that Reid would remain part of her life when David was lost.

As long as she lived, Livi would never forget the way Reid had thrown her trunk on the floor that day at the inn, the way he'd pinned her with those cold blue eyes and pronounced her unfit to wed his friend. That memory stirred the fierce, slow-burning anger Reid had always been able to rouse in her. The jolt of antipathy brought her to her feet with a burst of energy she didn't know she had.

She had a house to set to rights and fields to plow. She had a family to care for and animals to tend. Somehow she had managed to bring them to David's house and David's land. Somehow she would make a life for all of them here: for Tad and Cissy, for Violet and Eustace, but most especially for the babe nestled and growing beneath her heart. That baby and this house were David's final gifts to her, and she would treasure each of them to the end of her days.

And no matter when he came or what he said, she'd give Reid Campbell no part of this, no part of what was hers.

Settling the cabin took the rest of the day. Livi knocked down the spans of spiderwebs and washed the walls while Violet swept and scrubbed the floor. Eustace hauled the creels into the house for the women to unpack. They scoured and found places for the buckets, the basins and bowls, the pans and cups and trenchers. They tucked away extra shoes and clothes and bolts of cloth. Then Violet jumped down into the rectangular, stone-lined root cellar concealed beneath the cabin's floorboards. The "turnip hole" served as storage for the cold-weather foodstuffs, and while Livi and Cissy handed down turnips, potatoes, and the last of the carrots, Tad and Eustace ferried sacks of seed corn and meal to the loft. Together they saw to the animals. As the light waned and the birds winged home to their nests, the Talbots and the Hadleys downed a simple meal and dragged themselves to bed.

Weary to the marrow of her bones and secure in the house David had built for her, Livi should have slept as she had not been able to sleep in weeks. Instead she lay awake.

She listened to the hiss of the smoldering fire, to the deep, easy cadence of her children's breathing. She breathed air thick with resinous pine and the lingering drift of the coffee they'd brewed for supper. She stared into the shifting dark, watching the shadows dance against her whitewashed walls. And she tried to tell herself all was well.

That was hard for Livi to believe when restlessness crawled across her skin and hummed in her veins like swarms of bees. She shifted and stirred in her fine new bed. She fought the urge to move, fought the need to escape, fought the raw desolation that bloomed around her heart. For weeks Livi had held tight to her anguish and despair, denied her loneliness and grief. But tonight, in the safety and the silence of David's house, those emotions crushed past the last of her fragile defenses.

As the turmoil rose in her throat, Livi fled the bed she was sharing with her daughter. She crept around Tad's pallet near the fire and took care not to wake the Hadleys in the loft. From habit as much as from need, she caught up her pistol and pulled her cloak off the peg by the door. Without making a sound, she lifted the latch and stole outside.

The moon was high, casting the clearing, the fields, and the woods beyond in shades of indigo and black. The air was chill, the stone steps cold beneath her feet. Wrapping herself in the folds of her cloak, Livi sank down on the top step.

She must be mad to come out here alone, she told herself. She must be mad to eschew the safety of her bed for the dark and empty night. Yet she'd fled the cabin instinctively, needing space for the emotions building inside her. Needing solitude to let them free. Needing her children tucked safely away so she could spare them the sounds of her grief.

"David." Her husband's name worked its way up her throat on a sob. "David."

She was more aware of losing David here, where his dreams were furrowed into every acre of ground, than she would have been any place on earth. He should be walking these fields, welcoming her to this house, filling the clearing with hope and joy and purpose. He should be here to hold her in the dark and spin the fragile span between this crude beginning and the glorious future he had envisioned for all of them.

But David was gone.

Livi curled in upon herself, shrunken by the scope of her despair. Her arms, her legs, her ribs, collapsed around the emptiness inside her. Tears scorched trails down her cheeks. She balled the cloth of her cloak in her fists, wept silently and openmouthed, shaking with spasms of hopelessness.

She was desolate in a way she'd never been before. The grief she'd felt on the trail had been tempered by fear and indecision. What stirred through her now was purer, cleaner, deeper.

David was dead. She could not deny it. She had held him as he breathed his last. She had buried him herself.

For her children's sake. For her own. For the sake of the journey she'd felt compelled to complete, she had tried to deny the truth. She had cloaked herself in David's ambitions, in David's dreams. For a time, she had been able to pretend that if she reached this patch of rich Kentucky earth, David would somehow be with her.

He was not here. There was only this valley, some fields, and a cabin. So little, when she'd fooled herself into expecting so much.

With the final acknowledgment of her husband's death came the realization that she was truly alone. No longer could she draw her warmth from the fire in David's heart, live her life beneath the arc of his embrace, claim his hope as her prerogative. Without David, there was no heat, no shelter, no yearning for tomorrow to come.

Grief twisted her insides, wringing from her pride and vitality and fortitude. It left behind a deeper and more terrifying truth. From the night they'd met, Livi had defined herself by what she'd seen reflected in David's eyes. Without him, she was formless, soulless. Without David to remind her who she was, Livi lost herself. She didn't know what she wanted or who she was. She didn't know where to go to find courage, perseverance, and strength. Realizing that frightened her more than being alone in the wilds, battling Indians, facing her own death.

David's passing had destroyed something way down deep where her own dreams lived. Each one of the sweet, fragile visions she'd harbored of the future had David at the heart of it. She'd drawn serenity and strength from imagining them standing arm in arm, surveying the life they'd built together; imagining them dancing at their children's weddings; imagining them dandling fair-haired grandchildren on their knees.

Nothing she wanted was extraordinary; hers were dreams all wives and mothers shared. Now that David was gone, those dreams became impossible. Now that there was no core to shape her life around, all she had left to cling to was the crumbling ashes of a life that would never be. Now that there was no one to give her substance, the Olivia Talbot whom David had known and loved had ceased to be.

She wept again—for David, for herself, for the destructions of every hope she'd ever cherished. She and David had had so much together: love and passion, unity and friendship, security and hope. They'd taken joy in the good times and somehow weathered the bad. On this cold and lonely night in the wilds of Kentucky, the days they'd shared in Lynchburg seemed suddenly so real to her.

Lynchburg, Virginia
November 1768

Loving David was easy. Making a life with him was the hardest thing Livi had ever done.

They'd been married less than a week when Livi got her first glimpse of David's home, a tired clapboard structure plopped down in the middle of a windblown field. It was then that Livi began to realize the scope of the change in store for her.

"I know the house isn't much," David began, his gaze not quite meeting hers, "but we'll fix it up. I promise you."

Livi nodded, taking note of the crooked chimney, the sagging steps, the barnyard shed that slumped against the south wall of the house. The interior was no more inviting than the outside had been. It was neat enough, but there were no curtains on the windows, no rugs on the floor, no sense that David lived here. The furniture consisted of a bed just barely wide enough for two and a table with one lone chair.

My father's slaves lived more comfortably than this, Livi thought and was instantly overcome with shame at her disloyalty.

"I'm sure the house will be fine," she hastily assured her husband, lying to him for the very first time.

But it wasn't fine. The roof leaked and the chimney smoked. There were mice in the cupboard, and the smell of the animals in the lean-to permeated the house. Dirt sifted between the clapboards and down from the roof, so that no matter how often she wiped the table or swept the floor, a fine layer of grit glazed every surface.

The nights when Livi lay in David's arms, enchanted and petted and cherished, filled her with unimagined joy. The mornings when she awoke alone, the cold and loneliness replaced the magic with boundless despair.

David worked at George Wilkins' blacksmith shop in town three days a week. The demands of the woods and fields and animals that were part of his rented property took up the rest of his time. His long absences left Livi with hours alone and nothing but housework to do. Her mother might well have overseen Livi's lessons in sewing and deportment, might have approved of her daughter learning to read and cipher. She might even have turned a blind eye when Livi sat in on her brother's lessons in Latin and Greek. But Jessica Chesterton hadn't taught Livi the first thing about cooking or cleaning—except that no lady dirtied her hands with such menial tasks.

In David's house there were no servants to do the work; domestic responsibilities fell to Livi herself. She was not taxed overmuch by making the bed, sweeping, and dusting. Cooking, on the other hand, seemed some mysterious alchemy, as complex and impossible as turning lead to gold.

Livi made beans and corn bread for their first supper in her new home. It seemed simple fare, something she could manage by herself. When David returned from the blacksmith shop that evening, he exclaimed over the table as if it were laid with porcelain and silver instead of with wooden cups and

trenchers. They took their places with Livi in the chair and
David balanced on a three-legged stool he'd brought in from
the barn. They bowed their heads for grace, then spooned up
the meal Livi had slaved over most of the afternoon. The beans
clattered onto the plates, hard as pebbles and swimming in a
pale but noxious broth. The corn bread, which was burned
black at the edges, ran raw in the center. The next night she
boiled the potatoes dry and charred the slice of ham she was
frying. The third night she caught the hem of her gown afire.

After each inedible meal, after each domestic disaster, Livi
wept and David took her in his arms. "You'll learn to cook,
Livi," he assured her, kissing away each tear. "All it takes is
a little time and practice. There are some simple things I can
show you that might help . . ."

The next time he went into town, David brought back the
cow Mr. Wilkins had been boarding. Minnie came with lessons on milking, on caring for the milking paraphernalia, and
on making butter.

The association between Livi and the cow did not progress
smoothly. Minnie kicked Livi the first time she tried to milk
her and refused to give her bounty into Livi's hands.

To make things worse, Minnie snapped at Livi whenever
she had the chance.

"Do I look like clover, you miserable bag of bones?" Livi
demanded, rubbing her shoulder after a particularly vicious
chomp.

It took a week for Livi and Minnie to negotiate an uneasy
truce. It was weeks more before Livi could make the butter
"come," though she did take great pride in the first pale,
watery lump she served up at supper.

No one could have expected the daughter of a plantation
owner to easily assume the duties of a sharecropper's wife.
Surely David hadn't. But Livi had.

During their courtship David had introduced Livi to facets
of herself she had never known existed. He had helped her
discover and define her beauty, her capacity for tenderness,
her joy in living. By holding up his love as if it were a mirror,
he had opened a world of possibilities.

Her failures at domesticity in the early days of her marriage
stole that fragile self-confidence and her burgeoning self-
respect. Burning the dinner for the third night in a row, or not

knowing how or where to wash their clothes, chafed at Livi and rubbed her raw. It convinced her she was failing at the single most important task she'd ever undertaken: being David's wife.

When her efforts went awry, Reid Campbell's apparition rose before her to whisper the condemnation he'd voiced the day she'd married David: "Any fool can see you're too pampered, too fragile, too damn weak to be the wife that David needs."

And Livi was coming to believe him.

It was early spring when Campbell himself stopped by on his way west, his packsaddles filled with goods to trade for the Indians' winter furs. He arrived sporting well-worn buckskins and leading three pack horses—more in his element here than he had ever been in her parents' parlor. That fierce, dark face seemed to glow with vitality, excitement, and enthusiasm for his impending journey. Those cold, judgmental eyes gleamed with what could only be unerring insight into Livi's many failings.

Reid wrangled an invitation to stay the night. So he could see for himself how ill-suited she and David were, Livi thought in consternation. To confirm how right he'd been about her prospects as a wife. By some small miracle, the squirrel pie Livi baked for supper was passably tasty, and even the dumplings on the top were golden brown.

There! she wanted to shout when Reid quirked one dark eyebrow in her direction. *I'm learning.* I'm getting better at being David's wife.

Still, she knew the palatable meal was a fluke. For all David's praise and encouragement, Reid saw the truth: that she would never prove herself worthy of David's love.

While Livi washed up after the meal, Reid produced a bottle of fine French brandy he had tucked away, and the two men went out onto the porch to share it. Some trick of the wind blew the door ajar, so that their voices and wisps of David's pipe smoke floated in to her. For a time they talked about David's mother and brothers and sisters, most of whom were still settled on James Campbell's plantation.

"And what do you hear of Livi's family?" David finally asked.

She could hear the hesitation in Reid Campbell's voice. "They're well enough, I suppose."

Elizabeth Grayson

"Well enough?"

"Do you want me to tell you that they've gotten over the shock of Olivia running off to marry you? That they've forgiven her?" Reid paused as if he were shaking his head. "They say that when Arabella returned to the house and told them that Livi had decided to go with us, Richard Chesterton called for the family Bible and blacked out her name. They say her mother saw to burning all her things."

Had her parents really done that? Livi wondered, her knees gone weak. Did they really hate her so?

David cleared his throat before speaking. "I thought that in time they might relent, might come to accept our marriage . . ."

"I wouldn't count on that if I were you," Reid advised. "Richard Chesterton's not a forgiving man."

The two men fell silent for a time. She could hear the gurgle of a bottle, the faint clunk of glass against the edge of a wooden mug. In the house, Livi took up her mending and settled herself by the fire.

"You said you'd come west with me this spring," Reid offered up at last. "You said we'd go together and explore Kentucky."

This was the real purpose of his visit, Livi realized all at once. Reid had come to take David away. With her heart in her throat, she waited for her husband's answer.

"I said I'd think about it."

"The land you want is there, David. Lush and green. So unspoiled and beautiful it makes you want to dissolve yourself in the wind just so you can be part of it." Campbell's voice throbbed, low and compelling. "That land is ours for the taking. We could settle anywhere we want with no one to gainsay our choice."

"Except the Indians."

"You know as well as I do that the tribes will trade for land. They'll sell it as cheaply to us as anyone else."

"If it's theirs to sell."

Livi was well aware that land claims negotiated with the Indian tribes were under dispute all along the Blue Ridge.

Reid was undeterred. "Think about it, David. Where else can you afford to buy land of your own? Where else can you find any that isn't already half played out? You know all you've ever wanted is a few hundred acres to call your own. It's what you've always dreamed about.''

"Yes, well, sometimes a man's dreams change."

"And you've changed yours because you've taken a wife." Livi heard the condemnation in Campbell's tone.

"Aye, I have."

"And you can't leave her."

"I won't leave her," David corrected, and Livi wondered about the expression in her husband's eyes.

"Because she can't be left alone."

"Because I need to be here to provide for her. Because there's a great deal for her to learn." Even put as gently as that, David's words smacked of betrayal. "I can't just hie off into the woods as if I've no responsibilities. I accepted what I'd be giving up when I asked her to be my wife. And I'm especially responsible now that Livi's family has disowned her. I'm all she has."

"I knew she'd be a millstone around your neck," Campbell murmured angrily.

It was true, Livi realized, the acknowledgment snagging in her throat. If she were a stronger, braver, or more capable woman, she could urge David to go with Reid. Her ineffectiveness and inexperience were holding David back. She was preventing him from fulfilling his most cherished hopes and dreams. *Hopes and dreams he hadn't seen fit to share with her.*

Though she blinked furiously to hold them back, tears dripped onto the mound of fabric in her lap, shimmering like molten gold in the firelight. Angrily she stuffed the mending away. If she couldn't perform even this simple task, she might as well go to bed.

In the half-light, Livi slipped out of her bodice, skirts, and stockings and climbed into bed. Outside, the two men's voices rose, booming with shared laughter, blending in years-old camaraderie. Reid knew David far better than she, understood his motives and ideals, his foibles and strengths, his hopes and aspirations. The two men shared a common history, common dreams.

All she could ever be was David's wife. Until now, that had seemed a wondrous endeavor, one that could fill her days and nights to the end of time. Now she wanted more. She wanted to know David as if she dwelled inside his skin, wanted to claim her place in every facet of his life. She wanted to know the man who was her husband every bit as well as Campbell knew him.

Yet in order to protect her, David was holding back. He had stories she would never hear, laughter she would never share, a part of himself he would never let her see. David harbored dreams and hopes and ambitions he would discuss only with Reid. Because she was too dependent and weak. Because he couldn't entrust those dreams and hopes to her.

She pulled the bedcovers over her head to block out the sound of the two men's voices. She hated the warmth and intimacy in the rise and fall of their conversation. She hated the sacrifice that David was making in her behalf. She hated Reid for making her more aware than ever how badly she had failed. But most of all, she hated herself.

Reid rode out at sunrise, leaving behind a man who might well be clinging to his regrets and a woman who was once again uncertain of her place.

"You need to understand about Reid," David began as he and Livi stood together watching Campbell disappear up the road.

I don't want to understand, Livi thought. *Not any more than Reid wants to understand about me.*

But when they returned to the cabin, where their half-eaten breakfast awaited them, David continued, telling Livi about Reid whether she wanted to hear it or not.

"We were born just six days apart—him in the big house at Riverbend and me in a cabin out back. Reid's mother had trouble giving birth, so my ma tended both of us. The first clear memory I have is of Reid, of fighting over a painted wooden rabbit that someone must have given him."

Because David had given her no choice, Livi settled down across the table to listen.

"By the time we could toddle, Reid and I were all but inseparable. We played together every day, roamed through the fields and woods. It wasn't long before he was spending more time in our little cabin than he was at the big house. And after his mother died when we were five, there wasn't anyone who cared enough to come and round him up at the end of the day.

"Two years later, James Campbell married a beautiful young widow, fresh from England. It didn't take her long to convince the master to send away the first wife's get—especially when it was a defiant, half-breed boy who'd hated her on sight."

David winnowed one hand through his already tousled hair. "Reid was only seven when they sent him to school in Charles Town. I remember the morning the carriage pulled away. I cried into my mother's skirts. Reid sat there as if he'd been turned to stone, too proud to cry, too stubborn to admit he was scared to death."

In spite of herself, Livi felt a twinge of sympathy for the frightened child Reid Campbell must have been.

"I don't know what kind of school that was," David went on. "I do know that Reid came home reading Latin and Greek and quoting Scripture. But he also came home with his back scarred from being caned. And once the older boys at the school held him down and painted his face with indigo dye to mark him as a savage."

David looked up, as if seeking in Livi's eyes the compassion he felt for his friend.

"Every time he came back to Riverbend, it took longer and longer for Reid to find his place. As often as not, it was with my family in our cabin out back instead of with his father and stepmother, where he belonged. It was shortly after my father was killed in an accident that Reid got expelled from school for fighting.

"By then Reid's stepmother had whelped two children of her own, and she convinced the master that Reid's presence in the house would somehow corrupt her darlings. It was Reid's grandfather, Andrew McTavish, who suggested he take the boy to live with the Creeks."

"How long was Reid with the Indians?" Livi asked in spite of herself.

"Four years," David answered. "I didn't see him once in all that time. And when he came back, he'd changed. He was fierce and angry and aloof. A man in a way I wasn't yet. It took us some time to find our common ground, and by then he was preparing to leave.

"He was only seventeen, but Reid was determined to make his own way in the world just as his father and grandfather had done, by trading with the Indians. Reid finally convinced James Campbell to give him the stake he needed to set out on his own. But James's wife wanted Reid to relinquish any claim he might eventually have to Riverbend in exchange for the money, and in the end he did.''

"But why would Reid give up his inheritance? Riverbend is one of the richest plantations on the James River."

David shrugged. "Reid doesn't care for the plantation or the riches. He'd rather be off trading with the Indians or exploring land no white man has ever seen."

"But he's been back to Riverbend," Livi observed, thinking of her life-altering meeting with both David and Reid some months before.

"Just as I've been back," David answered. "But never for long. It's a young man's way to leave his father's world and strike out on his own."

Livi reached out and took her husband's hand. In a way, she'd done that, too. She had left her parents' home and a life of luxury to marry the man she loved.

"What I want you to understand, Livi," David said, deliberately seeking her gaze, "is that Reid doesn't have any place to go but here. He doesn't have anyone he can rely on but me. He needs to know he's welcome, and I need to know you accept him."

Livi looked down at their linked hands. She loved David and she wanted to do as he asked. Still, she knew that making peace with Reid was impossible.

"I *will* try," she hedged.

But she could never bring herself to abide a man who made it clear she didn't measure up, that she wasn't worthy of David's love. Nor had she and Reid ever been able to temper their demands for David's time and attention, and the resentment between them grew.

After that first visit to the cabin in Lynchburg, Livi and David's life seemed patterned by Reid's comings and goings. In spring he'd ride west with goods to trade; in early autumn he'd return, his packs filled with furs. And every time that Reid rode in with tales of the rich valleys and endless forests, Livi was terrified that David would pack his belongings and leave. If she were a better wife, it would be enough for him to have a home and her. If she were a more capable and competent helpmate, David would be able to go. If she were a braver and stronger woman, she might be willing to settle beyond the mountains. But how could she let David take her where life would be even more difficult than it was here? She couldn't survive a place where wild animals roamed the forests, where Indians raided and killed, where each day meant facing new hardships, new dangers. She'd had to struggle to learn to cook a meal and milk a cow.

As Livi grew round with their first child, her fears began to recede. This babe would give her a hold on David that neither Reid nor the call of the wilds could break. It gave him a second reason to stay with her.

As fate would have it, Reid was in Lynchburg the night Tad was born. When the midwife escorted David into the bedroom of the modest new house beside the blacksmith's shop, not even Campbell's presence could keep Livi from weeping with elation as she presented David with their son.

"You did well, Livi," he told her, his voice choked with emotion as he took the baby in his arms.

"I think we should call him Thadius," Livi offered, taking fresh joy in the love that flared in her husband's eyes.

"My father would be pleased to have such a namesake," he mused. "Thadius. Tad."

Livi looked beyond her husband into Reid Campbell's sun-darkened countenance. There was jealousy in the depths of his sky-blue eyes—and bitter resignation. David was wholly hers now. Even Reid conceded it.

But life wasn't that simple.

"Don't you understand?" David demanded mere days after Tad was born, mere hours after Reid Campbell had ridden away. "I want that land in Kentucky now more than ever before. We have a son, Livi, a fine, strong boy. I need that land so I can make a life for him, for you, for both of us."

"I'm happy with what we have," she insisted quietly.

David looked past her as if he hadn't heard.

"I want to give my son things I never had—property, a future, something to call his own. This land in Kentucky is my chance to do that. I've never had anything to offer you, Livi. Why won't you let me give you this?"

She turned away, angry that she could not make him see, terrified that he would concoct some crazy plan in spite of her.

Even if they argued for fifty years, she would never change her mind about Kentucky or understand the hold it had on him.

The argument simmered, through three devastating miscarriages and two stillbirths. It smoldered while David's blacksmithing business grew and flourished. It seethed while talk of revolution kindled into war. Reid's periodic visits fanned the flame, but it was not until Campbell rode in early in the spring of 1778 that the argument flared out of control.

With each report of the hostilities in Massachusetts, New York, and Pennsylvania, with each rider who came through with word of Indian atrocities against settlers in the west, David had grown more restless. He believed in independence and wanted to do his part. Now Reid came with the bait to lure David away from Lynchburg. Away from her.

"George Rogers Clark is putting together a company of rangers to fight the British in the west," Campbell blurted out as he stormed into the house, disrupting their supper. "Virginia is offering each man three hundred acres of Kentucky land in exchange for his service."

Livi saw the change in David's face, and knew that she had lost the battle for her husband's allegiance.

"David, I don't think—" Livi began, looking up to where he had risen to greet his friend.

David managed to keep his voice to a reasonable tone. "I'd like to hear Reid out, Livi, before I make my decision. This could offer a wonderful opportunity—"

"Or a chance to get yourself killed!" she shouted and jumped to her feet.

"Goddammit, Livi! Don't you understand this is war we're talking about? We need to drive the British back into the sea. We need to secure the safety of the settlers beyond the mountains. Without the Redcoats to stir them up, those Indians would leave the settlers well enough alone."

Livi had heard this speech before—from the recruiters who'd come to town, in the tavern and outside church, wherever men gathered. She had heard it from David's own lips, but this time was different. This time David was convincing himself to go and fight.

Livi glanced from her husband to Reid. Judging from the light in those ice-blue eyes, Reid knew he'd won.

Hot tears breached the rim of her lashes, tears she refused to let Campbell see her shed. Scooping Tad up, she rushed into the bedroom and slammed the door. While she wept, she could hear David offering Reid something to eat, hear the low, persuasive buzz of Campbell's promises. She realized that leaving the table was a tactical mistake; she'd forfeited any rebuttal she might have made. Not that it would have mattered.

When David came into the bedroom a good while later, Livi was darning socks by the flickering light of a Betty lamp.

"Livi, we need to talk," he began, stepping around the trundle bed where his son lay fast asleep.

She continued to stitch, her head down and her needle dipping. "And why should we bother with that? You've made up your mind what you're going to do."

"Livi, I want you to understand—"

"That you're succumbing to the demands of this fine and glorious cause, to the lure of adventure? Or to the promise of three hundred acres of land in your precious Kentucky?"

"Livi, I have to go. If I believe in liberty, I must stand and fight."

Livi refused to look at him.

"Don't you think it's important for our son to have a better life?" David asked. "Don't you believe in a country with peace and freedom for all?"

"Why have you chosen to go now, when you've been perfectly content—"

She could tell he was straining to be reasonable. "I admit that until now I haven't felt compelled to answer the call."

She looked up at him at last, felt the burn of anger in her cheeks. "No, you haven't felt compelled. Not until Reid Campbell came to entice you, not until you heard that there was land on the frontier being given in exchange for your services."

"And why shouldn't I take the bounty?" he demanded. "Reid and I are the kind of men George Clark is trying to recruit, the kind of men who can rout the British from the outposts in the west. This is how I can serve my country best, and I'll be proud to do my part with our independence at stake."

"And the land means nothing?" she countered. "Adventuring with Reid means nothing?"

"Livi, please." All at once David sounded unspeakably weary. "I'm going to fight because I believe in freedom. I'm going to do it with a man I can trust at my back. Is that so terrible?"

She knew what he was doing was bold and brave and honorable. She knew she should be proud—except that he was leaving her.

Livi crushed the darning in her hands. "How soon will you be going?"

David rubbed the back of his fist across his mouth. "Day after tomorrow. Colonel Clark is having the volunteers assemble at Corn Island in the Ohio River. It will take us more than a week to get there."

In the face of his departure, Livi's resistance crumbled. The hours they had left were far too precious and too few to spend them arguing. "Oh, David!" she cried and flung herself into his arms. "I'm so afraid!"

He wrapped her up so tight she felt all but swallowed by his strength. "Afraid for me? I swear, Livi, I'll be so careful . . ."

"You'd better be," she admonished him. "I couldn't make a life for Tad without you."

"You're more capable than you think."

She didn't believe that, but nestled closer. "Oh, David, hold me. Just hold me. I can't bear it that you're going—"

"Livi. Now, Livi," he whispered into her hair. "It's going to be all right."

He tumbled her backward onto the bed, his arms encircling her, his kiss tasting deep. She rose against him, trembling and eager, willing to let passion silence her doubts and fears for a little while.

Preparations for his leave-taking filled all the next day. There were goods to be gathered, both legal and financial provisions to be made, a boy to hire to see to chores around the house. David put the running of the blacksmith shop into his journeyman's hands and negotiated a monthly stipend for Livi and Tad. As the day progressed, neighbors stopped by to wish David well. Some brought gifts, a pair of knitted woolen socks, a sewing kit, a gleaming pocket telescope.

At dawn on March tenth, 1778, David and Reid Campbell rode west. David left Livi with the taste of his kiss on her mouth and a child in her womb. He left her with responsibilities she felt incapable of discharging and a loneliness that scarred her very soul.

Months passed without so much as a word. Reports filtered back that Clark's troops had captured a town on the east bank of the Mississippi called Kaskaskia and soon took several others. The following February the rangers laid siege to the fort at Vincennes and forced its surrender. She waited for word from her husband, but nothing came.

As time slipped by, Livi began to take an odd sort of comfort in knowing David was with Reid. Campbell would do his best to keep David safe, and if something happened, Reid would have the decency to let her know her husband was dead.

While the men were gone, Livi bore a girl-child and named her Cissy. She wrote both David and her mother about the blessed event. There was no reply from either of them.

Livi had been more than two years alone when David and Reid came thundering back. Livi heard the clatter of hooves coming up the street, the ring of neighbors shouting greetings, the melody of familiar voices in the yard. Brimming with anticipation, she scooped up Cissy in her arms and ran toward the front of the house. Tad brushed past her, shouting and dancing with excitement. She heard David greet his son, his tone different somehow now that the boy was halfway grown.

Livi halted, jittery and breathless, just inside the open door. Did she look all right? she wondered. Had she changed? Shifting Cissy on her hip, Livi slipped off her apron and tidied her hair. When David's footfalls came up the path, she stepped over the threshold to greet her husband—and stopped dead in her tracks.

It was David who had changed. He was a man in a way he'd never been before. He was harder and rougher, leaner and broader. A soldier instead of a husband. He loomed tall above her, all chest and shoulders, buckskin-clad thighs and swaying fringe. The sun had tipped his heavy hair with platinum, pinched fine, sharp lines at the corners of his golden eyes.

"Livi," he said and wrapped her up in his arms as if he were claiming some long-anticipated gift.

He found her mouth with the heat of his and ground the bristle of his beard against her chin. Livi curled her arm around his neck and held on tight. He was home. He was hers. She'd been waiting two long years for this.

Once she and David had recovered themselves, he looked down at the child in her arms. "And whose little girl are you?" he asked, as if there could be any doubt.

"David, I'd like you to meet your daughter, Christine Arabella Talbot," she said. "Tad and I just call her Cissy."

David reached out to stroke his daughter's cheek. She drew back against her mother's shoulder and wrinkled her nose. "My God, Livi, when . . ."

"Just before Christmas the year you left."

"Oh, Livi, I didn't know."

"I wrote, but I wasn't sure how to send you word." They stared at each other in regret, their gazes holding, their hearts in their eyes. In these two years they'd missed so much.

Then slowly, with reluctance, Livi shifted her attention from her husband to the man who was standing by the gate.

"Hello, Reid," she said.

"Good evening, Livi."

"Won't you come on into the house?" In her delight at having David back, she was willing to extend her welcome to Campbell, too. "Both of you must be hungry. I've a slab of bacon I can fry, some corn bread, and some apple pie."

"That sounds good," Reid answered. "Just let me head around back and see to the horses."

"Tad, you go give Reid a hand," David said.

"No, boy, stay with your pa," Campbell demurred. "With him just home, you've got better things to do than curry horses."

Protective as a brood hen with her chicks, Livi shooed her family into the house and shut out the world. Once David sat down at the wide kitchen table, Livi put a mug of just-squeezed cider in his hands and began to cook. Cissy stared at the newcomer with her fist jammed in her mouth, while Tad peppered his pa with questions. Livi had to smile just watching them.

Reid slipped in to join them a short time later. He was barely settled at the end of the bench when Tad draped himself around his shoulders. Cissy soon discovered the clutch of feathers in the band of Reid's black hat and set to plucking them, one by one. David seemed content just to sit back, smoke his pipe, and watch.

It was only after the two men had eaten their fill that they were willing to speak of the months they'd been away. "We reached Kaskaskia on the Mississippi in July, and except for the size of the mosquitoes, the campaigning wasn't bad," David recalled, bouncing Cissy on his knee. "It was Clark's little jaunt to Vincennes in February that tested our mettle some. We covered two hundred and forty miles in eighteen days, through chest-deep swamps, shivering so hard most nights we couldn't sleep, and going without rations for four full days."

"He threatened to boil up my old boots," Reid put in.

"It's only by the grace of God that we didn't lose any of our men, and then once we reached Vincennes, the British at Fort Sackville refused to fight. Colonel Hamilton—"

"The Hair Buyer?" Tad asked, wide-eyed. "The man who paid the Shawnee for settlers' scalps?

"The very same," Reid assured him.

"—took a day" or two to think about surrendering, called Colonel Clark to the fort, and handed over his sword."

Livi spoke up. "We had news of that, but it's a year or more since then."

"You didn't get my letter?" David asked. "I gave it to one of the men who took Hamilton to Williamsburg."

"In all this time I've heard nothing at all."

David reached across and took her hand. "I'm sorry, Livi. I didn't stop to think how it would be for you while I was gone."

"And after Vincennes?" Tad prodded his father. "What happened after Vincennes?

"We stayed on with Colonel—ah—General Clark, he was by then, trying to oversee the country we'd won. We had plans to attack Detroit, but the men and supplies Clark was promised never came. We raided the Indian villages north of the Ohio River where the British still have allies, but it didn't seem to do much good. The tribes were raiding in Kentucky anyway."

"And since our enlistments had long since run out, we came home by way of Williamsburg," Reid put in. "With my father's influence, we managed to get the land grants we'd been promised—and a good deal earlier, I warrant, than most of Virginia's soldiers will."

"So you did get the rights to the land in Kentucky," Livi murmured and felt her elation evaporate like morning dew.

"I've been telling David that if we're wise, we'll head west to Kentucky right away," Campbell said. "We can have our pick of land if we get there first."

Livi could see the viper in Campbell's smile. Abruptly she rose and gathered up their mugs. "Can't we set talk of land grants and Kentucky aside for a bit? My husband hasn't slept one night in his own bed, and already you're hurrying him off again."

That simple exchange drew new battle lines distinct and clear: Reid Campbell and the land in Kentucky on one side and Livi on the other.

"I told Reid I'd have to wait and see to my family and my business before I could do anything about staking a claim," David answered softly.

"Of course, what you choose to do, David, needn't hold Reid back. He can claim his land in Kentucky any time he likes."

Livi turned from the challenge in Campbell's eyes to the sleeping child in David's arms.

"I'll do it, Livi," he told her as he rose to go. "I'll put little Cissy to bed. I haven't had a chance before."

Clearly, their party was breaking up. Tad grumbled as he climbed the ladder to the loft above the kitchen, though the fact that Reid was sleeping up there, too, softened his sense of exile. Livi gave a final wipe to the kitchen table and blew out the candles.

When at last she and David came together in their room, the house had gone quiet. In the candlelit silence, Livi let down her hair. David unbuckled his belt. She loosened the laces at the front of her bodice. He tugged his shirttails free.

They stood there staring.

"It's good to be home," he said, his voice thick.

"It's good to have you here."

The air between them sizzled. It was as if they'd forgotten how this went. Or gotten caught up in remembering.

Livi could barely breathe.

A flush simmered in David's face.

She licked her lips.

He came toward her across the room. His hands were trembling when he raised them to cup her face.

"Livi," he whispered. "Oh, Livi. Livi." He lowered his head and kissed her. The kiss was fragile, delicate—and drew her home.

Her hands scaled the rise of his chest, the bulwark of his shoulders, the thick, strong column of his throat. His flesh was warm beneath her palms, vital and familiar. It reminded her how it felt to be fully alive to sensation, to emotion, how sweet loving a man could be.

She breathed his name.

He carried her to the bed and took her down. She could see the wonder in his face as he bent above her. It was as if this touching and tasting and communion were more than he remembered, more than he had dared dream it would be. He cherished her with the light in his eyes, the stroke of his hands, the depths of his kiss. She melted beneath his touch, opening to him, welcoming him, needing him. She sobbed with elation as their bodies came together.

Loving David had always been easy . . .

"Ma? Where are you, Ma?"

At the sound of Tad's voice, thick with confusion and concern, her memories scuttled away like mice before the lantern light. She left David and their life behind, David and her hope, David and her dreams. She scrubbed the last of her tears from her eyes and took a shaky breath.

"Quiet, Tad," she whispered, hoping he wouldn't hear the tremulousness in her voice. "We don't want to wake the others. I'm sitting out here on the steps."

"What are you doing, Ma?" Tad admonished. "This is dangerous."

"I do have my pistol." She lifted her gun so he could see.

Tad didn't seem willing to accept that as adequate protection in the face of this folly. He scanned the yard, the fields, and the woods before sitting down beside her.

In the pale wash of moonlight, he must have been able to see that she'd been weeping. "Are you all right?" he asked.

"I'm fine," she assured him. "I just needed some time by myself . . ."

Tad looked at her long and hard, a frown marring the

smooth, clean lines of his young face. He was clearly over-whelmed by the scope and complexity of the emotions he saw in her. They were things no twelve-year-old should have to see, facets of an adult's grief—disillusionment, anger, re-morse. Livi wished that she had been successful in sparing him her feelings when he'd lost as much as she.

Instead of turning away, Tad slung an arm around her shoul-ders. It was a gesture he hadn't quite mastered yet. He tangled clumsy fingers in her hair, had to adjust the span between wrist and elbow twice before he got it right.

As he fumbled, Livi's throat burned with a fresh assault of tears. She loved Tad's protectiveness. She loved his tender-ness, his sense of responsibility, yet no mother should ask so much of her child.

But she did. She took comfort in the warmth of him beside her, in the drape of his arm across her back.

They sat together in the night, looking out across David's fields. Fields that to Livi's eyes seemed black and barren in the cool spring night.

"This is what Pa wanted, isn't it, Ma?" Tad finally whis-pered, his voice tinged with awe. "To be here. To be part of this."

From the glow in his eyes, from the determination in his face, she could see that Tad understood—this place, this land, this dream—though Livi herself did not. It was Reid's part of David that wanted this, the part she'd never had, the part she'd never been able to comprehend.

"Yes," she answered, around the barb of disappointment lodged in her throat. "Yes, Tad, I think it is."

～ 10 ～

S tanding on the steps of the cabin in the cool, clear dawn,
Livi looked out across her land and realized all they had
to do. Somehow she hadn't grasped the scope of it before. She
hadn't foreseen the length and breadth of these cleared fields
and what it would take to get them planted. She hadn't fath-
omed the weeks and months of grinding work that lay between
the first slice of a farmer's plow and a successful harvest. She
hadn't imagined how alone they'd be—five little people in the
towering woods. Still, she knew they had to make their way.
They didn't have another choice.

Over the years Livi had cursed and resented and hated this
land. It had been the basis for David's restlessness, the source
of her fear. It had filled his head with dreams when Livi was
his reality.

All along she'd believed that when she reached the land
beyond the mountains, there would be a watershed—either
fulfillment of David's promises or vindication of her doubts.
Instead this far Kentucky was beautiful and terrifying, dangerous and life-affirming. But this was no longer David's Kentucky. It was hers—and it was up to Livi to make a life for
her family as best she could.

One by one, the others came to join her in the cabin doorway: Tad, his boyish enthusiasm dimmed by the task at hand;
Cissy, needing to be coddled and held; Eustace and Violet,
only beginning to grasp how high the price of freedom was.

They stood there in wonder and in fear.

"I think we need to start plowing today," Livi said in a very small voice, then glanced at Eustace for reassurance. "We're weeks behind the schedule David set. The corn should be sown and sprouting by now."

To David's credit, they'd come amply prepared for the task at hand. Once all of them had downed a hasty meal, Eustace and Tad hitched their strongest horse to the "jump and coulter" plow and began their work.

The plow was heavy and specially designed for breaking new ground. As they fought their way across the first of the fields, Tad urged the horse forward while Eustace drove the plow's blade deep into the soil, using his weight and all of his strength to slice through the web of tree roots that lay just below the surface. Even in the coolness of the morning air, they were both breathless and running with sweat in a matter of minutes.

Behind them, Livi and Violet hacked at the earth with hoes. Cissy dragged the roots they loosened into a pile at the edge of the field, to be chopped and burned another day. They worked their way around some of the larger stumps and dug up most of the smaller ones. They had barely finished that first field as darkness fell. In the half-light, they stumbled back to the cabin, ate a cold supper, and went to bed.

The next day was much like the first, as was the day after and the day after that. When Livi and Eustace agreed that the soil in each of the fields was sufficiently broken, they changed to the shovel plow and turned the earth for cultivation.

Now the women walked the furrows with bags of seed corn, digging into the humps between them with a long pointed sticks and dropping precious seed into each of the holes. It took them nearly a fortnight to complete the process: days sweltering in the sun and nights when their sore, knotted muscles robbed them of their rest. They laid in a patch of turnips at the edge of one of the fields, planted watermelons and pumpkins in the midst of another. Nature seemed to smile on their endeavors. A warm, soaking rain washed through the Kentucky hills the night they completed the planting.

Livi managed to bridle her curiosity about the other half of the house on the far side of the breezeway until the crops were in. Once they were, she set her sights on opening it. Perhaps, she reasoned, it was no more than an empty storeroom, locked to keep the varmints out. What seemed more likely was that David had laid in a cache of supplies. Until now Livi had done well enough with what they'd brought, but as the summer advanced, their stores might well run thin.

Livi and Eustace came together to consult on the question of the padlocked door one warm and rainy morning shortly after the corn had begun to sprout. They immediately established that the key David had left didn't work, and Eustace pried at the lock with a crowbar. The metal rasped and groaned but refused to give.

"David did pride himself on the strength of those locks," Livi said as Eustace groaned and rasped a bit himself.

"He sure did build 'em good, Miz 'Livia," the black man observed, blotting his brow on the back of his arm. He applied the same tactics to the door itself as soon as he recovered himself. Stout as it was, it didn't budge, either.

"Well, Eustace," Livi said when it was clear that the right side of the cabin was locked up tight, "there must be a station around here somewhere. Once we have a chance, we'll see about having a locksmith look at this."

"Maybe we can fin' someone who's got a file," Eustace offered, "though cuttin' through a hasp as thick as that will take a good long time."

They turned their energies to staking out a plot for the kitchen garden. Working together, Livi and Violet planted beans and squash, cabbage and potatoes, onions and radishes. Livi spiced the vegetables with a scattering of herbs and dug pennyroyal in around the foundation of the house to keep out fleas.

While the women worked, Eustace and Tad built a pen for the pigs, a coop for the chickens. A corral for the cow and the horses came next.

As they turned their attention to other projects, the plantings flourished. Green tufts poked up through the ruddy earth, sprouting with a vigor unknown in the played-out fields of Virginia's James River plantations. The women kept after the weeds on hands and knees or with freshly sharpened hoes. Eustace cut down one of the handles so Cissy could help.

The need for a barn loomed before them, a project far beyond their capacities. If they meant to build one, Livi would need to solicit help. David had mentioned that there were settlements in the area, but she couldn't bring herself to ride out alone to look for them. As odd as it seemed, she found this valley a small, inviolate world she wasn't eager to breach.

April slid seamlessly into May. The corn grew taller. Livi rounded out a little. Tad and Eustace worked together as if they could read each other's minds. Violet took both of the Talbot females under her wing, clucking gruffly over Livi and petting Cissy as if she were the most clever child on God's green earth.

David would be pleased, Livi found herself thinking one day as she squatted in the dirt, weeding the kitchen garden. She could hear the torrent of the wind spill through trees along the ridge, watch shadows scamper across the yard. She could feather the rich, rusty earth beneath her hands and feel satisfaction. This bit of Kentucky wasn't what she'd wanted, it wasn't all it would have been if David had lived, but she'd done her best.

She sensed a stroke of warmth along her back, caught the drift of what smelled like pipe smoke in the wind. And for one precious moment, Livi felt as if David were smiling down on her.

❧ 11 ❧

The man came out of the forest at midday. The first
    stranger Livi had seen since they'd been at the cabin.
The first intruder.

Livi spotted him from the doorway, noticing instantly how
tall he was, how broad. He was leading his horse and three
plodding mules across the track between the fields of rustling
corn, striding along as if he owned them. She could not see
his face for the distance and for the shadow cast by his wide-
brimmed hat, but a flare of impending menace fired up in the
pit of her belly.

Trusting her instincts, Livi stepped back into the cabin and
snatched the pistol from the mantel, taking time to check its
load. She moved back to the door and watched him approach,
glad that Eustace, Violet, and the children were away from
the house. They'd all gone to pick the wild strawberries on
the far side of the ridge and were well out of harm's way if
she had to defend herself.

As the man crossed the bridge, she noticed the spill of thick
black hair against his shoulders, picked out the familiar lines
of his fierce countenance, recognized his lithe, almost savage
movements. Even as far away as that, she could feel the blaze
of his nascent energy.

Reid Campbell crested the rise and stopped at the bottom
of the steps: a tall man, rangy and long-boned; a hard man,
his face weathered down to its elements. Even in dress he
flaunted the two worlds that had spawned him. He wore a

white man's trousers and boots, an Indian leather shirt that was fringed and heavily quilled. He sported a medicine bag on a thong around his neck and a clutch of eagle feathers in the band of his hat.

While they stood there, Reid had been studying Livi nearly as intently as she had been studying him.

"Hello, Livi," he finally greeted her, one corner of his mouth cocked up in a leer of pure derision. "So you did make the trip, pregnant and all. I wasn't sure you had the gumption. Where can I find David?"

Anger ripped up Livi's spine—anger that Reid Campbell could so easily dismiss her struggle to reach Kentucky, anger that Reid was here when David was not. The anger made her thoughtless, made her cruel.

"David is dead," she declared. She meant the words to shock Reid, to make him feel her pain.

She saw the corners of his mouth constrict, saw something flicker at the backs of his eyes.

"How did it happen?"

Outrage swept in behind her anger. "Is that all you have to say? Is that all you care about?"

Reid's eyebrows rose, conveying both surprise at her fury and frigid detachment.

"How did it happen?" he asked again.

Could Reid Campbell possibly be so unaffected by word of David's death? Livi wondered, searching his face for some shading of grief. How could he have demanded so much of her husband over the years and feel nothing at all?

"He was killed on the trail," she answered, fighting down the memory of digging David's grave, of wrapping him in her daisy quilt and lowering him into the earth.

"How?"

She refused to recall more than he had made her remember already.

"Indians," was all she said.

If Reid wanted more than that from her, he was going to have to crawl down her throat and pull the words out, one by one.

Instead of pursuing the matter, Reid dropped his horse's reins and went to the door of the locked-up cabin.

"What is it you're doing there?" she demanded, shifting

her grip on the pistol and coming out onto the steps.

He took a key from the medicine bag around his neck, unlocked the padlock, and pushed the portal wide. "That seems obvious, doesn't it? I'm unlocking my half of the house."

His half of the house?

For an instant Livi couldn't get her breath. David had built this house for *her*. He hadn't said anything about sharing their cabin with Reid.

But then, David wouldn't have told her—not until they had arrived, not until it was too late for her to object. Tears scoured her eyelids and she blinked them back. She wanted to shout and curse and throw things. When they met in the Hereafter, David was going to have to answer for this.

"I'd rather share this house with the devil himself!" she spit at Reid.

"I've heard the devil's busy elsewhere," he answered and began methodically stripping bundles of furs from the mules' backs and chucking them onto the floor of his cabin.

"Are both Tad and Cissy all right?" he asked, never pausing in his work.

"They lost their father. They saw him killed before their eyes."

Pure perversity made her want to wring a response from this unfeeling man. David deserved Reid's regret, Reid's grief. He had earned it a hundred times over in the long years of their friendship. For herself, Livi wanted the satisfaction of seeing sorrow in Reid's dark face.

"I was inquiring as to whether they survived the attack," he clarified.

"They're here with me in Kentucky."

With the packs and his saddle stashed in his side of the house, Reid finally turned to look at her. His eyes were glacial, that pale, translucent blue that always made Livi think of a fast-flowing stream beneath a sheen of ice.

"You seem to have come through everything—intact." His words were more accusation than observation.

Livi stood her ground and glared at him. She didn't care what he thought or said. This was her house, these were her newly planted fields, and she was not about to be intimidated by Campbell's presence. If he resented her being here, so be it. She resented him, too.

Reid said nothing more, only bent and picked up his rifle. "I'll tie up the animals out back and go shoot some game for supper. With David gone, you probably haven't had fresh meat for quite some time."

She wanted to tell him that Tad had been providing for them very well, that Eustace was better at barking squirrels than anyone she'd ever seen. But more than putting Reid Campbell in his place, she wanted him out of her sight.

With antagonism bubbling behind her sternum, Livi watched Reid feed and water his animals. She watched as he hefted his rifle and turned away. She didn't loosen her grip on the pistol or let out her breath until he'd stalked off into the hills again.

Reid blundered across the creek and up the hill. He scrambled over the boulders in his path and scratched for purchase on the grassy slope. He climbed until he was gasping for breath, until his heart was thundering in his ears.

Jesus, God! David was dead!

He looked back into the valley below. Back to the cabin he and David had built with their own hands. Back to the cabin Livi Talbot had quite obviously taken for her own.

Goddamn the woman, anyway.

How could she have broken the news of David's death to him that way? So coldly. So calmly. With venom in her eyes. She might just as well have blasted a hole clear through him with that pistol she'd been fondling. She might just as well have reached right in and torn out a piece of his heart.

David had been killed. Solid, rock-steady David. Strong, dependable David. David, who was more like a brother to him than any of his father's other sons.

Reid could scarcely take it in.

How could this have happened? On the trail that Reid had traveled a score of times. At a time when David had finally gained the land and security he'd been seeking all his life.

There was no mistake. The desolation in Livi's eyes, the anger and the blame, were real. Reid knew she had not lied to him.

He turned toward the top of the rise and kept on moving. Crashing through the underbrush. Beating back the bushes. Fighting his way through thickets and down ravines.

Grief pressed up the back of his throat, and he did his best to outrun it. His eyes stung and his chest ached, but Reid pressed on. He drove himself forward, climbing the spine of each hill, fighting instinctively upward.

The sun hung low in a hazy sky when he hauled himself the last few yards to the rocky outcropping at the top of a distant ridge. The land fell away around him under an ocean of shifting leaves. He could see miles of the land that David loved, from the mountains to the south to the rippled hills to the north and west.

Reid stood there panting, his lungs wrung raw, his muscles burning. His Indian heritage had brought him to this mountaintop to mourn a man who had been so much more than a friend. Here Reid would rage and weep for David. Here he would curse the men who had taken David Talbot's life and vow revenge. It was the Creek way. He understood it now. He understood it in a way he never had when the Panther clan killed his uncle in his stead all those years before.

Slowly he lowered his rifle, powder horn, and shot bag to the slight hollow in the top of the boulder beneath him. He flung away his feathered hat and tore off his shirt. He straightened joint by joint, locking his knees and hips, lifting his chest and shoulders. He sucked in a long, deep breath and raised his head.

"*David!*" he howled at the endless sky, tortured, anguished, as if he could call his friend's spirit back from the grave. "David! David!"

Echoes wailed back at him as the sun sank low. They blended with his cries, wove in circles through his head as the sunset dimmed.

At length, Reid staggered to his knees. His chest heaved; his throat burned raw from shouting. His hands were trembling. Yet with unerring precision, he took his knife from its sheath and rested the point at the base of his throat. He drew it slowly down along the midline of his body. Warmth welled up from the whisper-thin line. It gathered and pearled, deep, rich crimson in the fading light. He scribed a second line diagonally from right to left and a third from left to right. Shivering, Reid lay down on the rock to bleed.

The boulder was smooth against his back, cold in the gathering veils of night. The sky drifted above him, black overhung with gray, shifting and circling. Stars picked their way through the gauze of clouds. Sparks of ice, cinders of some cold and ancient fire.

Memories crept out of the dark. Visions of David Talbot flooded Reid's senses: the childish David, laughing when he'd been thrown from the back of James Campbell's stallion; David standing alone at the end of the plantation drive, crying welcome when Reid returned from the hellish school in Charles Town. He saw that same David uneasy and confused by the change in Reid after his years with the Creeks.

Since boyhood they'd been joined, working, playing, fighting, dreaming. Reid closed his eyes to shield himself, but the memories dwelled in his head and in his heart. They filled him and taunted him and tortured him. Now David existed only in his mind, only as part of the cosmos, only as part of the past.

As his blood seeped into the rock beneath him, Reid's soul drained and emptied, leaving a sparse, bitter residue of grief and regret. He came to his feet slowly, his head reeling, his body quivering. He bent to retrieve his gun, powder horn, and bag of shot. Raising his voice in the funeral chant he'd learned so long ago, Reid lifted his rifle and fired east into the night. Still humming, he reloaded and fired once to the north, once to the south, and once to the west.

Standing tall, he addressed the sky: "This is to herald the arrival of the soul of my brother, David Talbot. He is not a Creek, but his heart is pure. May he find peace in the World Beyond."

Alone on the rocky crest of a hill, Reid mourned his friend, his brother, his single tenuous link to the world beyond himself. As the moon rose, chasing the clouds to the west, Reid savored his memories of David Talbot and somehow managed to say farewell.

The children gave Livi ample warning of Campbell's approach. "Reid! Reid!" they cried, their voices rising in delight and welcome.

Livi glanced out the door into the bright morning sun just in time to see Campbell scoop up her daughter in his arms, to see Cissy press her fair, smooth cheek to his. Tad left off stacking the wood that Eustace was splitting and ran toward him, too.

"Ma said you came in yesterday," he greeted Reid, capering along beside him like a puppy eager for a scratch behind the ears. "Where did you go off to? We expected you back last night."

"I had some things I had to do," the big man answered. "And I told your mama I'd get us something good for dinner." A brace of rabbits dangled from a thong at his wrist.

"I've been getting some rabbits myself," Tad burst out. "With snares, mostly. But on the trail I killed a deer!"

"That's damn good, boy," Reid acknowledged. "Your pa would be proud."

Tad ducked his head. "That's what Ma said."

It was the only thing she and Reid were ever likely to agree on, Livi thought. She heard Campbell approach the door and renewed her efforts chopping the greens Violet had picked in the woods.

At least he had the courtesy to knock. "I brought those rabbits I promised you," he said.

"I expected them for dinner last night," she admonished, never looking up.

"Well, you always have accused me of being undependable."

"It's all right about dinner," Cissy put in. "We had wild strawberries instead. Violet and Eustace took us to pick them yesterday. They were very sweet."

Putting Cissy down and depositing the rabbits in the bucket on the hearth, Reid settled himself on the bench at the far side of the table, where Livi was working. Near as he was to her, the prickly warmth of his vitality danced across her cheeks and chest.

He cast a glance in Violet's direction. "I didn't think David held with owning slaves," he observed quietly.

Livi slowed her chopping and chose her words with care. "Violet and Eustace aren't slaves; they're my hired hands. I didn't think I could handle this place all by myself, and they agreed to work for me."

Just to prove her point, she made introductions. "This is Mr. Campbell, Violet. It seems he's just become our—um—neighbor. Reid, this is Violet Mae Hadley."

Violet looked up from where she was weaving baskets and skewered Reid with a single look.

toward the door. "Come on, Cissy. You can help me stack that wood now, if you want."

Livi watched her children go, telling herself that Tad was wrong about needing Reid's help. They'd been doing just fine. The crops were in and flourishing. Eustace and Violet had been doing more than their share. She couldn't think of a reason in the world to turn to Reid.

"You gots powerful feelin's for that man," Violet observed, coming up beside her.

"That I do," Livi admitted. "And with good reason. If it weren't for him, we'd still be back in Lynchburg. If it weren't for him, David would be alive today."

"He look like he know that, too. Look like he's takin' Marse David's death as hard as you."

"Nonsense, Violet. He didn't even flinch when I told him David was dead."

It surprised Livi to realize she'd wanted Reid to mourn David as deeply as she. She needed someone who understood the depth of her loss, who would share her pain and bewilderment.

Beside her, Violet shrugged. "Maybe he didn't say nothin', Miz 'Livia, but you look at Mr. Campbell up close. He's feelin' bad. An' your boy's right. We could use his help."

Having expressed far more of her opinion than Livi cared to hear, Violet picked up her pan of splints and the half-finished basket and went out into the yard.

Livi didn't have long to wonder what Reid wanted to discuss. He was back in a matter of minutes. While he was gone he'd discarded the filthy buckskin shirt for one of tow and tied back his hair with a leather thong. He looked more Campbell than Creek in this attire, more civilized than savage, except for the bit of tattoo peeking out from beneath his sleeve.

Still, apprehension simmered in the pit of her belly as she swept the greens into a pot of salted water to let them soak. She cast a glance toward where Reid was resuming his seat at the end of the bench. Maybe what Violet said was true. He did look haggard under his tan. The dark shadows beneath his eyes made it seem as if he hadn't slept.

But if those observations roused any softer emotions in her, Reid's first words obliterated any concern she might have felt. "I've given this a good deal of thought, Livi, and I've decided that it's best if you and the children leave Kentucky.''

"What?" Livi fought to catch her breath.

"Virginia's where you and the children belong," he went on, his forearms braced against the tabletop. "Whenever it's safe for you to travel, I'll be happy to take you back. You can find another house in Lynchburg and resume the life you've left behind. I'm sure that would be best for everyone."

Livi stared at him, anger rattling through her like artillery fire.

"Life here in Kentucky is hard, Livi," he continued, "harder than you can possibly know. There's land to clear and fields to plow, homesteads to build, expand, and defend. There's constant danger and very little help. No woman alone could do all that."

No one knew the truth of that better than Livi. Every day since they'd left Lynchburg had been a fight. Every day since they'd been at the cabin had taxed her strength. She and the children and the Hadleys had struggled to get those damned fields plowed. They'd worked to get them planted. They'd hoed the weeds and prayed for rain.

She'd battled this land with nothing more than her own finite strength and gritty determination. She'd done it with the help of others who understood the cost as well as she. Now Reid wanted her to simply give up and go away.

She might hate this land. She might yearn for safety and security and an easier life, but she could not leave this homestead. Not when the seeds she had planted with her own hands were growing. Not with a promise of seeing a fine harvest in the fall. She'd worked too hard, invested too much, to let Reid Campbell drive her off.

"The only thing you and I have ever agreed on, Livi," he went on, taking her silence for acquiescence, "is that you don't belong in the wilds. You're a planter's daughter, used to genteel surroundings, to having people do for you. You're not brave enough or strong enough to make a life for yourself and the children here. And you've got that baby to think about. The sooner you pack up and leave, the better for everyone."

Campbell was stating his case with a clarity even an imbecile could understand. Every word he said was true. A month before, she would have agreed with him.

She did not agree with him now.

"What gives *you* the right, Reid Campbell, to dictate where my children and I should go and what we should do? Why are you undermining decisions I've already made?"

Reid blinked, as if resistance were the last thing on earth he had expected from her.

"I'm only thinking about what's best," he fumbled. "I'm only doing what David would want—"

"What David would want?" she mocked him. "You never gave a damn about what David wanted. All you cared about was luring him here. All you cared about was defeating me. Now David's dead because of this land, because of this dream, because of you! And it seems a little late for you to have reservations—"

Reid shoved to his feet, a white line etched around his mouth. "I had nothing to do with David's death!"

"Oh, but you did! For as long as I can remember, Reid Campbell, you've come to us with tales of this wonderful place beyond the mountains, this eden of rich, new land all but free for the taking. You enticed David until the word 'Kentucky' became a promise of a better life, a prayer that only moving west could answer."

"It wasn't me or my tales that brought David here. He wanted this land for himself, for the children—*and especially for you.*"

Livi recoiled as cold sluiced through her. "He never wanted it for me. David knew exactly how I felt about Kentucky."

"He may have known," Reid answered, "but after marrying so high above his station, after making you choose between your family and him, David needed to prove himself. Out here he had a chance to do that, to make his fortune, to build his empire. Out here he had a chance to show everyone who shook their heads when you married him that he was worthy of a wife from such a *fine* Virginia family."

Oh, please, God! Livi prayed silently. *Don't let David have done this for me!*

Yet Reid's allegation held a savage sting of truth. She lunged at him in spite of it.

He caught her flailing hands and easily bound her to his chest. Livi twisted against him, panting, tears suddenly coursing down her face.

If they'd been anything but the most bitter adversaries, Reid might have wrapped her in his arms and offered comfort. If they'd been anything but staunchest foes, Livi might have curled against him and shared her grief. Old jealousies and the new accusation prevented them from doing that. Reid held her still until her tension drained away.

When at last he loosened his hold on her, Livi staggered to the bench and sat down hard. She knew there was no sense assessing blame. The David they loved was dead, and neither one of them could change that.

Though it made perfect sense to accede to Reid's urging and go home, Livi knew she could not leave. Not when this was all David had ever wanted. Not when he had bought this land with something so dear as his life.

"Well, then, Reid," she finally said, her voice both angry and cuttingly prim, "I thank you so much for your concern, but the children and I won't be going back to Virginia. We're staying on here. David left this land to us, and since it's ours—"

"Well, no, Livi," Reid interrupted, an expression she couldn't quite fathom on his face. "Strictly speaking, the land isn't yours."

Livi's world went dim around the edges. "What do you mean?"

"When David came to Kentucky last fall to stake his claim, I came with him. We decided to pool our acreage so there would be six hundred acres instead of three. We also made an agreement."

"What kind of an agreement?"

"We agreed that if one of us should die—or fail to come back from the wilds—the land would go to the remaining partner."

It took a moment for the import of what he was saying to sink in—that if David was dead, the land, *all the land*, belonged to Reid.

"I don't believe you," Livi whispered.

"I thought you might not." Campbell withdrew a folded paper from inside his shirt and extended it toward her.

As she read, phrases danced before her eyes. "In the event of one of the partner's death or his unexplained absence for a period of two years . . . the land surrounding Wilcox Creek extending on the north . . . shall duly fall into the possession of the remaining partner . . .'' The paper was signed by both David and Reid and witnessed by two men whose names she did not recognize.

Oh, David, what have you done? she wanted to wail, holding the page with trembling hands. *After all we've suffered, the land's not mine? After everything, you gave Reid Campbell a way to take it back?*

Yet the agreement made sense. Reid's expeditions into the wilderness for months at a time were perilous. If bears or injuries didn't get him, the Indians might. This agreement had been a way to protect David and his holdings. That Reid should use it against her now was a travesty of everything her husband must have intended this agreement to be.

Renewed anger nipped hot color into Livi's cheeks. She refused to let Reid Campbell take this away from her.

''And do you mean to evict us?''

''You don't belong here,'' he told her again.

''It's more that you don't want us here.''

A dull red flush crept up his neck. ''You can't survive alone in Kentucky. By trying to do that, Livi, you risk the children's lives as well as your own. I can't stand idly by and let you do that. If you think I won't enforce what this paper says—''

She didn't care what the paper said.

''Oh, I have no doubt you'll try to enforce it, but all it says is that you own the land. You can't take the crops I planted. They belong to me. You can't take the house that David built. That's mine, too. Consider me a sharecropper, if you like, but I'm staying. I'll be happy to pay you a stipend when our crops come in.''

''I don't want a stipend, goddammit.''

''Very well, Reid,'' she answered as reasonably as she could. ''We'll do this however you say, but I'm not moving from here until the crops we planted are harvested.''

''Christ Almighty, woman!'' he shouted. ''Can't you see that leaving is what's best?''

''And tell me, Reid, what will we live on if we go? The crops out there are my only asset.''

''For God's sake, Livi, I'll give you money—''

''Crossing the mountains is difficult at any time,'' she continued. ''Do you want me to go now and risk miscarrying David's child? Shall we leave as soon as I give birth?''

He glared at her from the far end of the bench.

Remembering belatedly what Tad had said, Livi softened her tone. "Please, Reid, try to understand. We've lost so much already, I can't let you take this, too. Once the crops are harvested, we can discuss it again. But for now—"

"Jesus, Livi!" Reid thundered. "I don't want you here!"

The truth at last.

"Well, I don't want you here, either," she shouted back. "Not on this land. Not in this house. And since David built at least this side of the cabin for me, I think I have the right to ask you to leave it!"

"Fine," Campbell muttered as he thrust himself to his feet. "Fine. But this isn't over, Livi. As long as you're on this land, it will never be over. And what are you going to tell the Hadleys now that you've got no land to pay them with?"

"You leave the Hadleys to me. Now get out of my house!"

Livi couldn't think when she'd gotten more satisfaction than she did from slamming the door behind him.

✦ 12 ✦

"**Y**ou sure this is where you saw those turkeys roost last night?" Tad whispered to Reid as he peered toward the dark stand of trees at the edge of the field.

"Just try that call," Reid insisted under his breath, "and see if I'm right."

Between them and their quarry lay a meadow thick with buttercups, cornflowers, and Queen Anne's lace. Each blossom seemed to glow in the rising sun, fierce blots of color spangled with dew. Both man and boy were hunkered low in the lee of a fallen tree, their guns primed and loaded at their sides.

With a skeptical sniff, Tad took a triangular piece of slate and a chip of wood from his trouser pocket. By rubbing the wood across the stone, he produced a loud *gobber-ruckk,* remarkably like a turkey's call. The two of them held their breath and waited. Reid nodded and Tad made the call come again.

This time a large tom answered, flapping out of the trees.

Reid grinned and poked the boy.

The bird gawked forward, his blue head iridescent in the dawn, his orange wattle quivering. Another turkey followed his lead. Two more came out of the trees. While Reid and Tad watched, better than a dozen of the ungainly birds flew and hopped and wobbled out of the woods. There were adults and a few pale pullets, looking vulnerable and naked without their full growth of feathers. The turkeys chattered among themselves, complaining and gossiping, oblivious of the danger that lurked mere yards away. They bobbed and scratched through the grass, looking for breakfast.

"Give us both time to sight before you fire," Campbell warned softly, picking up his gun. When Tad was ready, Reid whispered, "Now."

The rifles cracked simultaneously, shattering the morning quiet. Squawking and screaming, the flock of turkeys flapped back into the woods. Two of their number lay flailing in the grass. Tad and Reid reloaded as they ran to claim them.

Tad had just finished cleaning his tom when Reid loomed over him. "Good shooting, boy," he said.

"Pa let me practice when we were away from the house."

"Your ma think you were too young to handle guns?" he asked as they hefted the birds and turned in the direction of the cabin.

Tad shrugged. "She was pleased enough that I knew how to shoot once we were on the trail."

Tad's comment gave Reid the perfect opportunity to ask about the Talbots' journey to Kentucky. He was avidly curious about the trip, desperate to learn how David had died, and concerned about the medicine bag he'd entrusted to David's care. With difficulty Reid held his peace. Questioning the boy might stir up memories best forgotten, and he refused to risk hurting Tad.

Creek honor demanded that Reid avenge his old friend's death. His grief and bitterness drove him, too. David's killers would pay for what they'd done. But without learning more about the men who'd attacked the Talbots' camp, Reid didn't stand a chance of tracking them down.

Livi was the one who could tell him what he needed to know, but Livi wasn't talking—at least to him. She hadn't cast so much as a glance in his direction since she'd ordered him out of her cabin four days ago.

"If Pa and old Rusty were here," Tad said wistfully as they tramped the faint trail through the woods, "it would seem like things were right again."

Reid knew what Tad meant. Because a boy learned by doing, David had let Tad tag along when they'd hunted the woods around Lynchburg. Reid remembered the cool, crisp mornings spent in the hills, the easy camaraderie, the hound snuffling through the underbrush, scaring up birds.

"What happened to Rusty?" he asked.

"He died last fall while you and Pa were here."

"Then we need to get you a pup," Reid murmured, thinking aloud. "It's good to have a dog out here. They set off howling if there are Indians around."

"We haven't seen any Indians since we reached the cabin."

Reid gave a dubious snort. "They could pass within a stone's throw of your place and you'd never know. Maybe I'll ride on over to Logan's Station and see if Ben Logan's bitch has had a litter recently."

Tad perked up. "Logan's Station? How far is that?"

"Six or seven miles, maybe. Whitley's Station is closer, but not as big. You mean your ma hasn't searched out the settlements yet?"

Tad shrugged again. "We've been busy planting and all, though Ma's been wanting to meet some people out this way. She's got her heart set on a barn, and she knows she's going to need help to build it."

A barn? Reid thought, struggling to reconcile the idea that the bit of fluff and lace David had married could ever want something so mundane and practical. But then, the fact that Livi had managed to get the fields plowed and planted hinted at a side of her that Reid had never seen. As much as it chafed at him to have her and the children underfoot, he supposed she'd earned the right to stay until the crops were harvested, until her investment in time and effort was paid in full. Besides, once he'd managed to nail Livi down and make her tell him about the men who'd killed David, he'd be heading out.

"All of us could ride over there with you," Tad proposed suddenly, breaking the thick silence.

"What?"

"Ride over to Logan's Station."

"To Logan's Station?" Reid's thoughts had been tangled up in avoiding Livi and the children. The very last thing in the world he wanted was their escort. "Now, Tad," he began, "I don't think . . ."

Just then they topped the ridge behind the cabin. On the flat below, Livi was heading back to the house. She strode along with her back straight and her red braid swaying, a brimming bucket in one hand and her milking stool in the other.

This was not the woman he'd known in Virginia, Reid thought fleetingly. Livi had changed.

Before Campbell could realize what Tad was about, the boy took off down the path to the cabin. "Ma!" he shouted as he ran. "Ma! We got two big turkeys for supper. And guess what, Ma? Reid's taking us over to Logan's Station to get a dog!"

Livi refused to be grateful. She would have bucked up her courage and gone looking for neighbors eventually, or they'd have found her. She would have made her way to Logan's Station on her own. She hadn't needed Reid Campbell's help.

Nor was he a willing guide. "I'm only going to Logan's Station to see about transporting my furs to Virginia," he warned when he found Tad and Livi saddled up and waiting to accompany him. "I won't be there more than a hour. It's hardly worth the trip."

"We'll be there long enough to see about getting a dog, won't we?" Tad asked. "This morning you said—"

"I know what I said," Reid snapped. "We'll get you a dog if there's one to be had." Scowling in Livi's direction, he mounted up and led the way.

With or without Reid's blessing, Livi was glad she'd decided to leave Cissy in Violet's care and make the trip. Logan's Station, or St. Asaph's, as Reid told her it was sometimes called, was a wooden stockade fort built in what David had called the frontier style. Two dozen log cabins faced a broad interior field with spiked palisades connecting the cabins' high back walls. Large blockhouses guarded each corner of the fort, their slightly larger second stories overhanging the first to provide a deterrent to an enemy bent on scaling the walls. According to Reid, more than twenty families lived inside and tended the acres of gardens and fields to the east and south.

Livi, Tad, and Reid drew a surprising amount of attention as they rode in. The men returning from the fields for the midday meal paused to glare at them. Women appeared in the doorways of the cabins and watched with open suspicion. Livi was confused by their hostility until she realized it was Reid they were staring at, not Tad and her.

Livi had never considered how Campbell's looks might be construed on the frontier. Back in Virginia, where his father and grandfather were well-respected men, Reid had been an exotic. The obvious signs of his Indian ancestry stirred their share of gossip, but there had never been more to it than curiosity. Out here, dressed in his buckskin shirt and with feathers in his hat, he looked more savage than white. More like an enemy than a friend.

Just as they were dismounting, a tall, good-looking man emerged from one of the more commodious cabins. "Reid," he called out as he crossed the yard. "Reid Campbell. I didn't know you were back."

"It's good to see you, Ben."

"The trading go well?"

"Well enough." Reid took the man's outstretched hand warmly in his own. "I've come to see about shipping my furs."

Around them, the suspicion Livi had sensed melted away. The men picked up their tools. The women receded into the darkness of their cabins.

"And who is this?" the tall man asked, indicating Tad and her.

"This is Olivia Talbot, David's wife," Reid told him, "and their son, Tad. David was killed on the trail."

The man's thick eyebrows rose. "He wasn't caught in the massacre near Four Mile Creek, I hope."

"No," Livi answered, "but we came through there right after it happened."

Reid's head snapped around. "You didn't tell me that."

"You didn't seem very interested in our travels."

Livi saw a flush swell along Reid's cheekbones, but he bit down hard on whatever he'd intended to say.

"Well, I'm damned sorry to hear about David," Ben Logan said. "He was as fine a man as I've ever met."

His words brought the sting of tears to Livi's eyes. "Thank you," she answered.

"Let me welcome you to St. Asaph's. I'm Benjamin Logan, and I'm sure my wife will be pleased to offer you her hospitality while Reid and I conduct our business."

"I'd like that."

Logan turned. "Come right this way."

The Logan cabin was cool and dim despite the brightness

outside. The family was gathered for the noon meal, a sprout of a girl and two boys around Tad's age.

"Sit here, Mrs. Talbot," Anne Logan offered, motioning for one of the boys to make room on the puncheon bench. "We've nothing but mush and greens today, but you're welcome to some."

"That's kind of you," Livi demurred, "but I had a bite before we left the cabin."

"It helps to keep your stomach full when you're carrying," Mrs. Logan offered wisely as she dished up for Tad and her own three children. "When's the baby due?"

Livi took a moment to think. With the rigors of the trail and the work of settling in, she'd pushed her concerns for the baby to the back of her mind. "In the fall," she said.

"Well, don't forget there are women here to help when your time comes," Anne Logan offered.

If Reid insisted they leave once the harvest was in, Livi didn't know where she'd be when the baby came. "I'll keep that in mind."

"Sure I can't offer you something?" Anne Logan insisted. "A cup of sassafras tea, perhaps?"

"That would be nice."

While the older woman boiled and brewed, she quizzed Livi about Cissy and Tad, Lynchburg, the journey down the Wilderness Road, the cabin, and the crops. The boys gulped down their meal without saying a word and bolted from the cabin in search of Ben Logan and Reid.

"You seen any sign of Indians out your way?" Anne asked as she handed Livi the mug of tea.

"After our experiences on the road, I hope never to see another one," Livi answered honestly.

Mrs. Logan took a place across the table and drew her daughter onto her lap. "Ben thinks they'll be even thicker this year than last."

A shudder ran through Livi's frame. "What with the British defeat, David said the threat would lessen some."

Anne Logan shook her head. "According to Ben, it's the peace negotiations that will make this year so hard. The British figure the more land they control on this side of the mountains, the stronger they'll be when it comes to setting boundaries. Ben thinks those devils Caldwell and Weems are up in the

Ohio country convincing the Wyandot and Shawnee to continue raiding in the hope we'll all take our families and head back east.''

"That won't happen, will it?"

"Not with men like my Ben and your Reid putting roots down so deep.''

"He's not my Reid," Livi took pains to point out.

The other woman shot an appraising look in Livi's direction before continuing. "Well, I'm just as glad we're here in the fort and not 'settling out' like you all. We've come through more Indian attacks than a dog has fleas since we headed west in seventy-five, and it's a damned unsettling experience.

"We usually get word from the stations to the north when the Shawnee and Wyandot cross the Ohio, and we send riders out to the cabins. If I were you, I'd keep a few things packed in case you need to come into the fort sudden-like.''

Somehow Livi had convinced herself—or let David convince her—that once they reached the cabin, the danger of Indian attacks would lessen. That David had appeared to be wrong about the Indians frightened her. Could it be that he hadn't understood the danger the peace negotiations posed, or was Anne Logan exaggerating the possibility of attack? Was she a woman inured to living with the Indian menace, or had the man Livi trusted most in the world deliberately misled her?

Livi stared down into the pinkish tea, her stomach churning. If David had lied to her about this, what else had he told her in an effort to win his way?

"Ma?" Tad stood in the open doorway of the cabin, a wriggling black-and-brown puppy in his arms. "Ben said I could have the pick of the litter, and I want this one. I'm going to call him Patches."

It was a fitting, if not particularly original, name.

Behind Tad, Ben Logan and Reid loomed in the doorway. "I thought you needed a watchdog, Livi, and Ben says his bitch can smell Indians the minute they set foot on this side of the Ohio."

Livi nodded in both agreement and grudging appreciation. "To tell the truth, I've missed having a dog around. Old Rusty was part of the family."

Tad beamed and Campbell looked unduly pleased with himself.

"Oh," Reid added, "I've also spoken to Ben about the packhorses. He'll take them off our hands any time you like. There are always folks passing through here that have need of decent pack animals."

Livi stiffened, her voice going cold. "I don't recall that you and I ever discussed selling them off."

"Well, Livi, we both know they're too much work, and they'll eat you out of house and home."

Reid was right. She should have considered disposing of the pack animals long before this. There just hadn't been either the time or the opportunity. What rankled Livi most was that Reid had burst in and reordered her life when she'd been doing perfectly well without his help.

"Well, Mrs. Talbot," Ben Logan offered in a conciliatory tone, "whenever you're ready to sell them——"

"I'll see about bringing them over to the station in the next few days," she told him crisply, not sparing so much as a glance at Reid. "And while we're at it, there's another matter I'd like to discuss." Livi forged on in spite of Ben Logan's raised eyebrows and Reid's deepening frown. "I need a barn for my stock. It's one of the things David didn't have time to build, and I was wondering if you knew someone who would be willing to do it."

Logan looked at Livi long and hard. "Right now, Mrs. Talbot, most of the men have fields to tend. But come fall, when the crops are harvested, we might just put together a little barn raising out your way."

There would be no barn until fall, Livi thought. Not until after the crops were harvested. If Reid had his way, she'd be packed off to Virginia by then.

She set aside her tea and rose to go. "That sounds perfectly fine, Mr. Logan. Thank you."

They said their good-byes, and as they rode out of the gate, Livi studied Logan's Station with new eyes. She assessed the height of the walls, the bulk of the blockhouses squatting at the corners, the sentries surveying the countryside even on such a peaceful afternoon. It didn't assuage the fears that Anne Logan had roused, but now Livi knew they weren't alone here. If the British and the Indians came calling in the months ahead, she and her family were welcome to refuge at Logan's Station.

    *   *   *

Reid let his voice drop low and deep as he reached the climax of the tale he was telling Cissy and Tad. " 'And for your deception,' the Great Spirit told the serpent, 'you and your descendants shall slither on your bellies till the end of time.' "

"Is that true?" Cissy demanded as Reid's voice faded into the deepening dusk. "Is that really why snakes don't have any legs?"

"It's a story that goes back to the time when the world was young," Reid answered solemnly. "It has been told around fires in the winter house year after year, passed from one generation of Creeks to another."

Cissy looked patently unconvinced. Reid laughed and ruffled her silky hair.

"Tell us another story," Tad cajoled, gathering up the puppy, which was nestled on the step. "Tell us how the rabbit got his long ears."

Noticing Livi had come to stand over them in the doorway of the cabin, Reid shook his head. "There will be other nights and other stories."

The children groaned in complaint.

"Reid's right," Livi said. "It's time for bed. Wash your faces and say good night."

"Aw, Ma!" Tad grumbled and made his way to the basin in the breezeway between the cabins.

From her perch on his knee, Cissy wrapped her arms around Reid's neck. "It was a good story. I liked it very much." For the briefest moment before she wriggled free, the girl rested warm and trusting against his heart.

"Don't forget to wash your neck, young man," Livi admonished as she took a wet cloth to Cissy's face.

Females must be born knowing those eight words, Campbell thought, smiling to himself. He'd heard the very same thing in both English and Creek.

As Livi ushered her two damp-faced young ones into the house, Reid snagged the hem of her skirt. "I'd like a word with you once the children are abed."

She shot him a glance that implied she'd rather have discourse with a skunk. "I have to hear their prayers," she said.

Reid nodded and settled himself more comfortably on the

steps. The black velvet night wrapped around him. The air hung thick with the promise of rain. The wind hummed sweetly through the trees and set their branches dancing. At times like this, Reid was almost able to admit that he was more contented in this little valley than anywhere he'd ever been.

"You going to stay on with David's family?" Ben Logan had asked earlier in the day.

"Hell, no," he'd answered instinctively.

But Reid really wasn't sure. It all depended on how Livi answered his questions tonight.

Reid braced his forearms across his knees and stared out into the dark. If David were here, he would see this wilderness as a promise on the verge of fulfillment. He would remind Reid of the dreams they'd woven, and the plans they'd made on that arduous winter march with Colonel Clark.

Somewhere between Kaskaskia and Vincennes, Reid and David had agreed to pool their land grants, to find a little valley and call it home. They'd decided to come to Kentucky, to build something fine and bright and enduring. Reid was to trade and trap to provide their capital while David built the farm. This hollow with its creek and fields and cabin was to have been their great beginning.

David's death had ruined that. Now Reid carried the burden of land he had no desire to farm, a pregnant woman and two young children who might demand more than he could offer, and a future without the man who'd been his closest friend.

David had been his home, his family, his tribe. He was the only one who'd understood that a man's need for freedom could coexist with his yearning for something permanent.

The raw ache of loss rose hot in Campbell's chest. He would never rest until he'd avenged himself on the men who'd murdered David. And if Livi was able to describe them tonight, Reid would head off to track them down. He'd have his revenge on David's killers if it took to the end of time.

Livi's voice came low and wary, scattering his thoughts. "Reid?" she said. "Reid?"

He shifted on the steps, shoving over, making room. She sat down beside him with a twitch of her skirts.

"What was it you wanted to discuss?"

He took a moment to study her in the soft, faint light from

the Betty lamp she'd left burning in the room behind them. Olivia Talbot still possessed the most extravagant looks he'd ever encountered: hair with all the brilliance of a winter sunset; skin as fresh as virgin snow; a wide, soft mouth that invited seduction. No wonder David had fallen in love the first time he set eyes on her. No wonder Livi had proved to be such an able nemesis for Reid himself.

Campbell deliberately shifted his gaze to where fireflies flitted and sparked among the trees. "I want you to tell me how David died."

Livi sucked in air as if he'd slapped her.

"I want to know where you were camped, and how the Indians managed to surprise you. I want to know what they looked like, what weapons they carried, and how they behaved."

For a few moments he wasn't sure whether she was going to answer or bolt back into the house.

"How can you ask that?" she whispered at last. "How can you ask me to relive the most devastating moments in my entire life?"

His voice deepened with conviction. "Because it's necessary."

"Necessary how?"

"So David's death can be avenged."

He heard a rush of breath, her thready laugh. "I don't want him avenged. I want him back."

Reid's clasped hands tightened, the joints of his fingers going knobby and white. "I can't give you that."

"I know."

"No one can."

Without so much as a whisper of contact, Reid could feel emotions wax and wane in her: outrage bled to anger and anger into tears. He made no move to offer comfort; she'd never accept it from him anyway. What she wanted was a reprieve, from the questions he would ask, from the things he would make her remember. And he couldn't give her that, either.

He guessed she knew that, too.

"We were headed for the Block House," Livi finally said, "camped well back from the road. The weather had been fair and fine. David shot two fat pigeons during the afternoon, and we roasted them for supper. He said they were nothing compared to the bounty we'd find in Kentucky, but he said that about almost everything. No grass was as sweet, no sky as blue . . ."

She curled her fingers as if she could somehow grasp and hang on to those happier times.

"When it came time for bed, David lay down with me in the tent. He had done that every night since we'd left home. The noises in the woods frightened me and having him beside me helped. After I'd fallen asleep, he'd go out by the fire and keep watch.

"I don't know what happened that night. All I know is that both of us came awake to the sound of footsteps. Soft, they were, and stealthy. Moving past the head of the tent.

"David looked outside. He didn't tell me what he saw. He just handed me the pistol. 'It's going to be all right,' he said."

When Reid glanced at her, he saw wet streaks crawling down her cheeks. He saw that her eyes were dark and haunted, and he wished that somehow he could spare her this.

"What happened then?" he asked instead.

"David left the tent, yelling for all he was worth. He was trying to scare the Indians off, I guess. But they didn't go."

"How many of them were there?"

"I could see only the two who were going through our packs, but there were more. One of them spoke to David in some language I didn't understand. And David answered."

Reid straightened, anticipation crackling through him. Here was something he could go on. David knew a good deal of Creek and a bit of Shawnee.

"Then David and one of the Indians began to argue. He came at David with a knife. David shot the man in self-defense.

"The sound of gunfire roused the children. Cissy woke up screaming. Tad kept yelling at me to get out of his way."

Livi's voice crumbled and broke. Her breathing stuttered. She began to sob.

Reid twitched with an urge to hold her, an urge completely foreign where Livi was concerned. But more important than trying to sop up grief that no one on earth could assuage was finding out what had happened that cold, dark night three months before. If he took her in his arms, he'd never hear the rest of it.

"Go on," he said.

She panted for a space before she could speak.

"There were more Indians out in the trees. One of them ran toward David, yelling and swinging his war club. David fended him off the first time. It was the second time he swung at David—the second blow . . ."

Reid had seen attacks like the one Livi was describing. He could almost hear the Indian's wild yell, the whistle behind his vicious swing, the hollow thud of contact. He could imagine the boneless way David must have crumpled to the ground, the way he'd lain there shattered and still.

Bile scoured the back of Campbell's throat.

He should have been there, Reid found himself thinking. He should have gone back to Lynchburg with David to get Livi and the children. If he'd been in camp that night, he could have kept watch. If he'd been there, he might have . . .

"For God's sake, Livi," Reid burst out, "you had a loaded pistol. Why didn't you use it?"

He wanted to grab her and shake her hard.

Livi lowered her head, tears still spilling down her face. "Don't you think I've asked myself that question a thousand times?"

"You could have shot that Indian. You could have saved David's life!"

She took a shuddery breath and swiped at the tears with the back of her hand. "Please, Reid, try to understand. David told me to stay in the tent, and that's what I did. He didn't give me that pistol so I could save his life. He didn't give it to me to defend myself."

"Then why in hell—"

"He gave it to me to keep Tad and Cissy safe."

It was a fine distinction, one Reid wasn't willing to qualify. "But you let David die!"

He could see the pain and culpability in those wide, fierce eyes. He could see the conviction in them, too. "He gave me the pistol to protect my children. I did exactly what David wanted. I protected my children," she shouted at him. "What is it you would have had me do?"

Reid had no answer for that. Still, he clung to his condemnation, boiling with regret.

"Ma?" Tad's voice came to them from the cabin loft. "Ma?"

"It's all right, Tad," Livi called back to reassure her son.

"Are you and Reid arguing?"

There was a soft, sad lilt to her voice as she answered. "Don't we always?"

Tad seemed satisfied by the answer, with the uneasy silence that fell between them.

Beside Reid, Livi was fighting to compose herself.

He knew he'd pushed her farther than he should. He knew he should let her be. There was just so much he needed to know.

"What did the men who killed David look like?"

"Oh, Reid."

She looked exhausted, fragile, as if talking about that night had reduced her somehow, worn her down.

"Please, Livi, try to remember."

Livi scrubbed at her face with her hands and took a breath. "There were six or eight Indians in the band. Their faces were painted black and vermillion. They wore breechclouts and leggings. Their shirts were made of trade cloth, bright and new. One wore a matchcoat around his shoulders and a medallion of some kind at his throat."

"Tell me about their headgear, about their hair."

"Most of them had scalp locks braided with quills and feathers. Several others wore their hair longer, hanging loose."

A frown of confusion drew Reid's brows together. "What weapons were they carrying?"

She breathed a sigh. "Muskets and war clubs, mostly. At least one of them had a rifle."

"And what did they take?"

"Nothing."

He regarded her long and hard. "Livi, Indians don't raid a camp and take nothing."

"These Indians did," she insisted. "After David fell, they picked up the man he'd shot and crept away."

"Did they threaten you and the children?"

Livi shook her head. "Tad went sort of wild when he saw what they'd done to his father—cursing and sobbing and trying to get at them. I wrapped my arms around him and hung on tight. I was sure they'd kill us all if we did anything more to resist.''

"Then if they didn't take goods," Reid reasoned aloud, "they must have taken livestock."

"Not even one of the chickens was missing."

"Goddammit, Livi, that doesn't make sense. None of this makes sense," he admitted, raking his hand through his hair. "War parties shouldn't be raiding that far east. Indians don't attack in the middle of the night. And they never ransack a camp without taking something. Are you sure there was nothing missing?"

"We unpacked everything in the creels when we arrived."

"And you didn't find anything—unusual?"

"Only the things we packed in Lynchburg."

Reid climbed to his feet, needing to move, needing to pace. Frustration was eating a hole in him.

He had next to nothing to go on: a snatch of speech, behavior inconsistent with every tribe he knew, no cohesive description of the attackers. He wondered if Livi had really told him everything. Even if she had, there had to be more.

He'd talk to the scouts at the stations up north. Maybe one of them knew which Indians had been raiding east of the mountains back in March. He'd send word to John Anderson at the Block House and see what he'd heard. Reid could ride the Wilderness Road himself, maybe even follow the Warriors Path up the back side of the mountains toward the Ohio country. Even if Livi couldn't help him, there had to be a way to track down the men who'd attacked the Talbots' camp.

Still seated on the step, Livi suddenly stiffened. Her eyes widened. Her hands rose to cradle the small, firm rise of her belly.

Reid's heart snagged at the back of his throat. "What is it?" he demanded. "Tell me what's wrong."

She sat there barely breathing, utterly still.

Oh, God, he thought. If he'd pushed her too hard or demanded too much—

Slowly Livi lifted her gaze to his. "It moved," she whispered. "The baby moved."

He could do no more than stare at her.

"I was so sick at the beginning of the pregnancy," she went

on, smiling and crying all at once, "and we went through so much on the trail that I was afraid . . ."

"Afraid of what?"

Flushed and soft and luminous, Livi looked up at him through her tears. "Don't you understand, Reid? This is wonderful. David's and my baby is moving. That means it's all right!"

David and Livi's baby.

The dart of resentment was scurrilous, unworthy—but Reid couldn't seem to help what he was feeling. Livi was carrying David's child. She would always possess the last and best of the man that David Talbot had been.

"Of course, I—I'm—pleased," he fumbled, scrambling for equilibrium. "This news is—very—"

Hot color crept up his neck. Reid knew he should apologize, then couldn't scrape up the courage to admit what he was sorry for.

To his immense discredit, Livi seemed to understand.

Before his eyes, her excitement dimmed. The glow seeped out of her face. Disappointment doused the light in her eyes. Slowly, gracefully, and completely without his help, Livi rose to her feet and went into the cabin without saying a word.

He stood at the foot of the steps staring after her. He might own the cabin and the land. He might have the power to make her leave, but Livi was carrying David's child. Livi had what mattered most.

⚜ 13 ⚜

Reid looked up from the log he was splitting just as Tad rounded the corner of the cornfield. The way the boy's stride lagged when he saw Reid already at work seemed to indicate that Tad had more than split-rail fences on his mind. Reid took another swipe with the maul, anticipation brewing in his belly.

He'd come out here just before dawn, figuring this was as good a way as any for a man to spend his energy if he couldn't sleep. Already a score of logs lay split into fence-length rails.

"Is Eustace on his way?" he asked as the log he had been working groaned and fell apart.

"I guess," Tad answered, peering out from under the brim of his battered hat. "But before he gets here, I've got something I need to say to you."

Reid set the handle of the maul against his leg and wiped the sweat from his brow with the back of his arm. "Oh?"

The boy's mouth narrowed before he spoke. "I—I just wanted you to know that—that you really don't have to stay on here if you've a mind to go."

Reid admitted to a hitch of surprise. "And why is that?"

"Well, with Eustace and Violet here, we're doing well enough, and Ben Logan promised to help us raise a barn come fall. So I reckon we can do without your help."

Reid looked at the boy and saw in him the echo of the man his father had been. Tad had the wheaten hair, the golden brown eyes, and the beginnings of that powerful broad-

191

shouldered build. He even had the stubborn stamp to his jaw, the one David always wore when he knew he was about to do something crazy and intended to go ahead with it anyway.

"So you want me to leave?" Reid asked.

"I think it's best."

"Best for who?"

"Best for all of us." Tad lowered his eyes. "Best for Ma."

"You heard us arguing last night."

Tad nodded.

"Your ma and I always argue."

"I know," the boy acknowledged. "But with the baby and all . . ."

With the baby and all. Concern for his mother's welfare was reason enough for Tad to ask him to leave. It was also reason enough to give Campbell pause. It they were Creeks, there wouldn't have been any question about where his obligations lay. A man took responsibility for his brother's wife and children. But what would David expect of Reid in all of this?

He'd lain awake half the night pondering that. Reid had no doubt that with time and persistence, he'd track down David's killers. Someone knew who they were and why they'd attacked the Talbots. Eventually he'd figure out who killed David, and then he would avenge him. Tracking and killing were things Reid had always been good at.

But after talking to Livi last night, something stayed him. Something that went against every instinct he had. Something that brought him perilously close to accepting responsibility for someone beside himself. No matter how hard she might try to deny it, no matter how hard he tried to deny it to himself, Livi needed him. It was acknowledging that that made him so itchy and hot this morning.

"Jesus!" Reid said under his breath.

The curse brought Tad's head up so Reid could see his eyes. They were level, matter-of-fact. They were the eyes of a child who'd become a man before his time.

"It's not as if Ma's ever wanted you here," Tad told him. "I can look after her well enough."

It was convenient having everyone's permission to leave. Livi didn't want him here; she'd made that clear enough the day he rode in. Now Tad was telling him he could go. Then why the hell wasn't he back at the cabin packing his saddle-bags?

Instead Reid bent to pick up the wedge and glut and rolled another log into place with his foot. "Is this something I have to decide here and now, or can we get this fence laid up first?"

Tad let out his breath. A grin tweaked the corners of his mouth. "Ma gets mad as hell when one of the animals gets into the field. I guess we'd better work on the fence."

Reid wished he hadn't been able to hear the relief in Tad's voice.

Well, relief or not, he sure as hell meant to give leaving a lot of thought. With every hour that passed, that course looked more inviting. Out in the woods he was free, completely his own man. He had no alliances, no responsibilities. Out there he'd only have guilt to carry around with him like an extra bag of shot.

He set the wedge and tapped it into the log with the maul.

He'd have a damn sight more than guilt dragging at him if he stayed at the cabin. He'd have Livi and her hostility. He'd have two children and whatever mischief they managed to make. He'd have the fields and the house and the animals. And in an odd way, even Eustace and Violet would come under his care.

Damn it, David! You know I'm not cut out for this. He drew back the maul and hammered the wedge for all he was worth.

At the edge of his vision, the cool, dark forest beckoned.

I'm going to go, he promised himself. *Just as soon as we get these goddamned fences built.*

The dog was barking, sharp, insistent yaps with a puppy's yowl at the end of them. Livi glanced up from the corn pudding she was mixing.

"Dog's puttin' up quite a fuss," Violet said from the far side of the table, where she was cutting up the last of the turnips for dinner. "Haven't heard much from him till just now."

"I'll get him," Cissy offered from where she was practicing letters on her slate.

"No, I'll go," Livi said, wiping her hands on her apron. "You keep after that writing."

"Dog prob'ly got wind of a possum off there in the woods," Violet observed.

It was warm in the cabin, and Livi welcomed the breath of breeze as she stepped outside. She could hear the menfolk splitting rails across the creek. The fence they had begun the previous day had already progressed to encompass the front and half of the left side of the nearest field. With a nod of satisfaction, she headed down the breezeway to where Tad had tied Patches to a post to keep him from running off the way he had on his first night at the cabin.

"You certainly are making a lot of noise for such a little dog," Livi complained as she hunkered down to untie the rope. Instead of Patches greeting her all wag and slobber, he yapped and growled, straining in the direction of the woods behind the house.

Livi tried to reel the dog in to ease the tension on the knots. "Patches!" she admonished him, then lifted her gaze to see what had him so riled up.

For an instant all she could see was the shimmy of brush along the face of the ridge. Then a lithe brown body broke cover halfway down. He moved diagonally down the bank. A second and a third man stole along a dozen paces behind. Two more were just easing over the crest of the hill.

Indians!

A ripple of dread ran the length of Livi's spine. She left the dog yowling at the intruders and bolted for the cabin.

"There are Indians out back!" she announced as she burst inside.

Violet leaped to her feet, her dark eyes widening. Cissy wailed in fear. Livi's first impulse was to slam and bar the cabin door. It was the thought of the men working across the creek that stayed her hand. They had to be warned. They had to have time to reach the cabin if they meant to mount a defense. Yet she couldn't leave Cissy and Violet alone in case the Indians doubled back.

The trapdoor to the turnip hole gaped open in the floor of the cabin. Without taking time to think, Livi grabbed Violet's arm.

"Down there," she urged, pulling the smaller woman toward the opening. "You and Cissy hide down there while I go and warn the men."

Violet's eyes lit with both understanding and dread before she leaped into the stone-lined, yard-deep hole. She turned and reached for Cissy as Livi tried to hand her down.

Cissy balked when she saw what her mother meant to do. "No! No!" she cried. "It's dark down there. There are prob'ly snakes—and spiders, too."

"There are no snakes or spiders," Livi hastened to assure her. "And it's not all that dark. Light comes through the floor-boards. And Violet will be there with you. Please, Cissy, do this for me. All I want is to keep you safe."

Snuffling, the child looked from her mother to where Violet stood chest-deep in the hole. "I don't want to," Cissy whined, but didn't resist when Livi eased her into Violet's arms.

Livi waited until the two of them were seated amidst the remaining baskets of vegetables. "Don't come out unless one of us says it's all right," she instructed. "Or unless you smell smoke."

Tales of Indians torching cabins over the settlers' heads were rife along the frontier. If Livi had a choice, she'd rather see Cissy and Violet captured than burned to death.

Livi was just easing the trapdoor in place when she heard a yell and the crack of rifles from somewhere across the creek. Shoving the table a few feet to the left to hide the seams of the turnip hole, Livi snatched up her pistol and raced outside.

From the top of the steps, she could make out half a dozen Indians swarming over where the men had been working on the fence. She charged down the rise, fear backing up in her throat. She raced across the bridge and ran the breadth of the field, cradling her belly with her left hand. By the time she reached the corner, she was gasping for breath.

Beyond it, a haze of smoke blurred the struggling, half-naked bodies. The men had stripped off their shirts as they worked on the fence, so she could barely determine who was who.

As she raced nearer, she saw Eustace swing his rifle, beating back several of the Indians. Reid fought off three attackers with nothing more than his wooden maul. Crouched at his feet, Tad rammed a load into Campbell's rifle. Reid blocked the swing of an Indian war club while Tad aimed. The gun spit fire. The blast boomed through the woods and fields. One of the Indians attacking Eustace yowled and fled.

Reid wielded the long-handled mallet as if it were a weapon he'd been trained to use. With a vicious backhanded blow, he hammered one Indian's ribs and sent him sprawling. He slammed a second man in the chest. He wasn't quite quick enough to bring the mallet around to defend himself from the third. Tad dropped the half-loaded rifle, prepared to launch himself into the fray.

Livi ran forward instead. She raised her gun and fired at point-blank range. The impact of the ball spun the brave backward. She watched him fall. Blood poured from the hole in the man's bare shoulder, bright against his dusky skin.

She caught her breath; her stomach heaved.

She had a fleeting impression of Reid jerking around, caught a look of astonishment on his face. Then one of Eustace's attackers threw himself at Reid, and the two of them went down in a tangle of arms and legs. The battle ebbed and flowed around her, but Livi couldn't take her eyes off the Indian writhing on the ground. She didn't know whether to offer him help or knock him senseless with her empty gun.

With difficulty he gained his feet and staggered off.

Bellowing with rage, Eustace battered his knife-wielding attacker aside. The man Reid had been fighting gave up and scrambled away. Both braves ran for the woods.

As they vanished into the trees, everything stilled. The breeze died away. The sun beat down. The acrid taint of powder hung heavy in the air. The Negro, the trapper, the boy, and the woman stood waiting, not knowing if they had won a decisive victory, or if more Indians would come howling out of the forest to cut them down.

The stillness held. When he was certain there was no imminent threat, Reid bent to examine the two Indians who lay in the trampled grass.

"Shawnee," he said. "A raiding party come from up north. Two dead, one wounded, and five who'll be back to claim the bodies—if they can."

Livi was barely aware of his words. She looked at the smoking pistol in her hand. She stared at the bloodstains on the ground. She couldn't believe she'd shot a man. That she'd done it to protect her own somehow didn't justify the brutality. Beneath his paint, the Indian she'd wounded had seemed so young, only a year or two older than Tad.

Suddenly the gun in Livi's hand seemed too heavy to hold and dropped with a thud to the ground. Light flared before her eyes. Numbness rose through her. She heard Reid curse and shout her name, but she couldn't seem to answer him. Darkness billowed in Livi's head and carried her away.

Voices drifted over her, soft and muffled with concern. Somewhere a child was crying. Livi was almost too tired to wonder who. It took nearly all her strength just to lie there and breathe.

She opened her eyes anyway and blinked the world into focus around her. Violet was perched on the edge of the bed, a bowl of water in her lap and a cloth in her hand. "Miz 'Livia? You all right?"

"M-m-m-m," she answered. "Did I faint?"

"Dead away."

"That was a damn silly thing to do."

Memory was slowly coming back. The Indians. The attack. The pistol. Livi didn't want to think about the pistol—or what she'd done with it.

"Is everyone safe?" she whispered, seeking out Violet's wrist, tightening her fingers around it. *Please, God, let everyone be all right.*

"Eustace got his'elf cut on the arm, but that's the worst of it," Violet reported. "Marse Reid's stitchin' him up just now."

Livi nodded and let out her breath. As she did, Tad peered at her over Violet's shoulder. Worry had pinched harsh, deep lines around his mouth. "Ma?"

"Yes, Tad, I'm fine." She smiled and tried to push herself up on one elbow to reassure him.

Violet pushed her down again. "Jus' let your ma rest. She an' that baby been through a lot today."

The baby. Livi found herself smiling in spite of everything. Lying quiet like this, she could feel the baby moving, faint flutters of new life astir in her.

Again Livi became aware of a child's shivery, gulping sobs. "Where's Cissy?" she demanded. "I want Cissy."

Violet and Tad made room for the little girl at the side of the bed. A jolt of fierce protectiveness swept through Livi at the sight of her daughter. She was smudged with dirt from being shut up in the turnip hole. Her eyes were red from crying.

"Hello, Mama," she said in a squeaky little voice. Though she was trying very hard to hold them back, two big teardrops rolled down her splotchy cheeks.

"Hello, sugar," Livi greeted Cissy and drew her baby girl up onto the bed beside her. She knew how frightened her daughter must have been, hearing the Indians' war whoops and the gunfire, being shut up in the dark. After what Cissy had heard and seen on the trail, not even having Violet to comfort her could have been much help. So Livi held her younger child tight; she rubbed her back. For a time she held the rest of the world at bay.

Finally Cissy raised her head. "When Reid carried you in here," she said in a very small voice, "I thought you'd gone away like Papa did."

Livi drew her daughter close again, stroking her tumbled hair. It broke Livi's heart, knowing that her four-year-old had to worry about her parents "going away." No child this young should be so well acquainted with death.

"Well, I'm not like Papa was," she answered, raising her daughter's chin so she could look into her eyes. "I'm just fine. And I'm not going anywhere."

"Are you sure?"

Livi gave Cissy the reassurance without a qualm. "I'm very sure."

From the far side of the room, Violet had been listening and nodded as if she approved of Livi's answer. "Now, come on over here with me, little girl," she urged Cissy. "We'll see if we can brew up the last few scraps of this tea for your mama. She sure seems like she needs a cup."

Livi lay back and closed her eyes, aching, trembling, bone-deep weary. Though she yearned for sleep, she knew there was one last person she needed to see. Livi hated having to ask for him, hated needing to talk to him at all. But she did.

As if she'd conjured him up, Reid appeared at her bedside.

"Violet said I should come in and thank you for what you did," he explained.

"What I did?"

"Over there by the cornfield. With that pistol. You saved my life."

Livi's stomach curled. Weakness rippled down her arms and legs. "I never shot anyone before," she confessed on a long, uneven breath.

"Well, Livi," Reid offered with a certain chagrin, "I'm just as glad you made that Indian your first. He'd have hacked me to pieces if he'd had the chance."

Even knowing that her actions had kept Reid safe didn't seem to take the edge off what she'd done. "I never hurt anyone before. I never deliberately—" She swallowed hard. "I could have killed him, Reid."

His blue gaze held hers. "Yes, you could."

"But if I did . . ."

"Then you'd have to decide if it was worth it. You'd have to decide if you really had another choice."

This was what she'd needed to talk about, the terrible responsibility, the bottomless regret. Reid was the only one here who could possibly understand.

"But I don't want to be—the kind of person who—who could do—do that." Livi stammered, feeling as if she were dissolving before his eyes. "I mustn't let myself become—"

Tears rose and pooled and slid into her hair. Sobs climbed the back of her throat.

Reid stared at her, his brows notched down over the bridge of his nose. His mouth narrowed, the corners softening. She could see that he was doing his best to remain aloof. Then, mumbling what must surely be his vilest curse, Reid gathered her up in his arms.

Her head reeling, Livi lay with her temple pillowed on his broad shoulder, her face turned into the warm, whiskery crook of his neck. His hands splayed across her back: broad, rough hands holding her together while she cried; strong, capable hands offering consolation. For this moment, he seemed gentle and solid—and safe. Livi hadn't felt safe since David died.

"It's all right," he said, an odd, begrudging tenderness tinting his tone. "It's all right."

But it wasn't all right. Livi didn't want it to be all right. She didn't want to be able to dismiss shooting a man by telling herself it was justified. She didn't want to know that if her aim had been true, she could have killed him. She didn't want to be the fierce, hard woman the wilds were demanding she become.

Reid would say that if she weren't strong enough to defend her own, she wouldn't survive in Kentucky. He would tell her that if she weren't brave enough to face the hardships, she should go back to Virginia, where survival didn't cost so much. He would inform her with that hard, knowing quirk to his lips that until she'd made David's dream her own, she had no right pursuing it. And perhaps he was right.

But just this once, Reid Campbell held his peace.

Tucked up in his arms, she wept for what she'd done, for what life on the frontier might force her to do. She shed tears for the decisions she had made, for the responsibilities she had taken as her own. She cried because she had someone to hold her close.

In time, her weeping ran its course. She swiped at her eyes with her hand. She snuffled piteously until Reid produced a proper gentleman's handkerchief from the pocket of his trousers. Now that the worst was over, Livi was mortified that she had fainted, more embarrassed still that she had cried all over Reid. He was the very last man in the world she wanted near when her weakness got the better of her.

It took more than a dollop of courage for her to raise her head and meet his gaze. "Will the Indians be back?"

She saw a flicker of admiration in his eyes, as if he knew what facing him was costing her.

"They'll come back to claim their dead, but I think that's all. Unless I miss my guess, these were a few hotheaded young bucks bent on mischief, not part of a war party. I sent Eustace over to Whitley's Station and St. Asaph's to let them know what happened, just in case. But I'd say the danger's passed . . ."

"For now," Livi added, his implication clear.

"But *just for now*. What happened today should prove to you that no matter how peaceful it seems, this valley isn't inviolate. Indians will be through regular-like, and they won't come to parlay or trade a few skins. You need to accept that if you stay on in Kentucky—even just until the crops are in— you're going to have to fight."

His admonition to leave lay unspoken between them. In truth, he didn't need to put the warning into words.

Feeling suddenly compromised by the comfort she was taking and how good it felt to be held, Livi eased out of his arms.

Yet as she withdrew, she took with her a bit of Reid's warmth, his scent, the vitality that hummed beneath his skin. She felt stronger for those few minutes of contact, more able to face whatever came.

It surprised her that when she made as if to rise, Reid curled hard, restraining fingers around her arm. "You just fainted," he pointed out. "You're pregnant. You need your rest."

She shook her head. "I'm perfectly fine. Besides, Violet can't keep Cissy and get supper pulled together."

"I'll take Cissy myself if need be," he offered. "Now, for the love of God, Livi, just lie down!" His tone was gruff with annoyance and utterly implacable.

Deep inside her, a spark of their usual antagonism stirred to life. Campbell had to be the most obstinate, high-handed man she'd ever met. He had absolutely no right to order her around. Though when she thought about it, that shuddery, gone-at-the-knees feeling might go away if she could get some rest.

Perhaps Reid was just trying to be nice. Nice, she thought, closing her eyes. Reid Campbell being nice—the novelty of the concept made her smile.

❧ 14 ❧

R eid had to admit he'd been wrong. Once the raiders claimed their dead, no other Indians breached the peace and solitude of their little valley. Nearly a month passed, and though he and Tad hunted the hills and hollows for miles around to augment their dwindling food supply, not once did he see any sign of Indians in the woods. Nor, as Campbell rode from station to station asking questions that might lead him to David's killers, did he hear any indication that the tribes to the north were astir.

To his way of thinking, that didn't make sense. With the peace treaty still being negotiated in Paris and the boundaries in question, the English should be recruiting tribes to raid Kentucky. Certainly there was as much at stake now as there had been in 1777, when the British and their allies had come howling down across the Ohio River to lay waste to the forts and homesteads. The year of the bloody sevens, they'd called it, and hundreds had lost their lives. Reid's conviction that it could happen again stoked the tension constantly simmering in his gut.

That Livi and the rest went on about their lives, when death and destruction could sweep out of the hills at any moment, riled Campbell beyond all provocation. He knew that Livi took her pistol when she tended the fields or weeded her garden, but considering she'd fainted the first time she shot an Indian, Reid wasn't sure she'd use it. Instead of erecting a stockade as he'd suggested, Eustace and Tad turned their energies to building a corncrib and an ash hopper so there would be lye for making soap and hominy. Violet still gathered greens in the woods, and when Cissy wasn't practicing her letters or helping her mother, she went with her. Dangerous practices, all of them, yet part of daily life at the Talbot cabin.

In spite of Reid's concerns, everything in the valley flourished. The corn was high, and in a week or two they'd be plucking the first of the roasting ears. They were already eating from the vegetable patch, and the first of Livi's pole beans were sweet as honey. Livi was rounding out a little more every day, her belly protruding, her breasts growing lush and full. Though Reid knew she'd be mortified if he let on he'd noticed, it seemed to him a wondrous ripening. Somehow he'd put his uneasiness to rest where the baby was concerned and took pleasure in knowing she was keeping David's legacy alive.

His frustration at not being able to find the men who'd killed his friend took on a presence of its own. It fed his bitterness and grief, his anger and regret. In the thickest part of the night Reid would jerk awake, wet with sweat. In his dreams he knew the identity of the men who'd murdered David, but when he woke he could never quite remember. The nightmares kept the restlessness astir, kept him riding out, searching and questioning. Yet he couldn't seem to put the little valley behind him for more than a few days at a time.

Though being at the cabin chafed, Reid kept busy. He helped Livi whenever she let him, though in truth, she rarely did. She seemed to think that accepting his aid compromised the agreement they had made or nullified her own accomplishments. She worked harder and longer than he'd imagined any Chesterton could, and refused to give an inch in the demands she made on herself or on anyone else.

Reid didn't know what had happened to the hapless child David had married, but the woman who had faced him and refused to leave wasn't the wide-eyed girl he'd known back then. The only way he could think to explain the change in her was that the traits he'd long ascribed to Livi Talbot had been wrapped around a core of something stronger.

She so seldom asked for help that Campbell was surprised when she came to him one morning while he was sharpening the axes with a whetstone.

"Since you're on about household tasks," Livi began, com-

proached the water. He looked in both directions, to where the brook ran clear and swift, rippling over its bed of stones.

Thoughts buzzed through Reid's head. If an animal had carried Cissy off, he would have heard it. If she'd encountered Indians, she should have been able to cry out. If she'd wandered away, he'd be able to pick up her trail once she left the rocky streambed.

He headed west, trotting along the bank, anxiety soaring through him. He was halfway to the trees when he caught sight of Cissy's shoes, set carefully on a rock at the water's edge.

She'd gone wading in the stream. God knows he'd watched her do that often enough, with her skirts carefully hitched up in front and trailing the back in the water. But then, she'd always gone wading in the shallows closer to the house.

Cissy wouldn't have known this part of the creek so well. Looking for pretty rocks in the streambed, she might not have seen the drop-off hidden at the edge of the shade. There was a tiny waterfall just under the lip of the trees with a chest-deep pool beneath it. But what was a pleasant spot for a man to bathe in could be deadly for a child of Cissy's years.

"Christ!" Reid muttered and bolted along the bank. He needed to be wrong about where Cissy was.

In the dimness under the canopy of trees, shadows fell across the shimmering surface of the pool. As he came nearer he saw the shadows shift with billowing skirts and gossamer webs of floating hair.

"Oh, Jesus! Oh, God, please!" Reid muttered as he ran the last few steps and threw himself into the pool. Cissy drifted faceup, just below the surface, her eyes open wide; her tiny, fragile hands extended, reaching toward the light.

Reid scooped her up against his chest. She was white and cold. Slack and still. Limp as a broken blossom.

Dead. The word screamed through him. Dead. Like David. Dead.

Reid couldn't let that be. He groped his way onto the bank, bent Cissy over his arm, and rapped her sharply between the shoulder blades.

"Breathe, Cissy!" he ordered. "Breathe!"

Water drained out of her nose and mouth.

"Goddammit, Cissy, breathe!" he rasped and smacked her back again.

Cissy choked twice and twisted a little in protest of her rough treatment. She wheezed down a ragged draught of air.

He struck her again, then held her tight as she coughed and gagged and gasped. He held her and helped her clear her stomach and lungs of the water she'd swallowed. He held her as she gulped down air and gagged again.

He felt the life flow back into her body. He felt her muscles tighten, her body warm beneath his hands. It wasn't until Cissy began to squirm against him that Reid realized how tightly he was clutching her.

He closed his eyes, light-headed with relief. "Thank you," he whispered, though he wasn't sure to whom.

Cissy pushed at him again. "Let go, Reid!" she croaked, her voice raspy and raw. "You're squashing me. You're squashing the stone I found!"

He was breathing hard, laughing and shaking, and smoothing back this baby's hair.

"I'm squashing your stone," he repeated, and laughed again.

"See my stone? I never found one with a picture on it before."

Reid took the smooth, flat piece of limestone in one trembling hand.

"It's a fish," she prompted him.

He looked down, trying to focus, trying to loosen his hold on Cissy a little at a time. "A fish," he said.

"It's—a—fish!" Cissy repeated with some exasperation.

Reid nodded, his mind stirring again, returning from that place where panic and instinct were all he had.

He nodded and took another shaky breath. "This kind of picture in a rock is called a fossil," he told her.

Cissy squirmed to look at him. "How do you know that?"

"I learned it in school, I guess," he answered, still quivering inside and out.

"You didn't go to school! Mama said you lived with the Indians."

"I lived with the Indians, too."

"Then if you went to school, you tell me how the fossil got in that rock." Trust Cissy to make something as simple as this into a test.

"Well, when the fish died," Reid began, "he got buried in

the mud. And when that mud hardened into rock, it make the impression you found today.''

Cissy nodded, momentarily amazed, momentarily satisfied.

Still feeling battered, Reid managed to set Cissy on her feet and come to his own beside her. It was time to head back to the cabin, though he wasn't looking forward to explaining any of this to Livi.

"Reid?" Something about Cissy's tone made him squat down beside her again.

"What is it, Cissy?"

Her face screwed up; her eyebrows pursed. "Will my papa be a fossil, too? When he died, we buried him in the mud.''

Reid felt the air in his lungs go stale and thin, felt the world wheel wildly around him. With her forthrightness, her innocence, and her childish logic, Cissy had loosed all the grief he'd been holding inside. He ached with it, his chest heaving and his eyes blurring with tears.

Howling at the moon hadn't helped assuage this terrible pain. Looking for the men who'd killed David hadn't. Neither had running away from the world of responsibilities David had left behind.

Livi, Livi's baby, Cissy, and Tad were David's legacy. They were David's bequest to him. Reid had to stop denying it. As he stood there holding this wet, bedraggled child between his hands, this child he'd nearly lost, he wondered if he was worthy of David's trust. Was he strong enough and brave enough to watch over David's family? Was he wise enough and kind enough to give what each of them might demand of him? He'd asked Livi these same questions weeks before and judged her lacking. How could he claim to be any more able than she, especially after what had happened today?

Reid felt daunted by the prospect of keeping David's family safe. Yet he knew David was alive in each of them, and as long as Livi and the children flourished, a bit of David would live on. It was up to him to keep them together, keep them happy, keep them whole.

"Reid?" Cissy was growing impatient. "Will my papa be a fossil, too?"

Reid swallowed hard. "It takes a long time for a fossil to form," he answered carefully. "A very long time."

"Until I'm all grown up?"

"Even longer than that."

"Until I'm married?"

"It takes lifetimes, Cissy. More years than you can count."

"I can count pretty high," she warned him. "One. Two. Three. Four—"

"Cissy? Cissy!" A frantic voice came to them through the shiver of windblown leaves and the spatter of the waterfall. "Christine Arabella Talbot, you answer me!"

Cissy broke off counting and looked at Reid. "She never calls me that unless she's mad."

Reid heard not anger but desperation in Livi's tone.

"It's going to be all right," he told Cissy as he rose and took her hand.

"We're here," Reid shouted back as they moved along the far bank toward the cabin.

They met Livi just beyond the trees. She was clutching Cissy's discarded shoes and stockings so hard her knuckles were white. Her face looked ravaged, blanched, and stark.

"Cissy and I decided to take a little swim," he told her, trying to make light of something far more serious.

Livi wasn't fooled. She splashed across the stream and caught her baby tightly in her arms. Reid could see how Livi's hands were trembling as they smoothed back her daughter's straggling hair, as they skimmed up and down her limbs, seeking any sign of injury.

He understood her anguish in a way he never had before.

Finally she knelt back on her haunches and set Cissy before her. "Cissy Talbot! What have I told you about wandering off by yourself? It was bad enough when you did it in Lynchburg, but here in the wilds—"

Livi left the thought unfinished and dragged her baby close again.

Reid watched the two of them, Livi's arms enfolding Cissy, her hands splayed across her daughter's back, her face buried in the soft, warm curve of her little girl's neck.

A thick protectiveness rose in him, a fierce determination to keep them safe. Reid freely made the pledge to David he'd been fighting to avoid.

At length Livi rose and lifted her daughter in her arms.

Reid waited, anticipating Livi's smile, her thanks.

She scowled at him instead. "I'll deal with you later!"

With a glare that promised retribution, she spun back in the direction of the cabin. Reid watched Livi and Cissy go, feeling angry, unjustly accused, and all of ten years old again.

It wasn't as if she were snooping, Livi told herself, her hand on the door latch to Reid Campbell's half of the cabin. It wasn't that she didn't have a right to go inside. She'd finished the mending she'd offered to do. All she intended was to put down the stack of neatly folded clothes and leave. How could Reid take exception to that?

But then, he probably could—especially the way he'd been behaving these past few days.

Since Livi had taken him to task the morning Cissy had nearly drowned, he'd seemed less restless, more affable. He'd begun to take his meals with them, staying at the table after Violet and Eustace were gone, playing checkers or telling tales to Tad and Cissy.

Then, after sharing their noon meal two days ago, Campbell had inexplicably gone sullen and solitary. He'd either kept to his cabin or been off in the woods. He hadn't spoken to anyone or come by to eat. The children didn't understand why he'd withdrawn from them, and Livi didn't, either.

That was part of the reason she was poised outside his cabin door, ready to assuage her curiosity about the room that lay beyond it and the man who lived there. She'd chosen her time with care, waiting until Reid had vanished into the trees. She should just go on in, she told herself, have a look around, and leave the clothes for him to find. It wasn't as if she were doing anything wrong; she'd discovered *him* snooping in *her* cabin a few weeks back.

Huffing away her reticence, Livi lifted the latch. It was cool and dim inside. The scent of sweet grass and cedar welcomed her. She stepped across the threshold and pulled up short.

Livi didn't know what she had expected. Not a cabin so neat it belied the familial clutter of her own. Not a hand-hewn bed and soft, woven rugs on the floor. Not shelves of books suspended above a writing desk. Some things were not so startling. There were skins on the walls, a musket and two fowling pieces hung on pegs above the mantel. Basic cooking utensils sat at the edge of the hearth or to the right of the fireplace.

That the fireplace itself was swept bare surprised her. That it had been sprinkled with something powdery and white made her even more curious about what Reid had been doing.

She lay the mending on the woven blue-and-white coverlet and moved further into the room. Once she'd taken a closer look at the firebox, it was the books that attracted her. Reid had several dozen fine, leather-bound volumes, some of them edged in gold. There were books on science and philosophy, on astronomy, economics, law, and poetry. Some were in Latin and a few in Greek. Reid Campbell had never struck her as a man who read. He had always seemed too restless, too impatient for intellectual pursuits. It made Livi suspect that there was far more to Reid than what she'd imagined.

But before she could reach for the first slim volume on the shelf, she saw what was laid out on the writing desk. On a bed of pure white sand was an object unlike anything she'd ever seen. It was a disk about a handspan in diameter, with the velvety patina of fine, old copper. Its surface had been worked in concentric circles with complex, almost mystical designs. She reached out to touch it, but something stayed her hand.

An aura of some ancient culture rose like a warm, soft glow against her palm. She sensed its power on a more-than-physical plane, though she would have been at a loss to explain it to anyone. It was as if the copper disk resonated with a calm that was ages old, a tranquility that spread through Livi like a balm. She stood as if mesmerized, able to move but choosing to remain within the sphere of this inexplicable force.

"Livi?"

Reid's voice broke the mood, the serenity. Livi spun toward where he stood in the cabin doorway, excuses clamoring in her head.

It was evident he had come from bathing in the stream. His hair shone slick with wet. His tow shirt clung in darker patches to his shoulders and chest. She could smell the freshness on him, the green of the woods.

"I—I—didn't touch anything," she stammered. "I only brought the mending."

He came nearer, filling the cabin that suddenly seemed too close a fit for his height, his breadth, the force of who he was. She retreated half a step.

"No, Livi. It's all right."

"Is it?"

He nodded. "I should have known you'd come, that you'd be curious about why I've behaved as I have these past few days."

"And why have you?"

"Do you know anything about Creek traditions?" he asked, surprising her. When she shook her head, he continued. "The most important time of year for the Creeks is now, when the first corn is ready to be harvested. It is a time to prepare for another year, to right past wrongs, to purify oneself by cleaning and fasting."

"Is that what you've been doing?" She couldn't imagine why he was telling her this.

"The Green Corn celebration has several parts. The first is to clean the house and carry out the ashes from the old year's fire. The next is to prepare to lay a new one. Then a man must fast to be certain he's ready to begin a new cycle of life, to eat the new corn."

"And what part does the copper disk play in all of this?"

"To the Tuckabahchee Creeks, these plates are sacred. They are to be taken out for display on the second day of the Busk and put away the following morning. For a woman to touch one of the plates profanes it."

"I swear I didn't touch it," Livi hastened to reassure him.

"Well, in this case, I don't know how much it matters. David and I found two of these disks in the possession of the Hair Buyer when he was captured in Vincennes. We each took one of the disks with the intention of returning them to the Tuckabahchee Creeks when we had the chance. David must have had his with him on the trail."

"I never saw it if he did," Livi said. "But why would Colonel Hamilton have had them at Vincennes?"

"He might have held them in order to exhibit his control over his Indian allies, or to force the Tuckabahchee to fight with the British during the war. Are you sure you didn't find one of these disks among David's things?"

Livi shook her head. "I've never seen a plate like this before today."

A flicker of uneasiness came and went between his brows

as Reid carefully lifted the circular plate and slid it into an ornate doeskin medicine bag.

"I am ready to light the new fire now," he told her. "You may stay if you like."

"Are you sure?" she asked, strangely fascinated by the Creek customs and by seeing a side of Reid Campbell that she never imagined existed.

"I wouldn't have asked you if I weren't sure."

Taking up a bow drill and some tinder-dry scraps of wood, Reid knelt before the fireplace. Holding the base of the drill steady with his knees, he worked a pointed stick in a central hole with the string and the bow.

"I didn't know that you even acknowledged your Indian heritage," Livi offered, hoping to draw him out.

"And wouldn't knowing it give those Tidewater aristocrats something to laugh about? James Campbell's son still honoring the old ways, still clinging to traditions that have long since become diluted in his blood."

She heard the bitterness in him and knew that it was justified.

"But you lived with the Indians, didn't you?"

Reid continued his work. "After the master at the school in Charles Town declared me unmanageable and expelled me, after my father and his new wife threw up their hands in despair, my grandfather took me to live with my grandmother's people. The family ties are far stronger in Creek society, and my grandmother had been an honored woman in her clan.

"I was thirteen when I went to live with them, angry and impatient and full of myself. One of my uncles chose to befriend me, and he taught me everything I needed to know. How to hunt and fight and be a man. He taught me honor and respect and self-control. At seventeen, I became a warrior. Because a flock of ravens circled the encampment just as I was proving myself, they gave me the name Ravens Flight."

"It sounds as if you were happy with the Creeks. Why didn't you stay with them instead of coming back to Virginia?"

Reid shook his head. "I came back because I didn't belong with my grandmother's people, either."

"But why?" Livi knew full well she had no right to question him, no right to ask him things that he must have confided only to David. Still, she wanted to know. Reid was developing dimensions she'd never seen, shadings and striations. He was also showing her the other side of David's life. Now that David was gone, Livi yearned to glimpse the parts of her husband she had never been able to possess.

"It was my fault that I had to leave," Reid answered softly, intent on the bits of wood in front of him.

"How could it have been your fault?" Livi asked, instinctively defending him. "At seventeen, you were hardly more than a boy."

"I was old enough to kill, and that is what I did. I killed one of the other young warriors. It was an accident, but the Creeks believe that any death demands a death in answer. Like with David," he said, looking up at her. "It's the reason I can't rest until I've tracked down his killers and made them pay for what they did."

Livi nodded. In her mind's eye she saw how Reid must have been back then, bony and broad, all arms and legs. Reckless and intense, not knowing his own strength.

"But it wasn't me the other brave's clan chose to kill," Reid told her, his voice gone low. "It was my uncle, my strongest link with the tribe. Even though the Creeks consider it an honor to give your life for another, I couldn't accept that Soaring Eagle was killed because of me. I couldn't accept that Creek tradition forbade me to avenge him. And without doing that, I couldn't continue to live with my clan."

Livi stared down at the man who knelt before the empty fireplace, working to honor traditions he thought he had denied, living by a code and beliefs he told himself he'd given up. This was someone Livi had never seen in Reid before. She had feared and despised and fought this man for almost fourteen years, and she'd never really known him.

As she watched him work wood against wood in his quest for fire, one thing became very clear to her: whatever else might be in his heart, his birth and his upbringing had made Reid Campbell a dark and lonely soul, a strange and unlikely dichotomy. For reasons she could never admit or justify, Livi wanted to change that somehow.

Then all at once the hole where the pointed stick made contact with the base began to smoke. Still working the bow drill with one hand, Reid added bits of wood and char with the other. A small orange flame flared up, flickering and glowing as he breathed the fire to life.

He looked up at her, triumph on his face, a warmth in those clear blue eyes she had never imagined he was capable of generating.

It set off an answering glow in Livi's chest.

"You've begun a new fire," she said, her voice breathy and low.

Reid nodded and transferred the flame to the chalk-white center of the firebox. He fed it and stoked it and blew on it until the new fire cast flickering golden lights against the throat of the chimney, against his skin.

"Is the ceremony over?" Livi asked as he rose from his knees. "You've lit a new fire, begun a new year."

"I must keep to myself today and tonight. If this were a Creek village, there would be speeches and dancing. We'd drink the sacred drink to further purify ourselves and bathe again tomorrow."

Livi nodded, acknowledging what he'd told her, his beliefs. "Thank you for explaining, for telling me all this."

"And thank you, Livi."

"Why? What have I done that you should thank me for?"

He looked down at her for a very long time, his eyes unfathomable, his bright gaze holding hers. "For doing my mending, of course," he said.

"Now that I'm thirteen, I don't think I should have to milk the cow," Tad announced as he set the brimming bucket on the bench at the far side of the table. "Milking is women's work."

Livi couldn't help her start of surprise. "Whatever gave you that idea?"

"Well, Pa never milked except when you were sick," the boy reasoned. "And you never ask Reid to tend to Brownie."

"Brownie isn't Reid Campbell's cow," Livi pointed out, looking up from where she was separating the eggs she would use to make Tad's birthday cake. It was the first proper baking she'd been able to do since they reached Kentucky. The day before, Reid had ridden over to Logan's Station and come back with both cone sugar and wheat flour, frontier luxuries he'd managed to get from a French trader who was passing through.

"Turning thirteen should mean something special."

Livi heard the wistfulness in her son's voice and wished she had the means to make this day one he would remember. In these past months, Tad had taken on responsibility far beyond his years, faced hardships and dangers and heartbreaks that would cow a full-grown man. He deserved something to mark his fortitude and his courage. Instead she had nothing to give him but the truth.

"Tad, we've all got the same job on this homestead," she said as gently as she could. "That's making it through till harvest. It doesn't matter if I split rails or cook meals. It doesn't matter if you milk the cow or set snares as long as we're here to bring in the crops. As long as we have something to build our future on come fall."

Livi didn't dare think where that future might be. She had set her sights on a corncrib filled to the top, on a loft and a turnip hole bursting with bounty. She hadn't let herself look beyond that. She just hoped she'd made her son understand that those goals were all that could matter to any of them.

Livi expelled her breath in relief when Tad nodded. "All right, Ma. I understand. You want me to pour while you strain the milk?"

Livi shook her head. "I'll ask Violet to help me once I get this cake mixed up."

She knew he was pleased to escape the confines of the cabin; she would have been happy to leave it, too. The full, ripe heat of August lay thick across Kentucky, and the fire burning on the hearth made it unbearably hot. In deference to Livi's increasing girth and awkwardness, Violet had begun to take on more of the weeding and hoeing and gathering, leaving Livi to cook and tend the cabin. It was not a division of labor either of them particularly liked, but it was necessary.

Outside she could hear the ring of Eustace's hammer and knew that he was driving spikes into the shingles at the edge of the roof, a job every bit as hot and miserable as her own. She could hear the slop of water as Tad brought buckets up from the spring, and the steady thunk and tear of Reid splitting firewood.

He must have taken his shirt off as he worked, for all at

once she heard Cissy's ever-inquisitive voice. "How'd you get that snake twisted up your arm?"

Livi smiled. She well remembered the shock she'd felt on seeing that tattoo for the very first time. It had come peeking out from beneath the ruffled cuff of Reid Campbell's shirt the night of her sixteenth-birthday fete. She had been fascinated and appalled by the dark blue pattern coiling against his dusky skin, by the exotic, pagan look of it. Since then, she'd had more than one chance to study the tattoo up close, and it still had the power to make her go all squeamish and warm inside.

Livi moved to the doorway to hear the rest of the exchange and to take advantage of any breeze. Reid was squatting with his broad, sun-darkened back to her. Beads of sweat crawled along his ribs and down the valley of his spine. He had extended his arm so Cissy could see the pattern more clearly. Coiling around his arm from the back of his hand to just above his elbow, Reid's tattoo was meant to represent a snake, though the arrow-shaped head and sinuously patterned body seemed to Livi based more in fantasy than in fact.

Cissy stared openmouthed as she examined it.

"You like him?" Reid asked. "He's a diamondback rattler."

Cissy reached out to touch the dark, damp skin of Reid's forearm. "Is he painted on?"

"Sort of. It's something the Indians do. It's called tattooing."

"Does it hurt?"

Reid nodded, clenching and unclenching his fist, making the snake appear to writhe.

"E-e-e-w!" Cissy wrinkled her nose in distaste and took a step back.

Reid chuckled at her reaction. "Before you could get a tattoo like this, you had to prove you weren't afraid of snakes."

Livi leaned against the doorjamb. She had to admit she'd always been curious about the tattoo. Tad drifted closer, pail in hand, and even Eustace stopped hammering to listen.

"What did you have to do?" Cissy asked.

"You had to stick your hand into a rattlesnake nest—all the way up to here." He made a gesture that indicated a spot just below his elbow. "It wasn't a very smart thing to do, but I was full of piss and—ah—I was full of mischief then."

"And you got a snake tattoo if you could do that and not get bit?"

"Who said I didn't get bitten?"

Livi felt the shiver to the base of her spine.

"The snake got me right there." Reid pointed to a spot between his thumb and forefinger. "I got so sick I nearly died. Most snakes are harmless, but rattlers aren't something to fool with," he admonished Cissy.

And then he laughed.

Somehow Livi had been waiting for that laugh, anticipating, tensing, almost dreading the sound. She recognized the aggressive bark of challenge, of triumph, of unholy daring. It was a laugh that always set her teeth on edge. Perhaps that was because it was the only time Reid revealed so much of himself, the energy, the combativeness, the wildness that ran deep in blood and bone. Perhaps she'd hated that laugh because she had come to view it as a harbinger of danger, because it bore the intoxicating lure of freedom in the sound. And there had always been in it, in him, a threat to all she valued and held dear. At times that laugh had made her blood run cold.

Now it moved through her in a different way, a vibration that set something deep inside her aquiver, a challenge that quickened something hot and vital in her blood. Feeling that set her world a little out of balance. It made her wonder if he or she had changed.

She watched for a moment more: her daughter's winsome curiosity, Tad's openmouthed admiration, Eustace's answering grin. Then she turned back into the heat of the cabin, rubbing the gooseflesh from her arms.

She had just put the cake to bake on a slab of ash wood at the edge of the fire when she heard the shout of someone approaching the cabin.

"Hullo the Talbots."

She returned to the doorway just as Benjamin Logan cantered across the bridge. She waved and descended the steps to where Reid and the others were gathering to greet their guest.

"I was headed over this way, and I thought I would deliver some of the stores Reid ordered when he came to the fort." Logan swung down from his horse and handed a burlap sack to Livi. "There's some bacon in there to hold you until you get a chance to butcher those pigs, a length of blue fustian Reid said you had need of, some salt, and—a canister of tea.''

"Tea?" Livi breathed as if he had just offered her gold and pearls. "Real English tea?"

"Reid said you set high store by English tea."

Livi didn't know how Campbell had found out that tea was the single thing she'd craved all through this pregnancy, but she was grateful that he had thought to get her some. She'd run out shortly after Reid had arrived, and sassafras and walink tea made damned poor substitutes when what you craved was a cup of dark, rich brew.

"I do thank you." She bobbed her head, including both men.

"And then, let's see," Logan went on, loosening the ties of the long, flannel-wrapped parcel he had tied to the skirt of his saddle, "there's this. Is there anyone here who's old enough to have a rifle of his own?"

"Me?" Tad breathed. "Is it for me? Because I'm thirteen today?"

"Thirteen seems old enough for a boy to have a gun of his own," Logan said, a grin crinkling the corners of his mouth. "At least Reid seems to think so."

Logan handed the parcel to Tad, who dropped to his knees to unwrap it. He loosed the string and slid a classic Kentucky rifle out of its makeshift case. It was a fine piece, well balanced and graceful, with a curly maple stock. The octagonal barrel had been browned with acid, as had the flintlock, plate, and pan. The butt plate and the cover of the patch box were polished brass. The hickory ramrod that slid into the stock beneath the barrel was banded and tipped with horn.

Livi watched Tad's eyes widen with surprise and delight, watched him run his hands over wood and steel and brass as if he couldn't believe a gun as fine as this could possibly belong to him. She watched him raise the stock to his shoulder and sight down the barrel.

He's too young, she thought. *Too young to have a gun of his own. Too young to be so grown up. I remember when I held him to my breast.*

"Ma, look!" Tad exclaimed, alight with excitement and pride. "Look what Reid gave me for my birthday!"

Jealousy streaked through Livi, a jolt of envy and disappointment that suddenly turned her day to dross. *This* is what David would have done to make Tad's birthday special. This is how she should have rewarded Tad for overcoming all they'd faced on the trail. The gift of his first rifle would have told him in a tangible way how much his help and grit had meant to her.

Instead it was Reid who had marked Tad's passage into manhood, Reid who understood what her son needed and wanted far better than she. It was Reid who offered validation when all she'd given Tad today was lectures on hard work and responsibility.

"Yes, I see," she said.

Something of what she was feeling must have been evident on her face, for she saw her son's enthusiasm falter.

"Ma?" he asked, suddenly uncertain.

"I don't recall that Reid asked *me* if it was all right to give you a rifle for your birthday," Livi heard herself say. She shifted her gaze to where Campbell stood. "You didn't ask me, did you?"

For an instant before his eyes iced over, Reid looked as startled by her reaction as Tad.

"I had no idea I needed your permission to give the boy a gift," Campbell answered.

"This isn't an ordinary gift, though, is it? A rifle is something special. Having a gun of his own marks Tad as a man, and I don't know that he's ready—"

"Ma, please." Tad tried to intervene. "I'll be careful."

"He handles a rifle a good deal better than you," Campbell challenged her. "If anyone ever earned the right to have a gun of his own, Tad has in these past months."

Livi knew it was the truth and didn't care.

"Please, Ma. Pa would have let me have a gun this birthday if—"

"If he were here," Livi finished for him. "A great many things would be different if your father were here."

Livi stood stiff and brittle. If she bent so much as an inch in this, she'd surely shatter. "Wrap up the gun, Tad—"

"But, Ma, I'm not too young!"

"—and give it back to Reid."

She was vaguely ashamed that they were having this out in front of Ben Logan, but she couldn't seem to back down.

"You heard what I said, Tad. Wrap up the gun."

Campbell glared, his anger palpable. "This isn't about the gun, Livi, and you know it."

"It isn't about tea or fustian or bacon, either." She flung the burlap sack at his feet and spun back toward the cabin.

Once she was inside, the tears came in a torrent. They were tears of fury and frustration, tears of fear and confusion and self-loathing. They were tears that seemed to come from deep inside.

Reid was right; this wasn't about the rifle.

It was about everything. It was about land that didn't belong to her, crops she didn't want to sell, a future she didn't dare contemplate. It was about a boy who'd had to grow up far too quickly, and Livi's inability to make him stop.

It was about loyalties and power and intent, about jealousy that was taking on new life and form. She saw what Reid was doing with his gift. He was buying Tad's affection, and she couldn't bear to lose her son the way she'd lost his father. She had no strength to wage that war a second time.

Livi wept for a good long time. No one came to disturb her. No one dared to brave the house. And when she finally thought to check on Tad's birthday cake, she found that she'd burned it.

Reid thought he'd seen Livi at her best and at her worst, but he'd never seen Livi as she was today. Her reaction to the gift he'd given Tad was volatile and out of all proportion to what had actually happened. Her outburst had shaken Reid, and judging from the expressions on their faces, it had shaken Tad and Cissy, too. Reid was torn between following Livi into the cabin and letting her be. Letting her be clearly seemed the safer choice.

"It's going to be all right," he said, reassuring the children as best he could. "For now, though, Tad, would you take these things and put them in my cabin? And would you keep an eye on Cissy, please, while I have a word with Mr. Logan?"

As the boy did as Reid instructed, the two men ambled toward the stream. Though it didn't seem his place to do it, Reid apologized for Livi's behavior. "She's a bit high-strung these days," he murmured, "with the baby and all."

"Not once in carrying our young ones did Anne ever get

so—'high-strung' as that," Ben Logan observed. "Does Livi know the land's not hers?"

Ben Logan had been one of the witnesses to the agreement Reid and David had made.

Reid nodded. "I told her as soon as I got back."

"Then what's she doing here, working as hard as she is?"

"She refuses to leave until the crops are harvested."

Logan registered surprise with a shift of his brows. "Refused, huh?"

"She insists she won't have a mite to bless her," Campbell went on, "until she sells off the corn she and the children put in. Once she has her price, I expect they'll head back to Virginia."

Logan stopped at the edge of the stream and slanted a look in Reid's direction. "You're not going to marry her, then?"

Campbell spun to stare at Logan. "Marry her? Marry Livi Talbot? For God's sake, no!"

Ben looked at him long and hard. "Doesn't it seem the fair thing to do?"

"So she can have her share of David's land?"

"You and David didn't make that agreement to deprive his wife and children of what's rightfully theirs."

"No, of course not. I intend to pay her what the land is worth, *but only when they're ready to leave*," Reid insisted.

When Logan said nothing, Campbell went on. "God Almighty, Ben, they don't belong here. You've seen what this land can do to women, and Livi's not like Anne. She doesn't know the first thing about making a home in the wilderness. It would have been hard enough for her if David had survived, but now—"

Logan's snort of derision cut Campbell short. "Look around you, Reid. Beyond building the cabin and clearing the fields, most of what's here is her doing, isn't it?"

Reid didn't need to look at the corn waving lazily in the slow, hot breeze; at the vegetables flourishing in the garden out back; at the corral, the sty, and the chicken coop. Reid felt the warmth come up in his face.

"They don't belong here," he insisted.

"You don't want them here."

"No, I don't. I'll take responsibility for them for now. I'll go back and see them settled safely in Virginia. I'll do what

David would expect. But I can't watch over them while I'm off trading for months at a time. Besides, Livi and I have always been poison to each other. You saw the way we were just now. I don't want to live at daggers drawn for the rest of my days.''

''What I saw back there,'' Logan said, ''was a woman who doesn't know where her future lies. You hold the land she thought was hers. You're making her give up her husband's dream. You're trying to buy her son's loyalty with presents.''

''I wasn't buying his loyalty.''

Ben hesitated just long enough to make Reid think. ''The fact remains, Reid, that you control her destiny. Livi doesn't even know where she's going to have the baby she's carrying, and women set high store in knowing things like that.''

Reid remained stubbornly quiet, staring at the creek. Stoicism ran in him, and he practiced it now, hoping Logan would give up his lecturing and ride away. He didn't need the other man's meddling.

It seemed that Ben Logan had inherited some stubbornness of his own. ''How do you think Livi got herself and her family here?'' he asked pointedly.

''They came over the mountains with a pack train, I suppose, like everyone else.''

''Except the way I hear it, the party Livi was traveling with abandoned her and the children just this side of the Cumberland Gap because the little girl fell ill.''

Reid swung around. ''What?''

''From what Eustace told me, Livi and Tad took shelter in a cave and kept body and soul together while Cissy recovered from what everyone on the pack train seemed to think was smallpox.''

''Jesus!'' Reid whispered, scrubbing one hand across his face. ''Why wouldn't Eustace tell me any of this?''

''You figure it out,'' Logan challenged him. ''And you know, Reid, in the end, it was a damned good thing Livi and those kids got left behind.''

Anticipation pressed up beneath Campbell's ribs. ''Why?''

''Because the party they were with, the party of churchmen from Petersburg—''

''Yes?''

''—got massacred at Four Mile Creek.''

Reid's hands went cold; his stomach pitched. He had seen what marauding Indians could do, how they tortured the men, how they raped the women. God knows what they might have done to the children in that company. Coming upon that massacre must have been like riding through hell and back.

"And Livi said she and the children came through right after it happened," he murmured half to himself.

There must have been friends among the people who were killed: women with whom a widow like Livi would have had to form alliances, children Tad and Cissy must have called their friends.

"Jesus!" Reid muttered again.

Ben bent to pick up a handful of stones and skipped them, one by one, across the stream as if to give Reid more time to think.

"And just so you know—Eustace and Violet think the world of Livi Talbot. It seems she saved them from some slave catchers bent on taking them back to Virginia . . ."

When Reid said nothing, Ben Logan dusted his hands on the seat of his pants. "Well, I've got to be getting back," he said.

The words shook Campbell from his thoughts. "I'll just keep the things you brought out, Ben. And I appreciate you riding over."

"I've already had Erskine credit all that to your account." Ben Logan grinned and headed toward his horse. Halfway there he paused and turned. "Livi Talbot's quite a woman, Reid. See that you don't sell her short."

Reid nodded once and hunkered down on his heels at the edge of the stream. He watched the water skim past, darting and leaping over the stones.

He couldn't quite absorb all Logan had been telling him. Why hadn't Livi ever confided what their journey to Kentucky had entailed? Why hadn't she given him any idea of what they went through after David died?

Because you never asked. Because you never gave her the chance. Because she wouldn't have told you anyway.

How had Livi stood what she'd been through?

She's stronger than you thought, stronger than you ever credited her with being.

Now that he gave it some consideration, there might have

been more than obstinacy, more than antagonism in her refusal to leave.

After the struggle they'd endured to reach this land, the effort they'd made to plow and sow the fields, Livi must have felt this land belonged to her—agreement or no. It made him wonder if she really meant to leave when the crops came in. It made him question his own motives in demanding that she go. Ben Logan had deliberately stirred up this hornet's nest and Reid Campbell had the feeling he was going to get stung.

✺ 15 ✺

𝒫atches's barking and the sound of someone banging on the cabin door jerked Livi from a sound sleep. She floundered toward the edge of the bed, trying to make some sense of what was happening. The weight of her belly dragged like an anchor as she swung her feet over the side.

"Yes, who is it?" she called out.

The answer came muffled through the heavy door. "I'm from Logan's Station, ma'am. We had news of Injuns headed this way."

Though the warning sounded genuine, Livi glanced up to where Tad stood looking down from the loft. "Go see who's there," she whispered, "before I open the door."

While he checked the lookouts beneath the overhang at the edge of the roof, Livi snatched the pistol from the mantel and checked its prime.

Patches continued barking as if he meant to tear someone apart.

"Looks all right," Tad called down.

Livi slipped the bolt and peered outside. The man who stood before her was swathed in clothes that were one with the night. All she could make out beneath the brim of his hat was the gleam of huge, uneven teeth.

"It's Lige Higgins, ma'am," he told her. "Ben Logan sent me over this way to warn the folks who's settlin' out that we got word from Boonesborough. A party of Shawnee and Wy-

225

andot is sweepin' down from the north. Ben says pack up what you can carry and come on into the fort.''

Livi's heartbeat staggered with the news. ''Now? In the middle of the night?''

'' 'At's what Ben said.''

''And that's what you would do?''

Higgins flashed a grin that took up most of his face. ''I'd be halfway to the fort by now—in my nightshirt if need be!''

Livi nodded, trying to assimilate what Higgins had told her, trying to think what she must do to prepare to leave.

Reid appeared at the far side of the breezeway, solid, calm, and still tucking the shirttail into his pants. ''How long ago did Logan get word, Lige?''

''Hour and a half, maybe two.''

''Then they'll be here by morning,'' Reid said, thinking aloud.

''Lessen they stop to do some raidin' on the way,'' Lige agreed. ''If there's nothing more you need, I best be on my way. I got two more cabins to find.''

Reid nodded. ''Then go ahead.''

No sooner had Higgins leaped into the saddle of his lathered horse than Reid began issuing orders. ''Livi, pack up a few clothes and what food you can carry. Tad, go wake Eustace and Violet. Tell them what's happened and—''

Livi spoke up. ''Now wait just a minute. I'll not have my son chasing around in the dark, especially if there are Indians—''

''Jesus, Livi!'' Reid exclaimed. ''Didn't David ever teach you sometimes it's just better to do what you're told?''

Tad took the argument out of their hands, pushing past where his mother stood in the doorway. He disappeared into the dark at the back of the cabin with the dog at his heels.

Livi bristled for a moment, stung by Reid's tone and Tad's defiance. But there was more than enough to do to get ready without wasting time trying to put Reid Campbell in his place.

Cissy had herself half dressed and was full of questions when Livi turned back into the cabin. She answered them as best she could while she tucked clothes for each of them into a sack.

''How come we're going to the fort?'' Cissy demanded.

''Because we'll be safer there if the Indians come.''

"When will the Indians come?"

"Tomorrow, Reid thinks."

"Tomorrow?" Cissy mulled that over. "Have we ever been to the fort?"

Livi dumped the never-ending pile of mending from one of the baskets Violet had made and began filling it with food-stuffs from their stores.

"Tad and Reid and I went to the fort. That's where we got Patches. It's kind of like a town with a wall around it. Lots of families live there all the time. Others, like us, will be moving in until the danger from the Indians passes."

Livi spared a thought for what staying in the fort would be like. *It's bound to be overcrowded, overwrought, and unbearably hot.* She took one of Tad's shirts out of the sack and exchanged it for a thinner one.

"There should be lots of children to play with, Cissy," Livi told her daughter, putting the best face she could on what lay ahead. "And there might even be a school where you can show everyone how well you write your letters. You're going to like it."

"What about our cabin?" Cissy asked.

What about it? Livi wondered, pausing with her hands full of summer squash. Undefended, it would be easy prey for any Indian band that might pass by. She knew Indians had burned cabins all along the frontier, and she couldn't bear the thought of the home David had built for her going up in flames. Of the bed he'd made for them to share turned to ashes. Of everything gone.

And the fields. Oh, God! What if the Indians trampled the crops? They'd spent the whole summer tending them. They'd spent these past three days stripping back the corn husks in preparation for harvest. She couldn't bear to see all that work, all that struggle and determination, come to naught. Those crops were the only future she and her children had.

"My God, Livi, you're not even dressed!" Reid strode into the cabin, impatient, almost angry. "Tad and Eustace are saddling the horses. What have you got that's ready to go?"

"Reid, I've been thinking—"

"There isn't time to think."

"—about the cabin, about leaving the farm. If we're not

here to protect it, will the Indians burn it? Will they destroy the fields?''

"If you're not out of here come morning, they may burn the cabin over your head. Is that what you want?''

"But, Reid!''

He stopped and spoke calmly, though she had the sense he'd like to take her by the arms and shake her hard. "Do you want us to try to fend off an Indian attack all by ourselves? That's what it could come to if we stay. If the Indians come in force, the only way anyone on this frontier is going to survive is by being in one of the stations.''

"But David built this cabin. Everything he was or hoped for is in these walls.''

Though Reid's face softened, she could see the flint in his eyes. "Everything David was or hoped for is in Tad and Cissy, in that baby you're carrying. Do you want to stay here and risk something a lot more precious than a few bits of wood?''

Livi nodded as understanding dawned. Reid was right. What had she been thinking?

Before Livi could agree, Violet breezed into the room, her dark eyes snapping. "You leave off bullyin' her, Marse Reid. We be ready to leave 'fore you know it.''

"I'll hold you to that, Violet,'' Reid told her and left the rest of the packing in Violet's capable hands.

"Now go on,'' Violet admonished Livi, nudging her toward the peg where she'd hung her clothes the night before. "An' don't you go bein' mad at him. He's just doin' what he knows is best.''

By the time Livi had struggled into her bodice, skirts, knit stockings, and a sturdy pair of boots, Tad and Eustace had the horses saddled and waiting out front. Reid's three pack animals were tied to the back of Eustace's saddle, and Patches trotted impatiently between their legs.

"Where's Reid's horse?'' Livi wanted to know as she mounted her buttermilk mare. Eustace handed Cissy up to her.

"I'm staying on until morning,'' Reid answered, coming out of his door with a small keg of powder and a sack of balls under one arm and that shiny new rifle tucked beneath the other.

"But you said—'' Livi protested.

"I know what I said,'' he answered, stowing the powder

and balls on one of the creels. "That was before the damn cow turned up missing. She's probably just wandered off somewhere. As soon as I find her, I'll come in, too. Probably before you've had a chance to dish up breakfast."

He handed the rifle to Tad as if daring Livi to protest the return of the gift. She acknowledged the exchange with a scowl, but held her peace. There might be Indians lurking in the woods between here and Logan's Station, and another rifle could help to fend them off.

"You go on now," Reid urged them. "I'll see you at Logan's Station tomorrow. Tell Ben I'll be glad to ride scout if he needs me."

Reid stood at the edge of the breezeway, his feet planted and his thumbs notched into the waistband of his trousers. He looked fearless and resolute, as if he hadn't just committed himself to do exactly what he'd warned Livi against. By the jut of his chin and the energy radiating around him, she could tell that he wasn't about to be dissuaded, either.

Livi felt her face get hot. Damn him for taking this kind of chance. Damn him for doing exactly what he'd warned her against. Damn him for acting as if he were invincible. Was he so addicted to the wild, sharp taste of danger that he'd risk his life for the sake of a cow?

Then Livi suddenly understood. For as long as she could remember, Reid had always held back, remained aloof. Now all at once she saw the alienation and ambivalence at the core of him. She saw that not only was the solitary path the one he'd chosen for himself, it was the only one he dared to follow. What he was doing now—staying behind, sending them off without him, risking God knew what—was part of that.

His self-imposed isolation fired Livi's anger, firmed new resolve. She meant to reach out and challenge him, meant to set this infuriating backwoodsman on his heels.

Jockeying her mare a little closer to where he stood, Livi leaned toward him and ducked her head. Reid tried to step back but wasn't quick enough. There, in front of everyone, she did something she never dreamed she would do. She kissed Reid Campbell—her rival, her devil, her nemesis—full on the mouth. It wasn't all that deep a kiss, but Livi made enough contact to be aware of the taste of him on her when she retreated.

She wasn't ready to acknowledge to anyone else why she'd kissed him, or to examine her motives too closely. Nor was there time. It was enough that she saw a bright flare of incredulity in Reid's eyes as she turned her horse away. It was enough that as the night and the forest closed around them, she could still feel his gaze burning into her back.

Reid didn't make it to the fort for breakfast. All over Logan's Station, people ate their mush and johnnycake, while Livi Talbot paced the narrow walkway on the wall above the front gate. She'd been up there since just before dawn, watching, waiting, and calling Reid Campbell every name she knew.

The ride through the forest the night before had been harrowing. Without Reid to guide them, it had been impossible to stick to the trail in the dark. Afraid to use lanterns to light their way, they straggled cross-country, stumbling up and down ravines, pushing through brush, riding almost aimlessly until they came upon the main road as much by accident as by design.

Livi had been sure that at any moment she would hear the whoosh of arrows and a piercing yell that heralded attack. She had been sure that every copse of trees along the roadside was bristling with savages. In spite of that, they'd made it to the fort and been immediately welcomed. They were assigned a place on the ground floor of the northeast blockhouse where they could put their belongings and blankets. It was there they bedded down amidst a clamor and wail of more than a score of other displaced families. Livi had left Eustace, Violet, and the children asleep in the blockhouse more than two hours ago.

She was standing with her elbows braced against the pickets to the left of the gate when she heard two of the sentries call to each other.

" 'Ay, Will, what d'you make of that?''

" 'S an Injun brave leading a cow, ain't it?''

Livi turned to where the men were pointing. The sentries' assessment was right. Far across the open fields, she could see Reid leading the cow.

She could see right off why the sentries might imagine that he was an Indian. Reid was dressed in his buckskin trousers and trade-cloth shirt. He wore a clutch of eagle feathers tucked into his hat. There even seemed to be a bow and arrows strapped to the back of his saddle.

"Prob'ly up to no good," one of the sentries speculated. "Prob'ly some kind of a trick."

"Wait till he gets a little closer and I'll pick him off."

"You'll do nothing of the sort!" Livi exclaimed. "You call down and have them open the gates. That's Reid Campbell, my—ah—my partner, bringing in my cow."

Both men turned and looked at her. "Ma'am?"

"You heard me!" Livi insisted.

The men looked at each other for confirmation and finally called down.

Livi was waiting when Reid rode in with Brownie in tow. All four of the pigs were trotting along behind, and once he had dismounted, Reid set a pot of gruel on the ground. It had apparently enticed the pigs into making the journey from the cabin to the fort.

"Hello, Livi," he greeted her, an odd uneasiness around his mouth.

"Damn fool," she answered back.

A grin gathered and broke across his features.

"Don't you know you nearly got yourself shot coming here dressed the way you are?" she admonished him. "If I hadn't been up there on the wall—"

"Watching for me, were you?"

He picked up the iron pot and carried it toward the crowded pigpen in the near corner of the fort. Once he'd ushered Livi's pigs inside and closed the gate, he set the pot down and waited for them to eat it clean.

Livi felt herself color up at his question, but refused to answer. "We're over in the northeast blockhouse," she told him.

"So you did make it here all right."

"It would have been a damn sight easier if you'd been with us," Livi grumbled.

Having handed off the horse and the cow to one of the boys tending the corral, Reid turned to her. "Do you have any idea where I can find Ben Logan?"

"There's supposed to be a meeting in the front blockhouse first thing this morning. I'll warrant he's there now, or soon will be."

Reid nodded and moved in that direction. Livi tagged along. She'd meant to attend the meeting anyway.

The large first-floor room was crowded and noisy and swiftly filling with pipe smoke. Reid elbowed his way to a place by the wall. Nearly as many women as men were in attendance, some with children on their knees, others with bits of sewing they planned to do while they were listening. It seemed to Livi an indication that women were considered an important part of the community.

When Ben Logan began to speak, the room went still. "George Essex came in from scouting half an hour ago. He said he didn't see any Indian sign this far south, but that there's something stirring up north. He thinks we need to be ready, either to come to the aid of another station or to defend our own. While he's not the tracker Essex is, Phillip Wyant rode out this morning to see what he can see. If there's anyone willing to scout for us who's more experienced—"

"I'll be glad to do it, Ben," Reid called out.

Heads swiveled in their direction. A boil of speculation ran through the room.

"Let a goddamned red bastard scout for us?"

"How do we know we can trust the likes of *him?*" someone asked.

"Which side is he on anyway?"

Reid certainly heard the comments, but there was not so much as a quiver of acknowledgment in his face.

He must be used to the censure, Livi thought. This must be part of what makes Reid the way he is. Certainly the men's behavior confirmed much of what Livi had surmised the night before. Still, she wasn't about to let anyone disparage Reid's parentage or his abilities.

She drew in breath to defend him just as Ben Logan spoke up. "For those of you who don't know, this here's Reid Campbell. His pappy and grandpappy were two of the traders who explored the land beyond the Blue Ridge and helped open it up for settlement. Reid fought with General Clark and a few of the rest of us during the war. He and the Talbots have gone into partnership down along Wilcox Creek. *And* he's one of the best damned scouts I've ever seen. We should be pleased that he'll ride out for us."

Livi glared around her as Logan spoke, furious that in

Reid's case Ben had to give credentials to prove his loyalty.

Reid remained silent, his face like stone.

There was another stir of whispers when Ben was done.

"Now," he went on, "I intend to take Reid up on his offer to scout—unless there are any objections."

There were none, though Livi sensed there might have been if Logan had been a less forceful or respected man.

"I'll need a fresh horse," Campbell said, acknowledging only Ben.

"Then by all means, Campbell, take one of mine," Logan offered, his gaze every bit as intent as Reid's. "And I'm pleased that you'll be riding out for us."

Reid nodded once and swung away. His boot soles rang in the quiet as the others watched him go.

Livi followed him out and went to gather up a meal of parched corn and jerky for him to take on the trail. She caught up with Reid and Tad at the picket line a few minutes later.

". . . get any crazy ideas in her head about going back to that cabin while I'm gone. You hear me, boy?"

"I won't," Tad promised.

"And take care of everybody else."

"I will."

"I brought you some food and water," Livi said, breaking in.

"Thanks," Reid said and took the packet, tucking it into his saddlebag.

Their single brush of hands as he took the food warmed Livi to the elbows. The energy in Reid was blazing now, focused and controlled and compelling, but leaping higher and hotter than she'd ever sensed it in him. Perhaps danger did that. Perhaps it was the thrill of facing the unknown. Perhaps he dared to burn so brightly because he wasn't afraid of burning out.

She didn't know if the thought made her feel better or worse.

Reid didn't give her time to contemplate. He swung into the saddle and with a wave of farewell kicked his mount in the direction of the gate. By the time the doors had closed behind him, he was hunkered low over his horse's neck, galloping full out toward the edge of the woods.

*   *   *

Livi hated Logan's Station. She hated the sun that beat down from a ruthless sky. She hated the smell of cows and pigs and horses, of unwashed people and overused privies. She hated the constant buzz of conversation and the restriction of staying within the station's walls. She hated not knowing if her cabin was standing or burned to the ground, if her crops were drooping in the heat or had been trampled into the earth.

She missed the cool, thick green that greeted her when she stepped out of her cabin door; the taste of water dipped fresh from the spring; the soft, hollow call of doves at sunset. Sometimes she even found herself missing Reid.

He'd been back to the station only twice in a fortnight, arriving in the purple and gold of lingering dusk. Both times he'd come in dirty, silent, and glassy-eyed. Both times he'd required only a hot meal and the use of Livi's blankets. Both times he'd slept like the dead and been gone at first light.

Livi almost wished she could ride out with Reid. Beyond the walls there were Indians, uncertainty, and danger, but out there she'd have something to do besides wait. She knew that staying at Logan's was the safest course, the one she must follow for her children's sake, but the days were interminable. Never could Livi remember feeling so restless, so confined.

"As close as you are to birthing that babe and as hot as it is," Anne Logan observed as she watched Livi fold the laundry she was taking off the line, "you shouldn't want to do anything but sit."

"I feel better if I'm moving," Livi answered, spanking the wrinkles out of Tad's extra shirt. "I keep thinking of all there is to do at the cabin while I'm stuck here."

"Well, there's no sense going back before they're sure it's safe. You may as well stay on with us for as long as it takes to chase those Indians back across the Ohio River."

"And how long will that be?" Livi whispered under her breath.

That the children objected to the confinement more than anyone didn't make things easier. In the hope of giving them something to do, several mothers strung canvas between two of the cabins to provide a shady place to meet, and three or four others agreed to give lessons. There were only five slates and less than a dozen precious books, but somehow they managed. Livi took her stint as teacher by using stones and acorns and buttons to show the younger children how addition and subtraction worked. She taught the older students the rhymes and songs she'd learned from one of her brother's tutors that made multiplication and division tables easier to remember. She impressed the children with her ability to work out any problem in her head and challenged them to do the same.

Eustace kept busy helping the station's blacksmith, a position that paid better than Livi ever could. Violet set herself up cooking for the unmarried men around the compound. The couple's industriousness made Livi wonder if they couldn't do better living and working at a station than they ever could with her. That harvest was fast approaching meant the decisions she'd put off in the spring would now come due. She and her family would either pack up their belongings and take to the Wilderness Road or find a way to make Reid agree to let them stay. In either case, she had Eustace and Violet to consider, too. She had promises to keep to them, though she wasn't sure how.

One day as the two women sat together peeling onions and potatoes for one of the vats of stew made each day to feed the refugees, Livi raised the question of the future with Violet.

The woman looked at Livi long and hard before answering. "We's happy with that piece of ground," Violet admitted, her deep, smoky voice gone even more raspy than usual. "We come to like havin' somethin' t' call our own. Here in the fort, it don' matter if we's free. Them seeing us the way they do makes us slaves again. You gave us somethin' when we was nothin', Miz 'Livia, and we owe you."

Livi only hoped that she wouldn't have to betray the Hadleys' trust once the crops were harvested.

So much depended on what happened in these next weeks. The success or failure of her crops would determine where and how well she and her children would live. Her last and most precious child would arrive. Livi was surprised how much she wanted David's baby born in the place that had been both the beginning and the end of his father's dreams. This land, these hills, this wild, unforgiving place had been second only to his family in David's heart. No matter what the future might bring, Livi meant for this child to touch his father's legacy.

I won't let Reid send me away until after you're born, she promised the babe who kicked and stretched inside her. *Somehow I'll find a way to wait. Somehow I'll find a way to make you part of the land your father loved.*

As the second week at the station threatened to turn into a third, the equanimity that had held the diverse populace together came unglued. One of the guards for the detail of men bringing water up from the stream swore he saw something move on the opposite bank and fired at it. Spooked, the other guards discharged their weapons, too, leaving the group unprotected and well beyond rifle range of the men on the palisaded walls. One woman dumped a nearly full pail of milk over another for some real or imagined slight. Tad managed to pick a fistfight with an older, larger, and significantly stronger boy.

Livi clucked over him and stitched up the gash to the left of his eye. "You've got to find a way to get along with these folks, Tad," she admonished him. "We have to stay here until we know it's safe."

"How soon will that be?" he demanded belligerently.

All Livi's questions came back to haunt her at Tad's sharp words. "I just don't know," she snapped at him.

The answer came that afternoon with the thunder of hoofbeats that heralded George Essex's arrival. The scout flung himself off his horse into the unruly crowd that had gathered as soon as it heard the call to open the gates.

Ben Logan elbowed his way through to where Essex was just handing off the reins of his lathered horse. "What's the word?" Logan demanded.

"A party of about fifty British rangers and three hundred Indians under William Caldwell has crossed the Ohio," Essex reported. "They've got Bryan's Station under siege, and the fort needs reinforcements."

"Three hundred Indians!" The words went through the assembled settlers in a single gasp. It was as large a party as the British had mounted against them during the war.

"The British bring artillery?" Ben wanted to know. When Essex shook his head, Logan nodded. "Fair enough. I'll lead the relief party myself."

He dispatched riders to the other southern stations: Whitley's and Twitty's and as far west as Glover's, over on the north branch of the Green River. "Tell them we'll be leaving at first light," he instructed.

The whole compound turned out to see them off: the men and boys cheering, the women wringing their handkerchiefs and trying not to cry. Livi and her children stood with all the rest, wondering what would happen, if they would be safe.

Logan and his volunteers had been gone only a matter of hours when Phillip Wyant came in from scouting. His news was a good deal better than Essex's had been.

"It's all clear to the south and west," he reported. "Things may be hot at Bryan's Station, but that's near fifty miles away, and I haven't seen Indian sign for at least half that way."

"All the British and Indians are up to the north?" someone asked in confirmation.

"I imagine the raiders at Bryan's will turn tail and run once our boys arrive," Wyant boasted. "I'll warrant there won't be anything left for our men to do but chase the savages back where they came from."

"It's safe, then?" Arthur Johnstone asked. He and his family had been sleeping in the same blockhouse the Talbots had. "We can head on back to our farms without losing our hair?"

"Looks safe as a featherbed to me," Wyant assured him.

It was better news than Livi had dared to contemplate. They rolled up their blankets and saddled their horses, rounded up the cow and the pigs, and said their good-byes.

"You sure you're doing the right thing by leaving the station so soon?" Anne Logan asked. "Don't you think you should wait until Reid comes back?"

"Phillip Wyant says it's safe, and I'm eager to see how our fields and cabin fared in these past days," Livi answered. Her need to return felt like a good deal more than that, but she wasn't prepared to examine her feelings more closely. "Since the Indians never penetrated this far south," she continued, "things at the cabin should be fine. I'll just feel better once I get there and make sure."

"Well, take care of yourself," Anne said, walking with her out of the blockhouse into the close, still air of the compound. "Send for me when the time comes for that young'un to make an appearance."

"I'll do that," Livi answered. "And thank you, Anne, for everything." She accepted Eustace's help clambering into the saddle and shifted until she found a position that was relatively comfortable.

It was not quite noon when Livi Talbot and her entourage left the station: the two children, a Negro man and wife, three packhorses, a cow, four pigs, and a half-grown hound. They were eager to reach the cabin on Wilcox Creek, eager to reach their home.

"Rider coming in!"

Reid heard one of the sentries call out the warning as he galloped his horse straight toward the gates of Logan's Station. He'd been in the saddle for four full days and couldn't think of much beyond filling the hole in his belly with something warm and finding a place to sleep. But he had to talk to Ben Logan first.

The compound didn't look so packed with people as when he'd ridden in the other times. There didn't seem to be the usual number of men on the walls. What could Ben Logan be thinking of to ease back on his defenses, especially now?

Reid swung out of the saddle and handed the reins to one of the boys hovering nearby. "See that he gets an extra ration of oats," Campbell instructed.

Reid had expected his arrival to draw more attention. Ben usually came running when a scout rode in, and there were always people eager for news. Campbell had to admit to a twitch of disappointment that neither Livi nor Tad had come to welcome him.

"Where can I find Ben Logan?" Reid demanded of one of the men who was tending the gate.

"More'n halfway to Bryan's Station, I'd say."

Reid spun around. "What do you mean?"

The man snorted and spit before he answered. "Got word last night that British rangers and Indians got Bryan's Station under siege. Captain Logan gathered up those men we could spare and sent riders to ask for help from t'other stations to the south that ain't been threatened. They lit out b'fore dawn. 'Bout four hundred men altogether."

Reid swore under his breath. "Then Logan doesn't know about the splinter force?"

"Splinter force?"

With an effort Reid shook off his weariness. "Who's in charge with Logan gone?"

"That'd be Jake Prescott."

Campbell turned just in time to see Prescott hurrying toward him.

"They told me you'd just ridden in," the short, bespectacled man greeted him. He didn't look like much of a fighter, but Reid knew better from the months they'd spent with General Clark.

"I just heard about Logan heading for Bryan's Station—which is fine as long as he hasn't weakened our forces here too much."

Prescott's eyes widened. "We've been told that everything to the south is clear. Essex came in with the word about Bryan's Station yesterday afternoon, and Ben left at sunrise with volunteers. Then Wyant rode in this morning and said that the British and the Indians were concentrated up north. He said he hadn't seen any sign of Indians since he crossed Redbird Creek."

A stitch of concern jerked tight in the hollow beneath Campbell's ribs. "And you believed him? Christ, Jake, you know Wyant couldn't follow a trail in new-fallen snow!" Reid blurted out as they crossed the compound.

"From what I saw, I'd say the British and the Indians split their forces just south of Blue Lick. The main body headed west for Bryan's Station. About a third continued south. Every few miles a group of eight or ten would splinter off—for raiding, unless I miss my guess. I passed four or five burned-out cabins on my way, one of them still smoldering. I expect the families had come into the stations, because, aside from a few dead animals, I didn't see any other loss of life. Now, if everyone just has the sense to stay put—"

Prescott's brows came together. He shook his head. "When Wyant came in and told everyone it was clear, a number of families headed back to their homesteads."

Reid stopped dead in his tracks. He knew how reluctant Livi had been to leave the cabin, how worried she'd been about the crops. He'd sensed how unsettled and restless she was the last time he'd ridden in.

"Were the Talbots one of the families that left?" he asked, already suspecting the worst.

Prescott dipped his head and glanced away. "Livi Talbot and her family pulled out just short of midday."

❦16❦

The sight brought tears to Livi's eyes: the corn drooping in the fields, the squash and pumpkin vines gone yellow with the heat and lack of rain, the pennyroyal she'd planted around the foundation of the cabin lying prostrate in the sun. Though it seemed brooding and sad without a family to give it life, the cabin itself stood intact. To Livi's mind, no place on earth could have appeared more welcoming.

She'd lain awake each night at Logan's Station wondering if they'd return to a burned-out cabin and trampled fields. She couldn't imagine how they'd live if that had happened. But it hadn't. Thank God it hadn't.

Laughing, suddenly ebullient with relief, Livi urged her mount down the rise and across the bridge. It took her only seconds to dismount in front of the cabin and throw open the door. Heat billowed out of the house like a blowsy embrace. Though it was hot enough to set bread to baking, Livi pressed inside. Everything was as they'd left it: the bed unmade, the mending dumped hither and thither on the tabletop, a bag of meal lying forgotten on the floor. She let out a long, uneven breath, feeling as if she'd been keeping it stored up inside her ever since they'd left.

Without discussion, each of them fell to work. Tad and Eustace unloaded and cared for the animals. Violet lit the fire. Livi unpacked their belongings and put them away. Once they'd set things to rights, Livi and Tad began hauling water from the stream to the languishing vegetable patch. Violet and

Cissy headed out into the fields to pick a few ears of corn so they could make gritted bread for supper. Eustace climbed the ridge to see how his own small house had fared while he and Violet were away.

"How long do you think it will be before Reid gets home?" Tad asked, handing his mother another bucket so she could dole out water to her thirsty plants.

"I can't imagine that he'll be back before whatever's going on at Bryan's Station is settled and the Indians are back where they belong."

"I don't know why you wouldn't let me ride out with Ben Logan and the rest of the men."

Livi paused and glanced across at her son. She wanted to tell Tad what any mother would tell her thirteen-year-old: that he was too young to go, that he didn't know the hardships he would face. But Tad knew. He probably knew more about death and dying, about danger and courage, than many of the young men who had ridden out with Logan that morning.

"I couldn't let you go with Ben Logan because I needed you here with me," Livi answered, glad she'd been able to protect him this once. "If the baby comes early, I want to be able to count on you for help."

"You know you can count on me, Ma," Tad assured her and passed another pail her way. "Just like always."

"Just like always," Livi echoed. Tad wouldn't hear the regret in those words, but she felt the shame of them way down deep. Once the baby came, once she knew if they would be staying or going back to Virginia, things would be better. She wouldn't have to depend on Tad so much.

As they worked, the afternoon went hot and still around them. The trees stood listless and silent. The murky sun slipped behind a bank of clouds. The air took on a weight and presence of its own.

While they lugged more sloshing pails of water around the corner of the house, Patches set off barking somewhere up on the ridge. "Sounds like he's treed a coon again," Livi observed, pausing to swipe sweat from her forehead.

"I think he missed hunting when we were all at the fort."

"And you did, too."

Tad ducked his head. "You're not still mad about the rifle Reid gave me, are you?"

Livi took a breath. "I wasn't angry with you. I wasn't really angry with Reid. I was angry that I hadn't either the money or the sense to buy that rifle for you myself." It was a hard admission, but she figured she owed it to her son.

"It's all right, Ma."

"I want you to know that it wasn't because I didn't think you were ready," she went on. "God knows you've earned the right to have a rifle of your own. God knows you've proved—"

"It's all right, Ma," he said again. "I understand."

That was the worst of it. Tad almost always understood.

With a weary nod, Livi straightened and braced her hands behind her waist. Her back ached clear around into her ribs these days. Or maybe that ache was from the baby's kicking. She'd never carried a child who kicked and turned and jabbed her the way this one did.

Tad seemed to sense she was about done in. "Why don't you let me finish up? Eustace will be along soon enough to help me."

Up on the hill, they could hear Patches barking again. They paused to listen, the sharp, staccato yaps coming harsh and close together.

"Maybe that's Eustace coming now," Livi suggested.

"Maybe not," Tad murmured, shifting on his feet, peering up the hill.

"I think I'll head on over to the cornfield and see what's keeping Violet and Cissy."

"Fine, Ma. I think you should do that," Tad said.

A restless wind kicked up as she started toward the creek. It set the water beneath the bridge to churning and rippled through the tree branches. It tugged at the loose strands of Livi's hair and batted them against her cheeks. It carried a faint, earthy promise of coming rain.

Livi sniffed appreciatively. Oh, Lord, how they needed that rain!

She clambered heavily over the split-rail fence at the edge of the nearest field and was enveloped in the sweet summer scent of growing corn. She set off along the ends of the head-high rows, looking for Violet and Cissy. The turned-back husks scraped and rattled in the wind as she padded past.

By the time she'd reached the sixth row of corn, concern

for the two of them had begun to prickle down Livi's back. She couldn't imagine why they would have gone so deep into the field when any of the half-dried ears would do for making supper. When she reached the twelfth row, Livi's itch of concern turned to nettles of outright panic.

Three rows later, she spotted what looked like a pile of rags lying near the opposite end. She stopped and stared, trying not to let her imagination get the best of her. She ran the width of the cornfield anyway, dread building with every step. The closer she came, the more familiar that faded blue fabric seemed to be. Her heart pumped hard as she approached. She was less than a dozen steps away when she saw that the fabric and the earth beneath it were stained with blood.

Livi churned hot with horror, cold with fear. "Violet," she whispered, tears spilling from her eyes. "Oh, Violet, no!"

The wind winnowed down the rows of corn, ruffling the hem of the dead woman's petticoat. She lay sprawled half on her side, her shoulders hunched, her face turned into the dirt. There was red where her hair should be.

Livi swiped at the tears with her hands. She couldn't tell if Violet had died alone or if she was sheltering Cissy's broken body in the protective arc of her own.

Livi closed the distance and reached for Violet's arm. She pulled the dead woman onto her back. Violet came slowly, her head lolling. Her throat lay open in a single slash. The bodice of her gown was red with gore.

There was no child beneath her.

Livi stumbled to the ground, her knees gone weak. "Where is she, Violet?" Livi demanded around her sobs. "Where has my Cissy-baby gone?"

There was no answer in the rising wind.

Hunkered there in the dirt, Livi forced herself to think. She wanted to shout her daughter's name and knew she dared not. She wanted to run screaming toward the house and held herself still. Abhorrence of how Violet had died backed up in Livi's throat. She'd died violently. Alone and afraid. Livi wanted to take the woman in her arms and comfort her, but she had to find her daughter first.

Skirting Violet's body, Livi crept to the end of the row of cornstalks. She had no way of knowing where Cissy was. She had no way of knowing if the Indians were gone or lying in wait a handbreadth away. All Livi knew was that she couldn't return to the cabin until she'd searched for her child.

She mustered her courage and inched around the end of the corn row. The next lay long and empty. So did the one that followed it. Each time she peered down the length of another row, Livi grew more certain that, as hard as she'd tried, she had failed to keep her baby safe.

Livi throbbed as if a vital part of herself had been hacked away. She shook with self-loathing and remorse. She should have stayed at the station a few more days. She should have waited for Reid. Her little girl was lost and Violet was dead because she'd been in too much of a hurry to return to the cabin. Still Livi kept on walking, looking down row after silent row of cornstalks.

Then she caught sight of a tousled head just barely visible amidst the tangle of weeds and wildflowers on the far side of the fence.

"Cissy." Her child's name was in her mouth before Livi could bite it back. "Cissy?"

The little girl raised her frightened, tear-streaked face.

Livi struggled over the fence. She caught her daughter in her arms and held her amidst the wind-whipped grass. She shivered as she held her. She sobbed silently into Cissy's hair.

"I didn't want to see," Cissy confessed in a whisper. "I didn't want to see the Indians hurt Violet. I ran away."

"It's all right," Livi whispered.

Cissy shook her head. "Violet's not all right. I could hear them hurting her."

Livi crushed her baby closer.

Cissy's tiny, tear-choked voice came muffled against Livi's bodice. "The Indians made Violet go away, didn't they, Mama? They made her go away like Papa did."

Livi nodded, not knowing what to say, how to lighten the burden her child was carrying. "There wasn't anything you could do to help," she whispered, stroking her daughter's hair. "You were such a smart, brave girl to find this place to hide. It's what Violet wanted you to do."

But her baby refused to be comforted. They knelt together at the edge of the field. Cissy sobbed softly. Livi looked around, figuring what they should do.

They couldn't stay crouched behind the fence post where

Cissy had taken shelter. Even tucked up in the shadow of the trees, Livi knew they were vulnerable. The Indians could be anywhere, in the corn, in the woods. At any moment they could double back.

There were others to think about, too. Tad and Eustace must be warned. They'd have to barricade themselves inside the cabin to have a chance.

Livi took her daughter's hand and motioned her to silence. In a crouch, they stole toward the cabin. They moved slowly, clumsily, silently, knowing one footfall, one flash of movement, could betray them.

Livi and Cissy came to the notch at the end of the fence. There was cover here, a modicum of safety among the weeds. Livi knew they had to reach the cabin. It stood on the far side of the creek, across what seemed like acres of open ground.

Above them, the trees creaked in the wind. The sky loomed dark and threatening. Perhaps the Indians would leave if it began to rain. Perhaps if they stayed where they were for a little while, she and Cissy would be safe.

Then Tad appeared at the cabin door. "Ma!" he yelled. "*Ma!* Where are you, Ma? There are Indians!"

Livi realized they couldn't wait it out.

Grabbing Cissy's wrist, she broke for the house. Her gait was lumbering at best and the little girl managed to keep up. As they ran, a whoop erupted from the far side of the field. A brave lit out after them. In the doorway, Tad swung his rifle to his shoulder and drew a bead.

Livi felt the report of the rifle break over her. She didn't look back to see if Tad's aim was true. She didn't slow when the Indians' rifles barked in answer. She didn't falter when water spattered to their right as they crossed the bridge. Livi charged the last twenty yards in a hail of gunfire. Dirt erupted on either side. A ball slammed into the cabin above her head as she rushed her daughter up the steps. Tad banged the door closed behind her and jammed the bolt in place.

Livi sagged onto one of the puncheon benches and sat there panting. Her heart was racing. She couldn't seem to suck enough air into her lungs. The baby kicked as if he were none too happy with her recent activities, either.

And suddenly Livi laughed—breathless and relieved. For

the moment, her family was safe. For the moment, they were here together.

Then slowly she raised her head and looked around. "Where's Eustace?" she asked, though she wasn't sure she wanted to hear Tad's answer.

He looked up from reloading his rifle. "He never got back from their cabin."

Mindful of what Cissy had heard and seen, Livi nodded. "I found Violet out in the cornfield."

Tad's face shaded even grimmer than it had been before. He removed the plug from one of the loopholes on the front of the cabin and peeked outside. "Looks like they're gathering on the far side of the creek."

Livi hauled herself to her feet and went to check the loopholes around back. Directly in her line of sight, one of the pigs lay in a pool of blood. There were chicken feathers everywhere. She couldn't help but wonder how the rest of the animals had fared. Still, that was the only evidence she could see of Indians at the back of the house.

Tad fired the second rifle, sending a spiral of acrid smoke twisting toward the rafters. "What the hell are they doing out there?"

Livi went to peer out the loophole just down from his.

There were not quite a dozen braves gathered at the end of the bridge, talking and gesturing toward the house. They clearly intended to make some kind of assault.

Livi looked around the room, trying to think how they could fend off the band of Indians. They had a pistol and two rifles, a keg of powder, and plenty of shot. They had a fresh bucket of water and some food Anne Logan had packed for them.

They had a chance: if the Indians didn't stay too long, if they didn't attack from all sides at once, if they didn't decide to burn the cabin, if someone came to the Talbots' rescue. Which was about as likely as pole beans sprouting roses.

The room was becoming dimmer as clouds built and thickened overhead. The air grew close and oppressive. Thunder rumbled somewhere off to the west.

"Will the Indians go home if it rains?" Cissy asked, rolling tear-wet eyes toward the roof.

"We can hope they will, sugar," Livi said. "Now, come give me some help with this."

Cissy wiped her face on the hem of her skirt, and went obediently to where her mother was sitting.

"I'd like you to lay all these leather patches out here on the table," Livi instructed, needing to keep her daughter occupied, needing to prepare to reload as fast as they could. "Then put a ball in every one. You can do that, can't you?"

Cissy nodded and set to work. Livi bent to refill their powder horns while Tad kept watch.

The room grew so dark they could barely see. They worked and waited in silence.

"Ma?" Tad's voice sounded strangled when he called her to the loophole a few minutes later. "Ma, I think they're up to something."

When Livi looked, the light outside was gray and thin. Clouds shivered bright and dark in sharp relief. The air crackled with the threat of the coming storm, with the threat of the coming attack. Livi shivered, though she ran with sweat.

On the far side of the bridge, the Indians had begun to congregate again. Two or three worked intently over something on the ground, their heads down, their bodies hunched. The others waited, glancing over their shoulders at the cabin.

"Can you see, Ma?"

"Not nearly well enough." Livi fought to hold herself together as they watched, praying she was wrong about what the Indians had in mind.

Then shreds of diaphanous white began to dance upward in confirmation. They turned gossamer pale as they rose and dispersed in the whipping wind. Livi saw flares of orange and yellow lick across the ground within the ring of Indians. With terror in her heart, she watched yellow light flicker on the Indians' faces, saw torsos and bodies cast in deep relief.

Fear squirmed beneath her breastbone as she turned to her son. "Oh, Tad, they mean to burn us out."

Reid smelled smoke in the gusting wind, tasted it acrid and raw deep in his throat. He knew what it meant. He'd come upon burned-out homesteads more times than he could count. He'd just never known the families' names.

Fear for Livi and the children grabbed him hard—so hard he could barely breathe, with a force that jolted him to his fingertips. Reid forged ahead, needing to see what had befallen David's family—the people he'd vowed to protect.

Thunder rumbled overhead as he and the men who had ridden with him from Logan's Station crested the rise. Spears of fire whipped skyward from the blaze at the edge of the creek. Flames shot along the perimeter of the nearest field. Through the swirling smoke, Reid could see Indians with torches ablaze fanning out to touch off the other fields.

His gaze swung to the cabin on the rise. A fire arrow flared beneath the roof's deep overhang, sending tendrils of yellow dancing along the eaves. Another had found purchase in the breezeway, so that flickers of orange nipped and crackled up the walls. A third arrow sparked and fluttered to the left of the steps.

There was no sign of Livi and the children.

The men from the station cursed. Reid tasted their oaths in his own mouth. Sour and metallic. Bitter and ineffectual. He wanted blood. For Livi and the children. For David. For the nameless, faceless families who'd been killed like this all along the frontier.

"Ready?" Reid asked and raised his rifle. Howling with rage, he led the charge into the hollow below.

He thundered past the yellow blur of the first blazing field, past the bonfire that flashed orange and hot in the semidark. He fired as he rode. An Indian went down as he swept past.

He jerked his horse around to the right. Swinging his rifle like a club, he battered one Indian aside. He slammed another with a backhanded jab.

Another brave grabbed Campbell from behind. He felt the man's hands tighten on his arms, felt the drag of the Indian's weight and strength. He struggled to reach his saddle pistol. Once he had it in his hands, Reid jammed it into the warrior's chest and fired. The brave's hands and body dropped away.

Around Campbell, other men from the station fought as fiercely as he. One chased down a man with a torch. Another wrestled an archer to the earth. Dark figures writhed and merged in the firelight. Guns boomed around him. The air filled with shouts of fury and of death.

Reid turned back to the cabin. Fire had clawed its way toward the peak of the roof. Flames were leaping at the side of the cabin door.

He flung himself from his horse and raced up the rise. Reid didn't delude himself. He couldn't put out that fire on his own. He couldn't salvage anything inside. The cabin he and David had built was lost. The homestead and the dream were lost. But none of that mattered. Reid didn't know where Livi and the children were. He didn't know if they were safe. All Reid wanted was to find them.

As he approached the cabin, an Indian loomed up from around the corner of the house with torch in hand.

"Ravens Flight." The man addressed him in Shawnee as he came nearer. "I told them this cabin was yours. I told them it was your woman and children we had trapped inside."

Reid glanced toward where the roof at the left of the cabin had begun to blaze.

"They are burning, Ravens Flight," the Indian taunted. "Can't you hear them screaming?"

Reid launched himself toward the Indian.

The brave swung the flaring torch in hasty defense.

Campbell heard the whoosh as the torch brushed past, felt the heat blast across his face. The brightness all but blinded him. He stumbled back. The Indian waved the torch again.

Reid charged toward him. He reached past the heat, past the flames. Somewhere in the darkness beyond the blaze, he grabbed the Indian's forearm and tightened his fingers around it. The torch swung wildly. The flame swooped past Reid's cheek. He felt the wave of heat, smelled the singe of burning hair. He forced the torch to the left and dragged the Indian with him as he rolled.

Thunder detonated and lightning tore across the sky as the two sinewy bodies crashed together. They landed hard. Embers from the torch burst around them. Sparks bounced and flared, biting into Campbell's cheek, singeing his shirt at the shoulder.

He bit back a curse and tightened his grip on the other man's arm. The torch wavered, thudded to the earth, and rolled away. Deprived of his weapon, the Indian slammed his elbow into the hollow beneath Reid's ribs.

While Campbell fought for breath, the Indian squirmed away.

Both men scrambled to their feet. Each came up with knife in hand.

The cadence of their fighting abruptly changed. They circled slowly, arms extended, shoulders hunched. Each waited for the other to move, to challenge, to reveal his weakness. They hovered, panting, delaying the moment of contact.

Then the warrior lunged. He forced Reid back. Campbell gave ground, shifting to the left. His opponent advanced, pressing hard. His knife snagged the fabric at Campbell's shoulder and sliced down across his chest. Blood spilled hot from the open wound.

Reid jerked his blade up as he twisted away. He ducked and spun. He drove beneath the Shawnee's guard. He buried his knife in the Indian's belly. The man crashed backward, grabbing Campbell's arm as he fell, dragging Reid down.

The brave gripped hard as life seeped from those cold, dark eyes. "Your family is dead," he whispered. "When you find them in the ashes, Ravens Flight, there will be nothing left but their bones."

Reid raised his head and bellowed into the night, a cry of both victory and defeat. It echoed fury and anguish, unbearable pain for those he'd lost. It howled with an agony of sorrow and shattered dreams.

As if he'd called it down on all their heads, the clouds ripped open high above. Rain poured out as if a dam had broken wide. The deluge battered Reid, the dead Indian, and the bloody earth.

A blaze of purple burst across the sky. In the pulsing after-image, Reid saw what this place might have been. He saw the farm David had envisioned, green and peaceful and prosperous. He saw David and Livi happy together and proud of what they'd built. He saw Tad and Cissy with children and lives of their own. Reid saw himself settled and content after so many years of wandering.

He howled again and let the beat of the rain against him purge the savagery and carnage and death. He retrieved and sheathed his knife. He climbed slowly to his feet. He dashed the water from his eyes and turned to where the ruins of the cabin should have been.

Instead the building stood scarred but intact. The roof at Livi's end of the house smoldered in the wet. The breezeway was a cavern of black, steaming as the rain washed in. The door to Livi's cabin was dark with smoke.

Then, as he watched, the soot-blackened door opened. A woman stepped to the top of the stairs and stood gasping.

Livi! Oh, God, Livi! Joy and relief jarred Reid. He ran toward her across the cabin yard. He needed to grab her and hold her to be sure she was real.

Reid caught her to him at the bottom of the stairs. He closed his hands around her shoulders, seeking out the solidity, the warmth, the life in her. He slid his palms along the length of her back.

They stood together with the rain washing over them, soaking them to the skin, running in rivulets down their faces and through their hair. They let it purge his fury and her tears.

She stared up at him, amazement and exhaustion in her eyes. "How did you know to come?" she asked, her voice raw and raspy with emotion and smoke.

"When you weren't at the station, I knew," he answered. "I knew I had to get here as soon as I could."

He pulled her closer, smoothed back her hair. "Where are Tad and Cissy? Are they safe?"

"They're under the house. We dug some rocks out of the wall of the turnip hole. Tad and Cissy squeezed through, but I was too big to fit. They're supposed to stay down there until I say it's all right, or tell them to crawl out from under the cabin and run for the ridge."

It was a resourceful plan, as good as any Reid himself could have devised.

"*Is* it all right?" Livi asked above the groans of thunder and the hiss of rain. "Are the Indians gone?"

Reid looked around. The fields also seemed to have been spared the worst of the destruction. Across the creek, the men from Logan's Station were rounding up the wounded Indians and stacking their dead. The years of the war had taught them well.

A big blond fellow slogged across the yard and came to report. "The savages took heavy losses. There are two wounded and eight dead, counting that one over there," William Harris said with a jerk of his thumb. "Jim Langdon took a ball in the arm. Frank Marshall ended up on the wrong end of an arrow, but he'll be all right. There's a Negro woman, dead off there in the field."

"Violet," Livi explained. "And we haven't seen Eustace

since he went up the ridge to check their cabin.''

"I'll have someone look for him," Harris offered. "And your young ones, Mrs. Talbot?"

"They're under the house."

"As good a place for them as any."

"Then carry on," Reid acknowledged. "We'll be leaving as soon as we can gather up some things and bury Violet Hadley. You might want to put someone to digging a grave. There are shovels here that you can use."

Standing there in the rain, Livi didn't offer up so much as a word of resistance. Her quiescence should have been enough for Reid, but suddenly he was shaking inside, pushed to anger as overwhelming as it was irrational.

Harris was barely out of earshot when Reid turned on her. "Jesus, Livi! Couldn't you wait at the station until everything was clear? Did you have to risk yourself and everyone else coming back to the cabin?"

"But Phillip Wyant said—" Livi began, struggling to break his hold on her, struggling to defend herself.

"It doesn't matter what Wyant said," he shouted at her. "You should have had enough sense to stay put. You and the children were safe at Logan's Station. You had food and protection and a place to sleep. While you were there I didn't have to wonder . . ."

A stab of sick, helpless fury turned his stomach inside out. He didn't know if he wanted to hang on to Livi and thank God she and the children were safe, or shake her until her teeth rattled.

Tad spared him the decision.

"Ma? Is it all right, Ma?" he asked, peering at them through the rain. He stood at the cabin door with Cissy in his arms.

Reid felt Livi glance his way before she answered. "It's as all right as it's going to be for a while. We're going back to Logan's Station."

✧ 17 ✧

*L*ivi needed Reid. As much as she hated to admit it, as
much as it rankled her to ask him so much as the time
of day, Livi was systematically turning Logan's Station upside
down in search of him. She didn't seem to have another
choice. It had been three days since they'd returned to the fort,
three days since she'd slept.

She spent those days coddling her children. Livi had indulged both her need to hold her baby girl and Cissy's need
to be held. She had talked to her and read to her and petted
her, hoping that somehow the tenderness and the stories and
the affection might dim the memory of what Cissy had heard
and seen at the cabin.

She spent time with Tad, conveying—with what she hoped
was appropriate subtlety—her pride in him. Tad was thirteen
and a boy to boot, so she hadn't been able to tell him right
out how brave she thought he'd been, how clever and resourceful. She'd had to couch her praise in gruff half-
compliments. She'd had to pat his shoulder instead of hugging
him tight and stroking his hair the way she wanted to.

She spent the nights sitting with Eustace. The men had
found him tortured and half dead on the floor of the cabin on
the ridge. It was a wonder he'd survived the journey back to
the station, a miracle he was holding his own against the fever
and his injuries.

As she'd bathed him and fed him and crooned to him, Livi
came to believe that Eustace's recovery had less to do with

his injuries and more with accepting Violet's death. In the depths of those black eyes she could see the agony of knowing his wife was dead, of realizing that the future he'd struggled to make for both of them was irretrievably lost.

Livi understood what he was feeling. She knew how hollow life could be when the core of your world was gone, when you'd forfeited the other half of yourself. Livi still woke up some mornings feeling empty inside, yet she'd lived long enough without David to know that somehow you survived. Somehow you came to believe that a new life lay ahead. Somehow you came to realize that though you never forgot how much you'd lost, it stopped hurting to remember.

Just as surely as Livi knew all that, she knew Eustace wouldn't believe her. His shock at losing Violet was fresh and breathless and unbearable. His pain was vivid and soul-deep. All Livi could do for him now was see that he received proper care and hope that he found the courage to face the rest of his days without the woman he loved.

Livi was nearly as haunted by Violet's death as Eustace was. It seemed impossible that in these few short months she had amassed so many memories: of Violet's calm, smoky voice; of her sharp-edged wisdom; of her initiative and her willingness to work. Livi hadn't realized how much that wisp of a woman had lightened her load. Or how much she would miss her. Every time she closed her eyes, she saw Violet's face. Every time Livi tried to sleep, the horror of Violet's death crept into her dreams.

Livi needed to talk to Reid. She thought he might understand.

When she heard he was back from scouting, she began threading her way around the perimeter of the fort. She checked the blockhouses, one by one. She glanced into the Logan and Prescott cabins and stopped down by the gate. A hot, choky ache climbed the back of her throat as she searched.

She finally spotted Campbell currying his big roan in the area that had been roped off for the riding horses. As she lumbered toward him, Livi couldn't help remembering how Reid had been the night of the raid on the cabin. He'd flared as harsh and elemental as the fire and rain.

She'd sensed it as he'd stormed toward her up the rise. She'd smelled the anguish and the blood and the fury on him.

When he'd closed his hands around her arms, his ferocity had licked through her. That blue-white intensity had shaken and shamed, yet energized Livi. It had given her the stamina to gather up her children and her wounded, to bury her dead. It had given her fortitude to take what she needed and leave the cabin behind.

Tonight she needed something else, something she wasn't at all sure Reid knew how to give. She just didn't know whom else to ask for help.

"I heard you were back," she said as she approached him.

Reid's head snapped around, his brows clashing above the bridge of his nose when he caught sight of her. "Good God, Livi! You look like hell."

She took in the deep shadows beneath his eyes, the creases clearly visible around his mouth in spite of a ragged growth of beard. "You don't look a whole lot better."

"I rode out an hour after we got back to the station. I look like this for a reason."

She steeled herself to tell him she had a reason, too. "I haven't been sleeping."

Reid's rhythmic motions slowed. He rested one hand on the gelding's rump and turned his full attention on her. "And why is that?"

Livi's throat closed up now that the moment of truth was upon her. "I can't get Violet Hadley off my mind," she hedged.

Reid waited for her to continue, standing utterly still.

"I see her every time I close my eyes," she admitted. "Every time I sit with Eustace, every time I hold Cissy in my arms, I remember how Violet looked lying dead in that cornfield. I keep thinking how she died."

Reid stood silent, concentration sharp in those ice-blue eyes.

The words came hard in spite of Livi's need to confess. "I feel—" Her voice dipped, going raspy and low. "I feel as if it's all my fault. As if I'm responsible for Violet's death."

Once she'd spoken, found the courage to acknowledge her complicity, Livi wanted to be absolved and comforted.

Reid stood unmoved.

Livi waited, holding her breath, a new kind of panic winding her nerves and muscles taut.

Reid gave a snort of what might have been impatience or

derision and set the currycomb aside. "What do you want me to say, Livi? That nothing you did put her in jeopardy? That going back to the cabin was a wise and well-considered choice?"

His words lodged deep, sharp-edged and painful. Feeling bewildered and betrayed, Livi instinctively defended herself. "But Phillip Wyant said—"

"I'll grant you," Reid interrupted, "Phillip Wyant read the signs all wrong. He made a grave mistake in telling everyone it was safe to leave the fort. But you made the decision, Livi. You chose to go back to the cabin. When you did that, you accepted responsibility for everything that happened there."

Hot tears breached the rims of her lashes. Her voice frayed. "But I didn't think anyone would die."

He came a step nearer, closed his hand around her arm. His grip was inexplicably compelling.

"Of course not," he said gently. "Of course not. But, Livi, this isn't a forgiving land. Out here, every choice has consequences. Out here, mistakes come dear."

"And Violet paid for my mistake."

Reid said nothing. There was nothing to say.

A sob squirmed its way up Livi's throat. "But how do I live with Violet's death?"

Her belly nudged against him as Reid gathered her in. She heard him sigh, felt his hand stroke the length of her braid. He smelled of dust and horse and a stale, heavy weariness of his own.

"You never forget," he told her, his voice gone low, "but eventually you find a way to forgive yourself."

It was as if he spoke from experience, as if he were remembering when he faced this same realization, accepted this same horrendous responsibility. "You vow never to make that same mistake again, and you let it go."

"But is that enough?" she whispered.

"Nothing's ever enough, but you go on."

She sensed the ring of both resignation and truth in his tone.

She stood with her still-damp cheek pressed to his sweat-stained shirt, felt the stroke of his hand on her hair. She was exhausted, hurting, but calmer somehow. There was comfort here. Not the kind she had hoped for or expected. Not the kind David might have given her. What Reid offered was acceptance and understanding. And Livi seemed suddenly able to breathe again.

By degrees Reid released her and stepped away.

She knew he was worn every bit as thin as she was, and she needed to find the words to thank him for the wisdom he had shared with her. But when she looked up into his face, Reid's expression had changed. Instead of finding empathy in his eyes, she saw sudden determination. Where before there had been understanding and tolerance, there was now inexplicable anger. She stared back, stunned.

"Or consider this, Livi Talbot," he told her, his voice gone cold. "If you can't face up to what's happened, go back home. If you can't accept responsibility for your decisions, head back to Lynchburg, where mistakes don't cost so much. Go back to Virginia, Livi, for everyone's sake. You never belonged in Kentucky anyway." With a curse he spun away.

Livi stood there with her hands clasped together, watching him go. And thinking, as she had so often, that Reid Campbell was probably right.

Livi and her children gathered with the other families to welcome the Logan's Station militia home. They had received word the night before of the fighting at Bryan's Station and the defeat at Blue Lick that followed it. But even if they had not heard, the hopelessness and grief on the militiamen's faces spoke eloquently of the outcome. Still, Livi didn't fully grasp the disaster that had befallen the Kentucky settlers until Ben Logan allowed his troops to break ranks.

As the weary men waded into their loved ones' arms, they brought word of brothers and fathers and uncles who were lost. Though the Logan's Station militia had arrived at Blue Lick after the battle was over, men from almost every other frontier station had been struck down. Losses touched almost every family.

Near where Livi stood, Anne Logan was sobbing against Ben's chest. "Not Israel," she was saying, shaking her head. "Not Daniel and Rebecca's Israel."

"Daniel Boone's son must have been killed," Reid explained, appearing at Livi's elbow just as if they hadn't spit bitter words at each other two nights before. "Everyone's connected here in Kentucky, either kith or kin."

"What will our Martha do at that cabin all by herself?" one woman demanded of a man who was weeping as freely as she. "What will our grandson do without a father?"

As she tightened her grip on Cissy's hand and scanned the scene to locate Tad, Livi felt herself draw closer to Reid. She needed someone to lean on in this time of communal grief, someone whose calm was second nature, whose hand rode so naturally at the small of her back.

"All these folks came west about the same time," he went on in an undertone. "They cleared their bit of land, then banded together to fight the Indians and build their homes. Depending on each other for survival made them lifelong friends. Then the youngsters began to marry, binding everyone together." Campbell shook his head, his face gone grim. "The losses at Blue Lick will be felt on this frontier for decades to come."

Livi knew that no matter what the outcome of the battle, Reid would rather have been with Logan and the others than here at the fort. She could see the regret that shaded the blue of his eyes, the frustration that tightened the corners of his mouth.

She allowed her gaze to skim over the crowd. If she stayed, these people would be her friends and neighbors, would share her joys and sorrows as she was sharing theirs tonight. She saw the hardship in their faces, the loyalty, concern, and compassion they felt for one another's losses. Part of her reached out for that, wanting and needing to belong to something bigger and stronger than she was. Part of her shrank away. She realized that adversity and struggle had bound these people together. She knew grief and misfortune gave them this common bond. Livi had experienced enough of all those things to last a lifetime. Why should she stay on to experience them again?

Bit by bit, the crowd dispersed. Some of the families went back to their cabins and shut out the world. Most milled around on the wide, dusty expanse at the center of the station, drawing comfort by sharing their anguish and shock. Cook fires flickered to life in the gathering dark. Strings of rabbits were set to roasting over one open blaze. A haunch of venison turned on a spit above another. Huge blackened cauldrons of stew soon trailed delicious-smelling steam. A ham appeared on a makeshift table, as did breads made from rye and corn and squash. One woman brought out butter and wild persimmon jam. Several arrived bearing dishes of vegetables. Another served up greens she had been brave enough to gather at the edge of the woods.

Livi heard the particulars of the battle at Blue Lick while she worked with the other women preparing the meal. One grizzled man fortified with a ramekin of whiskey propped himself on a keg at the end of the table where his wife was slicing meat and commenced regaling her with the details. Livi listened in spite of herself.

Once the main force of British rangers and Indians had proved unsuccessful in forcing Bryan's Station to surrender, they abandoned their attack. They burned and trampled the fields around the station and killed what livestock they could find. Then, gathering up the smaller raiding parties as they went, they headed back toward the Ohio country. They crossed the Licking River on the buffalo trace and took shelter behind the ridge on the far side of the Blue Lick marsh. There they lay in wait, knowing the frontier militia would follow.

The men from Bryan's Station joined forces with the group that rode in from Boonesborough and several other stations. Together they set out to chase the raiders back across the Ohio River. The trail had been easy enough to follow. A force of nearly three hundred Indians and fifty British rangers left ample sign.

According to the man telling the tale, the Kentucky militia had hesitated on the east edge of the marsh. They knew the land. They knew that the woods at the top of the rise and the gullies behind it could hold a legion of the enemies—or nothing at all. A conference ensued. Some of the men had wanted to send out scouts before they ventured into the salt flats. Others counseled waiting for Logan's militia to arrive. But hotblooded Hugh McGary had issued the challenge and led the charge.

Their fate was sealed the moment the company fell in behind him. The British and the Indians laid down wicked fire from the safety of the trees, and when the badly outnumbered Kentuckians wheeled to retreat, their attackers chased them to ground. The rest of the battle was brutal and brief. The fighting with knives and war clubs was hand to hand. Nearly half the force of Kentuckians died in those few bloody minutes at Blue Lick.

Livi tried not to listen too closely to the descriptions of what the men from Logan's Station had found on the battlefield. Her memories of her husband being struck down, of the carnage at Four Mile Creek, of Violet's death in the cornfield, were far too close. When she shut her eyes, she still saw David lying broken and still, Violet Hadley's blood-soaked gown, Molly Baker's rucked-up dress and bright red shoes. She didn't need anything else to feed the visions in her nightmares.

Instead she concentrated on the music. On the far side of the field, someone had taken up his fiddle. He was sending sweet, sad music sailing into the deepening dark. The music, rich in minor keys, suited the mood in the station tonight. What the fiddler was offering was a tribute to those who had fallen, a lament for those who were lost. Livi's eyelids burned at the mournful sound.

She rounded up her children once the food was put out and saw that they got something to eat. People helped themselves from the dishes and platters and pots arranged on long trestle tables. Here and there they found places to sit, on the steps of the cabins, on the rough-hewn benches set up for the temporary school. The men clustered in the shadows, passing jugs of whiskey from hand to hand. They toasted fallen friends and drowned their regrets in a brew so raw that the tears they shed could be blamed on the liquor.

Livi filled a trencher of food and saw to Eustace's needs. She found her daughter playing with Tallie Logan and took her off to bed. Usually Livi lay down with Cissy, welcoming the chance to stretch out and rest her aching back, to get a little extra sleep. As she neared the end of her eighth month of pregnancy, her energy was dwindling. Some days she wondered how she would manage to harvest whatever corn was left standing. Some nights she was so tired she didn't care.

But tonight Livi was restless. The music and the stir of activity so long after the station was usually quiet drew her back outside. From the doorway of the blockhouse, she watched glowing, red-orange sparks lift from the fire into the ink-dark sky. She tasted the flavor of roasting meat in the smoke that hung in the thick, still air. The rumble of masculine laughter drifted from off to her left as someone tapped another firkin of spirits.

Livi stepped into the yard and was drawn toward where the first fiddler had been joined by another. A man playing a tin whistle sat in, too. With their arrival the tenor of the tunes changed. Where there had been sadness and lament, there was now grace and life and gaiety. Several couples began to dance. With a lump in her throat, she watched the men and women move together, silhouetted against the flames. That moments of such sadness and loss could blend so seamlessly into those of dancing and frivolity seemed proof of the optimism inherent in the wilderness. It was a tribute to the people who had settled here that they could mourn and then go on. Livi wasn't sure she was ready to do that.

Her mood heavy with memories, she wandered toward the fort's half-open gate. *What would you think about all this, David?* she wondered. *Would you want me to stay on here in spite of Reid, in spite of the Indians, in spite of everything?*

What is it you want, Livi? She could almost hear David speak the words. And he was right. She had to decide what she wanted for herself and her children. She had to decide what she was willing to fight to hold.

A scuffling sound behind her made her turn. She found Reid wending his way toward her, ever so slightly unsteady on his feet.

"What are you doing," he asked her, "staring out into the dark like that?"

"I was thinking about David."

That drew Reid nearer. As he came to stand a hairsbreadth away, she smelled the bite of whiskey on him. She saw the flush of high color along the crest of his cheeks and noted the slightly diminished clarity of his pale, bright eyes.

"I was thinking about him, too," he admitted. "He should be here with us tonight. He always believed in Kentucky, in the plans we made. He never lost faith, even in the darkest days."

Livi detected a regret in Campbell's tone that raked up the coals of her own emotions. "But David isn't here," she said almost angrily. "If there are plans to fulfill, it's up to us."

Reid stared down at her in surprise, as if seeing her for the very first time. "But don't you miss him?"

Tears welled up. Useless tears, tears Livi had grown impatient with shedding, especially when they did no good.

"I miss him every minute of every day," she admitted softly. "I wake up every morning needing to tell him what I think or how I feel. I lift my head from sweeping or baking or weeding and expect to see him standing there. I lie in bed at night and just before I drift to sleep, I wonder what plans he's made for tomorrow."

Reid nodded as if he understood, and again she sensed the loneliness in him. She saw suddenly what a singular and solitary life he lived, heading off into the woods alone for months at a time. Even here in the company of men with whom he'd served in the war, of men who respected the Campbell name and his skills as a woodsman, Reid didn't quite belong. He'd built a wall with his heritage and his demeanor that held him aloof. He'd staked out his claim in a no-man's-land between two cultures. Certainly there was reason for him to behave as he did; she'd seen proof of people's intolerance. Yet surely Reid wanted more from life than what he had.

When she thought back, she realized David was the only one who had accepted Reid for what he was. David had trusted him, encouraged him, and cared for him. Neither Reid's father nor his tribe had been able to claim Reid's loyalty, but David had. David had opened his life to Reid and invited him in. And suddenly Livi understood the scope of what Reid had lost when David died.

Livi loved her children and they loved her. She claimed burgeoning friendships here on the frontier and knew people would welcome her back if she returned to Lynchburg. She'd won the respect of Eustace and Violet. And the love of David himself.

Reid had never had anyone but David.

"Of course I miss him," she went on hastily, shaken by the insight, by the scope of Reid's vulnerability. "But I also miss who I was able to be when I was with him."

She could feel his gaze on her, sense the confusion behind his eyes. "What do you mean?"

"I've changed since David died. I've had to change. The children and I wouldn't have survived if I had remained the woman I was when we left Lynchburg." She drew a long and painful breath. "But I resent it. I liked being protected, cared for, and loved. I relished loving David in return. Loving him made me feel whole, complete in a way I'll never be again.''

Reid stood silent for a moment; then his hand settled at the small of her back. His touch set off ripples of awareness in her, just as his intensity always did.

"Livi—" he began.

"Rider coming in!" one of the sentries bellowed from the wall walk above their heads. Livi and Reid scurried back as the men swung the tall gates wide.

"It's John Gable from Harrodsburg," Reid told her as Ben Logan led a group toward where the rider had pulled up his lathered horse.

"We just had confirmation," Gable began in response to Logan's greeting. "The Indians are all tucked up tight in their village at Chillicothe. Near as our scouts and Boone's can tell, their raiding is over—at least for now."

"What does that mean?" Livi turned to Reid.

"It means we'll be able to go back to the cabin tomorrow," he said. "It means that you're going to be able to harvest whatever's left of your corn."

Abruptly he turned away from where the settlers were gathered around Gable's horse. "Let me walk you back to the blockhouse," he told her, his voice unusually gruff. "There will be lots to do come morning with half the families pulling out."

After the fighting and the dying, Livi had to struggle with the notion that it was safe to return to the cabin.

Each of them was silent as they crossed the compound. Livi's thoughts had to do with packing up, with making provision for Eustace until he was well enough to travel. She couldn't help but wonder if in the daylight there would be enough left of the crops and the cabin to make it worth going back.

God only knew what course Reid's thoughts had taken.

As they approached the blockhouse, Reid closed warm, rough fingers around Livi's wrist.

"Reid?" Livi sputtered in surprise as he pulled her into the shadows.

Then his lips came soft and full on hers, the strength of his grip incompatible with the hot, sweet tenderness of his mouth. He tasted dark, of whiskey and loneliness and yearning. Of confusion and need. Of masculine power and temptation.

With the sweep of his palm along the length of her spine he gathered her in, fitting her to the long, taut planes of his body. She arched into him instinctively, knowing just how to nestle her fullness into the bow of a man's embrace. Reid's energy enveloped her like a wave of heat, dancing along her skin, simmering through her veins. She felt his need grow full and hard between them.

Before she could draw breath, he deepened the kiss with the thrust of his tongue, dragging her into a maelstrom of sensation. A yearning of her own leaped up in answer. She tingled from scalp to toes, as if she'd encountered a force as fierce and elemental as a summer storm.

Livi curled her fingers into his shirt where it strained across his shoulders, needing to draw him closer. Her body cleaved to his, her breasts and belly, the length of her thighs. She opened her mouth, drinking him in to assuage a thirst she'd never thought to feel again.

Reid moaned and wrapped her closer.

And then the baby kicked. So hard that Livi gasped. So hard that Reid must have felt the jolt where their bodies came together.

His eyes widened. He jerked back, as if he weren't sure where the assault had come from.

Then he realized.

"Oh, Livi!" he whispered. "My God! I'm sorry. Did I hurt you?"

"It's all right," she tried to reassure him. "Babies kick like that all the time."

His face paled as if he'd only just realized who it was he'd been kissing. He let Livi go as if she'd burst into flames.

"It's all right," she said again.

But it wasn't all right. She could see that in his face. She could see it in his expression of shock and self-disgust. He'd been kissing David's widow. David's pregnant widow.

He backed away.

She fumbled for words to ease the discomfort he must be feeling. Words that masked the way she had responded to his kiss. Words that were distant and mundane.

"Shall I see you in the morning, then?" she asked. "Will you be taking us back to the cabin?"

Livi thought she saw Reid nod before he bolted toward the group of men gathered around the nearest jug of whiskey.

For herself, Livi didn't know whether to be glad or sorry that he'd been so quick to leave.

❦18❦

*L*ivi tensed with anticipation as they turned off the main road at the familiar outcropping of dun-gray stone. She clung more tightly to her horse's reins as they traced the course of the rocky stream. Her breath came hard as she guided her mount up the face of the hill. Then she topped the rise and her own sunlit valley sprawled before her. Her face flushed. Her chest filled. She drew a long, slow breath and swallowed hard.

The valley was not as pristine as it had been the first time she'd ridden in. But then, neither was she. The land bore the scars of struggle, of fire, of the harsh and hostile world. Livi bore those scars as well. But she had survived. Just as her valley and her house and her fields had survived. Her blood and bone resonated with the rightness of returning to this place. She knew now that she belonged here. This was home.

Reid pulled his horse up next to hers. "Looks to me like the roof of the cabin's pretty much intact," he observed, his outlook purely masculine, matter-of-fact, and practical. "It won't take Tad and me long to fix the parts that burned. Of course, we'll have to whitewash everything because of the smoke. And the fields . . ."

Livi shut out the sound of his plans. She sniffed the cool, green scent of the woods. She strained to hear the soft, hollow coo of her mourning doves. She sated herself on the rush of the wind through the trees. In time her own practicality would win out, but for now, there was only her cabin and her valley

267

and her stream and the love of a place she had once believed she hated.

For the first time, she understood what David must have felt when he found this spot. The awe and the elation. The wonder and belonging. It was odd how things turned out. Odd that this valley could come to matter so much, especially since she knew it wasn't hers.

That thought soured the sweetness of homecoming. It turned Livi from savoring her surroundings to evaluating and assessing them.

As they clattered across the puncheon bridge to the tune of Patches's barking, Livi could see that, except for singed places here and there and losing a score of rows of corn in the field nearest the cabin, they had escaped the fire amazingly well. Reid was right about the house. There was nothing that a few repairs and a coat or two of whitewash wouldn't fix.

Livi knew that Reid's arrival in the midst of the Indian attack was more than she could have dared to hope for. That the rain had rolled in when the fields were ablaze was little short of miraculous. Now she wondered if she dared ask one more favor—that Reid would let them stay.

Repairs to the cabin took three days. Reid and Tad reinforced the purlins on the west end of the house, then laid up clapboards and fastened them in place with lashing and poles. Livi tried to do her part with the scrubbing and the whitewashing, but she was slow and cumbersome with the bulk of her pregnancy, and she tired far too easily. In the end, Tad and Reid did them for her, while Livi resumed her household duties with Cissy's help.

Once the chores were done and the children were abed, Livi made it her practice to settle herself on the steps of the cabin and steep herself in the night. She would listen for the hoot of the owl somewhere off in the woods, for the faint song of the stream as it danced over its bed of stones. She'd savor the wind-washed quiet and a chance to be alone after the weeks at the station. She felt so comfortable here, so in touch with David's dream. It was a dream she was beginning to think of as her own, though she knew such thoughts were dangerous.

A night or two after they had returned, Reid came out of his side of the cabin while she was there. She shoved over to make a place for him on the steps. He put aside the bucket he'd been carrying and eased himself down in the empty place.

"It's good to be back," she said on a sigh. "I understand now why David loved this place. When we rode over that rise the other morning, it was as if everything in the world came right again."

Reid must have sensed the trend of her thoughts, the wish she was gathering her courage to voice.

"We agreed that once the crops were harvested, you and the children would head back to Lynchburg," he reminded her.

Livi took a long, uneven breath. "I feel as if this is my home now. I'd like to stay."

The corners of Reid's mouth drew tight in a frown. "That isn't the bargain we made."

"But I've proved I can make my way here," Livi insisted.

"You've proved nothing at all."

Livi felt the heat of impending battle flush her cheeks. "I've plowed and planted these fields. Soon I'll harvest my crops. I've kept my family well and safe and fed. I've made this cabin a home," she enumerated, fighting to be reasonable. "I've come as close as anyone could to fulfilling David's dreams."

Reid shrugged. "I don't know that that matters much. This land belongs to me, and I don't intend to let you stay."

"Why?" she demanded, anger singeing through her.

"Because you don't belong here," he began almost savagely. "This is too wild and dangerous a place for a woman like you. You don't know how to defend yourself. What's worse, you're too much of a lady to learn to fight. I tried to tell David that. I told him that if he loved you as much as he claimed, he'd let you stay in Lynchburg while he came here."

Reid's revelation dowsed her fury. Had David really considered leaving her and the children behind?

"Come fall," Reid went on, "I'll be heading west. I won't be here to take responsibility for you and the children."

"Damn you, Reid!" Livi spit. "Has anyone asked you to take responsibility for me and my children? Has anyone asked you to stay? You just take your trade goods and head off into the hills. Tad and Cissy and I will do just fine without you."

He shoved to his feet and glared at her. "Will you do *just fine,'* Livi? Can you run this place all by yourself? Will you do 'just fine' when the Indians attack? Will you be 'just fine' when someone you care about dies because you've decided to stay?''

Guilt over Violet's death rose up to haunt her.

''And what if it's one of the children?''

Reid didn't play fair. He knew her greatest vulnerability.

Though Livi's throat tightened with fear, she managed to raise her chin as if she were really as stubborn and strong as she longed to be. ''I'd have risked all of that if David were here. Doesn't it matter to you that this is what David would want—having his family farm this land?''

''No,'' Reid shouted, ''it doesn't matter at all! What matters is that the land is mine. What matters is that I have no intention of giving or leasing this land to you. Perhaps when Tad is old enough—''

He didn't finish the thought.

Livi couldn't allow herself to be placated by what he was offering anyway.

Instead he stood over her, glowering. ''Harvest your crops. Give birth to that child. But mark me well, Livi Talbot. As soon as you're well enough to travel, I'm taking you and your children back to Virginia. There's no debating that.''

With a muttered curse, Reid snatched up the bucket and spun toward the spring.

Go! she wanted to shout after him. *And don't come back! I'll hold on to this land one way or the other, Reid Campbell. I'll make my way in this world without you. Don't you think I won't!*

But making her way alone wasn't all that easy. As the days passed, Livi fretted about the harvest. She didn't see how a woman mere weeks from delivering her baby and two half-grown children were ever going to bring in the corn crop. She didn't have any idea how they could get it husked and shelled and stored away. She absolutely refused to ask Reid for help. If she did, she'd feel as if she'd compromised any profit she'd make.

Help came on foot and on horseback almost a fortnight after her argument with Reid.

''Hullo the Talbots!'' Ben Logan bellowed from the top of the rise one morning as Livi was getting dressed. She rushed to the cabin door just in time to see nearly twoscore of people troop out of the woods behind Ben and Anne. She recognized friends from Logan's Station, other families who were settling out, and a few of the scruffy single men who lived alone in the woods. They came with food and tools and songs and laughter.

The men and boys headed immediately into the fields, pulling the ears of corn that had dried on the stalks and ferrying bushelfuls back to the house. The women either sat in the breezeway and sewed, laid out long makeshift tables in the yard, or saw to the food. Cissy and the other children ran around squealing and laughing.

Enough time had passed since they had all been cooped up together in the station that the women were eager to renew their friendships and share the latest gossip.

"I hear that Susan Ferguson over at Harrodsburg gave birth to a fine baby boy," Margaret Chamberlain informed them.

"They named him Gabriel," Margaret's oldest daughter added.

"We sure could use another musician out here." Josette Adams giggled. "Or another trumpeter to summon the troops."

"My Frederick ran into old man Billings at the crossroads," Fanny Morris reported. "All slicked up he was, too. And when my Fred asked why, Billings told him he was courting Mattie Watkins's middle girl."

"Eliza?" Urilla Peters sniffed in disgust. "And him old enough to be her father!"

"Some old soldiers salute well into their final years," Granny Nichols offered up with a sly half grin that made all the women laugh.

"And, Livi, what about you and Reid?" Anne Logan asked.

Livi bent over the bit of sewing in her hands. She was aware that the other women had fallen silent, waiting for her answer. She felt herself color up.

"What about Reid and me? He'll soon be heading off to trade with the Indians, and once the baby is born, I'm going home to Lynchburg."

The flood of disappointment that met her announcement covered the distress Livi felt at the way things were between Reid and her. After the argument they'd had, Reid had withdrawn. Instead of sharing his meals with her and the children, he ate alone. Instead of offering to help around the cabin, he spent more time in the woods. She knew he was restless. She understood how much he wanted to leave. She and the baby were holding him here against his will, but there wasn't much she could do to change that.

"What's all this?"

She looked up to find that Reid had come around the corner of the cabin with his rifle in hand, Tad and Patches hot on his heels.

"I—we—" Fresh color bloomed in Livi's face.

"We all just came on over to visit," Anne Logan answered in Livi's stead, casting a long, measuring look at each of them, "and to get this corn crop harvested. If those pigeons you've got there are for supper, you might better take them down to where Prudence Wilson is doing the cooking. Then you head on out into the fields with the rest of the men. And take that boy there with you."

Reid stood his ground just long enough to make it clear he was making his own decision; then he did exactly as Anne said.

"Damned cocky rogue!" Anne muttered under her breath and winked at Livi.

The men ate a huge meal at midday and went back to the fields. As more bushels of corn were carried in, two boys emptied them into a pile in the cabin yard. It was here that a corn-husking contest would take place once the fields were stripped.

The men finished up just before sunset and came in to eat. While lanterns and torches were lit, Ben Logan and Reid negotiated the placement of the rail that would evenly divide the pile of corn husks, then chose up teams. In preparation for the contest, jugs of whiskey came out. Each man took a good swig from the gourd dipper and picked up his iron husking pin. Even Tad participated in the swigging, and Livi huffed with disapproval.

"Nimbles up the fingers," Lige Higgins assured her.

Her objections didn't seem to matter much as Tad shucked his shirt like all the men and boys were doing and found a place beside Reid on the near side of the mound of corn.

Everyone knew the rules to a husking contest. Whichever

team finished husking the corn on its side of the rail first, won. Cheating, while not officially sanctioned, was at the very least expected.

Anne Logan fired a pistol in the air to signal the start of the contest. A cheer went up as the men hunkered down and set to work. Husks flew in one direction while the stripped cobs of corn flew in the other. The men worked hard, their heads bent over their work, their bowed backs gleaming with sweat. The women shouted encouragement, laughing as two opponents began heaving husks at each other, clamoring in protest when the two began throwing the empty husks in the women's direction.

The gourd passed regularly from hand to hand. Undermined by skillful excavation, the rail that marked the center of the pile fell toward Ben Logan's side, dramatically shortening the work for the men on his team.

"Foul! Foul!" the men on Reid's side bellowed. It did no good. Instead the men worked harder, faster. Their forearms flexed, their wrists and fingers flicked back the husks and stripped them away in practiced movements. The pile of un- husked corn dwindled while the pile of dried cobs grew.

The men began to chant: "Faster! Faster! Faster!"

Ben Logan's team finished first. The men crowed their vic- tory, laughing, slapping one another on the back, and passing the gourd of whiskey again. While Reid's side finished up, the winners filled the corncrib that Tad and Eustace had built.

By the end of the evening, when the work of harvesting was done, Cissy had fallen asleep on Anne Logan's lap. Tad was swaying like a willow in the wind. Reid and Ben were brag- ging about how quickly they would husk the corn next time. Livi was so exhausted she could barely stand.

Still, she gathered herself to thank all her friends before they left. "I don't know what I would have done without you," she told them truthfully.

Anne and Ben were the last to leave. While Tallie slept against her father's shoulder, Anne drew Livi into a volumi- nous hug.

"That baby's dropping," Anne said and cast a discerning eye at Livi's bulk. "It won't be long now. You send for me any time of the day or night. You hear me, Livi?"

Livi nodded. "I will, Anne. And thank you for everything."

"That's what neighbors are for," Ben assured her as he helped Anne mount her horse, then handed their sleeping daughter up to her.

Livi stood at the edge of the breezeway and waved. Reid took his place beside her as if it were where he belonged. As they watched the Logans ride out, Livi became aware of the warm, comforting pressure of Reid's hand at the small of her back. His touch surprised her—and pleased her more than she could say.

The soft scratches on his cabin door jolted Reid awake every bit as fast as a howling horde of Indians would. He grabbed for his pants and the primed pistol that always hung on a peg above his bed, then stumbled through the darkness to the door. He slipped the bar and nosed the barrel through the opening.

A pale moon face greeted him, a woman with tumbled hair in a crisp white nightdress.

"Livi?" he said.

"I'm sorry to disturb you in the middle of the night—"

"What's the matter?"

"It's the baby. It's coming."

Reid's stomach dropped like a rock down a well. "The baby," he murmured and let her in. "What do you want me to do?" He sparked up the candles on his writing table and shrugged into a shirt. "Do you want me to ride to Logan's Station to get Anne?"

"I want you to stay with me."

No, he thought. Don't ask me that.

"How far along—how soon do you think—"

"I've been having pains since just after we went to bed. My water broke an hour ago."

Reid felt the heat wash up his neck. He didn't want to know this.

"Then I'll have Tad—"

"No!" She grabbed his arm for emphasis. "I won't have either of you riding six miles through the forest in the dead of night."

He could tell by her grip that she meant it. There was no arguing with her now.

"I don't want the children disturbed. I don't want them

worrying. It's going to be an easy delivery, if you'll just help.''

"Jesus, Livi! I don't know anything about bringing a baby into the world!''

She smiled, a smile that would have carried a lot more weight if he hadn't been able to see the sheen of sweat on her upper lip.

"You have the easy part," she told him. "I'll do all the work."

"Livi, please." In the candlelight he could see that her lips were red, as if she had been biting them.

"The pains," she continued, drawing a shaky breath. "The pains are five minutes apart. I timed them with David's watch. The baby should be here by dawn, and there's no sense rousing Anne Logan from her bed when I'll have brought this child into the world long before you and she can get back."

Reid hesitated, weighing her assurances against the fear that was turning him cold inside.

"Please, Reid. Don't make me do this alone," she whispered. "Don't make me ask my son to help me because you're gone."

There wasn't anything he could say to that.

"Well, then, what do you want me to do?"

"I've got what we'll need gathered up over in my cabin: blankets and twine to tie the cord. And a knife to cut it. We'll need flannel pads to put under me and a basin to bathe the baby in. When you do, you'll need to make sure the water's not too hot. Test it with your elbow first."

She sounded as if she knew exactly what to expect. She'd been through this before. Knowing that calmed his boiling anxiety to a simmer.

Then one of the pains hit.

He heard her gasp, saw her ball her fists. She started to sway. He caught her before she could fall, lifted her against his chest. Even with a baby inside her, she didn't weigh much. He could have carried her the six miles to the station. He carried her to his bed instead, laid her down on sheets that were mostly clean.

He watched her stiffen and curl up as if she were battling some demon inside her. Sweat popped out all over him.

It took barely a minute for the pain to pass. It was the

longest minute Reid had ever lived. He didn't belong here, but Livi was right. If he left her now, there wouldn't be anyone but a half-grown boy to see to her distress. And Tad would be even more scared by this than he was.

She smiled up at him when it was over. "See," she said, "that wasn't so bad."

Reid had to swallow before he could speak. "Well, now, where am I going to find those things?"

Livi told him and Reid tiptoed into her side of the cabin. She'd left a Betty lamp burning, and he checked on the children first. Cissy was asleep in the trundle bed. He could hear Tad's even breathing from the loft. The pile of damp linen on the bed and the pink-stained nightdress on the floor gave him pause, but he gathered up the twine and the blanket and the other things Livi had left in a pile on the table. He took David's watch, too. Livi seemed to set such store by knowing how long it was between the pains, he figured they'd have need of it.

He took a final look around the cabin before closing the door, considering whether he should send Tad off in spite of Livi's objections. But then, he didn't relish the idea of Tad picking his way through the woods in the dark, either. The forest was dangerous at night. With the weather so fair, there was no telling if there were Indians about or animals on the prowl. Something could spook the boy's horse or he could lose his way. The consequences didn't bear thinking about. Besides, Reid preferred to face Livi with a clear conscience if she asked about the children.

He could tell by the way the covers on his bed had been disturbed that she'd had another pain while he was gone.

"Back so soon?" she asked brightly, though he could see deepening lines around her eyes. "Would you put one of those pads under me? I'm afraid giving birth gets messy sometimes."

She leaned against the side of the bed while he spread the pad of flannel across his sheets. As he helped her lie back, he saw that her gown was wet and faintly pink where it dipped at the apex of her legs. Only then did he realize exactly what he'd agreed to do.

Reid felt the air in his lungs evaporate. Christ Almighty! If he delivered this baby, he would have to touch her *there!*

Reid Campbell had lain with more than his share of women since one of his stepmother's fancy friends had seduced him when he was thirteen. He'd held women and caressed them. He'd touched them and kissed them as intimately as any man could. He'd spent himself inside them. But, God help him, *this was different*.

This was Livi Talbot he'd be looking at and touching in places and ways he couldn't even contemplate. He would be drawing a life from between her thighs. Oh, Jesus God! *And she was David's wife!*

"Oh, Livi, I'm not sure—"

"A-a-ah!" she gasped, stiffening.

Oh, Lord! It was happening again! Reid swiveled his head around to where David's watch lay open on the writing desk. It couldn't have been five minutes since her last pain.

She rode this one out like it was some ornery, half-broken horse. Twisting and arching. Panting ragged and low. When she breathed easier, so did he. When she smiled up at him, he smiled back—though he had never felt less like smiling in his life.

She blew out a long, unsteady breath and promptly closed her eyes.

He stood there wondering what to do.

"Sit down, Reid," she said without so much as lifting her lashes. "Having a baby is a lot like fighting a battle. You get everything ready and then you wait."

Waiting wasn't something Reid Campbell did well. He sat. He stood. He shifted on his feet. He wanted to pace, but there wasn't room.

"For God's sake, Reid," Livi finally told him, "will you go outside!"

He went, but it didn't help. He could still hear Livi gasp when a pain came on, hear her stir against the covers as it tightened its grip, hear her sigh when it subsided. Only then would he dare let out his breath and stand in the breezeway quivering.

He went back inside. Another hour crawled by. The pains came harder and faster, in an increasingly steady rhythm. Livi rode the peaks and valleys, panting and lying back. She asked for water and he got it. She wanted her hair tied back in a braid and Reid helped her do it. She asked to be read to and he read.

Sometime later, he looked up from the page of a book he would never remember reading and saw that the flannel pad beneath her and the front of her gown were stained with red. Reid's heart seized up inside his chest.

"Jesus, Livi! You're bleeding to death!" he shouted and jumped to his feet.

She had the effrontery to laugh. "No, no," she told him. "It's all right. That's part of what happens when a baby's born."

"You're supposed to lose all that blood?" Reid glared down at her, unconvinced.

"It's really not that much, and there's going to be more. Maybe it's time I told you what else is going to happen so you're prepared."

Livi told him.

He tried very hard to listen, but words like "hemorrhage" and "stillborn" and "afterbirth" blared so loud in his head that he could barely make out the rest. He felt battered when she was done. Stunned and overwhelmed. He excused himself. He went outside and stood there trembling. He couldn't do this. And even if he could, how would he live with himself if something went wrong?

It took everything he had not to balk and run, not to saddle his horse and head for Logan's Station. He couldn't think of anything he wanted more than he wanted Anne Logan here to see Livi safely through this—not unless it was a long, deep drink of Jake Prescott's home-brewed whiskey.

Reid had almost convinced himself to go when everything that was happening to Livi started moving faster, getting worse. After that, no matter how much he wanted to, he couldn't leave.

The pains seemed to come one on top of the other with no respite in between. Livi moaned instead of gasping. She demanded that he tie two lengths of cloth to the head of the bed; then she clung to them as if they were her lifelines. She quivered and jerked and shook. Savage, angry, out of control. She cursed him, the baby, and herself.

More than once Reid had accused Livi of being weak, of having no spine, no courage. But as he watched the pains roll over her, Reid took all of it back. He couldn't have stood this agony, this relentless twisting in your guts. No man could stand what Livi was going through.

The pains went on and on. Livi ran with sweat, and so did Reid. She cried out and he didn't know what to do. She writhed and squirmed and sobbed. He hovered, helpless and hating it.

They had been locked in this room for a hundred years with no light, no air, no rest. It was torture for both of them, and he couldn't think of any way to make it stop.

Then all at once the frenzy ceased.

Livi lay back twisted, depleted, spent. She started to cry.

Ruthless, icy fingers crushed his heart.

Reid had never cared about his own mortality, but he cared about hers. He'd never understood what lay in the oily, impenetrable depths of fear, but he did now. He looked loss and pain and desolation square in the face and tried his best to stand against them.

"Promise me," she demanded in a whisper, clutching his hand.

"Don't do this, Livi," he warned her.

"Promise me that if I die, you'll take the children."

"Goddamn it, Livi! When you talked me into this, you didn't say anything about dying."

She almost smiled. "You will take them, won't you?"

She looked so fragile lying there in the middle of his big bed. Rumpled red hair escaping her braid. A face the color of paper. Slender arms and legs and a slackening belly that seemed to be squeezing the life from her.

He would have promised her anything.

"Of course I will."

"I know I can trust you to be good to them."

Reid felt words back up in his throat. Reassurances he needed to voice. Things he wanted to say about David. Praise for her courage and resourcefulness. Apologies—

"And about David—"

His heartbeat stumbled. "What about David?"

"I wasn't a very good wife to him," she confessed, moving again. "You saw and understood how badly I failed him."

"I never—"

"But even you didn't know the worst."

"This isn't the time to tell me."

"I was wicked, so wicked."

"Oh, Livi, don't!"

She couldn't seem to stop the words. "I kept getting pregnant, having babies to strengthen my hold on David. To keep him with me. To keep him from coming here. To keep him from you. I deliberately courted his passion to undermine his dream."

Livi was trembling, weeping silently.

Reid wanted to gather her up in his arms, but he was afraid. He wanted to take back all the bitterness and jealousy between them, but it was too late.

"No, Livi, no! You weren't wicked. You were only afraid. You probably had a right to be. This *is* a hostile land. It *did* cost David his life." He ducked his head, not knowing how she would react. "And I knew very well what you were doing."

Livi's sharp gasp of surprise seemed to stop her tears. "You did?"

He tightened his fingers around her hand. "I'm just sorry I made you have to hang on to him so hard."

"I'd do so much better if I had another chance."

He looked down into her eyes, dark and wet with guilt and strain. Jesus, what had he done to her, fighting for David's time and attention the way he had? Pitting himself against her when they both loved David.

"You loved him," he assured her, wishing he knew what else to say. "And David loved you with all his heart."

"He did?"

Reid nodded. He didn't tell her how threatened he had been by that. He didn't have to; Livi knew. He just wasn't sure she understood how much David's friendship meant when Reid was growing up or how afraid he was to let it go once he'd become a man. But this wasn't the time to tell her.

"Now, Livi, you have to try—" His voice frayed a little as he went on. "You have to try to get through the rest of this."

"I will in a minute," she promised, moaning again. "All I need is a little rest."

There wasn't any rest and both of them knew it. He felt the pain rise in her again, merciless and cruel.

"Ma?"

"Tad?" She raised her frantic gaze to Reid. "Oh, please! Please don't let Tad—"

Reid got to his feet and intercepted her son just short of the door.

"The baby's coming," he said, realizing suddenly that it was getting light. "I need you to ride to Logan's Station. Bring Anne Logan back as fast as you can."

"Is Ma all right?"

"She's fine," Reid said in a way that made Tad believe him. "But she's uncomfortable—and anxious to have another woman to help her with the birthing part."

Tad nodded and spun away. Reid waited to see him ride out before he turned back into the cabin.

Livi seemed different somehow when he got inside. She was sitting up a little straighter. There was a hint of color in her face.

"It's coming," she said through gritted teeth.

"What?"

"It's coming. I'm going to push the baby out. This is the part I need you for."

All Reid's blood drained toward his feet. He went tingly and light-headed, but stood his ground. "Just tell me what to do."

They worked together. Reid braced Livi's trembling legs. She groaned and twisted and dragged down on her lifelines with all her strength. They fought their way through a score of contractions, flushed and panting and running with sweat.

Then Reid saw a small ruddy dome emerge between her legs. "It's coming," he shouted. "I can see the top of its head!"

Livi stretched down to touch where the baby was crowning, desperate for confirmation. Reid reached out his trembling hands in wonder. Their fingers brushed at the crest of that downy head.

Reid felt the rush of connection to the marrow of his bones. The intensity of it shattered him, shattered everything he'd ever hoped, everything he'd ever feared. He and Livi and David were bound together by this new life, united by something so wondrous and mystical as this baby's birth.

"Oh, Livi!" he cried out. "Oh, God, Livi!"

She laughed and wept and pushed again. The head emerged, a tiny wrinkled face. She pushed and shoulders came into view. A belly and hips and drawn-up legs.

Reid caught the baby in his hands. Slippery and red and yelling. So small and so precious. Hands and feet and toes and fingers. So marvelously perfect.

He held life and joy and elation in his grasp. He held David's child as if it were his own. A sense of belonging washed through him, so wondrous and sweet, so tangible and strong, it stole his breath.

"It's a boy," he pronounced and laughed with the taste of tears on his tongue.

Livi reached out for her child and Reid laid him on her belly. She stroked the baby's fuzzy head, examined those tiny hands and fingers. She smiled up at Reid.

"Thank you," she whispered. "Thank you for giving me this."

His throat was too full to speak. He nodded; he smiled. Livi reached out and took his hand.

By the time Tad and Anne Logan clattered into the yard, both mother and baby were bathed and swaddled and tucked up tight.

Livi and Reid heard Anne stomp up the steps. "Might have known, Livi Talbot, that you'd wait until that harvest was in before you'd drop that child! Been holding that baby inside you with sheer will, now, haven't you, girl?"

Anne took one look at mother and baby curled together in Reid Campbell's big bed. "Well," she harrumphed. "I came all this way and there's nothing left to do. He looks like a fine, strong baby, too. You got a name for him yet?"

"David," Livi answered.

It's fitting, Reid thought, stepping back, giving the women room.

"I'm going to name him David Reid."

Livi's words caught and nestled in Campbell's chest. Hot and aching and precious beyond all bearing. Reid felt her gaze on him and couldn't make himself look up. She'd see everything inside him if he did. He knew he had to get outside.

He collided with Tad in the doorway. "Is Ma all right?" the boy demanded.

"You've got a baby brother," Reid told him and kept on moving.

He noticed Cissy sitting forlorn and half dressed on the floor of the breezeway and knew someone else would have to tend to her. He needed to get away too much.

Reid scrambled up the ridge behind the house. His chest ached and his vision blurred as he made the climb. His heart was pounding when he reached the top. He stumbled out of the trees and past the Hadleys' deserted cabin. He ran into the wide gold-and-green meadow beyond.

He managed to hold everything inside until he could see the sky. "David!" he shouted, tears running down his face. "David! David! We have a son!"

❧ 19 ❧

A Methodist parson who was passing through Logan's Station baptized David Reid Talbot on the second Sunday in December. Reid stood up with Livi in David's place, watching and listening as the minister intoned the appropriate words and dabbed the baby's forehead with water from a special cup. Campbell set no store by the Christian rite. His years with the Creeks had garbled whatever bits of the Anglican catechism had been drummed into his head during his years at school in Charles Town. But because Livi believed and took comfort in knowing her child had been baptized, Reid had agreed.

Livi had been in a state of nervous anticipation all week, worrying that the weather might keep them home, but the day turned out fair and fine. They'd ridden over with the sun strong and warm through the barren trees, and Reid meant to make sure they headed back before it sank behind the western hills. He didn't want to take any chance of the baby getting sick.

But for now, Anne and Ben Logan set out food and drink in their cabin to celebrate. Friends Livi had made during her stay at the fort and people who had come to the cabin to help with the harvest wandered in to eat and laugh and coo over the baby.

Reid watched from across the room. After being holed up with just Livi and the children for more than six weeks, even the modest gathering rankled him. He'd been doing for her,

284

too, and the way Anne Logan was hovering at Livi's elbow made him feel mulish and vaguely displaced. Reid hid his frown in one of the heavy pewter tankards Anne had brought out especially for the celebration and swallowed down a gulp of whiskey.

Livi certainly did look fine today, he reflected, with her hair brushed to a coppery sheen and tucked up beneath a lacy cap. The cream-colored bodice and deep green skirt showed off a figure that was quickly redeveloping every one of its dips and curves. The light in Livi's eyes and the glow on her face gave him pause. She looked contented, really happy for the first time since David died. She just never seemed to smile that girlish, carefree smile when she was with him.

Reid scowled again and turned away. He poured more whiskey into his tankard and went outside to squint at the sunny sky.

Maybe it isn't too late to head west after all, he thought. If he ordered his trade goods while he was here at the station, he could be on the trail by the middle of next week.

Since the summer he turned seventeen, he'd carried his whole world in his saddlebags, and now Reid squirmed with that old, familiar itch. He'd always had a hankering to see what lay beyond the next ridge. He'd always yearned to climb the mountains, to taste the sea, to touch as much of the world as he possibly could. And as long as he'd been wandering, he'd never once been disappointed.

Perhaps he should go, Reid told himself. He wasn't cut out for the quiet domesticity he'd sampled with Livi and the children these past weeks. He'd never been satisfied hunting the same hills day after day. He'd never been content sitting by the fireside in the evening. He couldn't imagine why being with Livi made him feel so settled and comfortable.

Well, it would sour eventually, he reflected, and drank again. He might as well get on his way before it did.

Livi would be safe at the cabin until spring. The Indians wouldn't be raiding any time soon. George Clark and his militia had burned Chillicothe and cleaned out the rest of the Shawnee villages up north of the Ohio. It would take the Indians months to rebuild, and the worst of the winter was ahead of them. Besides, Livi had made all these fine new friends while she was here at the fort. They could look after her when he was gone.

Reid almost had his mind made up to leave when Ben Logan joined him on the steps of the Logans' cabin.

"I wondered where you got off to," he greeted Reid, flushed and jovial with the pleasures of the day and the whiskey he'd consumed. "You have enough of breaking up fights among the children and watching all those women dandle that baby?"

"I've been sitting here thinking what I need to get together so I can head off trading next week."

"You're going now?" Logan turned to stare at him. "So late in the season? I figured you'd be around this winter at least, with Livi having the baby and all."

Reid swallowed deep. "I think she can do well enough by herself. She made it through planting without any help. She doesn't need me there for the winter months when all they've got is animals to tend."

"Livi liked having Eustace and Violet for company," Ben pointed out.

"Eustace is riding back with us today."

"Is he well enough to do that?"

"He thinks he is, and sometimes that's all that matters."

When Reid had asked the same question, Eustace had stared past him and said that a man needed to be near where his wife was buried to face up to the loss. In his way, Reid had understood.

"At any rate," he continued, "Eustace will be out there for Livi while I'm gone. And in the spring, when the baby is old enough to travel, I can take them all back to Lynchburg. I can sell my furs while I'm there, too, instead of trusting them to one of those crooked station traders."

Ben ignored the good-natured insult. "Well, damn!" he offered, taking a draught of whiskey. "Anne and I were hoping that while the parson was here, you and Livi would decide to marry up."

Reid's hands clenched around his tankard. "Livi's David's wife."

"And David is dead," Ben pointed out.

Reid took refuge in a long pull of whiskey and refused to answer.

"Don't you know it's up to the living to live?" Logan huffed with consternation. "For you, that means marrying Livi, now, doesn't it?"

Reid stared down into the murky depths of his cup and stubbornly shook his head.

"You love her, don't you?" Ben pressed him.

"I don't know."

"Hell, man! You love her!" he exploded. "Every time you see her, your eyes light up. Every time you look at her or those three children, your face says they belong to you."

"They don't belong to me. They're David's, not mine."

"But they could be yours."

It was the devil in the guise of a friend bartering for Campbell's soul.

God knows it wasn't as if Reid hadn't imagined how it would feel to claim David's family for himself. If he was willing to own up to it, he'd envied David for a good long while: having Livi to come home to, having children, having dreams that amounted to something. Thinking about stepping into David's place made him ache with hope and frustration and fear he'd fought with all his life. But David was David, and Reid was Reid. David always belonged with a home and family.

Reid never belonged anywhere.

"No," he said. "They couldn't belong to me."

"Why not?"

Goddamn Ben and his questions anyway. He didn't want to think about this—especially not when he'd mostly decided to leave Livi in possession of the cabin and head west.

"Because—because I haven't found the men who murdered David!"

Logan snorted in reply. "Reid, it's been months and months since David died. You aren't any closer to finding out who attacked their camp than you were when you started looking. You might as well accept it. The men are gone. You're never going to find them."

"I promised Livi I'd avenge his death."

"Did you promise that to her," Ben asked, "or did you promise it to yourself?"

When Reid didn't answer, Ben swirled the last of the whiskey in the bottom of his tankard and drank it down. "I think you're here because you want to be. I think you're holding back because you're afraid—of what Livi and those children make you feel, of taking on that load of responsibility. No man likes the clutch in his belly when he looks at his wife and his family and realizes what they mean to him, but every man feels it.''

Ben shoved to his feet and stood looking down at Reid. ''Don't jeopardize everything you could have because you're dead set on righting a wrong that doesn't matter anymore. Don't throw Livi and her children away because you're afraid of caring too much.''

Reid felt his face get hot. He wanted to tell Ben that until he had stood over the bodies of the men who killed his friend, it would always matter. He wanted to say that he wasn't afraid of what he felt for Livi and the children.

He nodded at the older man instead. ''You're a good friend, Ben Logan, even when you're wrong.''

''You're a damn fool, Reid Campbell,'' Logan answered, shaking his head, ''if you're just too stubborn to acknowledge the truth.''

''Has he asked you to marry him yet?''

Livi looked up from where her son suckled at her breast into Anne Logan's inquisitive face. They were in the little bedroom Ben had added to the side of their cabin to give Anne and him a little peace.

''Who is it that wants to marry me?''

''Why, Reid, of course.''

''Reid Campbell?''

Anne frowned and settled herself beside Livi at the side of the bed, reaching out to skim one finger over the sweet, silken skin of the baby's cheek. ''And who else are we likely to be talking about?''

Livi shrugged. ''You know as well as I do Reid's not a marrying man.''

Anne quirked a brow in Livi's direction. ''I would have agreed with you before, but now that I've seen him with you and that baby, I'm not so sure.''

Livi looked down at Little David again, not wanting the other woman to read the hope and confusion that shone in her eyes. ''What does he do that makes you think so?''

Anne gave a snort of laughter. "Why, it's as plain as the nose on your face! He can't take his eyes off you. He behaves as if you already belong to him. And he's every bit as possessive with Tad and Cissy and Little David here. He glowered at everyone who came near you today. If ever there was a man ripe for marrying a woman, it's Reid ripe for marrying you."

"He's been very good to us since the baby was born," Livi allowed, "and I know he's been neglecting his trading so he can stay on with us." A frown came and went between her elegant brows. "Or at least he's been neglecting it until now. He may head off into the woods once he's sure I'm feeling better."

"I don't think he's going anywhere," Anne predicted. "Besides, the kiss he gave you must mean something."

Livi sat up a little straighter, her cheeks flushed warm. "What kiss?"

"The kiss he gave you the night before you went back to the cabin."

"How do you know about that?"

Anne threw back her head and laughed. "My dear girl! Half the people in the station saw it. He kissed you like he wanted to make love to you right there in the yard. And with a man like Reid, I expect the fires burn pretty bright. Why'd he run off so fast?"

Livi figured there wasn't any point in denying what had happened. Besides, Anne was only indulging in a little good-natured teasing.

"The baby kicked him," Livi admitted, smoothing Little David's hair as he nursed.

Anne laughed again. "Serves him right. Has Reid approached you since then?"

"And when would he do that? Right before or right after he delivered this child?"

Anne was taking unholy delight in the situation. "Got a temper, don't you, girl? I wouldn't have expected that—not in someone raised up to be a lady like you were."

"It doesn't matter how I was raised. I'm not a lady anymore. I'm just a settler working to keep my family together."

"Marrying Reid would make that a good deal easier, I should think," Anne pointed out. "You care for him, don't you?"

Livi sighed. A few months ago she would have been happy to tell Anne how much she loathed Reid, how she'd thought of him as the devil incarnate for all of her married life. But today the answer was different. She wasn't sure exactly how it was different, but she couldn't hate the man who had helped her bring her last and most precious child into the world. She couldn't harbor enmity for a man who had welcomed that child with such all-consuming joy. When Reid first held Little David up for her to see, there were tears running down his face. It was a memory she would treasure all of her days.

Even if he wouldn't budge when it came to giving her the land, Reid had been good to her and the children in his way. He'd stayed by them while she regained her strength. He'd given them use of the cabin—at least until spring.

"I don't know how I feel about Reid," Livi told Anne honestly. "I don't have any idea how he feels about me."

"Don't be a fool, Livi. He loves you as sure as apples grow on apple trees. Just looking at him looking at you makes me recall how it used to be with Ben and me."

"Ben still looks at you like that."

Anne colored up. "Well, then, girl, since you think I know how good it can be between a man and a woman, take my word. If Reid won't ask the question, then maybe you should. Men need a nudge sometimes."

It was Livi's turn to laugh. "Asking Reid to marry me would be a lot more than a nudge. It would be a downright shove."

"Well, sometimes they need that, too. You mark my words."

Livi looked down at her child again, thinking about her life here in Kentucky. Thinking about Reid.

"I think marriage would be a whole lot more responsibility than Reid Campbell is willing to take on right now."

Livi could see that Anne thought she was right. "He could surprise you, Livi. When you put it that way, I wouldn't care to wager on the outcome, but he might just care about you and the children enough to take that chance. And if he did, Livi, it could be very good between you."

Damn Anne Logan, Livi thought at home later that evening as she undressed Cissy and put her to bed. What Anne had said earlier in the day made it impossible for Livi to ignore

Reid Campbell's presence in her cabin. She was vividly aware of him carrying in the armloads of wood she'd need to see her through the night, of him squatting before her hearth nursing the coals of the fire to life.

Livi couldn't help but steal a look at him when she had the chance, thinking how fine Reid had looked today in his blue broadcloth coat and buff-colored breeches, in his striped silk vest and soft cambric shirt. She had grown so used to seeing him done up in buckskin and trade cloth that she'd forgotten what an elegant figure he cut. Dressed in more conventional attire and with his hair tied back in a queue, he could pass for the finest Tidewater gentleman.

What Anne Logan had said also made Livi distinctly uncomfortable when, after getting the fire going, Reid took a place on the bench before the blaze as if he meant to stay.

Just as she was about to plead exhaustion and ask him to leave, Tad burst in from seeing to the horses. "Damn! It's cold out there!" he announced. "I had to break through ice on the water barrel in order to wash."

"You *did* wash behind your ears, though, didn't you, Tad?" Livi asked, indulging in what had long ago become part of their nightly ritual.

"You know I did, Ma," he answered and bussed Livi on the cheek.

"And have you made sure that we have water for the night?"

Tad complied, snatching up the bucket by the door and filling it from the barrel in the breezeway. Then, taking the stub of a candle to light his way, he climbed the ladder to the loft.

"G'night, Ma," he called down. "G'night, Reid."

They bade him good night. Because she couldn't think of what else to do, Livi settled herself on the bench before the fire and picked up her mending. Reid looked over with interest, as if she were up to something far more exotic than darning a sock.

They sat barely a foot apart, their backs against the table and their feet stretched out toward the fire's warmth. As she pulled a stitch taut, Livi glanced in his direction. There was a vee-shaped pucker between Reid's brows, a tightness at the corners of his mouth. She couldn't imagine what was bothering him. Unless . . .

Livi flushed hot with ire and humiliation. Surely Anne Logan hadn't been so foolish as to take Reid aside this afternoon and talk to him about marrying her, had she? On the off chance that Anne had, Livi meant to set things straight—though she wasn't quite sure how.

She had to clear her throat twice before she could squeeze any words past the knot in her throat. "I thought the christening went very well today."

"Indeed it did."

"It was good of Anne and Ben to invite everyone back to their cabin."

"You certainly took great delight in seeing all of your new friends."

She sensed undercurrents in Reid tonight, shifts and depths she couldn't quite fathom. Her heartbeat flickered and picked up speed.

"Yes, I did."

Silence fell, the air between them inexplicably thickening. Livi's stomach fluttered; her hands went damp. She felt as if she were missing something important.

"Reid, I was won—"

Little David's cry cut her short.

Welcoming the diversion, Livi rose to see to him. She had left the baby bundled up between pillows on her bed, and she changed his diaper before lifting him onto her shoulder. He was hungry again, but then, Little David always seemed to be hungry. Without thinking, Livi loosened the laces at the neck of her chemise and guided her nipple into the baby's mouth.

It wasn't unusual for Reid to be in the cabin when she put the baby to her breast, but the simple act seemed different tonight. It seemed so much more intimate, as if baring herself like this were somehow provocative. Color warmed Livi's cheeks as she resumed her seat on the bench in front of the fire. To do otherwise would have given credence to the tension bubbling between them.

Though she bent her head, Livi was aware that Reid was studying her as she nursed her child. Stealing looks at him, she watched as the hard planes and angles of his face softened with a warmth and affection he rarely permitted the rest of the world to see. She savored the notion that he trusted her. Instead of keeping all that gentleness and vulnerability hidden away, he allowed her access to his finer emotions. It made her think of how he'd wept with this child in his hands, made her remember that sometimes he seemed so weary and so very much alone.

Livi wanted to reach out. She wanted to soothe away the tension gathered between his eyes, the loneliness she sensed at the core of him even now. She wanted to find a way to make him whole. She knew the impulse was dangerous. To answer the need in him, she would have to risk emotions she wasn't sure she was ready to feel again.

Just when Livi would have drawn away, Reid shifted closer. He reached out one dark hand and stroked the baby's cheek.

"So soft," he murmured in wonder. "So fragile. So miraculous."

Suddenly Livi wasn't sure if he was speaking about the baby in her arms or the feelings growing thick and warm between Reid and her.

His knuckles grazed her breast, and with that simple touch, unexpected longing rose full and hot in her chest. It spilled through her, slow and honey-sweet. She caught her breath, aching with a need to claim the man beside her. This tender stranger. This other Reid.

She raised her head and saw her yearning mirrored in his eyes. Though she knew she was wrong to acknowledge it, Livi couldn't look away. Barely breathing, she shifted nearer and raised her lips to his, taking his wide, warm mouth with the fullness of her own.

Reid drew her and the baby to him with the strong, sure sweep of his arm. His fingers rose to stroke her cheek, to slide down the long, graceful curve of her throat.

"Livi." He whispered the word gentle and feather-light against her mouth. "Oh, Livi."

She closed her eyes and gave herself over to sensate enjoyment of his nearness. She curled into the protective breadth of his body, into his deep, sustaining heat. She savored the glide of his tongue against her mouth, savored the opening and the welcoming, the sweet and sinuous merging of his tongue and hers. She nestled closer and breathed him in, the scents of horses and whiskey and masculinity. She felt enveloped, sheltered, and, for the first time in months, exquisitely cherished.

He pulled her even closer, as if he were as hungry as she was for deeper contact.

Baby David yelled in protest at being crushed and jostled and deprived of his dinner. He shook his tiny balled fists like the tyrant he was.

Reid and Livi fell back laughing.

"I guess he's making his feelings abundantly clear," Reid said, shifting away from her. "He wants his mother to himself."

Livi hesitated before she spoke. "I guess I've never much held with giving a child *everything* he wants."

The air went sharp and thin between them.

Reid looked into her face, his eyes alive with questions. "And what about his mother?" he finally asked. "What does Little David's mother want?"

Livi realized how much she had to decide. If she followed her inclinations, if she made love with Reid, things would never be the same. She didn't know how they would be different. She didn't know how she *wanted* them to be different. She just knew that once they touched in that intimate way, once they shared the sweet, dark secrets of mutual passion, there would be no going back.

If she sent Reid away, the question would always lie unresolved between them. He would never ask again. She would never have the opportunity or the courage to reach out to this complex and solitary man. She would never have the chance to save him from himself.

He would never have a chance to offer all she believed he had to give.

Livi took a shuddery breath. "Little David's mother very much wants to be with you. *I* want to be with you."

Reid looked as if he weren't quite sure what to do with the miraculous gift she'd given him. He swallowed hard and shook his head. "We can't . . . be together here. Not in David's bed. Not with your children sleeping . . ."

"Could we go across to your cabin?" she asked. "Once I've finished feeding the baby and changed him again, he will sleep. We could . . ." The thought of just what they could do left Livi a little breathless. "We could be together then."

Reid didn't answer. He didn't have to. He just smiled and rose and picked up the basket they'd pressed into service as a cradle at the fort today. Before he left, Reid bent and kissed Livi long and slowly. He kissed her with a sweet, simmering intensity that made her head swim and her bones dissolve.

Oh, my, she thought when he was gone. *Oh, my!*

She took her time getting ready. She finished with the baby, stripped off her clothes, and washed herself, using her last precious bar of scented soap and a bit of the cold, clear water from the drinking bucket. She shivered a little as the droplets trailed over her breasts and belly and down her thighs. She followed them slowly, mopping with a length of cotton cloth, wondering what Reid would see when he looked at her. She wasn't the slender girl she'd been when David had initiated her to the rites of loving and being loved. This body was soft and broad from carrying babies, full and heavy from nursing them. If any man alive knew that, it was Reid.

Still, she wanted to be beautiful for him. She brushed her hair until it shone. She let it fall thick and straight to the curve of her waist. She took out the nightdress David had had made for her as a gift. It was soft as down, filmy lawn and trimmed with lace. She held it in her hands and remembered all the times she had worn it, all the lovemaking just wearing it had sparked between David and her.

Then she put the gown away. This wasn't about David anymore.

This was about Reid. This was about a man who had loved David as much as she had loved him. But it was also about a man who would never be content to live in David's shadow.

She slipped on another nightdress, threw her battered green cloak around her shoulders, and picked up her child.

It took her only a moment to tiptoe across the breezeway, only a moment for Reid to open the door.

His cabin glowed with candles. The fire was built up bright. Reid had set the basket on the writing table, well away from any drafts that might creep across the floor, and padded it with rabbit fur. She lay the baby down inside. He grumbled as she settled him in, but before she could tuck a blanket around him for warmth, Little David was already asleep.

Then she turned to Reid. From across the room she could see the tempest in his eyes. He was as aware as she of what they'd been to each other in the past, of what they could be to each other tonight. He knew as well as she all the things that would change if they came together.

He moved nearer anyway.

She felt the slow, sensual melody in his movements as he approached, the shift of his shoulders, the grace of his stride. Just watching him, Livi felt her body warm and bud in ways she had nearly forgotten.

He stopped before her, blatantly, potently male; tall and strong and powerful. She couldn't seem to raise her gaze from where his shirt lay open, revealing the smooth, dusky hollow at the base of his throat. She couldn't seem to tear her eyes from the pulse that tripped hard and fast at the turn of his jaw.

He breached the slight distance between them, slipping the dangling woolen ties she'd looped together beneath her chin. He drew the cloak from around her shoulders and reached to hang it on a peg behind her.

He was standing so close, Livi could feel his heat penetrate the fabric of her nightdress, reverberate against her chest and thighs. He lifted one hand to her cheek, feathered his knuckles along her jaw, and raised her face to his.

He was possessed of a harsh and stirring beauty: an angular face; a strong, straight nose; clear, bright eyes beneath heavy, angled brows; a firm but mobile mouth.

"Are you sure this is what you want?" he asked, offering her one last chance to change her mind.

Livi met his question with one of her own, as if it could hide her uncertainty and reticence. "Do you think I'd be here if I wasn't sure?"

He didn't challenge her answer. He just reached for her. He slid his palms along her ribs, spread his hands against her back. She felt as fragile as eggshells within his grasp, delicate and breakable. With only the slight, insistent pressure of his fingertips, he gathered her closer. Their thighs brushed. Their hips aligned. Her breasts nestled against the broad, unyielding wall of his chest. They stood there barely breathing.

"I always thought you were the most beautiful woman I'd ever seen," he told her softly. "Such glorious hair. Such pale, pale skin. Such a delicious, tempting mouth . . ."

She had never expected Reid to speak to her like this, never imagined there was anything like poetry inside him. The discovery sent delight spinning through her. Laughter bubbled up her throat.

Reid smiled in answer and lowered his head. She saw his lips part in anticipation as he closed the distance between them, felt the sweet, heated mingling of their breath. He took possession of her mouth, claiming and savoring, desirous and tender. The kiss pooled between them, lush and rich with promise.

She stretched up along the length of his body, fitting her breasts and belly more fully against him. She raised her hands to encircle his neck and encountered the queue he had affected to meet the demands of the day. With a flick of her wrist, she pulled the carefully tied ribbon free. The thick black silk of his hair spilled forward, spreading against the white of his collar and tumbling dark against his back.

It skimmed across his cheeks and brushed her jaw as he bent to deepen his slow, deliberate exploration of her mouth. His tongue glided along the widening O, tracing the delicate upper bow, the sinuous flare of her lower lip. He delved beyond the margin, tasting the soft inner corners, the pillowy softness inside.

Livi met the tip of his tongue with her own, learning his texture and his flavor, the essence that made him Reid. Bound together with nothing more than the contact of their mouths and the warmth of his hands against her back, they played the age-old games, touching and tasting and teasing, withdrawing and giving back. It stirred the restlessness in both of them, the questing and answering, the provocation and response.

Livi was quivering when Reid finally raised his head, and she could see that he was every bit as affected by the kisses as she. His face was flushed and he was breathing in sharp, staccato bursts. He looked down at her, and she saw wild, reckless hunger in his eyes.

Somehow she had known he would be like this when he made love, focused, intent, and so vital that when a woman took him inside her, he would fill her with his energy, his strength. It should have frightened Livi to offer herself to such a man, to fly so close to the sun. Instead it lit some answering passion in her, some compelling need to take all that he could give her. And offer him more.

She reached up and touched his face, letting her palm conform to the shape of his chin and cheek and jaw. He turned his head, pressed a kiss into her open hand, traced a spiral with the tip of his tongue.

Livi gasped at the tingling sensation that wound up her arm. Her knees melted beneath her and without a word, he swept her up in his arms and carried her to his bed.

He laid her gently atop the woven counterpane and followed her down.

"Livi," he breathed and nibbled his way slowly and deliberately from the curve of her temple to the corner of her mouth. He drizzled slow, sweet kisses down her throat, lingering in the hollow above her collarbone.

He raised his hand to cup her breast, circled the tight, engorged nipple with his thumb. Fierce, sharp pleasure coiled up the midline of her body. She cried out in surprise and delight.

"Livi?" Reid froze above her, his voice deep with concern. "Have I hurt you, Livi?"

She shook her head, incapable of forming the single, simple word that would reassure him.

"If I've hurt you, we will stop."

"No," she breathed. "No, I don't want you to stop. I want you to touch me and kiss me and . . ."

She curled her fingers into the front of his shirt and pulled him down. She raised her chin to fit the flare of her lips to his.

He moaned and gathered her up in his arms. He sheltered and warmed her with the bulk of his body; tangled his hands in the thick, shimmering mass of her hair; kissed her as if he never meant to stop. And as he did, his hands roamed over her, palms smoothing the length of her back, molding her hips to his; fingers sliding beneath the hem of her gown to trace slow, tickly patterns up the backs of her thighs.

She touched him, too, gliding beneath the hem of his shirt, tugging it upward over his head. His body was lean and hard and well formed, but marked. A straight, livid line ran the length of his chest. Two more lines transected it. He was marked with old scars, white and imperfectly healed. He was marked with the remnants of so many hurts.

Livi mewed with concern and would have demanded explanations if he had not silenced them with long, sultry kisses,

kisses that left her head spinning and her body taut with longing.

She was trembling and feverish when he raised his mouth from hers. "Oh, Reid," she whispered. "Oh, Reid, please!"

He stripped back the covers and laid her back on the chilly sheets. While she waited, he divested himself of his shoes and stockings and breeches. He came to her then, sliding along her body, lifting her nightdress as he went, staining her flesh with his heat.

Her hands moved over him, the yoke of his shoulders, the rise of his ribs, the hard taut belly. Her fingers curled around his shaft. She felt the pulse of life in him. Of power. Of pleasure—both his and her own.

He moaned and rolled over her, his fingers stroking to prepare the way. He touched her, lifting her on a swell of sensation, sending ripples rushing along her limbs. He petted her, circling and pressing, inciting sweet chaos in her blood. She shivered with each brush of his hands. Her breasts were full and heavy with delight, her belly abuzz with anticipation, the core of her wet and yearning for him.

He made her his. His fierce, focused energy flowed into her, relentless, compelling, and vital. He held her still, kissing her long and slowly, claiming and seducing and devouring.

She shifted beneath him, wanting more, wanting everything. She raised her hips and he sank deep, into the age-old rhythm of joining, into the life-affirming drive for mutual pleasure. He tangled his fingers in her hair and drew her to him with his hands and with his eyes, beckoning her to take all that he could give. The pleasure rose in her, the ecstasy eclipsing everything but the man whose body was joined with hers.

She called his name, needing him to follow her. He came, and she watched as he lost himself in her sweetness and in her eyes. The power of his energy coursed alive in her, filling her body with his seed, filling her soul with indescribable joy, filling her world with unimagined promise.

He bound her to him as if she were his prize, something wondrous and special, meant only for him. He held her tight, as if he were afraid that once the loving had passed, she would somehow slip away. His heartbeat jolted against her, tripping even faster and more erratically than her own. He buried his face against her throat and slowly let out his breath.

His long, dark body lay sheltering hers. She stroked his shoulder, the length of his back. He mumbled a string of sleepy endearments as his breathing deepened.

She hadn't known that this was how it would be between them. She had expected the intensity, but not the tenderness. She had anticipated the pleasure, but not the communion.

Anne Logan had spoken of a marriage between Reid and her, and Livi found herself wondering what that would be like. Different from anything she had ever known. Different from how it had been with David—just as this was different.

But Livi didn't want marriage now. If they spoke of marriage, there would be the question of the land between them. Of David. Of how the future would work out.

She didn't want anything to come between Reid and her and this wondrous thing they had discovered together. She lay feeling the fan of Reid's breath against her throat, the warmth of his body against her side, the possessive curl of his arm around her. And in the quiet, candlelit cabin, Livi smiled.

❧20❧

*L*ivi came to recognize Reid's smile. Reid's *special* smile. She came to recognize it not because she had seen it before, but because she had never seen it—not until he brought in an armload of wood from the woodpile the morning after they'd made love. It was a curled-up-at-one-corner smile, a cocky smile, a contented smile, a smile of security and belonging. To know that she was the one to make Reid smile that way filled Livi's heart to overflowing.

She saw that smile often in the following weeks. She came to recognize its smoldering intensity, feel its mesmerizing pull. She came to know that once the children were asleep, Reid's smile would deepen and his eyes would gleam. He would draw her into his arms, hold her, and touch her, and kiss her until she could not breathe. He would strip away her bodice and petticoats, and whisper that she was beautiful. He would stroke her in ways that made her writhe, press her back across the bed, and make himself a part of her.

As she shuddered beneath him in the depths of delight, she would see his smile change to one of deepest satisfaction, of strong and enduring passion. Behind it she could see the longing he could never admit, the emotions he didn't know how to express. She could see them glow in his eyes, hear them rasp in his voice, taste them in his kisses. She could absorb them through her skin as their bodies joined. But Livi was not willing to give those feelings a name. His smile was all she would acknowledge, though she had to admit that she was smiling, too.

As the storms blew in from the west, as the wind whistled around the corners of the cabin and the snow piled up in drifts, the pace of life in the valley slowed. There would always be wood to cut and animals to tend. There would always be meals to fix and sewing to do. Yet winter was a quiet time on a homestead, and Livi was glad for the respite.

Reid and Tad hunted, though game was scarce. Livi sewed until her eyes watered and her vision blurred. She shelled corn from her crop until the pads of her thumbs were raw and sore. Cissy mastered her letters and her numbers and read aloud as her mother worked. Tad struggled to stay ahead of his sister's accomplishments, though the book learning didn't come easily to him. That Reid, for all his adventures, was a lettered man gave the boy encouragement.

They all gathered at dusk for their evening meal, hominy and ham from the pig Reid had butchered in the fall, feather-light corn bread and rabbit stew, persimmons and walnuts Livi and Cissy had found in the woods. As often as not, Eustace came down from his cabin to join them. He sat silent for the most part, still struggling to make peace with losing Violet.

It was Cissy's reading and the child's willingness to "show him his letters" that seemed to spark new life in the black man's eyes. Livi took over teaching him, and in the long, cold spell after Christmas, they sat one night with rapt attention while Eustace read from the Bible for the very first time.

When the weather broke toward the end of January, they all bundled themselves in scarfs and cloaks and mittens and rode over to Logan's Station for supplies. The woods shimmered in the winter sun, the lacy underpinnings of snow at the base of the trees, the icicles along the banks of the stream that added their drip, drip, drip to the water's flow. The air was crisp and clear and delectable in their lungs, but they were shivering by the time they reached the gates to the fort.

It took Anne Logan all of two minutes to realize what had happened between Livi and Reid, and another five to get Livi alone so she could gloat.

"I knew the two of you were meant to be together," Anne all but crowed. "I knew the two of you would suit. So when's the wedding?"

Livi accepted the cup of tea that Anne had brewed while the menfolk and the children were busy out and around the station. "I don't know that there's going to be a wedding. Reid hasn't asked me to marry him, and I'm not sure what I'd say if he did."

Anne's face fell. "What do you mean, you're not sure what you'd say? Reid's a prime male specimen, isn't he? He cares for you and the children, and he's a good provider. He makes you happy, doesn't he, girl?"

Oh, Reid did make her happy! Livi loved having him around. She loved the sound of his laughter as they sat by the fire in the evenings; loved the way he took to the children, especially Baby David; loved the security he provided all of them when he was at the cabin. The loving between them had grown better each time they'd come together: the pleasure more intense, the communication between them stronger, the emotions deeper.

"It's just that I'm not sure he'd be content," Livi hedged.

"Can't you make him content?"

Livi wasn't sure anything she did could make Reid content if he took it into his head to leave.

"There's a wildness in him, Anne. A restlessness. A need to be free. How could I chain him to me by making vows, even if that's what he thought he wanted?"

"Isn't it what he wants?"

"I don't know what he wants," Livi admitted in frustration.

Anne reached across and patted her hand. "Well, never you mind. You'll tame him, Livi-girl. With a bit of sugar and a bit of pepper and a lot of love."

But Livi didn't want Reid tamed. She liked the wildness inside him, the restlessness, the energy. It made him Reid. It made him different from David. It spoke to the difference she was beginning to appreciate in herself.

That night after they had returned to the cabin, a storm blew in, and as Livi lay beside Reid in his big bed, listening to the wind, she could not help but wonder about the future. They had never discussed why Reid had stayed at the cabin for the winter when any other time he would be off trading in the west. He hadn't said anything about wanting her and the children to leave. She wondered what would happen in the spring when the road back to Virginia was clear again. Would Reid let them stay? She suspected that neither the serenity in his eyes nor the contentment in his smile would carry much weight when she measured them against the inevitable Indian attacks and the struggle it would take to make a life here.

She knew that eventually he would need to leave. He was a trader, a wanderer, not a farmer. The life here at the cabin would not hold him indefinitely. Could she convince Reid Campbell she was able to make a life here without his help? Could she loosen his tether and let him fly free?

Livi didn't want to risk their happiness by asking too many questions now. Time would bring the answers. While she waited, Livi meant to savor every moment. She'd learned that a man did what he had to do. She'd learned that a woman must take her happiness where she could. Those were hard, bitter lessons she had learned with David. She didn't intend to make the same mistakes with Reid. She loved him and this valley and this life, and she meant to store up every memory, every sound and sight and sensation, because she understood as never before how precious each moment of joy could be.

Beside her, Reid stirred and shifted and opened his eyes.

She took his wakefulness as an opportunity and trailed her hand down the long, livid scar at the center of his chest.

"Are you awake?" he asked, his voice still heavy with sleep.

"Indeed I am."

"And I take it you have something on your mind."

"Indeed I do."

He grinned at her, his eyes shining in the dark. "Shall I guess what it is?"

Her fingers skimmed lower, touching him in a way that made him catch his breath. "If you think you can," she challenged him.

"Oh, I think I can guess," he murmured, pulling her closer. "I'm very good at guessing games."

"Are you really?"

He answered her question with a kiss.

The hours and the days and the weeks of that winter sifted through Reid's fingers like so much sand. He tried to close his hands around them, to hold them fast. He tried to cling to the moments and the memories: of Cissy's soft, sweet weight as she slept in his arms; of Baby David cooing in the dark; of the victory celebration they'd given Tad when he mastered the vagaries of long division. Reid tried to store up the silvery spill of Livi's laughter, the gleam of her hair in the firelight, the silk of her touch on his skin. Those were all things David had experienced, but they were new to Reid, sharp and precious and overwhelming.

From the time that he could toddle, Reid had known David was different from him. David understood who he was and where he belonged. David had a family who loved him, a place in the world. When David's life expanded to include a wife and children, Reid had watched with envy in his heart. He'd seen the flush of joy in David's face when he drew Livi close, watched him roughhouse with Tad and Cissy and bundle them, giggling, in his arms. Reid had never aspired to any of that; there was no point wanting what he couldn't have. Now, with her touch and her kiss and the light in her eyes, Livi had opened the doors to this other world and invited him in.

Filled and sated and content in a way he'd never been before, Reid hardly missed the solitude of the woods, the far vistas that had once been so pleasing to his eyes and soul. Sometimes when he hunted far afield, he felt the pull of trails not taken and lands left unexplored. When he climbed to the top of the cliff where he'd mourned for David and looked out at a world as boundless as the sky, he felt his senses stir with the promise in that long horizon. Someday he might seek that world again, but for now, there was too much to experience and relish and explore within the walls of this one tiny cabin.

One evening in early March, when a late-winter storm howled around the house and muffled the world in drifts of white, Livi came to where Reid sat before the fire. The children were abed and the air hung redolent with the smell of the popcorn Reid had brought back from one of his forays to the station through the snow.

She settled herself on the bench beside him, her eyes alight. "I have something for you."

"Have you, now?" he asked. "Is it another of those wonderful molasses cookies you baked this afternoon?"

She shook her head.

"Is it a new pair of socks? I've noticed how diligently you've been knitting."

"It isn't socks."

"Is it a kiss?" he guessed hopefully.

He saw a flush warm the delicate pink in her cheeks, and experienced a slow, delicious rise of anticipation.

"What is it, then?"

From the folds of her skirt Livi withdrew a small, cylindrical case. Scarred though the shagreen leather was, the buckle at the closing and the brads that fastened the belt strap shone with recent polishing.

Reid knew instantly what Livi meant to give him and caught his breath. It was David's pocket telescope.

Reid knew the story of the telescope well; how Henry Dickerson, one of David's neighbors in Lynchburg, had brought the telescope to the blacksmith shop when he heard that David was joining up with Colonel Clark. Dickerson was a tough old bird who had fought against the French more than a decade before. "Take the telescope, boy," he'd said to David, "so you can see those demmed Englishers coming. Then part their hair with your best shot."

Scarcely believing that Livi would entrust David's most prized possession to him, Reid curled his fingers around the velvety, green leather case. He remembered that while they were campaigning with Colonel Clark, David was forever oiling and polishing that telescope; remembered how he'd bound it on a thong at his throat as they waded through the icy, chest-deep swamps on the march from Kaskaskia to Vincennes.

With hands that shook, Reid slipped the buckle at the top of the case and withdrew the small, elegant spyglass. Fashioned of gleaming brass, the two concentric cylinders expanded smoothly and locked in place with a tiny metallic click. Reid didn't need to put the glass to his eye to know how fine the optics were. He peered through the glass anyway, using the moment to blink away the sheen of tears.

"Are you sure you want me to have this?"

Livi simply nodded. "Tad and Cissy and I all have bits and pieces of David's life. I thought the telescope was something you would use, something you would treasure as much as David did."

Reid warmed with the wealth of her understanding and the depth of her generosity. "You don't know what this means," he began around the emotion snagged in his throat. "I don't know how to thank—"

Livi took his hand. "David couldn't have loved you more if you were his brother born. You were his friend, Reid, and his protector. I took comfort in that when you were off fighting with Colonel Clark. Even though I hated you for taking him away, I knew you'd look out for him."

"I would have kept him safe to my last breath."

"I know that," she said and seemed to hesitate, seemed to carefully consider her next words. "I wish you had been there the night the Indians came."

Reid fumbled to find an answer that successfully skirted the truth. "David thought it was better if he introduced you to Kentucky on his own." *He said he'd never get you out of Lynchburg if I was there.*

"He was wrong in that," she admitted, and Reid wondered whether she'd read his mind.

He stared down at their linked hands, tenderness and regret condensing in his chest. "We wasted so damn much time, Livi, fighting for David's loyalty."

She nodded slowly. Yet after the years of antagonism, there was more for them to discuss than that.

"You thought I was unworthy of being his wife," she accused.

Reid looked at her, seeing the vulnerable curve of her mouth. He saw that his accusations had raised doubts that dogged her still.

"I only said that," he told her, "because I was afraid. It felt as if you'd stolen my only friend."

It wasn't a defense. Too much had passed between them for him to have to defend himself. Still, he wanted to put his feelings into words. He wanted her to know he hadn't deliberately set out to hurt her.

"I would come to your house," Reid said, remembering. "David and I would share our dreams and make our plans—"

"You'd deliberately shut me out."

"Just the way you and David shut me out when you closed the bedroom door." He tightened his fingers around her hand. "I'd all but convince him to come west with me, to chase his dream, and there you'd be—so soft and fresh and beautiful, offering him enticements no man could offer another man.''

Reid watched her in the firelight. Her bright hair shimmered like molten copper; her pale skin warmed, burnished by the flames. He had always been able to see why David had fallen in love with her. Now, after all this time, he finally understood why David's love for Livi had lasted.

There was more substance to this woman than Reid had been willing to see.

''You had parts of David I could never have,'' Livi said, her voice shredding a little under the force of fresh emotion. ''You had all his wildness, all his dreams. You had the parts he denied to me. I wanted him whole and complete, but neither of you would let me have that.''

They sat in silence for a very long time, each knowing that David was gone, each seeing the chances they'd lost or thrown away, each realizing there was no way to recapture what might have been. Sitting there in the firelight a year after David's death, they each accepted their part in undermining a life that could have been better and sweeter and more nourishing.

''I'm sorry, Livi,'' Reid whispered.

''I'm sorry, too.''

He took her in his arms and held her close. ''Neither of us can change the past,'' he murmured, ''but we can make things better. We can work together for our own sake and for the sake of the children. And we will do that, Livi. I promise you.''

They sat for a time in silence. The admissions they had made, the grief they had shared, bound them as powerfully as the hope they both seemed to harbor for what lay ahead. It would have been as natural as breathing for them to gather up Little David and creep across to Reid's cabin to make love, but the baby was fussy tonight. Livi said he was teething, so when Little David began to cry, Reid returned the spyglass to its case and kissed Livi good night.

Once he had stirred up the fire in his own hearth and added wood, Reid sat fingering David's telescope. He could still see the fair-haired boy who had raced him to the uppermost branches of the oak that overhung the river, the laughing youth who had dared him to paint a mustache on his stepmother's bright new portrait, the rock-steady man his boyhood friend had become. It was impossible to believe that David was gone.

How could he be, when they'd faced so much of life together? They'd fought bullies who'd sneered at Reid's Indian heritage, hidden David's pet pig deep in the swamp when it was time for butchering. They'd drunk their first whiskey and smoked their first cigars, gone whoring together to celebrate their sixteenth birthdays. David had toasted Reid's success as a fur trapper long before he proved himself. Reid had been there when Tad was born. They'd kept each other safe during the war, pooled their land grants, and built this cabin. They'd shared a dream that somehow wouldn't die.

Reid braced his head in his hands and rubbed his eyes. But David was gone, and with his passing, so much goodness and strength and wisdom had gone to waste.

Tonight Livi had given him David's telescope. It was a keepsake Reid would treasure all his days, a remembrance so special that he could scarcely take it in. With David dead, he'd inherited the telescope. He'd inherited Livi and the children, the cabin and the land. He'd stepped body and soul into David's place. But Reid just couldn't let himself believe he deserved that. Not while David's death went unavenged.

Though he had accepted Ben Logan's counsel months before and given up his search for David's killers, Reid's conscience had never gone silent. That Creek law demanded a death for a death, that Reid himself subscribed to those beliefs, kept the questions alive inside him. He needed the answers now more than ever before. He needed to find David's killers, needed to be certain they paid for what they'd done. Maybe once he'd done that, he could accept what David's death had given him.

The very next evening, Reid cornered Livi after supper and asked her about that night on the trail.

"I don't know why you're bringing this up," she admonished him, both her hands and her voice trembling. "I don't want to talk about how David died. I don't remember more than what I've told you already."

"I need to know about the Indians, Livi," Reid prompted her. "Tell me about the Indians."

She went silent and resentful. With a glare that said that by asking about that night he'd betrayed her trust, she turned away. For the first time since Little David was born, Reid felt as if Livi were shutting him out.

He felt even worse when Tad sought him out while he was chopping wood the following morning.

"I heard you and Ma talking last night," Tad accused, "about Pa being killed on the trail."

Reid nodded, knowing why Tad was there. It wasn't the first time the boy had stood up for his mother. "And you don't want me asking questions that upset her."

Tad hesitated, casting a glance over his shoulder as if he didn't want Livi to hear.

"No," he said softly. "I want to tell you about the raiders myself."

Reid set aside the ax he was using, an odd, eerie shiver trailing the length of his back. "Your ma would skin me alive if she knew I was discussing this with you."

Tad nodded, his eyes reddening. "She doesn't understand."

Reid thought he might.

"All right, then," he said with a nod. "Go get your gun, and tell your ma we're going hunting."

They met in front of the cabin and tramped more than a mile through the melting snow before Reid pulled up beside a fallen tree. Leaning his rifle against the trunk, he gestured for Tad to take a seat.

"All right, boy," Reid said, bracing himself. "You tell me about the night your pa died."

Tad's nose got red. He swallowed hard.

Reid waited in silence. When someone had been holding memories like these inside for so long, it took a while to break them lose.

"It was the rifle shot that woke me up," Tad finally began, staring down at his hands. In a voice that shook, he described the sound of the single shot, the war whoop that followed it, and the beat of running footsteps. He'd heard the shouting, the clatter of a fierce, brief battle, and his mother's scream. With a tinge of frustration in his tone, Tad talked about how Livi had wedged herself in the opening at the head of the tent to block his path.

"When Ma went to see to Pa, I came out of the tent. He was covered with blood and lay so still I knew he must be dead."

The boy's face twisted as he fought for breath.

"I went after the men, the raiders. But Ma grabbed hold of

me and held on tight. She didn't understand I wanted to tear those men apart. She didn't understand I needed . . . to pay them back—for hurting Pa.'' Tad's voice frayed and tears broke free.

Reid pulled the boy to him and held on hard. Tad burrowed against Reid's chest, his shoulders heaving. He wept tears he'd been carrying around inside him for a year, tears he'd refused to shed in front of his mother and sister.

Reid hung on to the boy, feeling lost and helpless. He didn't know how to comfort Tad, what to say to make things better. No one had ever held Reid when he cried. Instinctively, he splayed his hands against Tad's back and bowed his body around him. He stroked the boy's hair, whispered words he barely understood himself. Out there in the woods, where the loneliness and the silence would keep the boy's secret, Reid let Tad be a child again.

At length the boy released a shuddery breath and pushed himself away. His face was flushed and tear-streaked. ''You won't tell Ma—'' he cautioned.

''No, Tad,'' Reid promised. ''I won't tell her.''

''It would upset her, you know?''

Reid knew.

''She thinks Cissy and I have forgotten what happened, but we haven't. We won't forget. We won't *ever* forget.''

Ben Logan had told Reid some of what Livi and the children had gone through on the trail, about the hardships they'd faced, about the massacre they'd ridden through. Reid couldn't help wondering what else this boy had tucked up inside himself.

''But it's the raiders I wanted to tell you about,'' Tad said, breaking into Reid's speculation.

''That night—the night Pa was killed—five of the men who came into our camp were Shawnee. I recognized the way they dressed and some of the words they said to each other.''

Reid nodded. ''Your mother said your pa spoke with one of them. I'd taught him some Creek and a bit of Shawnee.''

Tad sniffed and wiped his nose on the back of his hand. ''Was she able to tell you that the other two raiders were Englishmen?''

Englishmen? Reid felt his hackles rise.

"Tad, for God's sake, are you sure? Why didn't your mother realize who they were?"

"I don't think they spoke at all, and she was taking care of Pa. They weren't in camp very long, either. And the Britishers were done up in buckskin and feathers, too."

"Then how can you be so sure they were white?"

"They kind of didn't look right," the boy hedged. "Like you, you know? Even when you dress like one, you never quite look like an Indian."

Reid understood.

"And when I looked at their tracks the next morning," Tad went on, "I saw that two of the raiders were wearing boots."

Reid's suspicions bolted ahead. "What kind of boots?" he asked carefully. "Hobnailed boots?"

"Stitched boots," Tad said. "The one that killed Pa was wearing boots with the soles stitched on."

English officers wore stitched leather boots. Fine boots, expensive boots. The kind Reid himself wore.

If English officers had been in the group that came into David and Livi's camp, then it hadn't been a random attack. The raiders had come for a reason. Reid didn't have to think too hard to know what it was.

"Did they take anything?" he prodded Tad. "A doeskin bag? One embroidered with flowers and beads?"

The boy gave the question some thought and shook his head. "They didn't take anything. Nothing except the man Pa shot."

But Reid knew they had—somehow, without either Tad or Livi seeing them, the raiders had taken the sacred disk Reid himself had entrusted to David.

Reid sucked in a long, cold breath and let it clear his head. Tad had given him the answers he'd been seeking for nearly a year. Now he knew why David had been killed. It wasn't mindless brutality or happenstance that had cost him his life. Politics—England's last, desperate bid to maintain its power in the west—was the reason David died.

And Reid had a very good idea who had struck David Talbot down.

Tad hadn't told Livi any of this. Unless Reid missed his guess, Livi hadn't given Tad a chance to tell her. It was just as well. It wouldn't help either her or Tad to know that David had been sacrificed to the British cause in America.

It was only important that Reid knew—so he could extract the appropriate revenge.

He and Tad barked a couple of squirrels on the way back to the cabin to cover their long absence. While Tad skinned them and set them to soak, Reid gathered up the things he would need on his journey to the Ohio country.

As far as he knew, there were only two British officers still operating north of the river. Captain William Caldwell had led the attack on the Kentucky settlements and been in command of the troops and the Indians at Blue Lick. From what Reid had heard of him, Caldwell was an honorable man. He wouldn't involve himself in a raid like the one that had taken David's life.

But that other man, Captain Martin Weems, lived and intrigued with the Indians. He had deliberately fostered a reputation for ruthlessness and cruelty. David's murder had the stench of Martin Weems about it, and Reid meant to make Weems pay.

The next morning at first light, Reid led his horse to the top of the rise and paused to take a look back at the cabin. The last of the melting snow lay in ruffles at the edges of the roof. A sheen of rose and gold skimmed the puddles in the yard. The fields were broken and dark, the clods of earth frosted with a filigree of white. This place was the haven Reid never thought he'd find. The people who welcomed him home were the ones he'd grown to love.

He hadn't told either Livi or Tad where he was going. It wouldn't do for them to know, in case he failed, in case he didn't come back. In his way, he was protecting them. From knowing too much. From the men who had taken David's life.

If he succeeded in finding Weems, maybe Reid could convince himself that he deserved what he'd been give here in Kentucky. If he paid the debt of loyalty and honor he owed to David, maybe he could accept that Livi and the children and the happiness were his to keep. Either way, the confrontation with David's killers was inevitable. He'd put it off for far too long.

❦ 21 ❧

*L*ivi knew trouble when she saw it, and the men who rode into her little valley a fortnight after Reid had left were trouble. There were six of them, four Indians and two white men who were dressed in mismatched pieces of British Army uniforms.

While every instinct clamored for her to bolt into the cabin and bar the door, Livi couldn't do that. Not while Cissy and Eustace were off somewhere in the woods gathering early greens. She couldn't leave them out there to fend for themselves. She wasn't even sure that Eustace had taken his gun.

"Tad," Livi shouted, dropping the bucket of water she was carrying, "bring your father's rifle. We've got visitors."

Scrambling to the top of the steps, she grabbed one of the guns from her son and raked back the striker.

As Tad took his place beside Livi at the edge of the breezeway, Patches came hightailing out of the woods, yelping at the top of his voice. The troops were gathering, Livi thought. "What do you suppose they want?" Tad asked above the din of Patches's barking.

"I don't know—but damn Reid Campbell for heading off without telling anyone. This probably has something to do with him."

"It's going to be all right, Ma." Tad offered the assurance as if he meant it, though he watched the men approach as warily as she. "At least with them riding in like this, we know they haven't come to raid."

What Tad said was true. More often than not, it was the Indians you didn't see who did the most damage. Still, the appearance of either Indians or British soldiers boded ill for Kentucky homesteaders. Livi gripped her rifle tighter, hoping she was ready for whatever came.

The little band drew up not five feet from her door. The man in the lead, a big swarthy fellow with a hawk nose and hooded eyes, inclined his head.

"Mistress Talbot?" His low, cultured voice sent a chill down her back.

"Yes." She couldn't imagine how he knew her name.

"Captain Martin Weems at your service, ma'am."

Livi took a shaky breath. "You're fifty miles south of anywhere you'd be welcome, Captain Weems. What is it you want?"

"I was hoping you would help me."

"I'd be happy to give you directions back to the Ohio River."

Weems's mouth lifted in what might have passed for a smile. "The river's not what I'm looking for."

Livi waited, letting her gaze slip from Weems to the wiry lieutenant at his side and the four tall warriors dressed in deeply yoked shirts trimmed with ribbons and beads. Shawnee, she thought, judging from what she'd observed of the Indians since she'd come to the frontier. Though the Indians weren't painted up for war, they sat their horses with their weapons drawn.

She and Tad would be dead before they could fire a shot.

"Then just how is it I can help you, Captain Weems?"

"I want permission to search your cabin."

"Why?" The question was out of her mouth before she could think better of it.

"We're looking for something."

Not someone. Not Reid. Livi succumbed to a surge of relief.

"We're just poor homesteaders here," she said, in spite of the warning look Tad shot in her direction. "What could we possibly have that you would want?"

Weems seemed to take a moment to consider before reaching around into his saddlebag. He withdrew a square doeskin medicine bag dripping with fringe. The flap across the top was fastened with a loop and a bit of antler. Beaded designs swirled across the front.

Recognition niggled at Livi, but it wasn't until Weems opened the flap and revealed the blue-green disk within that she realized what he had.

The knowledge must have shown on her face.

"I see you recognize this, Mistress Talbot, as one of the Creeks' sacred disks," Weems observed. "That should make matters a good deal easier. All I want is the one that matches it."

"I don't have a disk like that one," Livi said, her mouth dry and her tongue gone thick as flannel.

"But you know where one is."

"No, I—" Livi knew the chance she was taking by holding back, but she just couldn't turn over something Reid had handled so carefully and protected so well. In truth, she didn't know where in his cabin he'd hidden the disk.

With a sure, swift movement of his left hand, Weems drew his saddle pistol and centered the barrel on Livi's chest.

Patches started growling at the base of the steps.

"Does this improve your memory, Mistress Talbot?" he asked. "Or does this?" He shifted the bead to Tad, to the place where his too-small shirt gaped across his breastbone.

Livi swallowed hard. "Please don't hurt him, Captain Weems. We don't have what you want."

Weems lowered the pistol and eyed her. "No, perhaps you don't. Perhaps you *did* have only one of the disks. That's all we could find that night on the trail."

Livi caught her breath, gooseflesh washing along her limbs. She thought she must have misunderstood.

"Surely you remember our last visit, Mistress Talbot," he taunted her. "The night your husband died?"

"You!" she whispered, though she couldn't remember seeing the sacred plate. She couldn't remember seeing this Englishman.

Beside her, Livi heard the cadence of Tad's breathing change.

"You goddamned, buggering bastard!" Tad yelled. *"You killed my pa!"*

He launched himself off the edge of the porch.

Livi brought her gun to bear on Weems.

From down among the horses, the boy jabbed his rifle into the Englishman's face. The big man battered at him with his saddle pistol.

The boy fired anyway. Weems's hat flew off.

Around Tad, the horses bucked and danced. The soldiers cursed. The Indians dismounted on the fly.

Patches barked furiously as Weems jerked back on his reins. He raised his arm. He clubbed Tad with the barrel of his gun.

Livi screamed as her son went down.

She got off one wild shot just as an Indian barreled into her. He slammed her back onto the floor of the breezeway. Her gun flew out of her hands.

The jolt of landing rattled up Livi's neck and down her limbs. Her stomach churned. She fought for breath. Darkness swooped in and out.

When she blinked the world into focus again, the Indian was straddling her heaving chest. He loomed above her, his eyes narrowed and his teeth bared. His knife lay like death against her throat.

Livi fought the constriction of his knees against her ribs. She squirmed beneath the cold, sharp blade. There was no sense fighting. She couldn't move.

At the periphery of her senses, Livi became aware of Patches's growling, of Weems's harsh curse. She heard a gun boom near at hand and the dog went silent.

From inside the cabin came the crash of overturning furniture, of pewter cups and plates being scattered across the floor, of broken bottles and crockery. Baby David began to wail, and Livi shifted instinctively to go to him.

The Indian's blade bit deeper. Warm blood oozed down the side of her throat.

Little David squalled again.

"Look in the cabin on the left," she whispered. "The copper plate is hidden somewhere in the cabin on the left."

The Indian turned and shouted a few sharp words to the others. Weems appeared at the man's shoulder.

"There, you see, Mistress Talbot." He leered at her. "You were able to help us after all. Things would have gone a good deal easier for both you and your boy if you had told us that at the outset."

Livi lay trembling, wrapped in the warrior's threat, in the warrior's stink of bear grease and sweat.

She could hear her baby shrieking and took comfort in the sound. If Little David was crying, he must be all right. She wondered if Cissy and Eustace were safe in the woods.

She stirred again, frantic to know where Tad was, to be sure he was safe. Was he lying somewhere in a pool of blood? Had the man who murdered David killed her son?

Tears tracked into her hair.

After what seemed like an eternity of thuds and crashes, she heard a crow of victory. Someone had found the copper plate.

Captain Weems bent above her a moment later. His eyes glinted with victory. "We found what we were looking for, Mistress Talbot," he told her, lifting the doeskin bag so she could see. "Our friends the Creeks should be quite cooperative now that we have both sacred plates. Odd, what store these savages set by something so simple. Still, trinkets like these do have their uses."

He spoke to the others in what must have been Shawnee.

The warrior guarding Livi drew the knife slowly across her throat before removing it. She felt the blood well up again.

As he rose, his gaze traveled the length of her body. It came to rest on her long braid. Livi knew red hair was a precious commodity among those who collected scalps.

She lay sprawled before him, barely daring to breathe.

Weems's command came blunt and sharp. The Indian stood over Livi for a moment longer. Then, with a nod of concession, he spun away.

She heard the scuffle of feet on the steps, the stamp of horses' hooves. Leather creaked as the English and their allies mounted up. Reins jingled. The rumble of hoofbeats moved away.

With an effort Livi pushed up on her elbows. Just as she did, a shot rang out from off in the woods toward the front of the cabin.

On the far side of the creek, one of the Indians toppled from his horse. Instead of stopping, Weems and his companions spurred their mounts to greater speed.

The raiders had disappeared by the time Livi managed to roll onto her knees. She hung there on all fours, quivery and light-headed.

Cissy broke cover from somewhere behind the cabin.

"Mama! Mama!" she shrieked, running toward her.

Livi sat back on her heels and caught her daughter in her arms. She crushed the girl against her chest.

"Oh, sugar," Livi breathed into the soft tangles of rose-gold hair. "Oh, baby, what a good, brave girl you were to stay hidden until the Indians were gone."

"Eustace said," Cissy volunteered, still hugging Livi hard. "He said not to move until the bad men rode away."

"You did exactly what you should have done."

Beyond her daughter's embrace, Livi saw Eustace come out of the woods on the far side of the creek and prod the man he'd shot with the toe of his boot.

As Livi shifted her daughter away, she became aware of Little David's wailing. "Why don't you go and do what you can to quiet that baby," she suggested, "while I see to Tad."

"But you're all blood!"

"I'm fine," Livi assured her and ushered the girl to the cabin door.

Tad lay silent at the base of the steps. Patches sprawled in a pool of blood not three feet away. He'd defended his master to the last.

Livi wobbled down the stairs and sank to her knees beside her son. "Oh, my God!" she whispered, the weight of fear heavy in her chest. "Tad! Can you hear me?"

Blood oozed down Tad's cheek and into the dirt.

Just like David. The thought came shrieking through her head. Just like David.

Eustace limped up the rise and stood over them. "He don' look none too good, Miz 'Livia."

Livi nodded and swallowed her panic. She lay her palm against Tad's chest. Instead of the ragged rasp of David's breathing, Tad's was slow and even. His heart beat strong beneath her fingertips.

Dashing fresh tears from her face, Livi gently probed the mat of red-soaked hair above his ear. The gash from the pistol barrel was still bleeding freely and a lump had risen that was nearly the size of her fist. But that was all. There was no depression in his skull, no sign of deeper damage. Livi let out her breath.

She shifted to assess his other injuries. Tad's left forearm was already swollen and bruised. She'd wager it was broken. She wondered if he'd cracked a rib or two.

As she probed along his side, Tad moaned and opened his eyes. "Ma?"

"It's all right, Tad."

"It hurts, Ma." His eyes were cloudy, unfocused, but he was awake and making sense. "My arm hurts and my head hurts."

"And it hurts to breathe," she finished for him. "I know, Tad. But it's going to be all right."

She dispatched Eustace into the cabin for water and bandages and splints.

"Ma?" When he opened them the second time, Tad's eyes looked clearer than before. Warm and golden and so like David's. She swallowed the lump that rose in her throat. "Are they gone, Ma? Did the men get what they came for? Did they find one of those Indian plates?"

Livi nodded. "There was one of them hidden in Reid's things."

Tad closed his eyes. "Those men killed Pa."

"I know, Tad."

"I wanted to kill them." Livi tried not to notice the grim set to her son's soft mouth and the tears that seeped beneath his lashes.

"It doesn't matter, Tad. Avenging your father's death won't bring him back."

She'd expressed the same sentiments to Reid months and months before. She sensed they'd have as little effect on her son as they'd had on Reid.

"Now that we know those are the men who killed Pa," Tad whispered, confirming her thoughts, "Reid will get them. He'll make them pay."

"We'll see about that," Livi acknowledged on a sigh. But she thought her son was probably right.

They'd been lucky. Considering that Captain Weems could have killed them all, considering that he could have let his savages take their hair, they'd been lucky. Livi murmured those words like a talisman as she bound Tad's ribs, stitched his head, and set his arm. She crooned them like a lullaby as she sat watching through the night while her oldest baby slept.

He might be uncomfortable and restless, but Tad would heal.

They'd been so lucky.

Livi only wished Weems hadn't found the sacred disk. It was the single facet of his Indian heritage she had ever seen Reid honor, and she knew he would grieve when he returned to the cabin and found it gone. Still, she hadn't had a choice about giving it up. He'd have to understand that.

The faint morning light seeping around the cabin door and Baby David gurgling in his bed brought Livi slowly to her feet. She was bruised and battered, but she was alive. All of them were alive, and she had to thank God for their escape. Bending stiffly, Livi picked up the baby on her way to the door.

She had slipped the bolt and stepped out into the sunlight before she realized they had visitors.

Eight Indians sat their horses not ten feet away.

Livi tingled, cold with shock.

In the split second when she might have ducked inside and barred the door, one of the braves sprang from his horse and up the steps. He grabbed her arm and wrestled her down and across the yard. Holding the baby prevented Livi from putting up much of a fight, and she refused to scream and waken Tad.

The rest of the Indians dismounted as they approached.

She realized immediately they were not Shawnee. These men wore cloaks of panther and beaver skin, and their heads were wrapped with wide woven bands heavily decorated with beads and trade silver. Though some of their faces were painted white and red, none wore the black-and-red patterns she'd seen on the Shawnee.

The leader, a huge man who sported a bright red face and porcupine quills entwined with tufts of his hair, glared down at her. Then, turning to an older man, he spoke at length.

"Red Hand would like to know if this is the cabin of the man who is known among the whites as Reid Campbell," the slighter man translated into surprisingly good English.

Livi bit her lower lip and nodded.

"We would speak with Reid Campbell, then," the man went on.

"Reid isn't here. I don't know when he will be back," Livi answered, regretting the admission the moment it was out of her mouth.

Red Hand seemed to understand what she said without translation. His glare intensified at her reply.

"Are you Reid Campbell's wife?" the translator asked.

Since it didn't seem like a good time to split hairs about her and Reid's relationship, Livi nodded again.

"Then we wish to look inside your house."

Livi started, as amazed by the translator's polite request as by what he wanted. Captain Weems had ridden in the previous day, made the same demand, and left havoc in his wake. Had these men come for the sacred disks, too?

She hazarded a glance toward the cabin door, wondering if she could make it inside before the tall brave stopped her.

"Is there something in particular you're looking for?" she inquired, hoping to buy a little time.

Red Hand, the translator, and the man beside him, whose face was painted white, exchanged long glances.

"If it's the copper disks you want," she continued, gambling she was right about why they'd come, "they are not here."

Her revelation threw the party into confusion. Shock and consternation ran from man to man. The babble of voices rose around her. Livi edged toward the steps. If only she could get inside the cabin—

As if he'd read her mind, the brave who had been standing guard grabbed her arm and hauled her back.

Red Hand, the man painted white, and the translator conferred heatedly.

"What do you know of the disks?" the translator finally asked her.

Livi tried to remember what Reid had said about them months before: that the disks were sacred, that they could be profaned by a woman's touch.

"I know only what my husband told me. I have not seen the disks themselves," Livi added as a precaution, "only the medicine bags in which they're kept."

"And where are those disks now?"

Livi lowered her head to hide her flush of satisfaction. If she could send these men off after Captain Weems, she might extract her own revenge on the men who had killed her husband.

"The British took them." Livi watched the Indians' faces.

"Captain Weems and several Shawnee warriors came—"

"Shawnee warriors!" the white-faced man gasped in English, quivering with agitation. "When the disks came to us from the Master of Breath, it was foretold that if the Creeks failed in their stewardship of the sacred plates, the Shawnee would take them from us! If it is true that the Shawnee have taken the plates, then even greater misfortune will befall our people than has befallen them already!"

"If it is true that Captain Weems has the sacred disks, he will try to barter them back to us for our continued loyalty to the British cause," the man who had been acting as translator offered in a conciliatory fashion. "Before the one with the hawk face gives the disks to the Shawnee, he will offer them to us."

Anger brought Red Hand's brows together. "It doesn't matter what Hawk Face does. It is the fault of Ravens Flight that the disks are lost," he pointed out. "Ravens Flight is the one who held the disks for all this time. Ravens Flight is the one who has dishonored us all by giving the sacred plates to the English. Who could expect a man with blood weakened by marriage to the whites to uphold our Creek traditions?"

"But Reid didn't give the disks to the British," Livi dared to interject. "They stole them from here only yester—"

"It does not matter how the plates were lost," Red Hand shouted, pacing the yard, letting anger stir the energy inside. "It only matters that they were lost by Ravens Flight. And it is he who should be held responsible."

"Someone must get the plates back," the man in white face insisted. "The future of the Creeks rests on the return of those disks. In the years since Hair Buyer took them from us, the Creeks have suffered many losses. If Hawk Face gives what has long been sacred to the Creeks to the Shawnee, the Creeks will suffer many more losses, many more deaths."

"Perhaps it is Ravens Flight who must see to returning the sacred disks," the translator mused, half to himself.

Livi felt the thud of alarm beneath her ribs even before she caught sight of Red Hand's malicious smile.

"But can we trust Ravens Flight to do that?" the white-face asked.

"Since Ravens Flight dishonored himself by running away when his uncle was killed, we cannot be certain he will do what is right,'' Red Hand answered, pacing again. "Perhaps we must find a way to make him bear the responsibility for giving up the sacred disks. And for bringing them back.''

As he spoke, Red Hand paced closer. Without warning, he snatched Little David from Livi's arms.

A cry of loss and outrage climbed the back of her throat. He might as well have torn out Livi's heart.

She lunged after him.

With the jab of his elbows and the breadth of his back, Red Hand easily deflected her. The brave who had been guarding Livi snatched her back.

Deprived of his mother's familiar scent and warmth, Little David squalled at the top of his lungs.

His cry sliced through Livi like a knife. She squirmed away from her guard and beat at Red Hand with her fists. She raked her nails along his forearm, trying to reach her child.

Another warrior intervened. Together the two men caught her arms. Livi scuffled, fighting to break their hold, cursing and kicking.

Tucking David beneath one arm, Red Hand swung at her.

Pain exploded along her cheek and jaw. Her head snapped back. Sparks flared and dimmed before her eyes. Her legs buckled. Livi sank to her knees.

She was hanging between the two warriors when her head began to clear. "Please,'' she begged, tears coursing down her face. "Please don't hurt my son.''

The man with the white face nodded as if in belated agreement with Red Hand's methods. "Perhaps it is wise to keep the child of Ravens Flight in our camp until the plates are returned.''

"But I told you,'' Livi insisted, though her head buzzed and her lip seemed swollen to twice its size, "Reid doesn't have the plates. Captain Weems took both of them.''

Red Hand turned to her, his eyes so filled with hatred she shriveled with the glance.

"Tell Ravens Flight that he must return the sacred plates in any case. He will have until the *Tasahtci iako*, the full spring moon, to return the disks. If he has not presented them to the council by then, we will sacrifice his child to the Master of Breath.''

"No!" Livi shouted, twisting against her captors again. "No! Please, no!"

"Tell him we will burn his child in the sacred fire. We will roast his child alive unless he returns both plates by the appointed day." The Indian paused, his eyes narrowing to slits. "Tell him it is I, Red Hand, who promises this. He will know I speak the truth."

Livi screamed as Red Hand mounted his horse with Little David in his arms. She fought her captors as he and the others rode away. When they stopped at the edge of the woods, the two men who had been holding her immobile threw Livi down in the dirt and ran for their horses.

From behind her, Livi heard the report of a gun. She turned to see Tad slumped against the cabin door, the smoking pistol in his hand.

His ball passed wide of its mark. The two Indians rode away. When they reached the others waiting at the fringe of the trees, they all turned and disappeared into the woods. They were taking Livi's baby, David's last and most precious child, away with them.

Cursing and sobbing, Livi fought her way to her feet.

"Ma?" Tad demanded breathlessly, easing down the steps. "Ma, what's the—matter? What did—those Indians—want?"

"They took David!" Tears poured from her eyes. "They took Little David!"

"Who did? Why?"

"The Creeks. The Creeks took him. They think David is Reid's son. They said they'd sacrifice him if Reid didn't bring the sacred disks to their village in time for the next full moon."

"Sacrifice who?" Eustace gasped, hop-stepping toward them from the direction of the ridge. He held his rifle ready in his hand.

Still weeping, Livi explained. She lifted her wide-eyed daughter when she came to her, hugging her girl-child close, trying to console both Cissy and herself.

"But Reid doesn't—have—the disks," Tad protested around the shallow breaths that were all he could manage. "And neither—do we."

"Then I guess we'll have to get them."

"But, Miz 'Livia, Marse Reid's not here to do that."

Livi shoved the hair out of her face and blew a shaky breath. "Then if you'll stay with the children, Eustace, I'll go after the plates myself."

Reid knew there was something wrong the minute he topped the rise. Though smoke feathered up from the chimney and the door to the cabin stood open invitingly, he could smell the malevolence in the air. He could feel the squirm of an answering fear deep in his gut. Instinctively he cocked his rifle.

He guided his horse forward with his knees, past the cornfields, across the bridge. That there was no sign of Livi or the children twisted anxiety taut inside him. That silence lay like a pall across the clearing raised a clamor in his blood. He had nearly reached the foot of the steps when Eustace appeared like a ghost in the cabin doorway.

Reid wasn't sure if seeing Eustace there made things better or worse.

"Oh, Marse Reid," the black man greeted him. "I sure am glad to see you back!"

"What the hell is going on here, Eustace?" Reid demanded. "Where's Livi? Where are the children?"

Eustace came out onto the steps and quietly closed the door behind him.

They're sick. Reid thought, his stomach rolling. *While I was out chasing phantoms, Livi and the children have been here sick and helpless . . .*

"I just got Tad and Cissy quiet. Sleep'll help that boy mend fast as anythin'. And poor Cissy's been cryin' ever since her mama left."

"Jesus, Eustace!" Reid exploded. "Will you tell me what happened here? Where has Livi gone?"

"She's gone after the copper plates," Eustace explained. "The ones the English soldiers took."

"English soldiers here?"

"Weems? Was it Captain Weems who came?" Reid demanded.

"Captain Weems, an Englishman lieutenant, and four Shawnee."

"And did they take the copper plate hidden in my half of the house?"

Eustace nodded. "They tried to keep him from takin' it,

Tad and Miz 'Livia did. That's how Tad got hurt so bad. That and findin' out they was the men who murdered his pa.''

Reid's own throat ached with the futility of that confirmation. "How bad is Tad hurt?"

"He got a bump on his head, a broken arm, and a crack in a rib or two, Miz 'Livia figured."

Still, Reid knew Tad couldn't be hurt all that bad if Livi had gone off and left him in Eustace's care.

"She didn't have to go after Weems to get the plate back," Reid muttered half to himself. "I know Weems wouldn't have given her any choice about taking it."

"It was the Indians and them takin' Little David that made her go after them soldiers," Eustace answered.

Reid felt the air leave his lungs as if he had been sucker-punched. "Who took Little David?"

"They was Creeks, she said. One called Red Hand took Baby David. He told Miz 'Livia he'd kill that chile unless he got the copper plates. That's why she went after Captain Weems and all. To get the plates."

Reid stood there, trying to make some sense out of what had happened in his absence, trying to think of what he'd do now.

"Miz 'Livia went after the plates herself 'cause she didn't know where you was or how soon you'd likely be comin' back."

They were Eustace's only words of reproach, but they flayed Reid raw.

He had long ago accepted Livi and the children as his responsibility. He should have been here to protect them, not riding the countryside trying to follow a trail that had long since gone cold. Coming back to find this disaster made Reid wonder what kind of a man put the dead and his own damned guilt ahead of the welfare of the people he loved.

"Which way did Livi go?" he asked, thrusting open the door to his cabin and stopping dead in his tracks.

Carnage greeted him. Clothes and books, firewood and utensils, skins and shot, were scattered everywhere. His mattress was slashed open and leaking corn husks onto the floor. His sheets were ripped to ribbons and his reading lantern was crushed flat. The room shouted of Weems's frenzied search—and of his utter ruthlessness.

Fear clamped talons deep in Reid's chest.

Seeing and hearing what Weems had done confirmed everything Reid knew of the man: that he was heartless, soulless, and cruel. Livi was no match for a man like that. Too much could happen if she confronted him. Judging from all of this, too much already had.

"Miz 'Livia went south," Eustace told Reid, joining him in the doorway. "She was goin' to try to follow the English captain's tracks."

South, Reid thought. South, toward the heart of the Creek nation. South, to where those two sacred disks could buy the British a few more months of Creek loyalty. South, where Livi's life and Little David's might well be forfeit to games of honor and politics they could never comprehend.

South—where everything Reid Campbell loved and everything he feared lay in wait.

"I'm going after her," Reid said, as much to hear the commitment aloud as to inform Eustace of his plans. He waded into the destruction that had been his home and began to gather all he'd need.

❧ 22 ❧

As the first orange spikes of rising sun probed the mouth of the cave, Weems and his men began to stir. One by one, they rolled out of their blankets, stretched and scratched, and righted their clothes. Weems's young lieutenant kicked the fire to life and added wood. The captain himself emerged from the shadows and lumbered into the trees to relieve himself.

From the hollow in the top of one of the boulders to the left of the cave, Livi took note of their activity. She had been following Weems's trail for two full days and had come upon the campsite the previous evening just at dusk. Hungry and aching, she'd watched the men build their fire and share a meal, watched them curl comfortably into their blankets' warmth. That was what Livi had been waiting for: a chance to steal into camp and take back the sacred disks. But no matter how careless Weems had been about covering his tracks, he'd been cautious enough to post a sentry.

She had waited out the night in the dampness and cold, keeping her own vigil. Beyond her worry over Tad and Cissy and her concern for Reid, Livi ached to know if her baby was safe. She needed Little David's warmth and weight against her shoulder, his tiny, perfect mouth suckling at her swollen breasts. She needed to breathe his baby scent and hold him close.

Watching the waxing moon track across the sky had stoked the urgency inside her. How many more nights did she have to recover the disks? Could she find Red Hand's village before the full moon rose? Livi had shivered and worried and waited. She'd prayed that something would even the odds, and when she saw a chance, Livi meant to be ready to take it.

The men had been astir only for a little while when the young lieutenant hefted his rifle and headed off into the woods. Not long after, the three remaining Indians gathered up the water skins and headed out of camp. Livi knew that Creeks purified themselves each day by bathing. Since the braves had left together, it seemed possible that the Shawnee subscribed to the same belief.

That left Weems.

Livi drew a shaky breath and scrambled down from her perch. These were better odds than she had any right to expect. She cocked her pistol and stepped into the clearing.

She had expected a shout of discovery, the report of a rifle, but nothing came. She could hear the shuffle and blow of the horses and the creak of the cedars in the wind. It seemed almost too quiet. Pushing the worry aside, Livi hitched up her skirts and sprinted toward the mouth of the cave.

Sunlight slanted in, illuminating a semicircle of sandy ground. Beyond the small, smokeless fire, a saddle, and two of the Indians' sleeping furs, the cave receded into darkness.

Gathering her courage, Livi slipped inside. For several unsettling moments she could not see. Sinister it was. Dank and cold. The air hung heavy, thick with damp and tension and malevolence.

Livi's muscles knotted as she stood with her back to the wall. She knew how vulnerable she was. Weems must be able to see her, even if the dark had turned her blind. Gradually she was able to pick out the details of her surroundings: another saddle and a bedroll, more blankets and furs, an empty rifle sheath. The only sign she saw of Martin Weems was a tattered captain's coat and vest folded across a pair of saddlebags.

Livi knelt beside the pile of Weems's belongings and looked around. He had to be here somewhere, somewhere she couldn't see. She had to be ready to defend herself. Then Little David's face flickered through her mind, and it didn't seem to matter where Weems was. She needed those plates to get her baby back.

Keeping one eye on her surroundings, Livi slipped her hand beneath the folds of Weems's red coat. His saddlebags bulged beneath her fingertips. She slipped the buckles and probed inside. The thick, rank odor of unwashed clothes assaulted her. She found a bag with the grainy texture of gunpowder and one of shot. She encountered a well-used deck of playing cards and a loaf of bread so stale it crumbled beneath her hand. In the other saddlebag she found more clothing, a sharp-edged gorget, a razor, a bar of soap, and a round of slimy cheese.

There were no copper disks.

Livi shoved the coat and saddlebags aside and rummaged beneath the captain's bedclothes. She found the doeskin bags tucked up at the head of the bed under the saddle that Weems must have used as his pillow.

With a jerk she pulled the two bags free. The plates inside were heavier than she had expected, the bags ornate and rippling with fringe. Livi slipped their plaited leather straps onto her shoulder.

As she rose, Livi's nerves whined in warning. Weems was lurking here, lost in the shadows. She could scent him the way horses did water at the end of a long day's ride. She tightened her grip on the pistol and started for the mouth of the cave.

The medicine bags bumped against her hip as she walked. The pistol weighed heavy in her hand. Chills rippled down her back. Escape seemed impossibly far away.

Livi kept moving.

Then he was there—looming up before her, an apparition from a nightmare. Livi halted and tightened her grip on her gun.

Weems stood in his shirtsleeves, his hair hanging tangled and loose from its queue. He balanced his infantry sword lightly in his left hand. "Well, Mistress Talbot," he said. "Imagine my surprise at finding you here."

"Indeed," Livi answered tightly. "It seems I was in the neighborhood."

"And you decided to come by for a visit. How very— sociable of you to come calling on such as we."

"You underestimate your attraction, Captain Weems," Livi answered, almost as unnerved by his pretense of civility as she was by her ability to answer in kind.

"You flatter me, Mistress Talbot. What could draw a

woman of your obvious refinements to lodgings as humble as
this?'' Weems asked. ''Indian antiquities, perhaps? Certain
copper disks?''

Livi glared her answer.

''But then, I see you've already helped yourself to them.''

''I need the disks,'' she told him baldly.

''A pity, that,'' Weems answered with a shrug. ''So do I.''

His implacable tone made Livi's muscles clench.

''Please, Captain Weems,'' she began, willing to beg. ''Red
Hand has taken my youngest child. He'll sacrifice my baby if
I don't take him the disks by the time the full moon rises.''

Weems lifted his eyebrows in mock concern. ''It seems the
Creeks will get their disks in either case. *I*, however, intend
to put them to a far better use than saving your squalling brat.''

''You intend to use them to buy back the Creeks' fealty to
the British cause in America,'' Livi accused.

''How very perceptive a woman you are, Mistress Talbot,''
he told her with a smile. ''The Creeks need to be reminded
of where their loyalties lie. They will continue their allegiance
with England, or I will effect the ancient prophecy and give
the disks to the Shawnee.''

Weems stepped toward her.

Livi raised her gun. ''If you want the disks, you'll have to
risk dying to take them.''

''My dear Mistress Talbot! I had nothing so theatrical in
mind. I can take those disks from you any time I like.''

As if to demonstrate, he raised his sword and with a flick
of his wrist sliced through the thongs of the medicine bags.
The doeskin bags and the disks inside thumped to the earth at
Livi's feet.

When she made as if to retrieve them, Weems's sword point
flashed to her throat.

''There, you see,'' Weems said with a curl of his lip. ''I
took the disks from you without the least unpleasantness. And
unpleasantness is the very last thing I want between us.''

''What *do* you want?''

''I think, Mistress Talbot, that you can guess. Women who
frequent gentlemen's bedchambers usually can.''

With a dip of his sword he nipped off the button at the neck
of her jacket. Livi gasped and stepped away. He moved closer
and flicked off the next. The fabric of her chemise billowed

up in the vee-shaped opening. Livi knocked his sword away.

As if in rebound to her movement, Weems closed the distance between them. He grabbed a fistful of her jacket and the length of her hair. He jerked her toward him and nestled the point of his sword at the base of her throat.

Livi jammed the barrel of her pistol against Weems's ribs.

He threw back his head and laughed at her.

"My comrades and I want three things of you, Mistress Talbot. We want the disks. We want your body. And we want your hair."

As if to underline the threat, Weems's sword blade danced to her right and sawed through Livi's long, thick braid. He dropped it to the ground at their feet.

She battered him with the nose of her pistol again. "You're wrong, Captain Weems. I'm leaving here, and I'm taking the Creek disks with me."

"And how do you propose to do that?"

"I intend to shoot you first."

Weems gave a derisive snort. "You had the chance to shoot me the night we attacked your camp. You saw me run at your husband. You saw me strike him down. You could have killed me then, but you were afraid."

Livi stood quivering inside as images of that night reeled through her head: the senseless brutality of Weems's attack, of David lying so battered and still, of an Indian—this man—standing over him.

"You didn't shoot me to save your husband," Weems taunted, sounding so sure of himself, "and you haven't the courage to shoot me now."

He was right, Livi thought. She hadn't shot him that night a year ago. She hadn't shot him to save her husband's life.

But this time was different. This time she was fighting to save her children. This time there was even more at stake. Unless she acted, she would never recover the disks. She would never save her baby's life. Unless she killed Weems now, Little David would die.

They stood poised: his sword against the pulse point raging in her throat, her gun tight against his ribs.

His words echoed in her head. *You didn't shoot me to save your husband, and you haven't the courage to shoot me now.*

"But you're wrong, Captain Weems." Livi whispered the

words and looked into Weems's startled face. "Any mother could kill to keep her babies safe."

And then she squeezed the trigger.

Reid heard the gunshots, four hollow, resonant booms that came close enough together that they couldn't have been someone hunting. At least not game.

He urged his horse to a faster pace along the narrow switchback trail at the top of the ridge. In among the trees and boulders, Reid didn't see the rider galloping hell-bent in his direction until it was almost too late.

Reid hauled back on his reins and turned his horse sharply to the right, sending them dancing into the underbrush.

The other rider never gave ground. She thundered past as if the devil were at her heels. And perhaps he was.

As she blurred past, Reid caught sight of flying skirts, a battered hat, a buttermilk mare—and knew exactly who it was.

"Livi," he bellowed, pleased as hell to see her no matter how much trouble she was in. "Livi!"

Livi never slowed.

Leaning low over his gelding's shoulder, Reid urged him after her. A hundred yards beyond the rocks, the trail dipped in a steep and treacherous descent. Reid took it at a headlong pace. Ahead of him, Livi rode even more recklessly, less in control of her mount than a rider should be on a course like this.

The narrow track poured out into a meadow between the hills, an expanse of yellow-green grass trampled by the force of the wind and weather. Once he gained the field, Reid spurred his horse to greater speed. He gained on Livi and relentlessly rode her down.

She turned as he came up on her horse's flank. He could see the panic in her face. She raised her pistol.

"Jesus, Livi! It's me!" he roared.

The gun exploded, spitting smoke and flame. The ball flew past Reid's arm, close enough to sting like fire but well shy of its mark.

Somewhere between pulling the trigger and looking back to see what damage she'd done, Livi must have realized who he was. She sawed back on the reins and the mare pranced to a stop. Reid surged past her, reined in his horse, and trotted back.

"Oh, my God! Reid!" Livi gasped, seeing the stain of red blossoming on his sleeve. "Did I shoot you?"

"Not anywhere that matters much," he answered. "You want to tell me what's going on?"

"Weems's men are after me."

Reid cast an eye back at the hill, wondering how many men were coming and how soon. He looked around for cover. A scattering of boulders lay clustered along the far side of the meadow near where the trail disappeared into the trees again. Anyone could see it was a perfect place for an ambush, but Reid didn't think that mattered.

Weems and his men thought Livi was alone, without resources. And Reid meant to make them sorry—for that and so much else.

With a gesture for her to follow, Reid led Livi toward the rocks. They'd barely gotten their horses tied back in the woods when Weems's men made an appearance at the other side of the field. Scrambling for cover, Reid sighted down his rifle. With her own rifle tucked beneath her arm, Livi joined him behind one of the boulders and reloaded her pistol.

On horseback, four men were making their way across the beaten grass. Four. Only four, and three were Shawnee. The one in the uniform coat was too short and too slender to be Martin Weems. Reid scanned the edge of the meadow, expecting treachery.

"Where the hell is Weems?" he whispered, half to himself.

"I shot him," Livi answered quietly.

Reid jerked around to look at her. "You what?"

"Shot him. When I took back the disks."

"You got the sacred disks?"

"How else was I to get my baby back?"

Campbell turned his gaze back to the field, feeling a little stunned, a little deflated. Somehow he hadn't expected Livi to succeed without his help.

"Did you kill him?" he wanted to know.

When she did not answer, Reid spared her another glance. She was pale enough that the few faint freckles spattered across her cheeks stood out like dots on dice. He noticed the bruise that marred one perfect cheek and wondered how she'd gotten it.

She swallowed hard. "Yes, I killed him."

"Good."

Reid drew a shaky breath and looked away. So David Talbot's death had been avenged, Reid found himself thinking. And not by him. Finding and taking revenge on the men who murdered David had been the focus of his life for all these months. It had been his way of coping with his loss, of answering beliefs he'd long denied. The knowledge that Livi had done what he could not left him feeling compromised, hollow somehow. Reid tried to tell himself that it didn't matter who killed Weems. He tried to tell himself that David's spirit had been appeased, but it didn't help.

He was your brother and you failed him. The words echoed deep inside him. He hadn't been strong enough or tough enough or persistent enough to do what had to be done. He hadn't proved himself worthy of either David's friendship or his—

"Reid?" Livi whispered. "How much closer do you intend to let those men get?"

"Not much." He sighted down the barrel of his rifle and squeezed the trigger.

The Indian on the left grabbed his shoulder and toppled off his horse. After a moment of surprise, the other three scrambled out of their saddles and took cover in the grass.

Reid snatched up Livi's rifle. Without Weems to spur them on, just how eager would these men be to continue their search for Livi? Not very, he thought, and deliberately sighted on the Englishman's hat. He blew the fancy cockaded thing to kingdom come. Then, in quick succession, he aimed and fired his pistol and Livi's, his rifle and hers.

He could almost hear the men conferring, speculating about Livi's arsenal and her marksmanship. They were wondering if getting back the sacred disks was worth braving the wrath of the woman who'd put a hole in Weems.

Reid left off firing long enough for the three of them to take a good, long look at how comfortably he and Livi were settled here in the rocks, at how little cover there was if they tried to approach.

Taking careful aim, he sighted on the one brave's feathered

roach, just visible above a clump of grass. He did his best to part the Shawnee's hair.

That seemed to decide them. Reid and Livi watched the men creep back across the field, leading their horses. They watched until they disappeared in the trees.

With a sigh, Livi leaned back against the boulder and closed her eyes. "I'll take a look at your arm in a minute, all right?" From the sound of her voice, he could tell she was trembling.

"It's nothing much. It's probably stopped bleeding on its own by—" Reid looked across at her and pulled up short. "What happened to your hair?"

Livi opened eyes that were blurred with tears. "Captain Weems cut off my braid with his s-s-sword."

Reid cursed under his breath. He reached to take her in his arms, but Livi held her ground.

"He said I didn't have the courage to shoot him. That if I had been brave enough, I would have killed him the night that David died."

"But you did shoot Weems," he offered softly.

Her eyes shone fierce and wet. "I had no choice."

Reid stared, stunned and awed by the change in her. Somehow Livi Talbot had learned to fight. She had learned to protect her own. She had proved herself worthy of this harsh new land. Yet the softness was with her still, the womanliness, the remorse and regret. She'd done what she had to do without compromising herself or her humanity.

They stayed there hunkered down among the rocks until Livi was ready to leave. When she was, Reid made sure all their weapons were loaded, helped her mount, and led the way out of the valley.

They traveled most of the day. Livi didn't ask where they were going. She didn't have to. Reid knew that after killing Weems to get the sacred disks, she wasn't about to be left behind while he went off to negotiate Little David's return. And she'd more than earned the right to come.

They stopped at dusk. The trails to the south were too treacherous to navigate at night anyway, and Reid could see that Livi was all but done in. Besides, there were things they needed to discuss.

While they ate parched corn and the fish he'd caught, Reid listened to Livi tell about the Creeks' visit to the cabin. He'd heard most of it from Eustace, but Livi filled in the gaps.

"The men who came, the three leaders, represented various factions of the tribe," he told her. "The one who was painted white was one of the Holy Men. He came with them to handle the disks, since not everyone can touch them. The one who translated was the Interpreter, an advisor to the Miko, the chief. The third—"

"Red Hand," Livi offered helpfully.

Reid's gut tightened. It was Heart of the Wolf, Red Hand's younger brother, he had accidentally killed all those years ago. It was Red Hand's clan that had taken his uncle's life in retaliation.

"Red Hand is a War Chief," Reid explained. "That's why he was painted red."

"Oh, Reid," she said, and he could hear the tears in her voice. "He said such terrible things. He said they'd sacrifice Baby David if we didn't bring the plates. He said they would burn him in the sacred fire to appease the Master of Breath."

Reid had heard tales of babies being sacrificed that way. If Red Hand made a threat, there was no question that he would carry it out.

"I won't lie to you, Livi," he told her. "It isn't going to be easy to get Little David back—even now that we have the plates."

"But, Reid—"

"You must do exactly what I tell you when we reach the village, Livi." He looked at her long and hard. "Everything depends on how the plates are returned. Everything depends on whether I can convince the council that the plates were not defamed while they were in my care. What I say and do will determine if they take them back. Not only is Little David's life at stake, but so is my honor. My acceptance by the tribe will affect whether the council will exchange the plates for your child."

She nodded and swiped at her eyes. "What must I do?"

"You must do nothing at all. I'll leave you with the women of my family, if they agree. You must stay with them and do as they say while I prepare myself to address the council. You must not admit to seeing the plates. You must not admit to touching them."

"I never touched the plates."

Reid nodded before continuing. "The Creeks believe that a woman's touch profanes the plates. They must never suspect that anyone besides one of their own has touched them. Even I am suspect after being away for all these years."

"Then why did you give one of the plates to David?"

It was a good question, one Reid wasn't sure he knew how to answer. It had to do with his ambivalence about who and what he was, with not wanting to accept responsibility for something so precious to his tribe. Though when he thought about it, that didn't make much sense.

"I thought that if anything happened to me," he said, "David could return at least one of the plates. And he knew where I'd hidden the other."

"But if you recovered the plates at Vincennes, why didn't you return them long before this?"

Reid drew an uneven breath. "Because there wasn't time. Because I never had the chance."

Because I'm afraid to go back. Because I've never been able to face that this is part of who I am.

"Are they taking care of Little David, Reid?" Livi asked softly, her mind moving to other things. "Are they holding him and seeing he gets enough to eat?"

"The Creeks love their children, Livi. Even the ones who aren't really theirs."

He saw that she was crying again and drew her toward the bed he had made for them earlier. She needed rest and comforting.

When they were settled, Livi raised her head. "Do you think Tad and Cissy are all right?"

"Eustace was doing a fine job of looking after them when I was at the cabin."

She nestled closer. "It's going to be all right, isn't it?"

Reid wished he knew.

"Of course it is," he lied and stroked her ravaged hair.

"Oh, Reid," she whispered after a moment and sought his mouth with hers.

He kissed her in return, emotion rising inside him. Tenderness tinged with regret. Sorrow and fear and elation. Loving so strong he ached with it.

He felt her hands on his skin. Felt her fingers skim along

his ribs. Felt the nudge of her swollen breasts against his chest. And he caught fire.

He rolled over her, needing the press of their bodies length to length. He needed the taste of her in his mouth. He needed the welcome in her touch. He needed the lift of her hips against him.

When she complied, they barely had time to remove their clothes. Then he was inside her, sharing sensation and emotion so deep that he wasn't sure where he ended and she began. Merging solace and elation. Blending sweetness and searing heat. Joining flesh to flesh and heart to heart.

He closed his eyes and felt her fly with him into something wondrous and undefinable. He felt her cling to him in the maelstrom as tightly as he was clinging to her. He felt her settle against him when the loving was past, languid and replete, all tenderness and trust.

He held her close in the aftermath, offering warmth and comfort and succor. He held her close because she needed to be held. He held her close because never before in his life had he been so very much afraid.

~23~

hey rode all the next day and half the night. They slept; they rose; they rode again. Livi clung to her saddle by dint of will, climbing steep-sided ridges and fording streams, plodding after Reid from dawn to well past dark. Sometimes only the conviction that her child was waiting at the end of the trail kept Livi riding when she was disheartened and exhausted.

It was late afternoon on the third day when they arrived on the crest of a river bluff overlooking the Creek settlement. Tucked into a wide, level spot at the bend of the river, the town was organized around two large buildings and a central square. Livi could see that in every direction houses clustered around individual quadrangles, with the rich. deep red of newly turned fields at their sides and backs. She stared at the village in surprise. She had never imagined that the savages who stole her son could live in such a peaceful and orderly fashion.

As her gaze ran over the compound, she knew Little David must be there. In one of those houses a Creek Indian woman was feeding him and petting him and seeing to his needs. Reid had assured her that no matter what Red Hand had threatened, the Creeks prized and nurtured their children.

Beside her, Reid sat silent. The set of his shoulders, the somber turn of his lips, the distance in his eyes all made Livi think that he was preparing himself to return to the village he had fled so long ago. Only the necessity of exchanging the disks for Little David could have brought him here. He would not have come alone.

Livi wanted to reach out, to thank him, to offer him what encouragement she could. That Reid had kept to himself these last three days made her hesitate. He had withdrawn in ways Livi might not have noticed if they had been back at the cabin but that were glaring and unsettling here. He hadn't touched her once since they'd made love. He hadn't helped her mount or dismount, hadn't so much as squeezed her shoulder or brushed her hand. He hadn't slept with her or spoken a word more than necessity required. Livi wasn't sure why he was angry; all she knew was that it had something to do with her, the sacred disks, and returning to this place. But it didn't matter if he focused his anger on her, as long as they got David back.

At length, Reid turned his horse down a well-worn path at the side of the bluff. They reached the edge of the village some minutes later, at the end of a wide, well-kept street that led toward the center of town. Houses stood in groups on either side. Some were sturdy, rectangular dwellings plastered with mud and roofed with bark. Some buildings were large and open, constructed with log uprights from which two distinct floors had been suspended. Other buildings seemed a combination of the two forms of architecture.

Without giving Livi any indication of where they were headed, Reid rode toward the center of the village and turned into a complex on his right. Their arrival in the courtyard caused a stir. Women cooking over the fire and scraping skins looked up in curiosity. Children ran into the house.

Just as Reid and Livi were dismounting, an older woman emerged amidst the spill of returning children. The thick black braids twined around her head were liberally laced with silver. Her lined face was etched with both the joy and the trials of life. For a moment she hesitated, staring at Reid. Then all at once she smiled and hurried toward them.

"Ravens Flight, you were barely more than a boy when I saw you last," the woman greeted him in English.

"And you were weeping for your brother, *tckutci,* because of my recklessness," Reid answered.

Livi watched them, freely indulging her curiosity about Reid's past.

She saw the woman's smile fade. "Though I wept, I knew it was our way. I accepted that. You did not." A moment of reprimand hung between them before the woman went on. "But why have you returned to us after so much time?"

"Don't you know why I'm here?" Reid asked.

For a moment the woman pursed her lips, as if deciding how much she would admit to Reid. "I know Red Hand has brought back a child he says is your son. He has promised that the boy will be sacrificed unless you return the sacred disks."

"That's exactly why I've come."

The woman's eyes warmed with what might have been wonder. "And you have the sacred disks?"

Reid lifted his brows in a gesture that indicated he had no intention of answering her. "Is the child well?"

"We have heard that he is being cared for by Red Hand's daughter."

"Here in the village?" Reid asked.

The woman shook her head. "In the red village upriver. Red Hand was afraid you would try to steal the child away rather than return the sacred disks. Now that they know you have come, the woman and child will be guarded night and day."

Livi saw the color come up in Reid's face as the woman spoke. "Does Red Hand think so little of my honor?"

"Red Hand and his clan have always wished ill to us of your grandmother's blood. And some will say you do not have the sacred plates." When Reid said nothing, she went on. "Some say the sacred disks no longer exist, that Hair Buyer had them destroyed. Some say that Hair Buyer gave the plates to the Shawnee to fulfill the ancient prophecy. Some say the hawk-faced English officer has promised that the disks will be returned to us only if we continue to fight the settlers."

"And what do you think?"

"I think," the woman answered slowly, "that you would not have come if you had no disks."

"Then will you help us?"

The woman smiled. "My door has always been open to you, *hopwiwa*."

Reid gestured Livi forward. "This is the boy's mother," he said. "She is known as 'Livi Talbot.' Livi, this is my aunt,

She Who Heals. You will be staying here with her.''

"What do you mean, *I* will be staying here with her?" Livi asked in a whisper, dread and confusion making her heart beat faster. "Where will you be staying?"

"Nearby," he said, and gestured for her to follow She Who Heals into the house.

It was dark and warm inside, though the coals in the fire pit at the center were barely burning. As Livi's eyes adjusted to the dimness and the veils of smoke hanging in the air, she could see that the large rectangular room was ringed with couches or beds made from a framework of sticks and covered with woven mats and skins. Raised nearly three feet off the floor, the beds provided a wide, deep space beneath which the occupants had crammed boxes and sacks. Simple clothing hung from hooks along the wall, as did assorted pots, bison horn dishes, and cooking utensils. The children who seemed to follow She Who Heals everywhere peeked at them with bright-eyed curiosity. Though the older men and younger women seated on several of the couches did their best to hide it, Livi could tell they wondered about their presence, too.

She Who Heals led Livi to a couch to the left of the door. "This will be yours," she said.

Livi nodded, feeling lost and overwhelmed.

"And this is my daughter, Bright Bird." She Who Heals indicated a woman seated on one of the couches with a child at her breast. "She will answer your questions and do her best to make your stay with us a pleasant one."

Livi ducked her head in acknowledgment. "Thank you for extending your hospitality to a stranger," she said. "When can I see my son?"

She Who Heals looked up at Reid, dismay and disapproval on her face.

Reid nodded, as if taking note of his aunt's concerns, and led Livi back outside. They crossed the compound under the sharp, assessing gazes of the women working in the yard. Reid stopped in a shady place around the corner of the house where no one could see.

"Now listen to me, Livi," he said with some exasperation. "You aren't going to be able to see Little David until all of this is settled. I thought you understood that. I thought you understood that you would have to let me do what has to be done.''

"But if he's so close, why can't I see him? All I want is to make certain he's all right and hold him for a little while.''

"That's just not possible,'' Reid's quiet words belied the intensity in his eyes. ''You've got to let me do this without your interference.''

"But you didn't tell me I'd be shunted away—''

"God damn it, Livi!''

He radiated tension, livid and hot. It crawled up her arms and down her back. She recognized how close to the surface the frenzy lay in him. She realized he was afraid.

She didn't know why, what it was about being here that could frighten a man like him. Was it what he had to do to get David back, or was it something else? Something deeper, something inside himself. That he'd been denying his own fears sent her own anxieties spiraling.

"I want to see my son!''

The cry came from the core of a mother's heart, from the place where hope and terror resided side by side. It came from the weight and heat that every mother carries in her chest, from her understanding of what it means to lose a child. Livi had lost other children. She lived with those hollow places inside her every day. She was haunted by the ghosts of bright young lives that might have been.

Livi didn't know if she could survive the loss of this beautiful child, this precious baby, the last of David's children.

Reid must have sensed what she was feeling, for he dragged her into his arms and crushed her close.

"Livi. Oh, God, Livi,'' he whispered into her hair. ''I'd take you to him if I could. Don't you know that?''

Livi muffled her sobs against the front of his shirt.

"Getting Little David back depends on what happens tonight and tomorrow. I can't concentrate on what I have to do if I'm constantly wondering where you are and what you're doing. By going somewhere you shouldn't go or doing something you shouldn't do, you could ruin everything. You've got to believe me, Livi. I'm not trying to shut you out. You just don't have a place in this.''

After a time, he unwound her arms from his waist and set her gently on her feet. Yet there was something about the crisp

way he withdrew his hands and stepped away that made Livi
think he hadn't wanted to touch her as he had, that she was
somehow unacceptable here, almost unclean.

"Will you promise me you'll stay here with Bright Bird
and She Who Heals?" he asked. "Will you promise to do as
they say?"

Livi stared at him, not knowing if she could give him her
word. Not knowing if she could keep it if she did.

"Will you promise me, Livi? Please?"

Not trusting her voice, Livi nodded.

He ushered her back to the door of the house, where Bright
Bird was waiting, and handed over her saddlebags. Livi
watched as he mounted his horse and rode away.

She saw how tired and vulnerable he suddenly seemed. She
saw how alone he was, even here where he should have belonged. A singular warrior against a nation of Creeks.

How could he hope to win against such odds?

Reid was surprised he remembered it all so well. He hadn't
expected the sounds of dogs barking, of children playing, of
women pounding corn to reverberate in his head the way they
did. He never imagined that the smell of curing skins and
mingled herbs could conjure up images from long ago. They
made him remember so much about the years he had spent
here: the warmth of being accepted by his clan, the solemnity
and the celebration of the Green Corn Busk, the kindnesses
Soaring Eagle had shown him. The sights and smells and
sounds also made him remember the helpless anger and grinding responsibility Reid had felt when his uncle was killed.

Still, if the reason for his return had been different, Reid
might have been able to put all that behind him and take joy
in the familiarity. As it was, he had Livi and Little David, the
sacred disks and Red Hand's threats to consider—fears that
left him cold inside.

Guiding his horse and Livi's along the Bird clan's large
block of houses, Reid turned in to another cluster of buildings
at the end nearest to the center of town. The old man sitting
in the fading sun enjoying his pipe didn't seem surprised to
see him. But then, that had always been Blue Feather's gift.

"Good day to you, *potca*," Reid greeted his grandmother's
only surviving brother.

Blue Feather exhaled a stream of pipe smoke as Reid dismounted. "So you have come, Ravens Flight. I thought you would. I knew that in time you would bring the disks to those who prize them most."

Reid didn't bother to deny that the disks were buried at the bottom of his saddlebags, beneath his Creek clothing and the gifts he had brought. Blue Feather saw into a man's soul as if it had no more substance than a shadow.

"If you knew that, then you know why I have come," Reid answered.

The old man had changed little in the years since Reid had left. Blue Feather was a little more wizened and his hair was now completely white. Yet his dark eyes were just as alive with knowledge of men and their secrets as always.

"You came to return the disks and to try to save the boy Red Hand claims is your son."

"He is the son of my heart," Reid corrected Blue Feather, knowing the old man would understand the distinction. "And will the council not accept an exchange of the disks for the child?"

Blue Feather shrugged. "Since the death of the Great Warrior Emistesigo last fall, Red Hand has been crying for a sacrifice to change our fate in battle. It will be hard to make the council listen to an offer of exchange when Red Hand's voice is so loud in their ears."

"Are you saying that he would rather sacrifice the child?" Reid asked, the cold in his belly seeping deeper.

"There are other ways to get the disks."

Reid considered the warning of treachery. He might hold the plates until his last breath, but a man had only one life to give.

"How did the council know I had the disks?" Reid asked after a moment.

"There were those who said that when Hair Buyer was captured at Vincennes you were there, that you took the sacred disks away. I tried to tell the council that you would keep them safe and return the disks when the time was right. But when the hawk-faced English captain came to us with one of the plates, when he threatened to give it to the Shawnee, it seemed wise for us to find you."

"And the council sent Red Hand."

"Red Hand was eager to go."

Reid scowled but said nothing. Red Hand had hated him for as long as Reid could remember. The animosity between them had swelled when Heart of the Wolf, Red Hand's younger brother, had died at Reid's hands. If Red Hand had had his way, Reid, not Soaring Eagle, would have died to avenge that death. But Red Hand had been younger then; he had not prevailed against the elders of his clan. Killing Soaring Eagle diminished the Bird clan's power in the council, and the Panther clan was shrewd and well versed in politics. Reid didn't have any trouble believing that Red Hand still carried a grudge for what had transpired so long ago.

"But can I convince the council to exchange the disks for the child?" Reid asked again.

Blue Feather didn't answer. He dumped the ashes from his pipe and rose with some difficulty from his bench.

"You must prepare, *osuswa*," the old man said, "if you are to plead your case before the council in the morning. You must purify yourself and then come with me tonight to smoke in the hot house with the rest of the old men. They are wise and put more store in regaining the sacred plates than in offering a child to the Master of Breath."

Reid wanted to ask if among the old men there were voices strong and numerous enough to sway the council, but he refrained. Blue Feather had made it clear he would not answer that question.

"I thank you for your help, *potca*," he said instead.

"You are my sister's grandson. You are a son to me. Of course I will help." The old man stopped as if there were something else he meant to ask. "And what of the woman you brought with you to the village?"

Reid had learned long ago not to question how Blue Feather knew what he did. Perhaps word had spread this quickly of his arrival with Livi in tow. Perhaps Blue Feather had seen their coming in a vision.

"I left the boy's mother with She Who Heals. To approach the council, I must lie separate from her and purify myself, as you well know."

The old man nodded. "It is good that you remember your duties, *osuswa*. Gather your things," he said, and led the way into his tiny lodge. "There is much to prepare."

While the rest of the village came together in the dusk, Reid made his way to the bathing place, a deep, protected bend in the creek to the south of the village. Reid had accepted that he must be pure in order to approach the council, especially on so important an issue as exchanging the sacred plates for a child. He had begun to prepare himself as they'd traveled. He had deliberately withdrawn from Livi and had taken no food since the evening before. Now he would bathe and dress himself as a warrior, a distinction he had earned in battle with the Cherokee all those years ago.

Though Reid's eyes teared and his skin stung as he waded into the frigid creek water, the chill seemed to sharpen his perceptions of what lay ahead.

Red Hand wanted blood. From what Blue Feather had told him, the War Chief had already stated his case to the council for sacrificing the child. By offering Little David, Red Hand meant to appease the Master of Breath and change the Creeks' dwindling fortunes—fortunes lost primarily through the misalliance with the British in the war against the colonists.

To save Livi's son, Reid would have to convince the council that returning the sacred disks to their rightful place was enough to alter Creek fortunes. He would have to make them believe that sacrificing the child was not necessary, and that as a reward for returning the disks, he deserved the life of his son. How he would do that remained to be seen. He just hoped he was skillful and eloquent enough to persuade the council to overrule the wishes of one of the most powerful men in the tribe.

In choosing to deny his heritage, in disparaging one of the Creeks' most closely held beliefs, Reid had made himself an outsider among his grandmother's people. How could he expect the council to decide in his favor against Red Hand?

Yet Reid believed that the future of the Creek nation resided in the council's choice to accept the sacred disks in return for the child. Everything Reid was, wanted, or hoped for lay in his ability to return Little David to his mother's arms. His actions and his words would determine so much. He felt the burden of that knowledge weigh down his soul.

Once he emerged from the stream, he dried and dressed himself in his Creek clothes. He wrapped the full, flowing breechclout and fastened it with a belt of braided deerskin strung with beads. He settled a buckskin mantle around him and tied it across his shoulders. He slid his feet into elk-skin moccasins. He wound a wide woven band around his head and secured it at the back. When he was ready, Reid returned to Blue Feather's lodge.

Together he and the old man made their way past the square ground where the council met when the weather was good, to the town house at the far end of the chunky yard. The big round building with its conical roof was the council's cold-weather home and a gathering place for men who wished to spend the evening talking and smoking their pipes.

They entered by way of a short, curved passage and were immediately enveloped by a cloud of heat and smoke. Both swirled upward and outward from the small fire laid at the center of the town house and the dozen or more men who were gathered on the woven benches around it. The men looked up from their pipes as Reid and Blue Feather moved past the tiers of benches toward where the group was gathered.

Rank and clan and veneration dictated who got the seats closest to the fire, and Blue Feather's place was right up front. He indicated that Reid should join him on the wide, deep bed and nodded to the other men gathered there.

"My grandson, Ravens Flight," the old man said by way of renewing acquaintance.

Around him, Reid recognized some of the men as ones he had admired when he was a boy: brave warriors, skillful hunters, the chief's wisest advisors. As they sat in the thin, orange glow of firelight, their bodies were marked by scars and age and tattoos that told of their bravery, of their service to the tribe, of their accumulated wisdom.

Reid found he was proud that his own body bore marks of living, too. The snake tattoo wound up his arm. There was a faded scar from a spear a few inches above his shoulder blade, the pucker where a bullet had grazed his thigh, the still-red knife slash he'd received defending Livi's cabin. He wore the scores he'd cut in mourning David as proudly as he wore the rest. The fresh bandage wrapped around his upper arm gave evidence of his continued daring.

He looked around him again and realized that all the men who were gathered here knew exactly why he'd come, exactly what he hoped to gain. Reid's nerves tightened with that realization.

He did his best to mask his feelings as Blue Feather went through the motions of packing his pipe and lighting it with a coal from one of the braziers kept smoldering between the benches. Blue Feather drew twice on the pipe and passed it to Reid.

Reid remembered the ritual well. He lifted the stem skyward to the Master of Breath, west for the thunder, north for the buffalo, east for elk, south for the Spirit of the Sun. He finally pointed it downward to the Mother of All Life. That done, he put the pipe into his mouth and drew deeply. The smoke raked down his throat, burned his lungs as he inhaled the pungent mixture of tobacco and herbs. With great effort he choked back the cough that rebounded from his diaphragm. He exhaled the stream of smoke with every semblance of enjoyment and handed the pipe back to Blue Feather.

It had been years since Reid had smoked anything at all. As they repeated the ritual of sharing a pipe, the strong Creek tobacco sent tingles dancing along his limbs and elongated the shadows cast by the fire into increasingly fanciful shapes.

As the air grew even thicker around them, one of the men from the Wind clan cleared his throat. "We were speaking of the sacred disks, the disks that Hair Buyer had stolen from us. We were speculating on where they might be today."

It was clearly an invitation for Reid to speak, but before he could think of how to respond, Blue Feather answered. "I sense that they are close at hand. I have sensed their presence these last days. Here." He touched the center of his chest with his closed fist. "I believe that they will come to us when we are ready to receive them."

"But how must we prepare?" asked one of the old warriors.

"I believe that we must purify ourselves," a third man answered. "I believe that we must sacrifice the child that Red Hand holds hostage to ensure the return of the sacred disks."

Some of the men muttered in agreement, while others shook their heads.

"I believe that it would anger the Master of Breath to receive the soul of an innocent child when all that is necessary to renew His favor is the return of the disks." Blue Feather spoke up and passed the pipe again.

"But how are we to ensure the return of the disks?" the first man asked.

Reid exhaled a plume of smoke. "If you believe that the sacred plates are no longer in the possession of Hair Buyer, I think that you should seek the favor of the man who possesses them now."

"We should seek the favor of the hawk-faced English captain?" a man with a scarred face asked. "He is a hard man and wants a continued alliance with the British in return for the disks."

"I refuse to seek the favor of a man who would threaten to give our sacred disks to the Shawnee," the man to his right put in. "It is wrong to allow the British to force us into an alliance that has brought nothing but grief and despair to our people."

"I believe that the hawk-face no longer holds the disks," Blue Feather observed after a moment.

Voices rose as the men exclaimed over this possibility.

"I have heard that the hawk-faced captain is dead," Reid offered quietly into the midst of the turmoil.

As one, the men turned to look at him.

"Did you kill him, Ravens Flight?" one of them demanded.

"No."

"Then who did?"

Reid remained silent. It would not do for word to get out that Livi Talbot had taken the captain's life. He knew that there were those in the camp who agreed with continuing the alliance with the British, and he refused to put Livi's safety in jeopardy.

"What is more important," the old warrior said, "is where the disks are now. Whose favor must we seek and what must we do to see that the sacred disks are returned?"

"I believe that the one who holds the disks wishes for them to be returned to the Creeks and for prosperity to return to the tribe. Yet such an important transaction must certainly come with a price," Reid answered, preparing to set the requirements as clearly as he could. "That price is that man's honor and the life of the child."

The men conferred among themselves, some agreeing out of hand, some speculating on the value of disks that had been held so long by men who did not understand their significance.

A few questioned whether the return of the disks would accomplish more than a sacrifice to the Master of Breath.

The first man spoke again. "Even if we agree, we are but a few voices in a council of many."

"Then it seems wise to express our beliefs to those in our clans, to use our wisdom to guide the council on a prudent course," Blue Feather offered sagely.

The men began to talk among themselves again, discussing the question, unifying their opinions, as was the Creek way.

As they did, Blue Feather passed the pipe once more. "You have done well, *osuswa,*" he whispered to Reid.

Reid accepted the pipe and drew the smoke deep into his lungs. As the men debated and nodded and saw to their pipes, he settled back on the wide bench in the town house. He had done what he could tonight. Tomorrow he must make the council decide the matter in his favor.

As he listened, his mind clouded with the effects of the strong tobacco and pungent herbs. His eyes drifted closed. His limbs fell lax. Yet even in sleep the fear lay with him.

∞ 24 ∞

*H*e stood alone on the crest of the ridge. Alone where he'd gone to mourn for David. Alone where he'd watched the moon set on a world in which his brother lived no more. He looked out across the swaying trees and endless skies, on lingering sunsets and glowing dawns, and felt the soul-deep sear of agonizing grief.

Around him, the wind picked up, tearing at the buckskin mantle across his shoulders, flattening his breechclout against his thighs. It swirled around him, lifting his hair, cooling his heated skin. Dispersing the loss and the sadness as if they were morning mist.

An eagle soared up from the base of the cliff, dark and magnificent against the blazing sky. His heart soared with it as it sailed and wheeled. Then, with a dip and a flutter of wings, the eagle came to land on a ledge a dozen yards below the precipice on which he stood.

She had built her nest on a narrow outcropping between the rocks. Three eaglets nestled inside. He had never seen the bird before, never noticed the nest, never realized that new life had begun in a place that seemed to him so steeped in sadness.

As he watched, the eaglets' mother offered each of her babies something to eat. They wriggled and flapped their thin, half-feathered wings. Their youthful eagerness and anticipation made him smile. It kindled a warmth in his heart that he had never expected to feel again.

While the mother winged away in search of more to feed her hungry brood, the three small birds jostled each other for room in the nest. They were more than hatchlings now, quickly outgrowing the ring of sticks that had kept them safe.

As he watched, one of the birds—the smallest, he thought— hopped onto the rim of the nest. It perched there, stretching and fluttering, its bony wings tufted with feathers and down. Then, as if driven by some instinct stronger than sense, it launched itself into the air.

Horror stole his breath as he watched it fall. Grief blossomed in his chest as the eaglet plummeted toward the rocks.

Without taking time to think, he spread his arms and leaped after it. He was Ravens Flight. He could save the tiny bird. The wind seemed to catch and rise beneath him, lifting him high. He soared out and away from the cliff and dipped to rescue the fledgling bird.

Then the wind that had carried him died. He felt only the sun and baking heat. He saw only his shadow on the boulders below. He flailed his arms like the birds that winged so gracefully. But he could not fly.

His chest contracted and a cry pushed up his throat as he plunged toward the rocks. He hurtled downward, knowing he had failed, knowing he could not fight forces so much stronger than he was, knowing he could not change nature no matter how just his cause. The world rushed up to meet him as he fell . . .

Reid awoke with a jerk, his throat raw, his chest heaving. He lay pooled in sweat. His muscles trembled and his heart battered around inside him like a wild thing trapped in a cage.

The images of the cliff and the eagles lingered at the backs of his eyes, woven through every level of consciousness, lodged in bone and muscle and sinew. His head pounded and muscles twitched. His body rippled with heat, though his skin was cold. He sat up, shivering and disoriented.

"It was only a dream," he told himself, as if hearing the words aloud might somehow convince him. But it was more than a dream. It was a vision.

A vision—something he had courted with fasting and chanting and purgatives when he was a much younger man. He'd needed a vision then to prove to his tribe and to himself that despite the white man's blood that coursed in his veins, he was still a Creek. The images he'd seen back then were every bit as vivid as these. They held the sting of prophecy.

Only this time Reid didn't need Blue Feather to interpret the signs. He knew what this meant: if he tried to save Little David, he would die.

Reid sat gripping the side of the bed, his lungs burning, his head reeling with the decision he must make. Few men received warning of their own death. Yet he'd been given this premonition—and, if he wanted to make it, a choice. He could approach the council today and offer the sacred disks for Livi's child, or he could breathe a few years longer, face a few more dawns, explore those far horizons.

He could have all that, or he could save a child born squalling in his two hands. A wondrous child, a precious child. David's child. Yet he'd had no sign that even if he offered up his life he would succeed. He'd had no assurance that if he went before the council today, Little David would be returned to his mother's arms.

Still, Reid knew he had to try. If anything he did could ensure that Livi and the baby returned to the cabin, he would welcome death. He would embrace it.

As long as they were safe.

Slowly his head began to clear, and Reid became aware that he was alone in the dark, smoky cavern of the town house. Blue Feather was gone. The old men were gone. Reid couldn't help wondering, To where? To their homes? To their beds? Or were they at the square ground, even now? At the square ground where his destiny, and Little David's, would play out before the council today.

Reid sought the entrance to the town house and made his way outside. It was dawn, a clear, cool, early-spring dawn with a pearly sky and the scent of the earth in the air. It promised to be a better day than most for a man to breathe his last.

But if a man knew he was going to die, he should prepare himself. He should prepare the people he loved. He should have the chance to say good-bye.

Reid reached the courtyard of She Who Heals's lodge only a few minutes later. Bright Bird was already stirring when he arrived and seemed surprised to see him. She did not ask why he needed to talk to Livi Talbot. She merely went into the house and brought her back.

"You must not touch him," he heard Bright Bird admonish Livi in a whisper that hissed with disapproval. "He has purified himself to address the council. It isn't right that he is here."

Livi came to where Reid stood. She was pale, dressed in only her shift. Her shorn hair was wild and rumpled with sleep.

"What is it?" she demanded in a whisper. "Is something wrong? Has something happened to David?"

"I've had no news of David," Reid assured her. "If all goes as it should, he will be brought to the meeting of the council this afternoon."

"Bright Bird told me. She said that is when the exchange will be made."

Reid nodded, stealing one more moment to drink her in. "I want you to promise me, Livi, that no matter what happens today, you will do as Bright Bird says."

"What do you mean, no matter what happens?"

"I mean that sometimes things turn out differently than what we hope. You must be ready to leave when either Bright Bird or She Who Heals tells you to."

He could see the flutter of panic in the pulse at her throat.

"Stop it, Reid. You're frightening me."

"It means that I may not be with you when you leave." He drew a shaky breath, wondering how she could have become so dear to him, wondering what else he could do to keep her safe. "And if I'm not with you, Livi, I want you to know how much I love you."

"Oh, Reid!"

"I love you," he repeated. "You and the children have brought joy into my life—joy I never dreamed I could feel. You gave me happiness for a little while, a place where I belonged."

"Why are you telling me this?"

"You gave back the meaning in life that I'd lost," he went on, saying what needed to be said, "and whatever I do today, I do because of that."

They stood a mere handbreadth apart: Livi trembling as if she understood far more than she wanted to acknowledge, Reid wanting so much more than he could have. He yearned to touch her, to hold her one last time, to breathe the scent of her skin, to stroke her ravaged hair, to bind her to him with all the love and passion inside him.

Instead he backed away. "I need to go. I need to prepare myself to meet with the council."

"Reid, please!"

She reached for him, and he put a few more steps between them. She looked so lovely standing there with the rising sun warm on her face, with the shimmers of gold in her hair. He would carry this image of her with him into whatever world came after this.

"I love you, Livi," he repeated and turned to go. He crossed the Bird clan compound with long, quick strides and never once looked back.

As he bathed and prepared himself to address the council, a sense of fatalism stole through him. With it came determination, a kind of peace. If he was to die defending Livi's child, he could hold nothing back in arguing his case before the council and against Red Hand. Having no future meant that there were no consequences, no responsibilities, no regrets. And suddenly Reid felt free.

The men of the tribe were gathering when he reached the square ground with its wide central plaza and four open-fronted sheds. The members of the white clans sought seats in the shed on the west. The warriors of the red clans claimed the shed on the north. The Second Men, advisors to the Miko, sat to the south; all the others occupied the shed to the east. Just as Reid was finding his place in the shed on the west where members of the Bird clan sat, he caught a glimpse of Blue Feather sitting at the opposite end of it. The old man nodded almost imperceptibly and glanced away.

As silence fell, the Creek men settled themselves and lit their pipes. The Miko, the chief's Interpreter, and the War Speaker filed in and took their respective places: the Miko and the Interpreter in the white clans' shed, the War Speaker in the red clans' shed.

The Second Men rose to prepare the purifying drink from the leaves and twigs of certain holly plants. The English called it black drink because of its color. The Creek called it white drink because it cleansed both mind and soul.

When the black drink was ready, the ceremony that preceded every meeting of the council began. Three waiters approached the Miko and offered a cup of the inky brew. The chief took it in his hands, and while the men sang a long, droning note, he put the cup to his lips and drank. When the chief finished, the men moved to the Interpreter, on the right, then to the War Speaker and each of the Miko's advisors. So the ceremony went around the square, the waiters pouring more of the drink from a hollow gourd and passing the cup from hand to hand. They moved from the highest-ranking members of the chiefdom to the lowest, replenishing the supply of the brew when it ran low, waiting while each man swallowed down the contents of the cup.

When Reid's turn came, he took the vessel with trembling hands. He knew this was the start of it. The end was just beginning.

Livi watched Reid leave, dressed and carrying himself like the warrior he was, his back straight, his shoulders squared, his stride determined. A man setting off to take on the world. She'd sensed the challenge in him, the recklessness. The desperation. And they frightened her.

Men who fought the world very rarely won.

And that was what he'd come to tell her: that though he meant to fight, he thought he'd lose. That though they were returning the disks, the council might sacrifice her baby anyway. That Reid was willing to offer up his own life to save her child.

Reid had come to say good-bye.

The realization battered Livi to her knees. It set her panting with fury and weeping with fear, breathless and inconsolable. She curled in upon herself and tried to deny how much of her life might be wrenched from her by the decisions the council made today. She didn't see how she could endure losing Little David. She knew she couldn't face losing Reid. There must be something she could do.

Bright Bird knelt beside her. She stroked one hand consolingly along the bow of Livi's back.

"You must accept what the council decides," Bright Bird offered sagely. "You must let Ravens Flight do what he must."

"He means to give his life to save my child."

"Then that is his choice. It is what the Master of Breath intends."

"You may believe that and he may believe it," Livi challenged on a shuddering breath, "but I won't accept it. I can't accept it."

She lifted her head to look into the younger woman's face. "You must help me find my baby."

"No, I cannot."

"You are a mother, Bright Bird. Could you stand by and watch your baby die?"

She could see the empathy in Bright Bird's face. "It is not a choice for me to make."

"Do you know where my baby is?"

"No, I do not."

"You *do* know where my baby is," Livi insisted.

Bright Bird looked into Livi's ravaged face. "She Who Heals knows where he is. She knows many things because she tends the sick in all the towns. She has not told me."

Sensing no duplicity, Livi believed her.

There had to be another way. "When will they bring my baby to the place where the council meets?"

"You cannot go."

"I must go," Livi insisted. "I can't stay here while they decide my son's fate. I can't sit and wait to learn what happens to him and Reid."

"Ravens Flight would be angry if you were there."

Livi knew Reid would be that and more.

"I will take his anger on myself," Livi assured Bright Bird, hoping she would relent.

The seconds crawled by. Livi sensed the struggle going on inside the younger woman as she weighed duty to her clan and tribe against what Livi was asking. All mothers shared a common bond, the necessity of protecting their young to their last breath. She knew Bright Bird understood that. It was the only reason for the Indian woman to accede to Livi's demands, the only reason for her to help a woman she had never seen until the day before.

"You would have to pledge your woman's honor that you will not speak," Bright Bird hedged. "That you will not show yourself, that you will do everything I tell you."

Livi would have pledged her soul—and lost it gladly if it

meant that she could save her baby or Reid Campbell from the council.

"I pledge my woman's honor."

Bright Bird glanced over her shoulder as if she were afraid someone would hear. "She Who Heals would bind you to the house posts before she would consent to this."

Livi waited, her heart like a rock in her chest.

Then Bright Bird nodded with sudden resolution. "If you mean to go to the council with me this afternoon, we must prepare. By now the men will be gone from the bathing pool."

Livi found she could breathe again.

While the others in the lodge slept, they collected the things they needed and went down to the creek. It had been a long time since Livi had bathed outdoors, since she had stripped off her clothes in front of other women. Those gathered at the bathing pool watched discreetly as she disrobed. They tittered among themselves.

"Are they whispering because my skin's so pale?" Livi asked, glad to immerse herself even though the water was biting cold.

"They are whispering because you have hair on your body in places Creek women pluck theirs out," Bright Bird answered.

Livi looked and it was true. She felt color rise in her cheeks, and she remained shivering in the pool until most of the women were gone.

Bright Bird's decision to help Livi turned her suddenly garrulous, when before she had treated Livi with courtesy but distinct reserve.

"Is Ravens Flight your husband?" Bright Bird asked as they dressed in deerskin skirts, trade-cloth shirts, and mantles of rabbit and otter skins.

"In a way," Livi answered, slipping her feet into a pair of calf-high moccasins.

"I was but a small girl when his grandfather brought him here," Bright Bird volunteered.

Reid had told her a bit of how he had come to live with the Creeks, but Livi had to admit to being curious. "His grandfather?" she prompted.

"They said that the trader McTavish came because Ravens Flight could not live among the whites."

"Was McTavish accepted as a friend?"

Bright Bird nodded again. "They say that many years ago, the trader McTavish saved the Miko's life while they were hunting. As a reward for his courage, McTavish asked only for permission to marry Light of Dawn, the Miko's daughter."

It was a romantic story, one that fired Livi's imagination every bit as much as the tales of brave knights and ladies in distress she'd read when she was a girl.

"What happened when McTavish brought Ravens Flight to the camp?" she asked.

"The Bird clan took him in. Blue Feather, Light of Dawn's brother, took his part. He made Soaring Eagle *pawa* to Ravens Flight," Bright Bird explained. "It is the duty of the *pawa* to take a young man into his home and teach him all a warrior needs to know."

"And it was Soaring Eagle, his *pawa,* who was killed when Ravens Flight left the village," Livi said.

"He was killed by Red Hand's clan, the Panther clan," Bright Bird confirmed. "There have long been bad feelings between our clan and his."

Livi was stunned by the insight. There seemed to be far more between Red Hand and Reid than the threats to Little David and the return of the disks.

"But why did the Panther clan kill Soaring Eagle?"

"Ravens Flight killed Red Hand's *teuci,* his younger brother, when they were practicing for war. Heart of the Wolf fell and hit his head while they were fighting. It is our way for a man's clan to retaliate when one of their braves is killed. Instead of Ravens Flight, the Panther clan chose to kill Soaring Eagle, because he had great power in the council. And once his life was taken in payment, the clans could fight no more."

But Reid hadn't been able to accept that. It was why he had left the only place where he had ever gained acceptance. He left because Soaring Eagle had been killed for something Reid had done. He left because of his guilt.

After Bright Bird had wound her own braids around her head and fastened them with a brooch, she began to comb and trim the uneven straggle of Livi's hair.

"You must understand what returning here requires of Ravens Flight," Bright Bird said, hacking at a recalcitrant lock with the blade of her knife.

"What does it require?"

"It means that he admits he was wrong to leave. It means that he accepts the taking of Soaring Eagle's life. It means that he will accept whatever other judgments the council makes."

Like sacrificing Livi's son.

But Reid wasn't willing to accept that, was he? Suddenly Livi wasn't sure what Reid's visit this morning had meant. Had he been telling her that he would fight for Little David's life, or that he was willing to give him up?

Livi's thought galloped ahead to the meeting that would be taking place in a few hours' time. She had thought she would be able to count on Reid to stand against the council to protect her son. Now she wasn't sure.

Reid had told her he would do his best. He had told her he loved her. But had he said that because he thought he was going to die, or because he knew she would despise him if he gave Little David up?

Livi's heart thundered and her hands shook as she and Bright Bird gathered up their belongings and returned to the house. She waited out the long hours of the morning with her heart in her throat. And when the time came for them to go to the meeting in the ceremonial plaza, she wasn't sure if Reid would champion or betray her.

~25~

Livi struggled to maintain some semblance of calm as she and Bright Bird sought seats in the council square. The place was crowded, the air thick with conversations and pipe smoke. People turned as they passed by. Their eyes shone avid, curious. They spoke in whispers and nodded their heads. That is Ravens Flight's wife, they must be saying. She is here to learn if her son will die.

Livi hated that so many had come—to see if the sacred disks would be returned, to see if the son of Ravens Flight would be sacrificed to the Master of Breath. Livi hated that she didn't understand the customs and the language. She hated that she must sit silent while the council debated the fate of her child.

Dread coiled inside her, twisting and writhing like a snake. She trembled in terrible anticipation.

They settled on a bench toward the rear of the eastern shed. Livi adjusted the narrow buckskin skirt and drew her cloak more closely about her. She knotted her fingers in her lap. She must hold herself together. She must hold her peace.

What she ached to do was hold her child.

Livi shifted her gaze to the square again. It was just as Bright Bird had described it—four mud-and-stick sheds facing the open plaza. She searched each of those sheds for some sign of her son.

She spotted Red Hand instead, speaking with two other warriors. His expression was obliterated by his bright mask of paint. Still, the menace in him rolled over her. She could feel it in the way he rested one hand on the hilt of his knife. She could see it in the lift of his chest, in the set of those mammoth shoulders. He wanted to take her baby's life.

She found Reid standing stiff and alone at the opposite end of the square. Since he'd come to see her earlier in the day, he had donned a rich mantle trimmed with fur, and tucked several white feathers into the woven band around his head. A belt made of silver disks encircled his waist and the moccasins he wore were thick with beads. The fine clothes made him seen grand, proud, imposing. They made him into someone she didn't know.

In desperation, Livi searched his face. She needed his reassurance; what she saw was his strength. She wanted to find hope and calm in the depths of his eyes. They were cold and far away.

She shuddered with uncertainty.

Bright Bird leaned nearer and touched her hand. "It is starting," she said.

Livi nodded. Anxiety washed hot as bile in her throat.

The Miko took his seat in the shed at the west end of the square, beneath a panel carved with birds and alligators. A heavily tattooed man of middling years, he wore a mantle of bobcat skins, a white breechclout, and a headdress adorned with swan feathers. The two men attending him had been at the cabin. One had translated the other men's words. The other had been painted white, as he was today.

Silence descended as the Miko stood. "Headmen, warriors, beloved Old Men, my brothers and sisters of all the red and white clans." Bright Bird translated for Livi in an undertone. "We have come together today to discuss a matter of great importance to the future of the chiefdom. It is a matter that has long concerned us, a matter that will determine the fate of our village and our people."

Livi shifted, already impatient with the Miko's rhetoric.

"In the early days of the war between the British and the colonists, Colonel Henry Hamilton, the one known to us as Hair Buyer, sent emissaries to our town to persuade us to fight for the British cause. While Hair Buyer's men were here, they took from us certain objects sacred to the Creeks. They took two of the copper disks that were granted to us by the Master of Breath for use in the ceremonies at the time of harvest. Through his men, Hair Buyer assured us that if we chose to fight for the English, he would keep these sacred objects safe. He told us that if we did not fight, he would fulfill the words of our most feared and ancient prophecy. He would give the disks to the Shawnee.''

Livi sought out Reid on the far side of the square. She had never seen him sit so impassive, so still. His focused silence frightened her. It made him a stranger to her in a way his Indian garb did not. It seemed to turn him into a man with no passion, no life. Was he gathering himself for the confrontation ahead, or did he know that saving Little David was impossible?

''For the sake of our trade with the British, and to keep the colonists from our land,'' the Miko went on, ''we agreed to take up our weapons in the English cause. For a time, Hair Buyer kept his word. He kept the sacred disks safe. But in the war, Hair Buyer was taken prisoner and our sacred disks were lost. With their loss, our fortunes as a tribe grew dark. Our allies, the British, withdrew from the land they call Virginia. Our Great Warrior Emistesigo was killed in battle with the colonists. Our hours and days grew heavy with mourning and fear.

''Then word of the sacred disks reached our ears. We learned that Ravens Flight, grandson of Light of Dawn and the trader McTavish, had protected the disks of our ancestors from harm. We sent our War Chief Red Hand to search out the lodge of Ravens Flight and return the disks to those of us who have mourned their loss. And so it is that I have spoken.''

Looking to where Red Hand waited, the Miko resumed his seat.

Livi went breathless, weightless inside. She could see how eager Red Hand was to speak in the way he braced his legs as he came to his feet. Casting one dark look in her direction, he sauntered to the center of the square.

''It is I, Red Hand, who was given the great honor and responsibility of finding Ravens Flight. I, Red Hand, who did what must be done to ensure the return of the sacred disks.''

For the first time, the crowd responded. Murmurs of approval rumbled around the square. Livi suddenly realized that the men's participation made pleading for David's life even more volatile and dangerous.

"We searched for many days to find the cabin of Ravens Flight in the far hills of Kentucky. When we arrived, we found that Ravens Flight had forsworn the blood of the Creeks that runs in his veins. We found that he had ignored the ancient prophecy he knows so well. We found that he had given the sacred disks to the English and the Shawnee."

Red Hand strode to where Reid sat and pointed at him with both anger and disdain. "It is the kind of treachery we have come to expect from men like him. Men whose Creek blood is thinned by mingling with the blood of the whites. Men who repudiate Creek beliefs. Men whose honor is tarnished by too many years among our enemies.

"It was his duty to care for the sacred plates. It was his responsibility to see that they were returned to the keeping of his people, and he did not."

Reid remained motionless. Only the flush rising in his face gave evidence that he acknowledged the accusations.

"He gave the sacred disks to others who would use their power to enslave the Creeks," Red Hand went on. "He gave our sacred disks to those who would bend us to their will. He betrayed us."

Livi heard a hiss of anger from the men around her.

"But I, Red Hand, undermined his treachery. I tore Ravens Flight's son from the arms of his white mother. I brought Ravens Flight's child back to the chiefdom to pay for his father's failure to honor our beliefs. I, Red Hand, demanded that this man, this tainted man, this dishonored man, recover the disks from the English and return them to where they rightfully belong. Here. Among the Creeks, who venerate their power.

"He is sitting among us now, but I do not see the disks. I do not know if he recovered them from the British. I do not know if he has brought that which we need to ensure a better future for our tribe. I believe he has not. I believe that the Master of Breath demands that Ravens Flight's son be sacrificed for his father's treachery."

Livi felt his threat pierce deep. It struck at her helplessness, spilled the worst of a woman's fears. She shuddered, clammy, breathless, and sick.

She couldn't let these savages sacrifice her child. She'd die instead. She shifted to stand and offer herself.

Bright Bird grabbed tight to Livi's wrist. "You must not act. You must let Ravens Flight answer the charges."

Livi fought the woman's hold, restless, frantic to somehow save her baby's life.

"You must put your trust in Ravens Flight," Bright Bird insisted.

She must put her trust in Reid. In Reid, who had fought for her and her family. In Reid, who had kept them safe. In Reid, who might have reasons of his own for acceding to the council's demands. Fear squirmed in Livi's chest.

Reid rose from his seat in the opposite shed and walked to the center of the plaza. As he stood there straight and still, the angles of his face showed in stark relief, like bones bleached white by the wind and sun.

"Have you brought the disks to us, Ravens Flight?" the Miko asked.

"I would see my son before I answer that."

The man beside Livi gasped in disapproval. Others around the council square were shaking their heads. Even Livi realized that in asking to see his son, Reid was questioning Red Hand's honor.

Reid stood like granite in a world of sand. He did not acknowledge the tumult. He made it clear by his presence and stature that he would not relent.

"This is not so unreasonable a request," the Miko offered in a conciliatory fashion. "Bring the child."

Stiff with indignation, Red Hand nodded to one of his emissaries. The man ran off.

Several interminable minutes passed. The crowd rumbled with speculation.

Livi's heart beat so hard she fancied everyone in the square could hear it.

Red Hand's man returned. A young Indian woman accompanied him. Livi looked past them both to the fair-haired infant in the woman's arms.

Livi devoured the sight of her son, from the dome of his downy head to his tiny moccasined feet. She took in the pucker of that soft, sweet mouth, his big dark eyes. She saw little David squirm and knew just how it felt to hold him while he wiggled and tested his strength. She heard his voice as if he called to her.

She rose to go to him, heedless of her surroundings, of Bright Bird's crushing grip.

The Indian woman looked up and saw her there. She glared at Livi. Livi glared back, anger boiling inside her. This stranger had taken her child.

Then David cooed and turned those wide dark eyes to the squaw. He wrapped his fingers around the bright beads that hung around the woman's neck and tried to drag them into his mouth.

Her baby's innocent gesture stung Livi like the most vile defection.

Slowly she realized others in the square had turned to look at her as well. She sensed their hostility and their censure. She was the stranger here. To them, *she* was the threat.

Livi sought out Reid in the midst of the crowd.

He stared back, stiff with anger and reproach. He hadn't wanted her here. He hated that she had come in spite of him. She read all that in his face. Then for one brief instant Reid betrayed himself. He let her see just how much she and David mattered.

The love and fear that shone in his eyes stole all of her strength. She sank to the bench, breathless and chastened and shuddering. She understood now what was at stake. If Reid failed today, he would lose not just the child, not just her love and respect, not just his life. He would lose himself.

Livi looked up at Reid. He deliberately turned away.

"Ravens Flight, grandson of Light of Dawn," the Miko said in a tone that was gruff with disapproval. "You have seen your son. You have seen how carefully we have guarded his welfare while he was here with us. Can you say you guarded the sacred disks as well while they were in your keeping?"

Instead of answering, Reid bowed his head for a moment, breathing hard. "I was assured that if I brought the sacred disks to my grandmother's people, my child would be returned to me."

Livi heard mumbles of outrage in the crowd. Clearly, none of them had heard this stipulation.

Red Hand rose from his bench to give focus to their mutterings. "No such promises were made," he declared. "Ravens Flight is wrong. The boy was brought here to be sacrificed.''

Livi stared at the others who had been at the cabin, the men on the Miko's right and left. They knew that Red Hand lied.

They did not speak.

"He promised," Livi insisted softly, her voice broken and thin. "Red Hand promised. Why else would we have gone through so much to bring back the disks?"

Red Hand moved slowly around the perimeter of the plaza, his gaze seeking out the members of the council. "Even if what Ravens Flight says is true, why hasn't he returned the sacred plates to us long before this?"

Livi saw the faint shift in Reid's stance. His shoulders seemed not quite so square. The angle of his jaw seemed not quite so resolute. This was the question he'd been dreading.

"When I received the disks from Hair Buyer," Reid answered, turning to the men in the sheds around the square, "I should have come to my grandmother's people and given them back. Instead I rode with Colonel Clark, to whom I owed a debt of honor. I went to the woods of Kentucky and built a home with a man to whom I owed a debt of friendship deeper than I can ever repay. Would you have me deny those responsibilities when it is here that I learned to bear their weight with honor?

"In truth, I was unaware of the distress the loss of the plates was causing my people. I was unaware of the privations the Creeks were suffering. I am sorry that in discharging other duties, I have not lived up to my responsibilities as part of this nation."

Bright Bird had said Reid would have to humble himself before the council in order to have a chance of recovering the baby. Livi knew that humility had never come easily to Reid. She understood, in a way she never had before, that sometimes Reid's pride was all he had.

"But what of the disks?" Red Hand demanded when it seemed that Reid's contribution might sway the men around them. "We still have not seen the sacred disks of which he speaks."

Reid's lips flared with fleeting disdain. "Would I bring them here and display them for all to see when they are to be viewed only at the time of the Green Corn Busk?"

"Where are they, then?" the Miko asked.

Reid's stance tightened even more. He glanced around the square. His gaze faltered only when he came to the place where Livi sat.

"The disks are where they should always be," he finally said.

"And where is that?" the Interpreter demanded in the Miko's stead.

"Have the Holy Men go and look in the sacred place where the disks have always belonged."

The men painted and dressed in white were on their feet almost before the Miko could nod his consent. They disappeared into the deep, dark compartment at the back of the western shed.

Livi's heart twisted with betrayal as she watched them go. Had Reid really given back the disks? Yet how could he have done that? Without the disks, they wouldn't have anything to bargain for Little David's life.

Reid waited in the center of the square with tight-lipped control. Though she willed it, he refused to look at her.

Livi turned to gaze at where her baby slept in the Indian woman's arms. Was this the last she'd see of her son? Once the Holy Men retrieved the plates, would they take her baby away?

Bright Bird tightened her grip on Livi's hand as if she sensed her desperation.

"Why is he doing this?" Livi whispered.

"Wait. Just wait," Bright Bird whispered.

"Without the disks, we have no chance of getting David back."

"You must trust him," Bright Bird counseled, though for the first time, Livi sensed the other woman's rising doubts.

Livi ached, raw inside. She needed her baby back. She needed for this to be over. She couldn't bear much more waiting.

The Holy Men were gone for a very long time. The people around the square whispered as they waited, anticipating, speculating. Shadows of clouds scudded across the center of the open plaza. The wind picked up, rattling the woven roofs over the daub-and-wattle sheds. It was a spare and lonely sound. Livi shivered.

Then all at once the men in white emerged from the shadows.

"The disks are here!" the leader among them announced, holding up two familiar doeskin bags. "The sacred disks have been returned to us."

Livi gasped and looked at her baby again. She stirred on the bench. She needed so desperately to go to him, to touch him, to hold him one last time. Bright Bird held her back.

Then Livi realized that around the square, some of the men were nodding. She could see approval and relief on their weathered faces.

Red Hand paced before the warriors' shed, his strides giving proof of his agitation.

Reid waited, his jaw hardened, his shoulders stiff.

The Miko rose again. Every eye turned in his direction.

"You have returned the sacred disks to us, Ravens Flight. For that we thank you. But why have you given them back when you have yet to learn what judgment the council will make? We could still decide to sacrifice your child."

"It is long past time for me to return to my people—to the Creeks—that which is rightfully theirs. I have no fear for my son's safety. The council's judgment is always just."

"Oh, God, no!" Livi breathed, tears spilling down her cheeks. How could Reid entrust David's life to the council now?

Bright Bird held Livi's hand tighter than before, though the Indian woman's fingers had gone suddenly cold.

Red Hand paused at the edge of the warriors' shed. "But how can we know that the disks have not been profaned in the years of Ravens Flight's stewardship? How can we be certain that the Master of Breath has been appeased by the return of the disks? We must sacrifice the child to ensure His blessings for all the Creek chiefdoms. We must spear the child and roast him over the sacred fire."

Livi fought to muffle the sob that clawed its way up her throat. Despair sluiced through her.

Livi saw the Indian woman draw Little David closer. She seemed as frightened for the baby as Livi was.

Reid's face softened, shaded with sincerity. "From the time I received the sacred disks from Hair Buyer," he told the council, "I have been ever mindful of the Creek traditions in regard to them. In all the time they were with me, they were never removed from their doeskin bags except when I celebrated the Green Corn Busk. They were never misused. They were never touched by women.

"I never gave the sacred disks to the English or the Shawnee. They were stolen, just as they were stolen from this place by Hair Buyer's men. And I got them back."

The Miko nodded as if he believed Reid's assurances.

Red Hand stood in counterpoint, the image of skepticism.

Slowly one of the old men rose to be heard. "By his good faith in returning the sacred plates to us, Ravens Flight should be rewarded with the life of his son."

"This is clearly a man of honor," a second said. "I believe we should heed his request. This child should be spared."

Livi searched the faces of the people around the square, seeking some sign that they agreed. When she saw that many of them were nodding, she crushed Bright Bird's fingers in her own.

Red Hand shook his head. "I say the Master of Breath is angry that Ravens Flight has withheld the sacred plates from His children the Creeks. I believe He will continue to withhold His blessings from this nation unless the child is sacrificed."

Livi looked at Reid, entreating him, begging him to save her son. He met her gaze, his eyes afire.

Reid stepped forward, his fists white and knotted at his sides. "Then if the council believes a sacrifice is necessary to renew the blessings of the Master of Breath, *I* am the one who should be burned. I am the one who kept the disks when my people were in such grievous need. If the disks have been profaned, I am the one who should accept the blame. Let the child go free. *I will give myself in this baby's place.*"

Livi's heart lumbered. Her head went light. This wasn't how she'd wanted Reid to save her son.

Around her, people shifted forward in their seats, their eyes glowing, their faces avid. Even the Holy Men whispered among themselves.

Red Hand watched with a smile on his lips.

"My Creek heritage may be tainted with the blood of my white father and grandfather," Reid went on, "but it is far more pure than the blood of this child. I have proved myself as a Creek warrior. Would the Master of Breath not be more pleased by the sacrifice of a warrior than the sacrifice of a child? Would the sacrifice of a man who goes to his death gladly not bring greater honor to this tribe? I will credit the Master of Breath in the way I die. He will smile on all the Creek nation when He sees my courage. If there is to be a sacrifice, it must be me.''

Livi stared at Reid with tears in her eyes. This man had held her and comforted her when she was hurt and afraid. He had given her tenderness and pleasure. He had helped her bring this child into the world. This man had made her find the strength to stand alone in this raw, new land. How could she bear to lose him now?

Red Hand moved toward where the Miko stood. His eyes gleamed with satisfaction. ''I believe that the Master of Breath would welcome the sacrifice of Ravens Flight.''

Men from the warrior clans rose to voice their agreement with Red Hand's words.

As they spoke, Livi realized that Red Hand hadn't been any more satisfied by Soaring Eagle's sacrifice than Reid had been. Now Red Hand meant to take what his tribe and his clan had denied him so long ago. He meant to take Reid's life. The baby and the disks were far less important to Red Hand than revenge.

''How do you answer, Ravens Flight?'' the Miko asked. ''The council is willing to accept you as a sacrifice in the place of your child.''

Reid inclined his head. Though his eyes burned bright, he seemed to be breathing easier. ''I have returned to the Creeks as a Creek. I have offered myself to the Master of Breath. If the council requires a sacrifice, I freely give myself.''

Voices clamored approval around the square.

''Then so be it,'' the Miko agreed. ''The child will be returned to his mother. They will be allowed to go in peace. In his place, you, Ravens Flight, will be given over for sacrifice to the Master of Breath.''

Livi sat quivering. She and Little David could leave. But how could she accept their freedom when she knew Reid had paid for it with his life?

He stood tall and spare in the center of the compound. His hair lifted in the wind. His clothing fluttered. The sun shone warm and golden on his face. Livi had long feared the wildness in him, the savage lurking in the depths of those bright, clear eyes. But there had always been honor there, too. Courage, love, and selflessness. No white man would have paid such a price for the life of her son. No man in broadcloth and lace could engender such pride and power.

She loved Reid. She needed Reid. How could the woman in her let him make this sacrifice? How could the mother in her refuse?

"I freely give myself," Reid repeated.

Livi could not stop him from doing this. She must hold her peace. Yet remaining silent when she yearned to speak was harder than anything she'd ever done. It was harder than giving birth, harder than shooting Weems, harder than burying David.

Tears coursed down her face. It took everything she had to accept what Reid was giving her.

Only when Bright Bird nudged her did she become aware that there were arguments erupting in the sheds around the square. She heard the hiss of strong opinions being expressed, the rumbling of consternation.

Shaking off the restraining hands of the men beside him, one old warrior came to his feet to be recognized. "I believe that we are wrong to sacrifice such a man as this. How can our tribe spare braves of such strength and nobility?"

"Who would expect a man with blood of the whites so strong in his veins to behave with such honor?" another asked. "I say Ravens Flight has proved himself a Creek, willing to do what is best for his people. Surely the Master of Breath would prefer for this man to honor Him with his life rather than pay tribute with his death."

Livi caught her breath, her heart fluttering with hope.

Red Hand bolted forward. His voice rang ragged with outrage. "But Ravens Flight deserves to die! Ravens Flight has profaned the disks. He has kept them for himself when he knew that we had need of them. He has never taken responsibility for what he's done."

The men looked up as Red Hand spoke, their faces arrested and still.

"Have the disks been profaned by Ravens Flight's stewardship?" one elder asked.

The Miko turned to the Holy Men to settle the question.

"You have examined the disks Ravens Flight returned to us. Do you see any impediment, any sign that they have been profaned? Have they retained their power to protect our people?"

Livi recognized the man who had been at the cabin rise to answer his chief. The white paint covering his face made his expression impossible to read.

"The power of the plates," he said, "appears undiminished by their years with Ravens Flight."

"Then if Ravens Flight grieves for his mistakes in not returning the disks," another man inquired, "why must we ask more from such a man?"

One by one, men in each of the sheds rose to speak, leaders, warriors, and administrators of the towns along the river.

Red Hand had to shout to make himself heard above the others. "Surely the men of this council can see that they are wrong in their judgment of Ravens Flight. Surely they can see that he deserves to die!"

The people in the square went utterly still.

"What is it?" Livi whispered to the woman beside her. "What is happening?"

"It is no longer Red Hand's place to argue. The decision is being made. No one may speak against it now. This is our way. By doing this, Red Hand dishonors himself."

The discussion picked up as if Red Hand had not spoken.

"Though objects of such importance to the chiefdom should have been returned long before this, I believe that Ravens Flight's heart is pure."

"By his good faith in returning the sacred plates, by his willingness to give his life, Ravens Flight should be spared this sacrifice."

"But he deserves to die!" Red Hand shouted.

One by one, the Creek men glanced at Red Hand, then turned their faces away.

"No! No! You must listen to me, my brothers," Red Hand continued. "Ravens Flight is evil. He must pay—"

At the Miko's nod, two of the other warriors came to where Red Hand stood and escorted him from the square.

Quivering with relief, Livi let out her breath. Her baby was safe now. Reid was safe. All she wanted was to go home.

But the council was not over. Other men came to their feet to be recognized. They spoke at length.

When they all had had their say, the Miko rose. "By decision of the council we thank you, Ravens Flight, for returning to us those very precious and sacred objects that we believed were lost. We appreciate the efforts you made to keep them safe. Take your son and teach him the ways of the Creeks, and return among us when you can."

Livi wept silently as the Indian woman approached where Reid was standing. Giving Little David a few last, gentle pats, she relinquished the baby with what appeared to be genuine regret. Reid took the child in his big dark hands. Holding Little David as he had on the night the baby was born, with the same elation on his face, Reid wrapped the child against his heart.

Then all at once people spilled out of the sheds. The square ground was filled with noise and rejoicing. Livi fought her way toward where Reid stood with her son, but Bright Bird barred her way.

"Now that Ravens Flight has had his victory, you must let him come to you," she admonished softly, grabbing hold of Livi's arm and nudging her toward the clan compound. "This, too, is our way."

While everything in her demanded that she rush across the square and claim her child, Livi knew that in these matters Bright Bird was far wiser than she. When Livi looked back one last time, Reid was cuddling the baby close. Beside him, smiling and watching over them like a benevolent spirit, was a wizened old man.

Reid hadn't expected to walk away from the council square with the sun in his face. To be the one to carry Little David through the village and deposit him safely in his mother's arms. To see the wonder in Livi's eyes as she bowed her body around her child and wept for his safe return.

He hadn't expected the fear that gripped his heart as he stood over them.

They were safe, Reid tried to tell himself. He'd keep them safe. He had offered his life to keep them safe. Seeing such tangible proof that he'd succeeded should have brought a sense of triumph, a moment of ease. Instead Reid shivered, knowing the reunion of mother and child was the result of a reckless plan and the whim of fate.

He eased away from the gentle domestic scene, out the door of the smoky lodge, and around the corner of the house. Once he was well out of sight of the women cooking in the courtyard, he braced his back against the wall and slid to the ground.

He'd almost lost them. He could admit that here, where no one could see his ravaged face, his shaking hands. He'd almost lost Little David. If the council had given more credence to Red Hand's arguments, if it had voted differently, he would have lost Livi, too. She wouldn't have allowed her baby to be sacrificed. She would have fought and died to save him. Reid had done everything he could to protect them. He'd offered his own life in the baby's place. What would he have done if that hadn't been enough?

He clenched his fists in his tangled hair. He sucked down air as if he couldn't get enough. His heart beat raw inside him. Livi and the children and that cabin had come to be the world to him. They were the place his heart called home. He would rather have given his life a thousand times than face what might have happened in the council square.

He'd been afraid for Livi and her children before. But somehow he had managed with skill and strength and will to keep them safe. This time he'd faced an enemy he couldn't anticipate or control. This time he cared too much. This time he'd come too close to failing.

And what about the next time? There were dangers in this wilderness he couldn't thwart—hunger and illness, fire, animals, and misfortune. He couldn't protect the people he loved from things he couldn't see or count or fight. He couldn't keep them safe from things that were amorphous and undefinable, shrouded in an unpredictable future. Yet he couldn't bear to lose them, either.

He'd known that kind of loss before. Soaring Eagle was gone because of his carelessness. David was dead because he had misjudged the English soldier's treachery and the dangers of the trail. Reid couldn't let himself make another mistake.

There couldn't be a next time. He couldn't let there be a next time. And if there was a next time, he couldn't stay around to watch.

The restlessness came with the force of a whirlwind, so strong he felt suffocated by this town, these people, this life. It came so hot that his skin itched and his muscles coiled with the need to move. It rose like panic in his blood. He wanted to run as far and as fast as he could. He craved a dose of solitude, some open country where he could breathe.

It was time to go.

Driven by an almost overwhelming need to get under way, Reid returned to Blue Feather's lodge. He donned his breeches and hunting shirt and boots, gathered up their guns and the food he and Livi would need on the trail. He arranged for their horses to be brought around and sent word for Livi to prepare herself.

"Are you in such a hurry to leave, *osuswa?*" Blue Feather asked when he returned to the lodge and found Reid in the midst of preparations. "Can you not stay with us a little while longer?"

"We have the baby back," Reid said almost gruffly, jamming his breechclout into one of the saddlebags. "There is nothing to keep us here. Livi has other children to see to once she gets back to the cabin."

Reid could feel the sear of the old man's gaze, and took care not to meet it with his own. Still, Blue Feather stood watching him, his scrutiny telling and deep.

"Are you so afraid of losing yourself, Ravens Flight," the old man finally asked, "that you cannot accept the love that others would give you?"

Blue Feather's words made the air in the lodge seem unbearably close. They made Reid's hands tremble and his muscles flex.

"Of course I'm not afraid."

Blue Feather hesitated just long enough to make it clear he knew Reid was.

"Then you will accept the gift I have to give?"

Reid didn't see how he had any choice.

The old man went to the bed nearest the fire and took down his bear-claw medicine bag. A man's most sacred objects were kept inside: his ceremonial pipe, his tobacco and herbs, all his most powerful fetishes. Reid knew that objects belonging to a man of Blue Feather's wisdom would be potent indeed.

Reid wasn't sure he wanted something that might bind him

to the tribe by the old man's magic, but the challenge had been issued and he could not turn away.

As Reid watched, Blue Feather took out a smaller bag that was exquisitely stitched with the shapes of flowers and birds. The old man withdrew a round, flat object from inside. When he turned, Reid could see it was a whelk-shell gorget.

"This belonged to your grandmother when she was a girl," the old man said. "After she married your grandfather and went away, she wore it every day to remind her how strongly she was linked to her clan, to the tribe, to her life here in the village. Her last request was that the trader McTavish bring the gorget to me. I have kept it all these years, knowing in time I would find a use for it. Now I believe Light of Dawn would wish you to have it, to remind you where you come from, to remind you that there are those among the Creeks who love you still." Blue Feather raised those wise, ancient eyes to look into Reid's face. "Will you take this gift from me, *osuswa*? Will you make a commitment to the parts of yourself you have long denied?"

Reid looked down at the graceful symbol etched into the pearl-gray surface of the shell, at the details of the bird's flowing plumage, at the ring of encircling symbols that represented truth and fidelity and courage. If he accepted Blue Feather's gift, he would renew his connection here, not just to his mother and grandmother's clan, but to the tribe, to the whole Creek nation. But then, hadn't he done that by coming here, by addressing the council, by returning the disks? Hadn't he courted—and received—the acceptance he'd been seeking all his life?

Reid had to swallow before he could answer. "I would be honored to accept this gift from you, *potca,* and wear my grandmother's necklace all my days."

The old man nodded in acknowledgment of his words, and Reid bowed his head so Blue Feather could reach around and fasten the necklace's carved bone clasp at the back of his neck. The old man settled the shell gorget at the base of Reid's throat and smoothed the long, spun strands of buffalo hair.

"It is done, *osuswa.* You are one with us again—in your heart and in your head, just as you have always been in your blood and in your bones. Now I know that though you leave this place, you will return. You are part of us, as we are part of you."

Reid felt both damned and redeemed by accepting the necklace. "I thank you for this, *potca*. I thank you for your wisdom and your help in returning the sacred disks."

The old man nodded. "But there is more, is there not, *osuswa?*"

"More?"

"More that you love, more that you fear?"

Reid thought of Livi, of Tad and Cissy and Little David. He thought of the commitment he didn't have the courage to make. "No," he said.

"There is a vision," the old man prompted him.

Reid let out his breath. "Of leaping from a cliff."

"In the vision you have already leaped, Ravens Flight. There is nothing left but to let yourself fall," the old man said. "Or to choose to soar as eagles do."

Reid stepped away, strangely shaken by Blue Feather's words. Before he could consider how he should interpret them, the old man was speaking again.

"Come back to us, Ravens Flight, just once again before I am called to the World Beyond. And bring your son, this child of your heart, and the others you will father in the years ahead."

Reid wished what Blue Feather said was true, that he would have sons of his own one day to hold and teach and nurture. He wished he were the kind of man who could embrace a home and family.

He wished that he were David.

But he was not. Reid had accepted long ago that he could never be what David was, never have what David had. He'd been reminded of that again today.

The fear prevented it.

The restlessness prevented it. Even now, the lure of lands not seen and worlds not yet explored left him trembling inside.

Reid grasped Blue Feather's forearm in the age-old gesture of farewell and felt the old man close his own knobby fingers around his wrist.

"I will try to return to the village, *potca*," he promised softly. "But for now, I need to gather Livi and the child and take them back to the cabin."

"Take them to the place that is your home, *osuswa*. Make a life for them there."

"I will try," Reid whispered, though even as he spoke them, he knew the words were a lie. "I will try."

❧ 26 ❧

S pring awoke in the mountains and the woods as they
rode north. The hills ruffled with lacy redbuds, and ravines brimmed with budding dogwood trees. Violets ran in the
shady vales at the edges of the creeks. Trillium shone like
fallen stars on the pale, fresh green of the forest floor. The air
chorused with birdsong.

Livi turned her face to the sky and reveled in the renewal
and rebirth. She held her son tucked safe in the crook of her
arm. She was headed back to a home and a life she'd wrestled
from land she once thought she hated. She was loved by a
strong and extraordinary man who had come to stand beside
her in David's place. A year ago she could never have imagined any of this. A year ago she would not have believed that
the heartache and the fear and the grief could give way to
contentment that ran so deep. Yet they had, and she clasped
the joy to her like a prize.

Livi wasn't sure when she began to sense that Reid didn't
share her wondrous delight in the world around them. She
caught a hint of his reserve in the way he shifted his gaze
away when she looked up. She heard it in his voice when he
spoke her name, felt something vital missing from his touch.
As they moved deeper into the rugged hills, back toward the
cabin where Tad and Cissy and Eustace waited, Reid's with-
drawal became more pronounced. He spoke in monosyllables
when he spoke at all. He made excuses to head off into the
woods as soon as they'd made camp. He kept watch through

the night, sleeping in snatches where he sat instead of curling into the blankets with her and the baby.

She worked to span the distance between them. She questioned Reid about the country they were riding through. She asked his help in tightening the cinch on her saddle or spreading their blankets for the night. She made certain he carried Little David at least part of the day, hoping his love for the baby would breach the wall he'd inexplicably erected around himself. But nothing broke him. His detachment made Livi afraid, and the world that seemed so bright and filled with promise went suddenly dark.

There was a time when Livi would have waited for Reid to explain, but she refused to do that now. That evening, just as they finished making camp, Livi caught Reid's arm.

"Please, Reid, can't the hunting wait a little while?"

"Only if you don't want anything for supper."

"Then I'd as soon eat corn and jerky than go another day without having my say."

He watched her warily, tightening his grip on his rifle as if he meant to leave in spite of her request. Instead of allowing that, Livi cast a glance at the blanket where Little David was sleeping and headed toward the fire. She settled on a log a few feet away. Reid relented, put his gun aside, and took a place on the ground beside her.

She reached across to claim his hand.

At first he resisted, but she pressed her thumb into the hollow of his callused palm and curled her fingers across the back. She could sense the tension in him, the determination, the power. And the fear.

She didn't know why he should be afraid.

"I wanted to thank you," she said after a moment.

"Thank me?"

"For taking me to the Creek village, for what you did while we were there. I wanted to thank you for speaking before the council in our behalf, for getting Little David back." Her fingers tightened. "For offering your life in David's place."

He stared down at their linked hands, quiescent, still.

"I didn't have a chance to tell you before," Livi went on, "how grateful I am that you would offer yourself for the sake of my child. I didn't have a chance to tell you how afraid I was that I would lose you, too."

Reid's breathing came heavy in the silence.

"I love you, Reid. There was a time in my life when I wouldn't have believed that I could care for you as I do now. But you've proved in a hundred ways how good and honorable a man you are. You've given me so much—"

Reid jerked his hand away. "Stop it, Livi!"

She felt the loss of his warmth the length of her arm.

"What is it you want me to stop?"

"Stop deluding yourself that you're in love with me," he told her. "Stop pretending that the two of us can make some sort of a life together."

"And why should I do that?"

"Because we can't. Because I don't want you at the cabin. Because you belong in Lynchburg, where it's safe."

"I don't want to go back to Lynchburg!"

"I'll pay you for David's land," he offered. "I'll take you back myself. I'll help you find a house. I'll—"

"Damn it, Reid, I've proved myself. We broke new ground on those fields. We plowed them and we planted them. We weeded and watered and harvested our crops. I've kept my family safe—"

"Safe!" Reid thundered. "By God, Livi! How can anyone keep a family safe when you've got Indians raiding every few weeks? How can anyone keep a family safe when there are sickness and wild animals and accidents that could take their lives? You've got to go back. It's the only way I can be sure—"

"I don't have any intention of going back!" She was bone-deep weary of arguing with him about the farm. "If you refuse to let us stay at the cabin, then we'll move on. We'll go and live at the station while I look for another piece of land." Until Livi spoke the words, she hadn't realized how much Kentucky had come to mean to her, how determined she was to stay. "I know Ben Logan will help me find—"

Reid surged to his feet, cursing, shaking, angrier than she'd ever seen him.

"God damn it, Livi! I don't want Ben Logan helping you find another cabin somewhere out here in the wilds. You won't be safe there, either. I need you safe."

He snatched up his gun and spun away.

"I'm not leaving!" Livi shouted after him. "You may as well get used to that!"

Reid kept on moving. He didn't come back until almost dawn.

The rains washed in a few minutes after Reid returned to the camp, dousing the last embers of their argument, forcing an uneasy cooperation on both of them as they prepared for the trail.

It took everything they had to keep moving the next two days. Downpours came and went. Streams swelled, swirling muddy and treacherous to the lip of their banks. The steep trails churned to quagmires underfoot. They sheltered both nights in caves with little to eat but their dwindling supply of parched corn and jerky. Livi scrounged in the wet for wood, then built up the fire against the chill. Reid sat staring out at the rain and refused to speak.

Trapped with Reid by the weather, Livi felt battered by his energy. It seemed distilled to its essence here, the currents running thick and relentless, confined by the rough stone walls. It was as if she could feel him squirming inside his skin, trying to escape both her company and himself. She sensed a high-pitched panic he could barely control. She didn't think he ever slept, kept awake not so much by the need to stand guard over her and her child as by whatever was boiling inside him.

The third day the sun broke through the clouds and the land became rolling and familiar. They traveled more swiftly here, reaching their valley in early afternoon.

From the top of the ridge to the south, they could see across the fields to the cabin on the far side of the creek. Everything was as it should be. The animals grazed in the stubbled fields. Tad and Cissy sat on the steps of the cabin in the sun, busy with their books and slates. Eustace worked turning the ground in the kitchen garden. It seemed so calm, so perfect, that Livi was reluctant to turn away. When she did, she saw that Reid had resolved whatever he'd been struggling with.

"Livi," he said when he'd dismounted, "I'm going away."

With those simple words, Reid dashed the hopes she'd been harboring for the future.

"And there are some things we need to discuss," he went on.

"Can't they wait until we get back to the cabin? Can't we talk there?"

Reid shook his head. "It will be easier for everyone if I just go."

Livi knew he was right. The children wouldn't understand why he was leaving any more than she did. With a nod of compliance, she handed Little David down to him and climbed from her horse.

"I've decided to deed the land to you," Reid told her once he'd given the baby back. "I don't want you looking around for another place. This land is as good as any you'll find and the cabin's already built. It should have been yours anyway. David signed those papers to protect you, not to deprive you of what's rightfully yours. While I'm at Logan's Station getting supplies, I'll see to drafting a deed and have Ben bring it by when he has a chance."

"But why are you going away," Livi whispered, "when we were so happy here last winter? If you stay we can clear more land, raise more crops. We can have a family that's yours and mine."

"That sounds wonderful, Livi," he offered gently, "but it wouldn't work. I've always been a wanderer. In time I'd get a hankering for the woods. I'd want to stay, but I wouldn't be able to help myself."

"I *would* let you go."

Reid shook his head. "You'd need me here when there were fields to plow and crops to harvest. You'd expect me to be with you when our children were born, and I couldn't even promise you that." He gathered up his horse's reins. "And I could never be the kind of husband to you that David was."

The last words came so softly she barely caught them, the tone disillusioned, resigned.

"Well," she declared with a lift of her chin, "I could never be the kind of wife to you that I was to David."

Reid paused and turned to stare at her.

"In case you haven't noticed," Livi went on, "I'm not the woman David married. I'm not the wife he had when he left Virginia. I've changed since David died. I've had to change. That change is what makes me want to stay here. It's what makes me able to love you. It's what makes me believe we could build a life together."

"God damn it, Livi, I can't stay." Reid's words were so filled with longing, they tore at her heart.

"I won't expect you to be David," she promised.

She saw the sag of his shoulders, the weary lines around his mouth. She saw the loneliness he never showed to anyone. "It's not just that."

"What is it, then?"

Reid fumbled for an answer, the silence swelling between them. But when he raised that clear blue gaze to her, she knew he intended to tell her the truth.

"I love you, Livi," he said, his voice gone low. "I love the children and this place and the life we had last winter. More than anything, I want to ride down this hill and go back to that. But I can't."

"Why?" Livi whispered.

"Because I can't protect you here. Because I can't keep you safe." His voice began to fray. "Because I couldn't bear losing any one of you."

Livi saw the frank, stark terror in his eyes and wondered how a man with Reid's courage could feel such fear. She wondered what she could do to assuage it. Reid wasn't a child to be soothed and cosseted. He needed the truth.

"Then you mustn't be afraid of losing us."

He gave a ragged laugh. "Why shouldn't I be afraid? I lost Soaring Eagle. I lost David. I came so close to losing you and Little David back at the Indian camp that I—" He looked away, breathing hard. "You and Tad and Cissy and Little David are all I have and I won't—"

"Stay and live in fear?" Livi finished for him.

"I'm doing what I have to do."

"You're running away."

"Well, maybe I am," he acknowledged, raising his gaze to hers again. "God, Livi, how do you bear it? How do you bear seeing how fragile those children are and knowing how little you can do to protect them? How did you bear standing helpless, watching David die?"

Livi took a shaky breath, wondering if she had the words to explain to him.

"I'll mourn David for the rest of my days," she admitted after a moment. "Just as I mourn the children I've lost. Just as I'd mourn Tad or Cissy or Little David. I'll guard those children with my life. But if I fail, I'll never for a moment mourn the time we had, the love we shared.''

Livi sought the tempest in his eyes. ''You live life or you fear it. You make a stand or you run away. Oh, Reid, are you really so afraid of losing us that you're willing to deny yourself the joy of sharing our lives?''

The silence thickened between them.

He couldn't seem to answer.

She had nothing more to say.

With a sigh, Livi adjusted the baby on her hip. She gathered up the reins of her buttermilk mare and lay her hand against Reid's sleeve. For an instant she pressed her cheek to his.

''Good-bye,'' she whispered and turned toward home.

Livi could feel Reid's gaze bore into her back as she led her horse down toward the cabin. She sensed Reid's longing to stay and his anguish at needing to go. She recognized his fear for what it was, a brave man's terrible weakness, and she loved him all the more for it. She loved Reid Campbell for his darkness and his fears, just as she loved him for his honor and his tenderness and his strength.

She hoped that the woods would give him no peace, that the hills would offer no sanctuary. She hoped that he'd be back. But if Reid never returned, she would make her life without him. She could do that now. This year with its tragedies and its loss, with its struggles and its victories, had given her a belief in herself. In her strength. In her ability to accomplish what she must.

For now she was going home. Back to her children. Back to her cabin and her fields. Back to a future that held hopes and aspirations.

She would grieve for Reid. She wanted the life they could have had together. She yearned for the love he had to give her. Tears burned against her cheeks. But as Livi wept, she wept less for the dreams she had lost than for the man who refused to dream at all.

Reid watched her go, down toward the cabin he and David had built, down to claim the children who might as well have been his, down into the valley that had been his only home. Livi went with her head held high, her shoulders squared, her baby riding gently on the curve of her hip. She moved along the path at the edge of the trees, leading her mare behind her.

She carried his heart away with her as she went. She carried the sunshine in a baby's smile, the unwavering trust of a fair-haired girl, the confidences of a boy half grown to manhood. She carried the only laughter and delight and tenderness Reid had ever been able to claim for himself.

Reid had never been more proud of her. David had given Livi a place to belong, a foundation to build a life on, a way to start believing in herself. When David died, Livi had taken David's gift in her own two hands and made it something beautiful. She was forging and forming it still: with her determination to hold this land, with her resolve to keep her family together, with the conviction that life must be lived to make dreams come true.

With his friendship and his loyalty, David had given Reid the very same gift. The freedom to seek lands yet unexplored, rivers flowing to the sea, mountains that reached the sky. But once he'd exorcised his restlessness, Reid had always come home—home to David. Home to shelter and acceptance and security.

If he turned away from this valley today, he'd forfeit any right he might have to that part of David's legacy.

Down below at the base of the hill, Livi came out of the trees. The children saw her immediately. Cissy leaped from the cabin steps and raced out to welcome her mother. Tad followed his sister down the rise. Livi waved an extravagant greeting and lengthened her strides.

Reid watched as they came together in the field nearest the bridge. Livi bent, catching up her daughter and holding her close. He smiled to himself. He knew how it felt to have Cissy's arms wrapped warm around his neck; to hold the fragile span of her ribs between his hands; to feel her soft, fresh cheek pressed close to his.

Then Livi rose and went to her son. Reid saw her brush back the wheat-gold strands of Tad's shaggy hair, run her hand the length of his bandaged arm. Once she had satisfied herself that he was healing, she drew the boy close against her side. Even from this distance Reid could see how alive David was in Tad. He was his father's image, with the same stance and build and coloring. He had the same solidity, the same inner strength. He would grow to be as fine a man as his father had been.

Reid wished he could be here to see that. He wished he could watch Little David grow. He wished he could see the children these children would have. He wished he could hold and laugh with and dwell with Livi all her days.

Below him, Livi and the children stood together in the midst of the field. This precious, insular family. The people Reid loved.

Then, as one, they turned to look toward the crest of the hill where he stood watching. Reid's heart tore in two when they turned away.

He was losing them. Not to Indians or snakebite or fever. Not to any of the calamities he could so vividly imagine. He was losing them because he was afraid. What difference did it make if some nameless threat stole away the people he loved or if he deprived himself?

Reid's head reeled with the implications of what he longed to do. Of all he would risk. Of all he could lose. Yet somewhere inside he must have the courage to share his life. To claim Livi and the children, and damn the cost.

"In the vision you have already leaped," Blue Feather had told him. "There is nothing left but to let yourself fall, or to choose to soar as eagles do."

He was falling now, hurtling toward oblivion.

Desperate to save himself, Reid grabbed for the whelk-shell amulet that hung at the base of his throat. He closed his hand around it, feeling its edges bite into his palm, feeling the flare of the charm's heat and power. He drew strength from the grandmother he'd never known and from the wisdom in Blue Feather's words. He drew courage from some final reserve inside himself.

He was trembling as he raised one hand and cupped it to his mouth. "Livi!" he shouted. Her name caught and echoed in the wind.

On the field below him, Livi turned.

"Livi! Livi, wait up!"

Dizzy and breathless, he scrambled down the path with his horse in tow. His heart was knocking against his ribs, and his knees turned watery beneath him. He felt shaky and scared and exhilarated, as if he were falling free.

But Livi was there to catch him. She came running across the field with her skirts flapping and her hair flying wild. She came with welcome shining in her eyes and tears spilling down her cheeks.

She surged into his arms, and he gathered her up in the breadth of his hands. He wrapped her into himself. He needed this woman more than breath, more than sustenance. More than life. He loved her to the very depths of his soul.

"I couldn't leave," he whispered into her hair.

"Because this is where you belong."

He took her mouth. It was sweet with joy and solace, lush with endless promises.

He was still afraid. He might never stop being afraid. But he had now. He had this. He had Livi and the children and this valley and this life. He had the joy of today and the dream of tomorrow.

With their arms around each other, Reid and Livi turned back toward the children, toward the cabin. Toward home.

Turn the page for an excerpt from
Elizabeth Grayson's new novel,
coming in early 1997 from Avon Books—
a powerful story of the American West,
of an extraordinary woman caught between
two worlds, and of the rugged frontiersmen
who seek to share her destiny.

Early March 1866
Department of the Platte

*T*rouble comes out of the west. Or so Hunter Jalbert's old Arickaras Indian grandfather had taught him in the years when Hunter was struggling to prove himself a warrior. Enemies loomed out of the lingering daylight for a final attack. Wild animals stalked down from the mountains in the dark. Whirlwinds tore out of the western sky.

Today trouble took the form of a white woman.

Hunter scanned the hills around the little draw where they'd agreed to exchange their wagonload of goods for a Cheyenne captive and felt his hackles rise. As sure as hellfire burned, they'd been set up for annihilation here.

A hundred Cheyenne and Sioux warriors could be massing on the far side of the ridge. A score more might have their rifles trained on them from the outcropping of dun-colored rocks just off to the north. And here they sat—twelve troopers, two mule skinners, a captain, and a scout—visible as gravel in an open palm.

When the messenger came to the fort offering to trade for an Indian captive, Hunter had urged Colonel McGarrity to negotiate a safer place to make the exchange. But McGarrity hadn't listened.

Drew Reynolds, the new spit and shine captain who was leading the patrol, hadn't heeded his warning, either. Hunter sliced his gaze in Reynold's direction. Word was that he had attended West Point and proved himself a hero in the war back east. But things were different here. Nothing the captain had seen fighting the Rebs would prepare him for the way these tribes made war. Nothing he might have experienced in the battles between the North and South could teach him about the trickery and barbarity he'd face fighting Indians. And Reynolds was proving himself too arrogant to consult someone as lowly as his half-breed scout.

Well, the captain would learn, Hunter found himself thinking. If an arrow didn't get him first, or if the Indians didn't scalp the lot of them while they waited for a meeting that might never occur.

It is a very good day to die.

The warriors' creed was as much a part of Hunter as his breathing or his heartbeat. It calmed him, enervated him. It made the waiting more difficult.

Just when they were ready to give up their vigil to the blowing and the cold, a party of Cheyenne emerged from a crease in the hillside to the right of the rocks.

Hunter stiffened in his saddle and shifted his gaze to where Reynolds sat on his big bay gelding. "Hostiles, sir."

"I have eyes," the captain snapped. Reynolds turned to his men and shouted the order. "Stand ready."

Hunter saw the troopers free the flap on their holsters and limber up their carbines. As the Indians approached, he did the same.

There were about a dozen Cheyenne in the party that cantered toward them. Because they were riding two abreast, it took a moment for Hunter to spot the woman in their midst. She rode as tall as some of the men, discernible from them only in the way her buckskin skirt flapped against her legs and by her ornate, high-pommeled saddle. As the party rode closer, Hunter could see that the woman's complexion was baked nearly as dark as the men around her, that her hair, slicked into braids with bear grease and dusted with vermilion along the part, was nearly black.

Hunter's breathing thickened with renewed suspicion. If this wasn't a white woman the Cheyenne had come to trade, then they were dead men. They might be dead men even if she was.

"What do you make of this?" Reynolds asked almost begrudgingly. He was probably having doubts about the woman, too.

"I think we play it out," Hunter answered.

As the Indians made their way along the draw, Hunter itched to spur his horse forward, to ride in shooting and howling like the warrior he'd trained to be. But years of fighting both Yankees and Indians had taught him patience.

The party of Cheyenne stopped less than a dozen yards away. The leader, a strongly built man wearing a war shirt trailing scalps and thick with beads, dismounted and motioned for the woman to do the same. Leaving their horses, they made their way to a midpoint between the two factions.

"God damned savages want us on foot," Hunter heard the captain mutter as he swung out of his saddle. "Come along then, half-breed," he added. "I'll be needing you to translate."

Biting back his reply, Hunter slid down from his horse and followed Reynolds across the matted grass. The captain paused a few feet from where the Cheyenne stood with the woman at his side.

"I am a representative of the U.S. Army sent from Fort Caspar, as you requested. Is this the captive you've come to exchange?"

The brave nodded, seeming to understand Reynolds's words without benefit of translation. But when the Indian answered, it was in his own tongue, accompanied by the appropriate sign language.

"I am Standing Pine, warrior of the Cheyenne," Hunter translated as the Indian spoke. "This is the captive we have come to trade. Have you brought sugar and flour and meal as we asked? Have you brought ammunition?"

"There is no ammunition in the wagon," Reynolds answered brusquely. "As you well know, the Army has refused to trade for powder and shot you redskins can use to attack the stage stations and wagon trains."

Reynolds's tone was belligerent, his words inflammatory. Hunter leveled a brief, quelling glance at the officer. Hadn't anyone told this man there was nothing to be gained by antagonizing the Cheyenne? Didn't the captain want the woman freed?

"We need ammunition to kill buffalo," Standing Pine insisted. "It has been a hard winter. The hunting has been poor. We only seek to feed our families."

"Well, I have no ammunition to give you," Reynolds said and turned away.

"There *is* food for your families in the wagon," Hunter put in, addressing the Indian, halting Reynolds where he stood. "There's flour and meal and bacon, potatoes and onions and canned fruit. There's cloth in colors that will please your women, knives and axes and cooking pots. Would you turn all that away for the sake of powder and shot?"

The brave paused a moment to drink in Jalbert's logic.

"Surely such goods would be welcome," Hunter hedged.

After a moment, Standing Pine inclined his head. "It is true that the Cheyenne would welcome such gifts. I must see for myself what you have brought."

With a nod, Reynolds granted permission for the Indian to approach the wagon.

The brave crossed the swath of grass to where it stood. He pushed back the flapping tarpaulin and looked at the boxes and barrels and sacks inside. Apparently what he saw among them pleased him, for when Standing Pine returned, there was satisfaction in his face.

"We will accept what you have given us in return for Sweet Grass Woman."

Hunter had begun to nod in agreement when Reynolds spoke up. "How do we know that this is indeed a white woman? She could be some squaw you're passing off on us for the promise of gain."

Hunter stared at Reynolds in astonishment. What he lacked in diplomacy, he made up for in pure arrogance.

Yet the Cheyenne met his demand with surprising courtesy. The woman had been standing with her face averted and her shoulders bowed, as if she were attending the words her betters spoke but never once acknowledging them. At a mumbled command from Standing Pine, the woman raised her head.

The woman's features were strong but more finely drawn than most Indian women's. She had a firm chin and a mouth that didn't seem meant for smiling; a short, straight nose with a spattering of freckles; and brows that flared at the corners like a bird on the wing. The eyes that locked with his were pale, clear green, ringed by a corona of some mysterious darker color that was neither green nor gray. As he stared, Hunter did his best to plumb the depths of her. He found no warmth or joy, no fear or enmity. Her passivity assaulted him, decimating some fundamental belief about the light that should live in a woman's eyes.

And then he realized what they had done to her. High on her left cheekbone someone had marked her. A tattoo the size of a silver dollar spread like a star burst against her skin, deep blue lines radiating outward from a small hollow circle.

Beside him, Reynolds sucked in his breath. The captain obviously hadn't seen an Indian tattoo before. He wouldn't know that they were worn as often for adornment as punishment. He would only see the disfigurement, the humiliation of being marked.

Even Hunter, for all his background and experience, tingled with shock.

Yet not so much as a ripple of acknowledgment disturbed the stillness in the woman's eyes. Either her captivity had made her as impervious as the surrounding hills, or she had retreated deep inside herself. . . .

The solid wood and stone structure of the North Platte Bridge spanned the wide churn of coffee-brown water. It breached the gap between the mat of yellow grassland that rolled off to the north and east and the wind-swept foothills that rose in humps toward the snowy, pine-capped summit of the mountain to the south. At the far end of the bridge, on a bend in the wagon road that had carried thousands of settlers to Oregon, stood the United States Army outpost recently dubbed Fort Caspar.

An unprepossessing cluster of log and rough-sawed buildings, of half-finished barracks and tents, the fort was still impressive enough to make Sweet Grass Woman stiffen in her saddle. She sat even straighter than before, though for the length of their ride she had refused whatever warmth and comfort might be afforded her by proximity to the cavalry officer whose horse she shared.

She refused to accept anything from such a man. He believed that she had helped Standing Pine and Red Wolf lure him and his men into an ambush. He had shamed her by forcing her to lie in the dirt, shamed her by thrusting his knee between her legs to pin her there, as if she were some common woman. Even now he rode with one hand twisted in the belt at her waist as if she were his prisoner.

But Sweet Grass Woman knew very well what she was and took no joy in it.

The sentries who guarded the gate at the north end of the bridge snapped to attention as they approached, but not even the strictest military discipline could prevent the troopers from gaping. Their reaction to the tattoo the Kiowa had etched into her cheek made the breath catch in her throat. Sweet Grass Woman knew very well that these were only the first of many men who would stare, speculate, and scorn her in the days to come.

The column rumbled onto the bridge's cottonwood decking. The thud of horses' hooves on the planks reverberated inside her chest. The cold wind tore at her hair and clothes, chilling her bones to the marrow. The crossing seemed to take forever.

When they finally reached the southern bank of the river, the captain gave orders for the troopers to be dismissed. In response they melted away, some to stables, some to dismount before tents and barracks, a few to seek the small separate building where there must be someone who cared for the wounded and prepared the dead for burial.

It was only her captor, the army captain, and his scout who continued around the end of a row of buildings and onto a half-built parade ground. A flag she'd once thought of as her own snapped in the stiff March breeze.

They were just drawing up before the large log building opposite the flagpole, when an officer came out onto the narrow, covered boardwalk that fronted the building. At the sight of them, a scowl gathered his mouth so tight it all but disappeared into the bristle of beard and mustache.

Sweet Grass Woman tried to make sense of his expression, wondering if it was focused on the captain and the scout, the skirmish they'd fought with the Cheyenne, or her.

The captain dismounted from his horse and dragged her down. His grip was painful, almost insulting. It took every bit of her determination to keep from twisting away. With a hand on her elbow, he maneuvered her to stand at the foot of the wooden steps.

The older man loomed over her, his gaze sliding up from her moccasined feet to her buckskin dress, from her vermilioned hair to the crest of her cheek. The star burst tattoo stung as if it had been cut and colored only the night before.

"... this ... captive ... goods for?" he demanded.

Sweet Grass Woman strained to make sense of the big man's words. She had spent three years as a slave to the Kiowa and five with the Cheyenne. It had been nearly six years since she'd heard English spoken aloud. She trembled in frustration at the sound of it, angry with herself for needing so desperately to understand, appalled by how little of her native tongue she had managed to remember.

"We ... gave ... wagon ... goods ... get ... captive back."

The big man nodded. "... said ... you ... trouble ... Cheyenne?"

The men's words came in a torrent after that, too thick and fast for Sweet Grass Woman to grasp. She knew they were discussing the meeting with Standing Pine, the ambush by Red Wolf and his men. She knew they were discussing her. Her return. Her fate.

She strained closer, aching to make some sense of what they were saying.

As the two men talked, a crowd gathered. There were troopers in sweat-stained shirts and dusty canvas pants, as if they'd dropped what they were doing and had come to gawk. A cluster of traders and buffalo hunters had wandered up and stood off to one side, their eyes alight with speculation. Three women in bonnets and swaying skirts came rushing from the far side of the compound. They stopped dead in their tracks once they got a look at her. Settlers jumped down from their trail-worn wagons and ambled over to find out what was happening.

The shame of being forced to stand on display sent humiliation seeping hot beneath her skin. She linked her fingers and held on tight, fighting to keep her hands from her burning cheeks, to keep from acknowledging to these men and women the many ways the Kiowas had marked her.

The murmurs came as she knew they would, tainted with

sympathy, disdain, and horror, in a language that shouldn't
have seemed so foreign in her ears. With that hiss, the crowd
and the buildings and the dread closed in. The smells of sweat
and onions and the white man's privies. The musky taste of
fear and the burn of bile in the back of her throat. Her muscles
twitched with a need to run.

Then she caught sight of the half-breed scout standing a
little way apart. His face was broad and impassive. In spite of
his expression, she recognized the pity in his eyes. And it
shamed her.

From somewhere deep in the bedrock of her soul, she
dredged up enough pride to glare at him. To square her shoulders, to lift her chin.

She had relied on pride to see her through worse times than
this. Pride had kept her from screaming and cowering when
she was taken by the Kiowa. It helped her endure the years
of beatings and servitude, helped her bear the shame of being
marked and traded to the Cheyenne.

But pride could not ease the turmoil in her blood or slow
the wild, fierce thunder of her heart. She was afraid, afraid in
a way she had never been before. Afraid of what she'd been
and what she'd become. Afraid of what might happen after
this. In the years of her captivity, she had learned to fear for
things not nearly so intransigent as her death.

The crowd fell still when the older officer turned his attention from the captain to her.

"You . . . English, girl?" he demanded, raising his voice.

Sweet Grass Woman shook her head, barely able to grasp
more than bits of what he was saying. She couldn't remember
nearly enough to make herself understood.

". . . you tell . . . name? . . . you tell . . . you come from?"

She shook her head again. She didn't know the words for
Víhˀ ō ŏts Héˀe in this other tongue.

"Me—" he thumped himself soundly on the chest—
"Colonel Ben McGarrity."

She nodded.

"You?" He pointed at her.

She stared back, realizing that before she'd misunderstood.
He wanted her English name, not the name the Cheyenne had
given her. He wanted to know who she had been when she

was fifteen and traveling down the Santa Fe Trail with her family—not who she was now.

To Colonel Ben McGarrity Sweet Grass Woman didn't exist. To him Pale Eyes, as the Kiowa had called her, had never existed. To him, to the captain, to these white men and women, she had not existed for eight long years. A shudder ran the length of her back. Only if she could give her English name would she exist for them again.

America Loves Lindsey!

The Timeless Romances
of #1 Bestselling Author

KEEPER OF THE HEART	77493-3/$5.99 US/$6.99 Can
THE MAGIC OF YOU	75629-3/$5.99 US/$6.99 Can
ANGEL	75628-5/$5.99 US/$6.99 Can
PRISONER OF MY DESIRE	75627-7/$6.50 US/$8.50 Can
ONCE A PRINCESS	75625-0/$6.50 US/$8.50 Can
WARRIOR'S WOMAN	75301-4/$5.99 US/$6.99 Can
MAN OF MY DREAMS	75626-9/$5.99 US/$6.99 Can
SURRENDER MY LOVE	76256-0/$6.50 US/$7.50 Can
YOU BELONG TO ME	76258-7/$6.50 US/$7.50 Can
UNTIL FOREVER	76259-5/$6.50 US/$8.50 Can

*And Coming Soon
in Hardcover*

LOVE ME FOREVER

Buy these books at your local bookstore or use this coupon for ordering:

Mail to: Avon Books, Dept BP, Box 767, Rte 2, Dresden, TN 38225   D
Please send me the book(s) I have checked above.
❑ My check or money order—no cash or CODs please—for $_____ is enclosed (please add $1.50 to cover postage and handling for each book ordered—Canadian residents add 7% GST).
❑ Charge my VISA/MC Acct#_____Exp Date_____
Minimum credit card order is two books or $7.50 (please add postage and handling charge of $1.50 per book—Canadian residents add 7% GST). For faster service, call 1-800-762-0779. Residents of Tennessee, please call 1-800-633-1607. Prices and numbers are subject to change without notice. Please allow six to eight weeks for delivery.
Name_____
Address_____
City_____State/Zip_____
Telephone No._____   JLA 0895

NEW YORK TIMES BESTSELLING AUTHOR

ONLY YOU   76340-0/$5.99 US/$7.99 Can

ONLY MINE   76339-7/$5.99 US/$7.99 Can

ONLY HIS   76338-9/$5.99 US/$7.99 Can

UNTAMED   76953-0/$5.99 US/$6.99 Can

FORBIDDEN   76954-9/$5.99 US/$6.99 Can

LOVER IN THE ROUGH

                      76760-0/$4.99 US/$5.99 Can

ENCHANTED   77257-4/$5.99 US/$6.99 Can

FORGET ME NOT   76759-7/ $5.50 US/$6.50 Can

ONLY LOVE   77256-6/$5.99 US/$7.99 Can

Buy these books at your local bookstore or use this coupon for ordering:

Mail to: Avon Books, Dept BP, Box 767, Rte 2, Dresden, TN 38225   D
Please send me the book(s) I have checked above.
❑ My check or money order—no cash or CODs please—for $_____is enclosed (please
add $1.50 to cover postage and handling for each book ordered—Canadian residents add 7%
GST).
❑ Charge my VISA/MC Acct#_____Exp Date_____
Minimum credit card order is two books or $7.50 (please add postage and handling
charge of $1.50 per book—Canadian residents add 7% GST). For faster service, call
1-800-762-0779. Residents of Tennessee, please call 1-800-633-1607. Prices and numbers are
subject to change without notice. Please allow six to eight weeks for delivery.

Name_____
Address_____
City_____State/Zip_____
Telephone No._____   LOW 0795